I0763350

Dawn Crescent

Also by David and Daniel Dvorkin

The Captains' Honor: Star Trek, The Next Generation

Dawn Crescent

David and Daniel Dvorkin

Editing, print layout, e-book conversion,
and cover design by DLD Books
www.dldbooks.com
Editing and Self-Publishing Services

ISBN: 978-1-7362886-2-7

Prologue

October 1981

He was sweating in his uniform, but the president stood erect in the sunlight as troops and armor passed before the reviewing stand. These were the units, even the men themselves, who eight years before to the day had scaled the eastern bank of the Suez canal, forced the Israelis to abandon the Bar Lev line, and restored the nation's pride. Now they celebrated that glorious moment.

Behind him, the president heard people complaining about the heat, the dust, the noise of tramping feet and roaring machines, and the raggedness of the band. To him, it was all sweet music, music that had brought him to the pinnacle and established him as the greatest leader in modern Egyptian history. Later, he had parlayed that military victory into a stunning peace treaty with the Israelis and had even addressed the Israeli parliament. He had earned respect in the eyes of the world as a statesman as well as a warrior.

He had much to be proud of. He had accomplished so much already.

But it was just the beginning. He planned far greater things for the future. For now, though, he was satisfied to watch the marching ranks and listen to the music of their boots. The sun, the heat? It was the same sun that had shone on the pharaohs of ancient times, the same heat that had warmed them while they conquered the world. The dust? It was perfume.

Anwar el-Sadat noticed two men break suddenly from the ranks. His surprise turned to alarm as they ran in his direction, unlimbering their guns. No one else seemed able to respond. Sadat felt frozen. The conversation behind him ceased. The soldiers on parade kept marching. The running men threw something toward the reviewing stand—grenades, Sadat realized—and then they began firing, and he knew nothing more.

It was a slum on the outskirts of Cairo: narrow alleys of packed dirt stinking of human waste, hovels crowding together on all sides so that even the sun of Egypt couldn't penetrate the dangerous shadows, a place where no plants grew and humans could scarcely be said to live. In a small, smoke-filled room, Ali ibn Daoud paced nervously. Two other men sat at a small table, smoking. One of them—the one producing most of the cigarette smoke—growled at Ali to stop. "You're even making me nervous," the other man said.

"So much depends on this, Hassan," Ali said.

"We all know how much depends on it."

"If we fail—"

"We'll die either way," Hassan growled. "Probably soon, in either case."

"It's not dying I'm afraid of," Ali said. "It's failure. So much depends on this."

The other man shook his head with the air of one who has realized the futility of arguing. He returned to his earlier rapid puffing on his cigarette. He wore an introverted look, as though he were divorced from the great events he was part of.

There was a quick, light knocking on the door—two raps, a pause, two more. Ali yanked the door open. "At last you're here!" Ali said. "What happened?"

A young man entered. His eyes gleamed with excitement and he breathed rapidly. "According to plan!" he said. "All according to plan! The traitor is dead!"

Now Hassan was on his feet. He gripped the young man's shoulders. "You're sure? There's no doubt?"

"Absolutely sure. They riddled him with bullets. I saw it myself, from a distance. Khaled killed him. Sadat is dead. The traitor is dead."

"Praise God!" Hassan said. The others echoed him.

Ali said, "And now—"

"And now we must leave," Hassan said. "Immediately. As planned. Scatter, tell your assigned cells, go to ground. The army will be out in force. There'll be no traffic in the city. All movement will be watched. Do what you must do. Go with God."

Ali could scarcely keep himself from laughing. What did God have to do with it? But he said nothing, nodded to the others, and slipped from the apartment.

Let the others waste their time and possibly their lives trying to alert cells of the Brotherhood. Ali had completed his assigned task, and now he had to report to another authority, a far higher one, and one these petty assassins had no idea existed. No idea *yet.*

By the following morning, Ali was in Damascus.

The house he went to was as different from the room he had left the day before as the neighborhood was from the Cairo slum. He was in one of the new suburbs well beyond the crumbling remnants of the old Roman wall. Here the streets were wide and lined with palm trees, and gardens surrounded the sprawling, gleaming white mansions.

But the outward appearance of wealth doing everything it could to imitate that of the West disappeared the instant the front door opened to Ali's knock.

The manservant who opened the door was dressed in a turban and flowing robes. To Ali, he looked like a character from a movie about the Middle Ages. Once inside, Ali found himself on the set of that movie. The hangings on the walls and ceiling mimicked the interior of a giant tent.

The manservant showed Ali to a large room where the leader he had come to report to was waiting for him.

The Grand Master sat behind a small, utilitarian desk—a jarring Western note, but the only one Ali noticed.

Ali bowed. "Master. We have succeeded."

Rashid, the Grand Master of the Ismailites, nodded. "I know. Television and radio are among the useful imports." He stood and came from behind the desk. He was a tall, slender man, an ascetic, a scholar, outwardly far different from the conquerors and politicians whose mantle he had assumed. But he radiated an iron strength of will that Ali was always aware of when in his presence. When he was away from Rashid, Ali often doubted that the self-styled Grand Master could accomplish his far-reaching goals. When he was with him, Ali had no doubts.

No doubts, that is, about the Grand Master's determination and the rightness of his goals, but perhaps Rashid needed some guidance, some steering in the right direction.

"What of those tools you helped create?" the Grand Master asked.

"The Brotherhood?" Ali shrugged. "They're of no more use. They're ideologues of limited vision. They plan more assassinations of the same kind, but each one is an attempt to avenge some imagined betrayal of Islam. They have no long-term goals. I imagine many of them will be captured and tortured and will confess. Then they'll probably be executed. Some will escape, and they'll wander around the region and cause trouble, but it will be minor, local trouble, and I think we can ignore them."

"Good. So now we've proven our ability to infiltrate a major Arab army at a high level. Next time, we'll do it without the use of any intermediaries. No more of these ideologues, as you call them. I must decide on the next target. The Jordanian king, I think."

Ali hesitated for a moment, then steeled himself and spoke. "Master, I think it would be a mistake to assassinate another leader. That causes temporary local disruption, but in the long run it gets you no nearer your goal. Infiltrate your men into another Arab army, yes, but then let them wait there for a signal from you. And infiltrate them into the middle ranks, not just the uppermost, and into the armies of many countries, not just one. Then some day when the moment is right, you can cause more than an assassination. You can change history in an instant."

"And what will that moment be? What if it never comes?"

"I think you will know the moment when it comes. As for whether it will come, perhaps you can arrange matters so that the crucial moment is inevitable."

"Those are interesting ideas, Ali, and perhaps you are right. You have outlined an immense project, though, a huge undertaking. You have so much faith in me."

"Master, I have every faith in you. That is why I have pledged myself to your service."

"Many others have made the same pledge because they believe God has chosen me to lead them against His enemies. But you've never believed that, have you?"

"I have always spoken to you with complete honesty, Master," Ali said. "You know that I have little interest in the question of God's existence or whether He intervenes in human affairs. It's up to us to make our own way in the world. And to make the world in our image." Ali was growing uncomfortable with this line of discourse and hoped the Grand Master would change the subject.

But the Grand Master continued to gnaw at the matter. "In our image," he repeated. "If I was not chosen by God as leader, then how do I differ from that debased and unworthy playboy who lives in Europe while claiming the same position I do? Why is my claim superior?"

"Precisely because he is debased and unworthy, Master. It wasn't God that chose you, it was your worthiness and strength that chose you. Your power comes from within you, not from God."

"So then if I fail somehow," the Grand Master said, "or if I decline in strength or worthiness in time, some other man, someone stronger and worthier, will have the right to dispose of me and proceed in my place."

Ali hadn't noticed any kind of gesture or other signal from the Grand Master, but he became suddenly aware that someone was standing behind him. "Master, no such thought has ever crossed my mind!"

"Al–Hasan would probably have advised me to make sure it never did. But I do believe you. You may leave."

Ali bowed, turned. To his astonishment, there was no one in the room beside him and the Grand Master. In his imagination, he had already felt the slender cord whip around his neck and the hard knot dig into his spinal cord.

With a shiver, he hurried from the room and then from the house. He didn't begin to relax until he had reached Tunis and was in his own home, where Leyla waited to comfort him. And even then he didn't relax completely.

One

January 1991
Saudi Arabia

"Fold," Rick said, and put his cards face down.

"So let us see what you have," Sharon said.

Rick shook his head. "You don't get to see those cards."

Sharon laughed. "I'm still in the game, big boy. You wimped out. Let's take a look."

"We've had this argument a million damn times..."

"And I'm still right."

Rick cracked his knuckles and looked at Harry for support. "Harry, would you tell this blue beanie I don't have to show her my cards if I fold?"

"That's another thing," Sharon broke in, before Harry could answer. "Security police know how to address our NCO's with respect. By rank, not first name. Unlike Club Med here."

Harry smiled. "Which is why you're playing cards with us instead of polishing your boots with your buddies, right?" He lowered his voice an octave. "Well, as the senior ranking NCO present at this time and place—"

"—please tell us the answer," said Ben, "Master Sergeant Elkins, sir—"

"—I insist that Airman First Class Welton and Senior Airman Alcazar answer a question which, in the fine tradition of senior NCO's everywhere, I have been pondering for some time."

Rick sat at attention in his chair: like watching a mountain straighten its spine. "Sir, Airman First Class Welton reports as ordered, ready to answer the question, sir."

"Airman Welton, Airman Alcazar, the question is this. Which of you two can do more push-ups?"

Rick and Sharon stared at him for a moment, then at each other. Rick was four inches over six feet, blond with chiseled features like an SS recruiting poster, and so muscular he had to have his uniforms tailored to fit. Sharon was a foot shorter, dark and delicate like her Arab and Iberian ancestors, and probably half Rick's weight—but that weight was composed of muscle like steel cable. She'd been a gymnast in high school; Rick had played football. No surprise either way.

Ben laughed and threw down his cards, a straight flush. "Pot wasn't that big anyway, and this is going to be *much* more interesting." The medic and the cop kept staring at each other, and Harry thought, with a sudden chill, that it wasn't going to be funny after all.

The moment broke. Rick shook his head and said, "Harry, you're kidding, right? No offense, Sharon, I know you're tough and fast. I've *seen* you knock a quarter out a tree with an M16. But come on." He flexed, perhaps unconsciously, and the sleeve of his fatigues threatened to pop.

Harry leaned back and took a puff from his cigarette. He wasn't in either of their leagues physically—never had been, really. He was no athlete when he joined the Air Force in 1970 to keep from getting drafted into the Army, and years of the Old Service tobacco-and-booze lifestyle hadn't helped any—but twenty years as a medic had given him a good understanding of the capabilities of the human body. And how those capabilities weren't always what people thought they were.

"No," he said at last, "I'm not. Indulge me here."

Rick shrugged, stood up, and peeled off the BDU shirt he'd been wearing for protection against the cold desert night. The light of the Coleman lantern threw his muscles into sharp relief, and even under his t-shirt—stretched skin-tight by his bulk—his washboard stomach and weirdly cut pectorals were clear. Have to put in a lot of hours at the gym to go around looking like an anatomy textbook, Harry thought, feeling his belt buckle cutting into his own stomach.

Sharon gave a quiet smile and did the same. She was a hill next to Rick's mountain, but equally impressive for her size: arms like carved and oiled hardwood, small breasts supported by ridged pectorals, the same washboard abdomen in a smaller size. Quite nice, Harry thought with the kind of impersonal lust which was all he was allowed to feel for women so junior in age and rank. Wish there'd been more like you when I was your age. Quick memory-flash of Joy, as pretty as Sharon but softer in the way typical of that generation of soldiers' wives, which he pushed away with the ease of long practice. This was already perilously close to not being fun anymore.

"Sergeant Carpenter," he said, and Ben took his eyes off Sharon for a moment. "Start calling cadence when they're ready, please. Airman Welton, Airman Alcazar, assume the position. These will be four-count pushups, on Sergeant Carpenter's call, until one of you stops."

Both of them got down on the ground, holding the ready position of straight arms and board-stiff bodies without any sign of strain. Christ, Harry thought, I'd already be shaking. "Whenever you're ready, Ben."

"*One*-two-three-four *two*-two-three-four *three*-two-three- four *four*-two-three-four..." Harry looked at his watch. Thirty seconds, forty-five, a minute. He'd had to do fifty pushups in two minutes to graduate Basic. These days he might be able to knock out twenty in a minute, and then collapse on the ground, if someone had a gun to his head. A minute and a half.

"*Forty*-two-three-four *one*-two-three-four..."

Eighty pushups in a minute and a half and neither of them was having any trouble at all keeping up with the cadence. Christ. He choked back laughter at the thought of Ben and him sitting bleary-eyed as the sun came up, watching these two automatons going up and down.

"*Nine*-two-three-four *sixty*-two-three-four..." Ben was getting hoarse.

Rick faltered in his rhythm, and Harry smiled. "You're falling behind, Airman Welton." He squatted beside the sweating airman. "Are you going to get beaten by a girl, Airman Welton?"

"No sir!" Rick's pushups picked up, running ahead of Ben's count for a moment before they settled into the same rhythm as Sharon's. Jesus, Harry thought, why did I do that? I start goading them on and they really will be at it all night, just to show the fat old sergeant what they're made of.

"*Seventy*-two-three-four..." Harry straightened and decided he was going to call the whole thing off in a minute. Rick and Sharon were both clearly in agony, and he regretted asking the question in the first place—it wasn't a joke anymore, and he'd never been the sort of NCO who took pleasure in torturing his subordinates. The only real question, he thought, is if they'd be angrier with me for calling it off than if I let them go on.

Rick faltered again, stopped, held himself stiff-armed for a whole count before resuming the rhythm. That's it, Harry thought with relief. Sharon had stumbled a bit too, her left arm refusing to straighten completely a couple of times, but he was ready to declare her the winner.

He'd just drawn breath to speak when the alarm siren made speech impossible.

The piercing wail cut off after a minute. Harry knew it would start again soon enough—one minute on, one off, until Headquarters decided everyone had got the message. Not the up-and-down banshee cry or short on-and-off blasts of an attack, though, at least it wasn't that...

"Shit!" came from both the airmen on the ground, as they collapsed into quivering heaps.

"Get up," Harry told them, in the sort of voice calculated to produce obedience in anyone who'd spent time at Lackland. They did it, even though they could barely use their arms to lift themselves from the ground, even though as they stood there at semi-attention their muscles twitched uncontrollably, already chilling in the desert night.

"Airman Welton, Sergeant Carpenter, get back and make sure the entire flight has their shit together before we get in the Blackhawks. The *entire* flight, you understand, and if it's necessary, tell them I sent you." They nodded; they knew who the troublemakers were, and how to deal with them. Ben's rank and Rick's size should be plenty, with Harry's borrowed authority to be used only as a last resort. "Airman Alcazar, if you want to get back to the SP barracks, I'll understand. If you don't, we've got a seat for you."

The sweat on Sharon's face was only partly the result of exercise. "If I receive an order from a senior NCO—well, the rest of my squadron isn't going anywhere. Sir."

They understood each other. "Is your weapon racked?"

"It's with the NCOD." Who was Linda Lewis, a tech sergeant who didn't much care for rifles and would be happy to give Alcazar's back before the choppers lifted. "Good. Retrieve your weapon and join me on Rodeo Three." Which was strictly speaking a violation, having combatants in a craft with a Red Cross on its nose, but no one was going to be checking ID cards. "We may find it useful to have a good shot along." And she spoke Arabic, some kind of getting-in-touch-with-her roots thing, and you never knew.

They turned and ran for the chopper pad.

Harry tried to ride with the rocking motion of the Blackhawk and keep his mind on his training. It was easier to think about this as a mass-casualty exercise than the collection of real cases it would inevitably become. He'd be one of the very top people on the ground—the Army sent flight surgeons out for this kind of work, but the Air Force didn't—and his first responsibility would be triage. Don't think about them as real casualties, he told himself. Just think of them as items, to be labeled green or yellow, red or black. Just tags.

That worked until the chopper shook so hard they all nearly went flying around the cabin.

Outside, flak came up like giant softballs from the toy-sized

ZSU four–barrel antiaircraft guns they could barely see in the pre–dawn light. None of the softballs came very close, but Harry knew their detonations could invert the choppers, and then everyone on board would die just as surely as if they'd been blown apart in the air. The Blackhawks were wonderful birds, much tougher and more stable than the Hueys they had recently replaced, but there were limits. He hoped the pilots got them down soon.

Something—several somethings—passed *under* them, moving too fast to see until they were some distance away, tailpipes glowing with afterburner exhaust. "Those aren't ours," Linda said next to Harry, her voice tight with fear.

"British planes," someone else said, as calm as it was possible to be under the circumstances. "Tornadoes. Going after the ZSU's."

He was right. The RAF pilots snuffed out the Iraqi AA, making it look as easy as shaking out a match, and the last half–klick of the medics' flight was smooth. When they hit the ground, the Marines were already driving out to meet them, vehicles packed with Navy corpsmen and their patients. Harry's mind rebelled at the word—"patients" were people with sore throats and twisted ankles, people you saw in brightly lit sterile rooms, people who talked to you instead of screaming and thrashing around or, worse, lying quiet and still.

Whatever these people were, they weren't just colored tags.

One of the corpsmen was covered in blood and looked like he was about to fall out of his vehicle. No matter what the rules say, medics always take care of their own first: if the medics die, after all, what happens to the rest of the wounded? When Harry got up to him, he shook his head and said, "The blood's not mine.

Here, help me get this sonofabitch out."

They lifted out a Saudi private whose left leg was hamburger from mid–thigh to knee. The corpsmen had done all they could for him on the ground, packing the wound with an ABD pad and what looked like fifteen field dressings, but he needed definitive treatment. The corpsman gave report as they ran for the choppers, lugging the stretcher with the Saudi on it between them and trying not to dump the poor bastard. "B/P's eighty by palp, resps twenty–eight, LOC responsive. Tried to get an IV in him but he's avenic."

The Saudi grabbed at Harry's sleeve and said something, quite loudly. "What's he trying to tell me?" he asked the corpsman.

The corpsman shrugged. "Been saying that ever since we picked him up. Hell if I know Arabic."

Linda was standing at the door of the chopper, her hands and forearms covered in blood and other body fluids. "We've got three red tags in here and a couple of black in the back," she warned them. "Dustoff in less than one. Your boy need to go that bad?"

"Might be a femoral. Hard to tell with the pads." He was still talking, but if there were a bone fragment too near his femoral artery, one twist or jolt in the wrong direction and he'd bleed out in minutes.

Decision flickered across Linda's face. "All right, bring him on board." She was loadmaster for this trip; although Harry and a couple of others on the rescue flight outranked her, there had to be someone with the authority to decide when to stop loading. On the ground, the loadmaster was God, the same as the pilot was in the air. Next time out, Harry thought, maybe I'll get to be God for a while. What fun.

They had him halfway on when they heard the M16 shots.

For God's sake don't drop him, Harry thought, and set his end of the stretcher poles on the floor of the chopper, where they should be all right for a minute or two. Then he turned, very carefully keeping his hand away from the butt of his pistol. They carried the weapons because even with the Red Cross on their arms they were still soldiers in a war, but no one expected ever to have to use the damned things, and it might still be possible to avoid such use even now.

Depending on why those shots were fired, of course.

Sharon knelt in a textbook firing position, her weapon still at her shoulder, still sighting in on a knot of Saudi walking wounded who had come in with the Marines. One of them wasn't walking anymore, and the neat hole in his forehead said he never would again. The other Saudis stood around him with expressions that promised more death in the near future.

"I'll tell the pilot to hold the dustoff," Linda said.

Harry nodded and walked slowly toward Sharon. "Airman Alcazar," he said, raising his voice to be audible over the engine noise but carefully not shouting, "what exactly do we have here?"

"Son of a bitch made a grab for me, sir," she replied in the same level tone, still aiming her M16.

"And you shot him?" Harry let his hand drift toward his pistol. He liked Sharon, thought she was a good troop and a good cop and a good human being, and if he had to shoot her to save the lives of a group of people he'd never seen before in his life and didn't particularly care for, he would.

"He was still armed. Grabbed at my tits with one hand, had the weapon in the other, told me to put down my weapon and do what a woman should do." A pause. "Doesn't translate well out of Arabic, but you get the idea. Sir."

Two ideas, Airman, he wanted to say but didn't. *One is that it was an attempted rape, in front of his God and his buddies, which I can well believe, and you did the right thing. The other is that you overreacted to a crude remark and killed an allied soldier and earned yourself a one–way trip to Kansas. God damn.*

"Yes," he said. "I think I do."

A shout behind him, "Get down, Gunny!" A hand in the middle of his back, pushing him off balance, and he fell hard and rolled away and tried to get his weapon out of the holster and there was more firing, from Sharon right in front of him and the chainsaw sound of a SAW somewhere to his right, and three more Saudis went down. The others scattered, half and half in two directions, taking up firing positions behind nearby vehicles and Blackhawks. More shots now, the general racket of a firefight instead of individual bangs. Bullets snapped over his head, as much felt as heard. Fifty meters downrange a grenade went off, muffled but immensely loud, throwing up a shower of sand.

What the fuck?

Someone grabbed at his leg. He crunched sideways in the dirt, finally got his weapon out, pointed it at a terrified face pale under Arab coloring and desert tan. The wounded Saudi, the one he'd been about to load for evac before everything went crazy. The guy was still babbling, gesturing with his free hand while he gripped Harry's ankle, but he didn't look hostile. Harry looked around, saw Sharon wriggling backward toward the cover of the chopper strut.

The Blackhawk's rotor started to spin up until a mortar round shattered the hub. Two blades flew away like huge javelins, almost too fast to see.

"Alcazar!" he shouted. "Get the fuck over here!"

She saw him, nodded, and wrapped herself around the strut, holding herself off the sharp edge of the wirecutter with one hand and still doing a decent job of aiming her M16 with the other, an unconscious display of strength. "What can I do for you?"

"Find out what this guy's trying to tell me." Maybe the Saudi could explain what the hell was going on. On the other hand, maybe he just wanted to say, "I'm dying, Sarge, tell my Mom I did my best." Whatever. Harry wanted to hear it either way.

Sharon's face went carefully neutral. "Yes, sir." She couldn't be happy right now about talking to an Arab instead of shooting him. Fuck it, Harry thought, she's a good troop, she'll do what she's told. And if she gets me good intelligence, something that helps us get out of here alive, I'll make sure she doesn't go to Leavenworth. Somehow.

Sharon put her face close to the Saudi's, then looked up at Harry in disbelief. "He wants you to, to take him back to the fight. He says he's not that badly hurt and he doesn't want people to think he ran away."

"Tell him he took a hit from a fifty–one–caliber machine gun and he's not going anywhere for a long time."

More Arabic, somehow guttural and musical at once, and Sharon said, "He still says it's not that bad."

"Fucking raghead wants to be a fucking hero? Get him to tell us why half his buddies are dead and the other half are trying to kill us, then. I'll pin a fucking Silver Star on his chest myself if he tells us that."

They talked in Arabic for a good while after that, or at least it seemed so to Harry, pinned down as he was in the largely illusory cover of the Blackhawk while bullets ricocheted off its metal skin a foot above his head. It probably wasn't more than a minute in real time.

Finally Sharon shook her head and switched back to English. "I'm not sure I get all this. There's some kind of guy, this... not a priest, but a religious leader of some kind—excuse me." She flattened herself against the wirecutter, ignoring the sharp metal for a moment of fierce self-control, and squeezed off three quick shots from her M16. The volume of fire in their vicinity seemed to slack off for a moment. "Okay. Or a politician, something like that. Whatever.

"He's got like a, a cult following with some of the guys. Some of the Saudi troops, I mean. They shouldn't be fighting Iraq, the Iraqis are their Moslem and Arab brothers, they should band together to fight the Great Satan instead. Same kind of shit you hear from the Moslem CO's back home. But these guys aren't CO's. They're the guys shooting at us. It's like half-and-half. Half the troops think this guy's an asshole, the other half think he's Mohammed incarnate. They've been waiting for this."

"Fuck," Harry said in the quietest voice he'd used since the shooting started, and rolled over to try to get a good firing position. The little nine-millimeter pistol wouldn't be much in this kind of fight, but it was what he had. And if they were going to be fighting half the Saudi brigade here at Khafji—with a battalion of exhausted Marines and a few Air Force medics armed largely with pistols—the Geneva Conventions wouldn't get much respect from either side, and every shot would count.

Not that it would keep them from dying in the end. They would tell stories about Khafji the way they did about Thermopylae, was all. It was something.

The Marine who had pushed Harry to the ground now wriggled forward to join them beside the chopper. "Gunny," he said, "I can see their MG gunner. He's set up behind that deuce over there. If you cover us, I bet we," a nod toward Sharon, "can get in a good firing position and take his ass out."

Gunny? Harry thought. The Marine must have looked at his rank stripes and come up with the best equivalent. It would work for now. "All right," he said. "Tell me when. Try not to die."

The Marine nodded, looked at Sharon for confirmation, and jumped up and started running. He and Sharon leapfrogged each other, one going to ground and firing while the other dashed forward a few meters, faster than Harry could have covered the ground at a run. I'm definitely too old for this, Harry thought. Should leave it to the young ones. Join the Air Force to stay out of Vietnam and look what happens. Then he gave up thinking for a while, tried to concentrate on giving what covering fire he could to the two superbly trained homicidal kids in front of him.

The light machine gun fire stopped, leaving only the heavy slow sound of the fifty–calibers and the chattering of the SAWs. He supposed that was a good sign. He squeezed off another shot for luck, the pistol bucking in his hand with familiar force, and realized with amazement that his magazine was empty. Where had all those bullets gone?

Without the machine gun, the turncoat Saudis didn't last long. The Marines had lived up to their reputation for fast action, and two RAF Tornadoes still circled this small section of the battlefield like hawks, dipping occasionally to unload napalm or high explosive. That would do for the local bunch of ragheads, probably no more than a platoon in total. Harry looked toward the center of the town, where there was still steady fighting going on. That was where the Iraqi tanks were, and their new–found allies if the wounded Saudi were to be believed, and they would come this way very soon.

Oh Jesus, he thought, the casualty. Back to being a medic for a moment. He turned to look at the Saudi and saw him lying slack, half–in and half–out of the wrecked Blackhawk, quite still. "Oh," Harry said, and Linda stumbled out into the dawn sunlight, blinked, started to speak, and fell across the Saudi's body with a fist–sized hole in her back showering red froth across Harry's face. There was no sign of air moving through the hole that Harry could see.

Sharon and the Marine walked back toward him, a movement quite different from either their bent–over, under–fire run or the swagger Harry usually associated with rifle troops. "Good work," the NCO told them as he tried to wipe the blood of his friend and his patient off his face.

"Gunny," the Marine said, his face tight and his voice thick with tears and very young. "Just got some people from Battalion. The ragheads, they—oh, shit." He stopped where he was and collapsed, going first to his knees and then putting his head to the ground as though imitating a Moslem praying to Mecca, and began sobbing.

Sharon looked at him with what might have been compassion, then back to Harry. "What he's trying to tell you is that the entire Marine Battalion command has been wiped out. Throats cut at HQ by Saudis. All the officers, most of the NCO's, all the Saudi officers who weren't part of the plan. And every senior ranker we had out here in this part of town is dead. I think," a cough, "you're in charge now, Master Sergeant Elkins."

Harry pulled himself upright and looked around. Iraqi armor

right ahead of them, in the center of town, that was a known quantity. But all around them, somewhere in the desert, were Saudi formations of unknown allegiance. They had a few RAF birds overhead still, no functioning choppers—those must have been the Saudis' first priority—and a shitload of wounded. What was left of the Marine Battalion and those Saudis who hadn't turned their coats was scattered for miles around. Unexpected assumption of command seemed like a minor problem if viewed in that light.

"All right," he said. "Thank you, Airman Alcazar. See about assembling the flight, and find me a Marine with a couple of stripes, would you?" She nodded and turned away.

Harry squatted beside the sobbing Marine. "Lance Corporal," he said, and then, louder, "Lance!"

"Gunny?"

"Get up. *Get the fuck up!"* The Marine straightened by reflex and stood at rigid attention. Tears and snot still streamed down his face.

"Good," Harry said, returning to a normal tone. "Now, listen. I am going to assemble every Marine and airman and Saudi good guy I can find, and I am going to march us out of here, and we are going to kill everyone who tries to stop us. Just like Chosin, you understand? Chosin, except with better weather."

"Aye aye, Gunnery Sergeant."

"Good. Go round up your buddies." Harry watched him go, then slumped against the chopper strut. He's taken care of, he thought, and Sharon, and whoever else they can find. Who's going to take care of me?

Two

January 1991
Washington and Moscow

"Mr. President, Mr. Speaker, members of the United States Congress. I come to this house of the people to speak to you and all Americans, certain we stand at a defining hour. Halfway around the world, we are engaged in a great struggle in the skies and on the seas and sands."

Bush looked down at the faces looking up at him—the depressed faces of those Democrats who had been harboring presidential ambitions, the glowing, cheerful faces of his fellow Republicans.

This is great, he thought. This is super. The kid'll be leaving for Norway right after the speech. Out of my hair. All's right with the world. Top of the world. Riding high.

"For two centuries we've done the hard work of freedom," he told the joint session. And the cameras. And the millions of watching voters. "And tonight we lead the world in facing down a threat to decency and humanity. What is at stake is more than one small country, it is a big idea—a new world order." He grinned at them, and they—the majority of them—grinned back at him. "The world has said this aggression would not stand, and it will not stand."

He talked about the end of the Cold War and about America's leadership. "My leadership" he could have said, but he didn't need to. This way, everyone could join in and feel proud and resolute, warriors bringing peace. But the implication of his personal leadership was clear nonetheless.

Payback's coming, he thought. Presidential election. *My* reelection. I'll show them a landslide. Out from the shadow. Come into my own.

"The principle that has guided us is simple: our objective is to help the Baltic peoples achieve their aspirations, not to punish the Soviet Union. In our recent discussions with the Soviet leadership we have been given representations, which, if fulfilled, would result in the withdrawal of some Soviet forces, a reopening of dialogue with the republics, and a move away from violence. We will watch carefully as the situation develops. And we will maintain our contact with the Soviet leadership to encourage continued commitment to democratization and reform."

Hold on, Gorby. Never, never, never let go. You can do it.

"Tonight, we work to achieve another victory, a victory over tyranny and savage aggression."

Good line. They love it. Now stuff about the legislative program. Thousand points of light. Help your neighbor. Free trade, jobs, competitiveness. Fighting crime, fighting drugs. Red meat. Lots of good stuff.

Some kinda trouble in that Saudi border city. Don't remember the name. Doesn't matter. Smash 'em up, grind 'em up, and move on. Probably all be over by the time I go to bed. Maybe by the time I finish this speech.

Okay, that's enough of that part. Back to the war. Make them stiffen their spines, throw out their chests. All warriors together.

"Almost 50 years ago, we began a long struggle against aggressive totalitarianism. Now we face another defining hour for America and the world. There is no one more devoted, more committed to the hard work of freedom, than every soldier and sailor, every Marine, airman and Coastguardsman—every man and every woman now serving in the Persian Gulf."

Lip service to diplomacy. Gotta do that. Name the foreign leaders who tried to prevent the war. Don't say they're pussies. Leave that for the commentators. Gotta pay lip service to the other countries' troops there, too. Then back to America. Leadership. Strength. Technology. Noble motives. We'll do the job, then we'll get out. No occupation for us. Warning to any other despot. We'll do it again, if we have to. We're riding high. We're top of the world. Eat our dust.

"Our cause is just. Our cause is moral. Our cause is right.... The winds of change are with us now.... We move toward the next century, more confident than ever that we have the will at home and abroad to do what must be done."

The applause that followed, the handshakes, the near adulation—he drank it all in, he gloried in it. He *was* the Commander in Chief.

Petty Officer Third Class Hans Zurcher raised his head slightly from the deck chair so he could look out over the ocean. The water was a blue so intense it almost hurt to look at it. He felt a touch of synesthesia, fancying he could *hear* the blue and the glitter of sun off the waves and the thin white line of surf, far away at the edge of vision, where the sea met the Iraqi coast. Between there and his seat on the deck of the *Bunker Hill,* fishing boats dotted the unreally calm water. Hans wondered how their crews felt, trying to do their jobs in the middle of a war. Their ancestors had fished this water for millennia, a span of time the American sailor could barely get his mind around; in a matter of months, or at most years, the Americans would be gone and the fishermen would still be here. If I were in their shoes, he thought, that wouldn't be much comfort. The whole damned US Navy was out here *right now.* If the shooting started, the boat crews would die in seconds, and their age-old traditions would provide no succor at all.

Growing up in Minot, North Dakota hadn't prepared him for any of it. Not the age of the traditions just about everywhere they put into port, not the endless open sea bigger even than the prairie back home, certainly not lying out on the deck of a warship sunning himself in sight of enemy territory.

Hans laid his head back down and prepared to cover himself with more sunscreen. Even in winter, the Gulf sun was murder on the milk-pale skin his own ancestors had bequeathed him. He got a tiny drop in the palm of his hand, then the farting sound of an empty bottle. "Damn," he said. "Chief, you got any more?"

Senior Chief Petty Officer David Ellis, a couple of feet away, shook his head and laughed. "Zurcher, why the hell you spend your time out here anyway? You look like a lobster."

"Gets me out of F-Division," Hans said. "You know, all that air conditioning, coffeemaker going all the time, nothing to do but tweaking the fire control systems..." His voice was earnest. "Hey, I just put on PO3, it's time for me to get more experience with the rest of the ship. Being out here teaches me a little about how the deck apes live."

"Bullshit," Ellis said, but Hans could tell he was trying not to laugh. That was the secret to dealing with chiefs, Hans had learned long ago. Make them laugh enough to like you, but not so much that they decided you were too much of a smartass. Ellis had more of a sense of humor than most. That came from his history, Hans thought. The petty officer turned his head fractionally so he could see the chief.

Ellis was nut-brown everywhere except his left leg, where a huge white scar ran from ankle to hip. It was a fascinating thing, that scar. It looked like an organism in its own right, a small tree or a vine, rather than something on a human body. It had its own knots and whorls and even branches. Ellis was the first gunner's mate on the ship, a hard job, and he could keep up with any of the younger men; but everyone had seen him limping badly after a long day, probably more than the Navy should have allowed. And no one ever said anything about it, because the experience inside Ellis' grizzled head was worth more than any set of whole legs.

Seaman Apprentice David Ellis had been a machine gunner on a PT boat in the brown-water Navy back in 1969, cruising up and down tributaries of the Mekong. That was hard work of a different sort, boring and tense and terrifying all at the same time. The US boats were the toughest thing out on the open water, an absolute terror to the sampans they were there to police—but the banks were dense jungle where anyone could be hiding, and heavy weapons could be dragged up almost to the water's edge and still be invisible from the river. An NVA rocket attack had blown Ellis' boat to hell and embedded pieces of metal all up and down his leg. Then the Communists had opened up with a machine gun, shooting the survivors in the water.

Ellis had submerged himself in the muddy water, yanked off his belt and tied it around his leg by touch to act as a tourniquet, then managed to grab an even more badly wounded crewmate and swim to the opposite bank. There the two of them crawled half a mile through the jungle to an Army firebase. Ellis said he remembered nothing between the attack and waking up in a MASH, but there had been a Silver Star hanging from the frame of his bed when that happened. Hans figured, and apparently the Navy did too, that the whole chain of events pretty much excused a man from a bum leg.

Which was why when Ellis' eyes snapped open and he sat up to look out over the sea at the fishing boats, Hans did the same.

"Something wrong, Chief?"

"I'm not sure," the older sailor replied, but the tone of his voice said something was *very* wrong, he just didn't know yet what it was. "See how those boats are arranged?"

Hans felt a chill, despite the heat of the Middle Eastern sun. Before, the boats had been scattered randomly across the waters of the Gulf. Now it seemed as though they were neatly arranged in a vast semicircle, its center nearly touching the Iraqi coast and its arms reaching for miles in either direction around the American fleet. "A lot of activity on deck," he said, trying to keep his voice calm.

Smoke billowed from the boats. "Uh–oh," Ellis said.

Hans felt his ears assaulted by a roar like he'd never heard before, not even when the *Bunker Hill* fired its five–inch gun, a huge sound felt as much as heard, and going on and on. Where only the sun had glittered on the waves before, now the sea was lit by red sparks trailing smoke, and as the sparks grew closer they became lean black shapes moving so fast they were just beyond the edge of clear vision.

Behind Hans, there was another roar, this one familiar and comforting: the Phalanx missile–defense system springing to life. Hans felt a moment of pride in his work, the endless hours spent fine–tuning the machinery for just this moment, the delicate circuits and switches which controlled the high–speed guns' monstrous power. In less than a second, many of the shapes coming toward them just *stopped,* blossomed into smoke and flame and then became pieces of scrap metal sinking into the suddenly oil–slicked water. But not enough of them, and not fast enough. Plenty of the shapes were still coming.

The deck heaved worse than in the heaviest seas. Hans was thrown from his chair, felt the breath go out of him as he slammed against metal. Chief Ellis was already rolling with the blow, rising very fast despite his leg, and then standing. "Antiship missiles on the fishing boats!" he bellowed over the noise. "Goddamn ragheads! Keep this fucker floating long enough for us to kill all those sons of bitches!" Hans had barely managed to get to his feet when he saw Ellis disappear down a hatch. Headed to his post, presumably, which reminded Hans he ought to do the same. The machinery wouldn't fix itself, and after this, it would need *plenty* of fixing.

Another one of those shapes streaked by him, very close, and the bridge disappeared in a shower of flame.

Some time later, Hans picked himself back up off the deck, which now seemed far from level. It was hard to be sure, because something was wrong with his balance: as soon as he stood up, he fell over again, and felt as though he were about to vomit. That didn't make sense; he'd never been seasick. And the battle h
somehow grown a lot quieter. He couldn't hear anyone sh

anymore at all, and even when the five-inch gun fired, its noise was only a mutter. He reached up to touch one of his ears and encountered something that felt like raw hamburger. He pulled his hand away and stared without comprehension at the red liquid and white spots, like paint chips, covering his fingers.

He had just begun to feel the pain when a wall of flame crossed the deck and tossed his smoking body into the sea.

Yazov entered without knocking.

Gorbachev looked up in surprise. He had been frowning over a diplomatic communiqué, trying hard to absorb the subtle complications it warned of. "Marshal, what— " He switched immediately to a different tone. "Dmitri, what's the matter?"

"What did you promise the Americans? Did you offer them the Baltic states?"

"Ah, that speech. Yes, I heard it, too. Bush gets carried away. Ignore him."

"But did you promise him the Baltics? He said you did. He said you had promised a withdrawal of our forces, and he said the Americans will open a dialogue with the Baltic republics. What else can that mean? You told him he can have the Baltics!"

Gorbachev stood up, walked up to the defense minister, and put his hand on the man's shoulder. He put all his sincerity into his voice. "Dmitri, I promise you I have done nothing to compromise our country's security. You should know me better than that, despite our disagreements."

"I do know you better than that," Yazov said reluctantly. "I know you mean well. But meaning well isn't good enough. Our forces are deteriorating, our country is crumbling, and now I hear these words from the American president. Even if I can trust you,

I don't know if I can trust your foreign minister. He's like his predecessor, too friendly with the American Secretary of State. Shevardnadze and Baker used to use nicknames with each other when they talked on the telephone. Did you know that? Jim and Shev." He grimaced. "It's an outrage."

And how do you know such a detail? Gorbachev wondered. No doubt from the GRU. It had its tentacles everywhere. It had even known of the Iraqi plan to invade Kuwait but had neglected to tell him, the president. No doubt they know what I say to Raisa over the phone, too, Gorbachev thought. A chill ran down his spine. "We have to get through the current crisis," he told the defense minister, "and then we can discuss these other matters."

"The current crisis," Yazov grumbled. "The current crisis isn't that the Americans wage war against one of our allies and we do nothing to stop them. That's just a symptom. The real crisis is that you have let the country grow weak and you refuse to stop the decline."

"As you have already said. Dmitri, you must let me deal with the most pressing matter, and right now that is indeed the American war in the Middle East. When that's over, then we can discuss longer range matters."

Bush was awakened at just after 1 a.m. on January 30 with the word that something had gone terribly wrong.

By the time he reached the Situation Room in the basement of the White House, Powell and Cheney were already there. Powell looked worried in that placid, almost bland way Bush had become used to. Cheney looked uncomfortable, as though he couldn't find a good position in his chair. Baker and Scowcroft came in as Bush was taking his seat at the conference table. Cups of coffee had been placed in front of each chair.

"All right, what the hell's going on?" Bush asked. "Some kind of setback? We've lost some troops?"

"It's more than that, I'm afraid, sir," Powell said. "Our friends have lost control of the ground in northern Kuwait, and we've lost contact with some of our ships in the Gulf."

"That's impossible! When I went to bed, our guys were rolling them back into Iraq. Out of that little town. Whatever it's called."

"Khafji, sir. Everything looked okay at first. We were taking their armor and artillery out from the air, and the Marines were retaking positions on the ground. Midmorning local time, we started having communications problems with the troops in Khafji."

"Local glitch," Bush said. "No big deal. Air power. Still in control."

"It appears to be a wider problem," Baker said. "We're getting reports of trouble throughout the region. Uprisings, mutinies, assassinations. I wish I could be more specific, but the communications problem Colin referred to is a general one."

Bush stared at him in horror. "What are you saying, Jim? The Coalition's shaky? My Coalition?"

"We just don't know for sure yet. That's the whole point: We know something's happening, but we're not getting the kind of information we usually depend on." He broke off and looked at Cheney. "Dick, are you all right?"

Cheney was pale. Through the combed-over hair, sweat gleamed on the top of his head. He waved his hand. "Yeah, fine. Just not awake yet." He picked up his coffee cup with a trembling hand. "This is awful," he muttered.

"Try more sugar," Bush said. "Listen—"

The Vice President burst into the room, face glowing with eagerness. "Sorry I'm late!"

"Why the hell aren't you in Norway?" Bush growled. "For the funeral?"

"I got a message from Brent about what happened in the Gulf, so I had them turn back. I knew you'd need good military advice."

Cheney said, "Awful."

Bush motioned toward the empty chair on his left. "Sit down, Dan. Listen carefully."

A Marine in dress uniform entered the room, saluted Powell, and said something quietly to him. "General Schwarzkopf is on the speaker, sir."

"Norm!" Bush said loudly. "What's happening there?"

Schwarzkopf's voice crackled from somewhere overhead. "We're in a shitload of trouble, sir. Something's going on out here. It's like an uprising, a general uprising. There's some kind of religious leader behind it. His people have taken over a bunch of radio and television stations, and they're broadcasting the weirdest stuff you've ever heard—all about purifying the Arab nation and brother not fighting brother and getting rid of the Crusaders. By which they mean us."

Bush looked at Baker, who held up both hands, palms up. "First I've heard about this," the Secretary of State said. He raised his voice, "General, how widespread is this? How good is your intelligence?"

There was a crackling sound from the speakers, through which the men in the Sit Room could hear only a few words in Schwarzkopf's distinctive voice. Then it cleared up. "Sorry about that, gentlemen. We're having all kinds of trouble. Jim, this was all new to us, a real surprise. Right now, our intelligence consists of a bunch of Saudi officers we captured when they tried to sneak in here and kill me. We're questioning them right now. I wouldn't have believed their stories, but—Hold on."

They could hear him talking to someone in the background. "Shit," he said loudly. "Fuck."

More background conversation. Then Schwarzkopf came back on the speakers. "Okay, here's the deal. We don't know who we can trust anymore. We're completely out of touch with about half our ground troops. Carriers are still okay, but we've lost contact with smaller vessels. One of the carrier pilots reports that he flew over the *Bunker Hill* in the Gulf, and it was listing badly and smoke was pouring out of it. Shouldn't be possible to get anywhere close to an Aegis vessel. Must be sabotage."

Powell cut in. "Norm, are you saying we've lost contact with, what, a couple of hundred thousand troops?"

"Yeah, something like that."

"But it's just a communications glitch, right? Just a problem talking to them?"

"I've got a feeling it's a lot worse than that."

"A *feeling?*"

"Right now, that's all I've got to go on."

Powell said, "Mr. President, I have to get back to my office. This is no time for a committee meeting."

"Sure," Bush said. "Go ahead."

Baker stood up. "And I have to find out what's really happening. My people will know the real picture."

One by one, they stood up and filtered out. Bush was left with his Secretary of Defense and his Vice President.

"Dick, we gotta know what's going on. The big picture."

Cheney stared back at him unblinking, a look of surprise on his face.

"Dick? Dick? Holy shit!"

"If he refuses to answer you, I think you should fire him," the Vice President said.

Quayle had skipped the funeral for King Olav V of Norway, but he would be forced to attend the funeral for Dick Cheney, whose weak heart had just given out.

The scope of the disaster became clearer during the hours that followed.

Obeying a summons, the Director of the Central Intelligence Agency arrived at the Oval Office at noon. Bush met him at the door and motioned him, not toward one of the chairs facing the large desk, but toward the couch in front of the fireplace at the other end of the room. Bush sat in one of the comfortable, armless chairs next to the couch, with his back to the crackling fire.

Given the circumstances, Webster thought, the setting was deceptively peaceful and inviting. In fact, at the best of times, he disliked the way sitting on the couch put him at a lower level, looking up at the man in the chair. It made him feel trapped, as though he wouldn't be able to escape if he had to.

"Bill, I've seen the reports your people have been sending me. What I want from you is an overview. Executive summary. Why in God's name didn't we see this coming?"

That last question was the one Webster had been sending down through the ranks repeatedly all day long. The replies had boiled down to little more than blank stares. Something more than that was required from him now.

"They were under our radar, Mr. President. I wish I could tell you more than that, but I can't. We've known for a few years that radical Islamists have been trying to infiltrate military organizations in the Arab world, but ever since the Sadat assassination, all the governments in the region have been on the lookout for them. They've become pretty good at finding those people and weeding them out. A lot of those terrorist outfits came out in the open too soon. You'll remember the big pro–Saddam demonstrations in Amman last summer. The Muslim Brotherhood was behind that. So they exposed themselves prematurely. This... this was something else. Much cleverer."

"And this guy, this Grand Mufti? Whatever he calls himself."

"Grand Master. The Grand Master of the Ismailites. He goes by the name Rashid–al–Din Sinan, which is surely not his real name."

"Why not? What do you mean?"

"Er, it's a reference to an historical figure, Mr. President. The leader of the Hashashim, the Assassins, during the twelfth century. Everyone was terrified of him and his men. Not just the Crusaders. The Arabs were scared of him, too. The Crusaders called him The Old Man of the Mountain. The mountain being the fortress of Alamut in what's now northern Iran, near the Caspian Sea."

The first broadcast had come an hour before, when it was evening in the Middle East, announcing to the world that a new government had been established, centered in Beirut, under the control of the Grand Master of the Ismailites. Rashid, the Grand Master, claimed the right to rule all of the Muslim world. It was an astonishing claim, and the CIA had at first dismissed it as coming from a lunatic who had managed to gain temporary control of a

Beirut radio station. But in light of the chaos into which Desert Storm had deteriorated, America's intelligence analysts had been forced to conclude that this was a lunatic who could not be ignored.

"Northern Iran, huh? That reminds me. Jim Baker got a call from the Iranian foreign minister. Suddenly, they want to be our friends."

Webster smiled. "That's the first amusing thing that's happened today. Maybe they wouldn't be so eager if they knew how little we're able to help our real friends right now. Or even ourselves."

Webster might have been even more amused if he had known that at that moment Jim Baker was on the telephone with his colleague and friend Eduard Shevardnadze, who was calling from an airplane over the Pacific, headed toward California. Also on the plane was Raisa Gorbachev. Shevardnadze was asking for diplomatic asylum for both of them—and in advance for Mikhail Gorbachev, who was expected to be following within hours.

"What about those friends?" Bush asked. "Can they hold on? Can we extract them?"

"Yesterday, I would've said, 'No problem.' Today... This Grand Master element throws everything up in the air. You can't put down a rebellion if your own troops have been infiltrated and you can't trust your own commanders. As for pulling the leaders out of there, you'll have to ask Powell to be sure, but I guess we're having enough trouble extracting our own troops right now. It's happening throughout the region. Looks like we'll have to write off Syria, Lebanon, Jordan. And Iraq and Kuwait, of course. Saudi—well, the whole damned peninsula. Even Turkey is getting worried. Egypt should be okay. But there've already been riots in

Tunis. We're getting reports of at least two attempts to assassinate Khadafi, and I don't think the people who're trying to kill him are on our side. We know they're not working for us."

Bush shook his head. "I don't know, Jim. We've been trying to be good friends to these people for years. Keep them on our side. They were supposed to keep things calm and level. Bring their people into the twentieth century. Be our friends. When Saddam invaded Kuwait and scared the piss out of the Saudis, I thought we were finally okay."

"We were pushing some very old buttons, Mr. President. Nerves that have been raw for a long time. To a lot of the people there, we're the Crusaders. They actually use that term. We're Christian invaders, just like the Crusaders in the Middle Ages. Maybe this Grand Master took that too seriously. Unfortunately, he's talked a hell of a lot of other people into taking *him* seriously. His people even seem to be using infiltrators for assassination, just like the historical Assassins. We've been getting word that the loyalist troops who were holding out around Damascus and in northern Jordan are being overrun or are switching sides to support the Grand Master, and part of that is because their commanders are being murdered."

"By who?"

"That's just it. We don't know. It's happening in spite of all their guards. Maybe it's being done *by* their guards." Webster considered telling Bush the story of Saladin's supposedly loyal bodyguards whom he had raised from boyhood but who turned out to be members of the Assassins. He decided not to bother. Reluctantly, he said, "We're losing touch with all of our people in the region, one by one. We've sent warnings to all of them, putting them on their guard, but it doesn't seem to matter. Someone knows who they are. Someone's getting to them."

"They're being killed?"

"Well, they're disappearing. Let's hope they're being killed. Quickly." He didn't have to remind Bush, himself a former director of the CIA, about William Buckley. Buckley, CIA station chief in Beirut, had been kidnapped by terrorists in March 1984, while the Lebanese civil war was raging. His "execution" was announced in October of the same year by the Islamic Jihad, but his body had never been recovered, and there were many in the CIA who suspected he was still alive somewhere... and still being tortured.

"Damn," Bush said. "I miss Dick."

Once again, Yazov entered without knocking or being announced. Others crowded in behind him—Plekhanov from the KGB, Vice President Yanayev, and even Gorbachev's own chief of staff, Valery Boldin.

This time, Gorbachev was half expecting it. Too late, he thought sadly. I'm sorry, Raisa. I waited too long.

He stood and, in a steady, calm voice, said, "Hello, Dmitri. What is it this time? And why such a crowd?"

"Mikhail Sergeyevich, I'm sorry it's come to this. I'm here as the representative of the State Committee of Emergency."

"I have authorized no such committee."

"We no longer wait for your orders! I've come to relieve you of your powers and to request that you place yourself in our custody. No harm will come to you. You must declare a state of emergency and then resign. You will be taken to your *dacha* in the Crimea and held there."

He went on for a while, speaking of the decline of the

country, the betrayal of a friend in the Middle East, the humiliating surrender to American power. Gorbachev heard little of it. He was pondering his future. He saw Yazov and the others as fools, but he thought he could believe them when they said he would not be harmed. Perhaps he would yet be able to join Raisa in exile after all! But what about this declaration of a state of emergency? He knew what that would mean—the end of all progress. He couldn't sign such a decree. He'd commit suicide first.

Yazov's face exploded, showering the room with blood and brains. His body jerked forward and flopped to the floor halfway to Gorbachev's desk.

Shouting, the others shrank back, trying to get away from their suddenly dead spokesman.

Through the now-clear doorway strode a young Army officer Gorbachev had never seen before. He held an AK-74 cradled casually in his right arm. From beyond the doorway came the sound of gunfire and explosions.

Gorbachev was overcome by relief. His knees gave way and he sat heavily in his desk chair. The attempted coup was over. He could have wished for a more peaceful ending, but at least it had ended, thanks to this young hero.

The young hero said, "I am Lieutenant Aleksander Vassilievich Slonimsky."

"And you're most welcome," Gorbachev said.

Slonimsky grinned. "Perhaps not." He swung left and right. His gun burped three times. Plekhanov, Yanayev, and Boldin jerked backward and fell motionless, chests bloody.

Gorbachev gasped. "That wasn't necessary! Even Yazov—you could have left him live. You could have let them all live."

Slonimsky shook his head. “Softhearted incompetents. You heard him say you would not be harmed. Hmph.”

The truth sank in. Too late. Gorbachev grabbed for the phone. He realized that the line was dead even as the bullets slammed into his chest.

In his office, waiting for Schwarzkopf to call on the secure phone, Powell was also missing Dick Cheney. No man was irreplaceable. That was the essence of careful planning: that the plans went forward on their own, each element, whether man or machine, playing its part. That was the idea, anyway. When it came to the political side of things, though, personality and contacts counted more than anything else.

The telephone on his desk rang, interrupting Powell’s thoughts. “General! What’s the latest?”

“Worse by the minute,” Schwarzkopf said. “There’s still something like twenty, thirty thousand ground troops we can’t reach. They’re in small groups. We know where they are, but ground fire is too intense to send in choppers, and we can’t reach them overland. We’re using close air support to keep them alive, but I don’t know how long we can keep that up.”

“Yeah. I understand.” All day, Powell had been getting reports of sabotage at air bases in Saudi Arabia and elsewhere—sabotage by Arab troops formerly believed to be friendly to the Americans. Nor was it limited to land. There had been numerous cases of explosions aboard ships, including carriers, in the Gulf. Bombs smuggled aboard somehow, or American munitions sabotaged. Exocet missiles, perhaps. Powell couldn’t imagine a plane getting close enough, undetected, to fire an Exocet. Nor could he imagine saboteurs getting through American security procedures. And yet it had happened. With the result that the air support Americans had come to rely on was thin and spotty and unreliable.

Something potentially worse had just been reported to him.

"General, I've just gotten word that someone managed to scuttle some ships in the Strait of Hormuz. Oil tankers. They're lengthwise across the narrowest part, just off the coast of Oman."

"Shit. How bad?"

"Looks like nothing the size of a carrier will be able to get through until we clear the obstruction."

"We need that air power. How long?"

"Hard to say," Powell told him. "The British and French have got their mine sweepers in the Gulf. They're sending them down to the south end to see if they can shove the junk aside enough to clear a passage. I don't know if that'll work. It's not what they're designed for."

"Hell, those minesweepers are up at the other end of the Gulf! They're hours away from there! We can't wait that long!"

"I don't know what else we can do. I've ordered the biggest bombs we have dropped on the obstruction. I don't know if that'll work."

"The biggest bombs? Nukes?"

"No, of course not. The long-term effects would be terrible. They'd hate us even more in the region."

"You've been dealing with politicians too long," Schwarzkopf said. "You're thinking like them. Order in the nukes."

"I can't do that."

"Can you lose tens of thousands of your kids?"

"General, for God's sake! I—"

Over the phone came the sounds of war. There was a scream,

and the line went dead.

Powell held the receiver, listening to the silence, praying it wasn't what he imagined, knowing it was. Knowing, too, that it was too late for nuclear weapons to matter. Too late, perhaps, for anything.

Three

February 1991
Saudi Arabia

They started moving again at dusk. It was the first rule of desert survival, to take shelter during the day and move at night, to avoid dehydration and eventual death. Even in the winter, the Saudi desert could be lethally hot. Harry had already started to wonder if what he'd said to the Marine, about the weather being better than at Chosin, was a lie.

He hunched around a map with Sharon and one of the Marine NCO's a little way from the main body of his troops. Air Force medics didn't have much need for map-reading skills, usually, and the lessons Harry had had years ago were barely a memory. Sharon was better at it. Staff Sergeant Leventhal, with ten years as a rifleman under his belt, was very good indeed. He was lanky, black-haired, olive-skinned. He looked like he belonged here, Harry thought. Of course, after a week in the desert, everyone looked like they belonged here. The desert did that to people, darkened and weathered them until racial and ethnic differences were worn away. Would have been nice if the

Arabs believed that.

This is my operation, he thought, *and the Marines and the Saudis have to remember that. But I'm not going to sacrifice useful skills for pride.*

The problem was that even for someone who knew how to read a map as well as Harry knew how to suture a wound, there wasn't much information out here. In one direction was the sea; in all others was an expanse of sandy dirt so flat that it could be distinguished from the sea only by color. The occasional gentle rise, like a long low wave frozen into rock, could provide cover for crawling soldiers. Anyone standing could see, and be seen, for miles.

"Not much to choose from," Leventhal said. "I figure we should stick close to the shore, about three hundred, three-fifty meters back, so we can use this here for cover if we need to." His finger traced the contour lines that marked one of the rises, running almost parallel to the shore for thirty kilometers or so. "Poke our heads up now and then and see what's out at sea. If they're friendly, we can signal them and they'll be able to pick us up in minutes. If they're not," a shrug, "we keep our heads down and keep going."

Harry nodded. "We have to assume we're not going to find anything by the time we get to the end of the rise," he said. "Is it worth setting up some kind of rally point, say here—" a tap of the finger at what looked like a spur on the rise, if the word could meaningfully be applied to terrain that never rose much more than a couple of meters above its surroundings "—and trying to bring in any other friendlies in the area? If we're going to be out here a while, we should maybe start thinking in terms of a command post, somewhere to pick up stragglers and plan for the rescue pick–up. Especially if they do it by air, they're not going to want to land 130's on the beach."

Leventhal's face, usually animated, went flat, a sign he didn't like Harry's idea. An airman would have just told Harry what he thought, but the Corps didn't encourage any response but "Aye aye, sir" when superiors proposed something dumb. At last the Marine said, "It's your decision, Gunny." All the Marines called him that now, which Harry supposed was a good sign.

"What Sergeant Leventhal isn't saying," Sharon said, "is that we can't think about this as an air operation, because it's not. It's a big hunt, and we're the deer. We'll get killed if we set up there, or probably anywhere. We need to present a moving target, and if there are other Americans out there, they can just find us on their own. If the people in charge of this clusterfuck decide to send in some air for us, we can worry about landing strips then, for God's sake."

Leventhal opened his mouth, then closed it again without speaking. Sharon grinned at him.

"Thank you, Airman Alcazar," Harry said, and stood up—slowly, and with the glance around the landscape that had become SOP for all of them. "You're both right, of course. Sergeant Leventhal, in any case, we need some more organization than what we have right now. In fact, what we have right now is, as Airman Alcazar put it, a clusterfuck." He waved his hand as she started to speak. "I know you weren't talking about us particularly, but it's true. We're a little clusterfuck in the middle of a big one. Let's do something about that.

"Specifically, we've got the numbers for an overstrength company. Sergeant Leventhal, I'd like you to take charge of integrating the Air Force and Saudi elements into your formations, with an eye toward spreading them around—about equal numbers of airmen in each platoon, and try to make sure that either the Saudis speak English or that one of the translators is around. No squads that are all Arabic-speaking, or we'll lose communications. If they have to, they can figure out what's going on by watching everyone else. And try not to mix them with the female personnel." Sharon looked away.

"The main body will travel by squads, staggered to provide overwatch. Let's try to maintain no more than fifty meters between squads. That may not be ideal for this terrain, but if we get too strung out at night we'll never find each other. Try to give each platoon its own mortar and anti-tank capability. If anything happens, it'll happen too fast for a separate heavy weapons platoon. The gunners should be able to coordinate well enough if they have to.

"Also, I'd like a couple of recon squads that can travel ahead of and behind our line of march, about a hundred meters up and out, which means a fair amount of crawling when they're on the rise. They'll move by bounding overwatch and I'd like them to be down to very light weaponry; keep the Dragons and M60's with the main body. If you want to use all Marines for that job, I won't object, though I'd like to recommend Airman Alcazar here, and an Airman Welton in my group, for the job if they'd like it."

Leventhal folded the map and stood at something that was almost attention. "Aye-aye, Gunny. I'll take care of it." He walked away briskly, not at all like a man who knew that he and his friends were most likely all going to die within a few days.

"Give them orders and they're like a kid on Christmas," Sharon said. "But you're good at that, sir. You're very good."

"Thank you again, Airman," Harry said. He wanted to say

more, a lot more, but he knew he couldn't. He wanted to put his arms around every single one of them, all these kids, and shelter them from the bad people who wanted to hurt them and tell them everything would be all right. All he could do instead was lead them, and he wasn't sure that was enough.

It would have to be. While there was still light enough to see by, he made his way back to his command.

They had almost burrowed in for the day when one of the recon squads reported the ship.

Harry made his way to the top of the rise, crawling for the last several meters until he lay half–buried in sandy dirt, with a clear view out to sea. There were things crawling around inside his clothing, tiny parasitical creatures that did not care in the least for his personal survival; most of them would cheerfully feed on him whether or not he was alive. He forced them out of his awareness and focused on the wreck.

That it was a wreck was immediately obvious, even though he could barely make it out. To the naked eye it was the size of a very small toy boat. The cloud of oily smoke rising from it was much larger than the ship itself. The smoke rose perceptibly above the horizon, then almost vanished as it hit a strong wind that carried it north. To Iraq, and points beyond.

"One of ours?" he asked, of no one in particular. One of the Marines handed him binoculars. He muttered his thanks, brought the binoculars to his eyes and found the focus.

Then he almost wished he hadn't. The lines and the paint were distinctively American, as was the inverted flag the ship flew. Whoever had raised that distress flag was probably dead now, or wished he was. The ship was dead, without a doubt. She was listing worse by the minute, and the many fires on board were spreading fast.

"Cruiser," said a Marine, his voice filled with a terrible awe. "I didn't think the Iraqis could sink anything that big."

"They couldn't," another said. "But the Saudis could."

Oh, Jesus, Harry thought, that's right. The Saudis have everything they need, mines, anti–ship missiles, torpedoes, the best stuff in the world. We gave it to them. Made in the USA.

"Aircraft coming in," someone said, tight and afraid.

Harry rolled over and squinted into the sky. Not far away, two Marines were breaking out Stingers. The antiaircraft missiles were most effective when aimed at the tailpipes of departing craft—wonderful weapons for guerrillas operating from good cover, as the Soviets had learned to their regret in Afghanistan, but very weak in open country. But it was what they had.

Then Harry almost sobbed with relief. The plane was an AC–130 gunship, in USAF colors rather than Saudi, and it wasn't a burning wreck about to fall from the sky. He jumped up, not caring how far he could be seen on the ground, not when that blessed bird was up there in the air. "Make an LZ!" he shouted, then realized that was silly; the pilot had nothing but perfect natural runway for miles around, and he could surely see where the troops he had come to rescue were. "Stay clear when they come in," Harry finished, feeling the need to say something.

"Oh, shit," Ben said. "Harry, I don't think he's landing."

"What? Of course he's—oh." The 130 wasn't slowing down much, nor coming in low enough. The troops on the ground had a brief glimpse of the crew before something tumbled out and the plane went into a hard banking climb.

They watched the 130 disappear into the clear desert sky,

the tiny dot it had dropped blossoming into a parachute with a crate suspended underneath. It was a good drop, the kind aircrews practiced on the range and got perfect scores for in exercises. I hope you're proud of that one, guys, Harry thought.

The troops broke cover and ran for the crate as soon as it landed. Harry thought about yelling at them, decided against it. It wouldn't stop anyone, and there was nothing for miles around, and the 130 crew would have shot at any Iraqis they'd seen. He hoped they would have, anyway.

He jogged up as some Marines and Saudis finished tearing it open. A few M16's and SAW's, four M60's and four Dragons, and a shitload of LAW's were on top, then several ammunition boxes. Well, that made sense—however little contact with the enemy they might have had since leaving Khafji, the time would probably come when they'd need everything they could get their hands on. This way everyone could have a rifle or a SAW instead of a pistol, at least. Except for the M60's and the Dragons, it was all light stuff, which was also good from a marching perspective. How good it would be against the armor–heavy Iraqis was another question.

Under that was a layer of MRE's and water bottles, which were just as important. Especially the water. Everyone was suffering, the big guys like Rick most of all. They could live without a great deal of food, but nobody could skimp on water. Harry had seriously considered mixing the few remaining IV bags with the water in their canteens... And under the food and water were some more medical supplies, including those blessed IV bags. Anyone who got badly wounded enough to need an IV out here was dead anyway, but a couple of liters of normal saline was still the fastest and best treatment for dehydration.

"Mail call, Gunny," one of the Marines said, grinning. Amazing that anyone out here could find anything to smile about, but this one looked like he should still be in high school. He handed Harry a single sheet of paper.

The note was handwritten, not typed or printed, and barely readable. Like it was written in a plane, bouncing around, Harry thought, which was probably no more than the truth. "Hostiles have everything north of 25 degrees. We have Qatar and Bahrain. Head for Qatar for evacuation. We'll get you sooner if we can. Maintain radio silence." There was no signature, indeed nothing at all except the messy handwriting to indicate that the note had come from a single, identifiable human being.

"Back down to Qatar's two hundred, two-fifty miles," Ben muttered. "This is a fucking joke."

"No," Harry said. He stared at the place in the sky where the plane had gone. "I don't think they're joking at all."

They came in over the desert under a waning sliver of a moon, mottled ghosts blending perfectly with sky and sand. They could be heard, there was nothing to be done about that, but they could not be seen unless they chose otherwise. And if the enemy saw them, it would be the last thing he ever saw.

Warrant Officer Tom Bateman watched his instruments and the featureless night around him with equal and complete attention. You couldn't split yourself between what you saw and what the readouts told you, not at all; that was suicide. The trick was to make it all part of the overall perception, make the VDU and the HARS and the IFF and all the rest of the alphabet soup just as much a part of your senses as the Eyeball Mark One, and then take it all in at once.

Whether there was going to be anything out here to see at all was another question.

They'd left from a Forward Arming and Refueling Point just north of Dammam, with orders to fly up the coast and find a group—maybe a few groups—of Americans who had supposedly made it out the clusterfuck up by Kuwait. Tom was vaguely aware of his squadron in the air just behind him, even without radio chatter, just from the feel of being in the air with more than sixty other choppers at once. On the ground before setting out, everyone had been confident. The 227th might not know what the fuck was going on, anymore than anyone else did, but they were a good team, they had the best equipment in the world, and they were the best helicopter pilots in the Goddamn US Army. Even the knowledge that as soon as they left the FARP was going to pull up stakes and head back to Bahrain on a boat hadn't dampened their mood.

That had been on the ground. It was different after almost an hour in the air with no sign of life, friendly or otherwise, down there in the desert sand.

It was the infrared, not the Eyeball Mark One after all, that first told him they were down there. The Apache pilots flying immediately behind him had the firepower, and behind them were the Blackhawks for the actual snatch, but his little Kiowa was the eyes of the whole squadron. "Ground movement eleven o'clock, over one hundred troops in the open, no vehicles," he said for his copilot's confirmation.

Truth be told, he didn't like Langston Thomas very much, in fact the guy was basically an asshole, but he had a very good eye and would make sure Tom was seeing what he thought he saw before the pilot made an idiot of himself on the whole squadron net.

"Tally movement... Vehicles, in column, nine o'clock. I count three, no, four ZSU-23-4's, SA-6's, BMP's—Jesus, that's a battalion down there, and they're going straight for our guys. We need to tell Squadron."

Tom nodded. "Do it. I'm going to try to reach them on the ground." Radio silence was well and good, but the Americans on the ground—if they were Americans, and right now he had to believe they were—needed to know what was about to hit them, and that help was on the way. They needed to know right now.

Harry had almost forgotten about the survival radio he carried. There were several of them, salvaged from the wrecked choppers—more specifically, from the bodies of dead pilots—and carried along almost as an afterthought. They were fairly short-range, though they were supposed to put out a beacon that any search-and-rescue team could pick up from some distance away, and he didn't think they were going to do much good. But they were light enough, compared to the heavy rucksacks everyone was carrying, and it couldn't hurt to have them along.

"Alpha Kilo Two Seven to all units on this net, all units on this net, do you copy, over?"

He dropped his rucksack and grabbed the radio. For a moment he couldn't remember how to make the damned thing work. He fumbled with it in the dark, found the "send" button. "November actual to Alpha Kilo Two Seven, go ahead, over."

"November actual, be advised unfriendly forces are less than three klicks from your position on your five o'clock. Contact is imminent. We will provide support and attempt evacuation. Can you hold your current position, over?"

Harry looked around. It could be a trap, he thought, there have to be Iraqis or Saudis who can speak good English, and the Saudis know our frequencies. No, forget about it, if the bad guys know where we are we're dead already. "November actual to Alpha Kilo, we'll try. Do you have an ETA for evacuation, over?"

"November actual, we're about three mikes out from your position. I can find an LZ and we have heavy firepower for the unfriendlies. Alpha Kilo Two Seven out."

Sound carried well in the desert night, and now over the usual noises of a unit on the march—the creaks and rustles of equipment, labored breathing, the occasional soft curse or muttered snatch of conversation—Harry could hear both the thumping of helicopter blades and the grumble of diesel engines. The diesels were closer, he thought, but what mattered was not distance but time. The helicopters could move much, much faster than the armor... which wouldn't matter at all if the armor rolled over them a minute before the air support arrived.

"Everybody get over the ridge and form a line!" he shouted. "Enemy's coming in behind us! Friendly choppers coming in but they're not here yet!" Then he shut up and put everything he had into the awkward, half-blind scramble up and over the ridge. His feet slid in the sandy dirt and he could see the ground only as a silhouette against the stars. Those stars were heartbreakingly beautiful, brighter and more numerous here in the desert than he'd ever seen them before in his life, and they did not care in the least if he lived or died.

He flopped down on the seaward side of the ridge, only then remembering that he'd left his rucksack back out there in what was about to become no-man's-land. Fuck it, he thought, the ragheads can have it for a souvenir. "Radio, someone got a real radio?" he asked the rustling, panting mass of troops around him.

"Here is one, Master Sergeant," said a heavily accented voice. Harry stopped himself from making a grab for his weapon, it was one of the Saudis who'd stayed loyal, that was all—but Christ, he thought, it's like a scene from a bad movie, the hero asks his buddies for help and finds out the villain's killed them all. And there's no scriptwriter around to give me a way out of the deathtrap.

He took the PRC–77 and clicked it over to the company push. It was a more familiar device than the survival radio, and more comforting, somehow. With one of these, on a clear night like this, he could probably talk to Qatar, if anyone was listening. More to the point right now, he could get his troops into some kind of order before the shitstorm hit.

"November actual to all November, count off, over," he said, and let go of the button so he could hear the responses. That was one nice thing about working with the Marines, he knew he'd get the right answers instead of undisciplined chatter.

"November One Zero, aye." Leventhal, speaking with flat professional calm.

"November Two Zero, aye." This voice was one he didn't know, younger and not calm at all.

"November Three Zero, good to go." That was an airman, of course: Baumgartner, a medic turned infantry platoon leader. He did that job with the same cheerful fatalism he'd always shown in the ER, whether suturing a wound or doing CPR.

"November Four One, aye." Harry wondered for a moment where Four Zero had gone, then put it out of his mind. If the Marines kept up their traditions of leading from the front, a lot of platoon and squad leaders wouldn't be answering their radio calls soon. Whoever the Four One was, he'd answered when his name was called, and that was all you could ask, really...

"November Alpha Zero, aye."

"November Bravo Zero, aye."

Those were the recon elements, last to answer but quite possibly first to fight. And sure enough—"Bravo Two to November Actual, I confirm two... four BMP's headed our way." Harry gripped the radio tightly. That was Rick's voice, and maybe it wasn't fair but he realized that he wanted his own people, the airmen who'd flown in with him, to live even more than he wanted the Marines and the Saudis to do the same.

"November actual, request permission to fall back to the main line, over." Still businesslike, as though he didn't quite comprehend what was bearing down on him.

"November Bravo, you are *ordered* to fall back to the main line," Harry said. "November Two Zero, you are cleared to fire a flare and two Dragons for targeting. All units, fire for effect when you confirm targets. November actual out."

The world exploded.

"Missiles on the ground!" one of the Apache gunners screamed, as though everyone couldn't see it anyway. The scene was clearly illuminated by the flare the Americans down there had fired, and by the engines of the antitank weapons—Dragons and TOW's, Tom thought—they were using to engage the Iraqi armor. Not a bad way to start, he thought, but it won't be enough. He brought the Kiowa down in a hard bank that ended with them barely three meters above the ground, skimming over the desert at seventy knots.

"Tom," Langston asked, "what the fuck are you doing?"

Tom shook his head and didn't answer as he armed and locked the Hellfires. The Kiowa rocked slightly as the first missile dropped away. "Shot," Tom said. Langston glanced at him, then back at the Iraqis as the missile augured in.

"ZSU destroyed," the copilot said. All business now, at least until they broke off. You are an asshole, Langston, Tom thought, but at least you're a smart asshole.

"SA-6, three hundred degrees, twenty-one hundred meters," Thomas added a moment later.

"In constraints."

"Shot... target destroyed." That was it for the Hellfires. Their other weapons pylon carried a fifty-caliber machine gun, which would be useless against all but the most lightly armored vehicles. If there were any soft targets down there, though—Tom felt his face twisting into something that was not really a smile. Killing individual Iraqis with the .50 would be no challenge at all.

"What the fuck?"

Langston's shout went unanswered, and no answer was really needed. One of the surviving SA-6's had drawn a straight line of fire to the Blackhawks three klicks behind the Kiowa. The huge flash as the missile exploded and ignited the chopper's fuel was followed a second later by a blast wave that threatened to tumble the low-flying Kiowa into the sand below. Tom fought with the controls and brought them up for a moment, then down again. Staying low to the ground was the only protection the scout helicopter really had.

"Oh, dear God," Tom whispered, "I think they just took out Command."

The noise was incredible, shaking Harry's bones, driving spikes of pain into his head. In the glare of a missile explosion he saw Ben shouting something, shook his head and pointed to his ears to indicate that he couldn't hear anything. Dragons and the company's few remaining TOWs screamed out from all around their position, while the Apaches above them and the Iraqis downrange added their fire to the barrage of sound.

The fire from the Iraqi positions, what little they could spare for counterfire on the ground, was blessedly inaccurate so far. Seventy–three–millimeter shells from some of the BMP's were falling far short, while the longer–range thirty–millimeters from others were mostly just kicking up sand. Harry thought, in the brief interludes in firing when thought was possible, that such luck surely couldn't last.

Ben put his face next to Harry's and screamed, "Third platoon says they've got infantry contact! BMPs unloaded some guys about fifty meters from the line and they're trying to infiltrate!"

Harry nodded and took the proffered radio. "November actual to November Alpha and November Bravo, actual to Alpha and Bravo," he bellowed into the microphone. "Move to third platoon soonest. They have enemy contact and they could use some help, over."

"November Alpha Zero, aye aye," crackled from the radio. Harry could barely hear the response, and when he waited for an answer from Bravo, he didn't hear anything at all—but he knew he might not have heard their reply over the noise, or they might not have heard him for the same reason. He hoped the noise was the problem, anyway.

And one fire team might not be enough reinforcement for third platoon, but it was what they had right now.

One of the choppers—he thought it was a Kiowa, not an Apache—roared by over third platoon, very low, tremendously loud even in the middle of the firefight. Fifty-caliber tracer streamed from one side of the chopper, like a laser beam in a science fiction movie, and Harry fancied he could see human figures falling where it touched the ground. That was one less thing to worry about, at least for now.

Then the fist of God came up from the ground and hit Harry along the entire length of his body. He was briefly aware of being airborne, then fell back to earth with an impact almost as bad as the first. He couldn't see much, couldn't see at all, and knew a moment of paralyzing fear—oh God, he thought, shell fragments to the head, I'm deaf and blind—before the feeling of having a wool blanket wrapped around his head started to clear.

Every part of his body still hurt like hell.

"—think they landed a seventy-mike in first platoon," Ben was saying as the world came back in. "I'll go see what I can do." He slithered away, and Harry choked back the order to stand fast he'd been about to give. He himself might have been cast as an infantryman, but Ben at least was still thinking like a medic.

All right, then, old man, he told himself, then you keep thinking like an infantryman. First platoon's anchoring our left flank. Can't send anyone from second or third out to help them, they've got their own problems, God only knows where Bravo is, and fourth is just too far away. He grabbed the radio again.

"Actual to Two Zero, shorten the line. Fall back on your right and watch the flank, over."

"Two Zero to actual, aye aye, over."

"Actual to Two Zero, watch for stragglers from First before you open fire." They'd know better than he did what had happened to first platoon, would hopefully have a pretty good idea where friendlies would be coming in from. If they started shooting each other in the dark it would all be over. "Use them to plug up the line and send One Zero or One One in to me if you can, over."

No response. Harry waited half a minute, clicked the microphone a few times. "November Two Zero, come in." Still nothing but silence from the radio, the only silence to be found.

"Fuck!" Whatever was out there was no longer a platoon in any meaningful sense of the word, he knew. It might be, at best, a collection of squads and fire teams struggling to hold their ground. Or it might be a collection of corpses.

"November actual to November Three Zero," he said into the radio, "shift one squad to second platoon. November Four Zero, shift one squad to second platoon. I say again, Three Zero and Four Zero each shift one squad to second platoon. November actual out." He clicked off and dropped the radio. If he came back for it, that would mean they'd won the battle. If not... well, some Iraqi could take it home to show his kids.

He slithered through the dirt toward what had, minutes before, been the anchor of his line. A few meters along the way he came to a corpse. He found its head, looked at its face in the glare of a rocket blast. Ben's eyes stared blankly back at him in the moment before the light faded.

Another kid he hadn't been able to protect. Ben had been too old to be like a child to him—more like a favorite nephew, a bright, funny kid with a wife and young daughter back home. Another corpse in a battle that would never have a name.

Then a living hand pulled him with astonishing strength into a shallow foxhole. "We've stopped them here!" Rick shouted.

"First and second platoon both got overrun, but Leventhal pulled what was left back together. There's a heavy weapons squad from third laying down a good line of mortar fire about half a klick downrange. The ragheads could probably break through it if they wanted to, but I think we've scared them. Third and fourth platoons saw some of their armor running away. Guess they don't want to fight those choppers."

Harry nodded. It seemed like the noise wasn't quite as loud as it had been at first. Maybe he was just getting used to it. "We in any shape to try and get back some ground?"

"Right now, no. Once we get rid of everybody inside the mortar curtain, yeah, maybe. If we're lucky we can just walk back over them." Harry felt a distant amazement that they could be having this conversation, with the blood of their friends all over them and people within shouting distance trying to take their lives, as casually as they'd once have discussed patient care in the hospital cafeteria. "'Course," Rick added, "if those choppers do their job, we can just fly away like little birds."

The Iraqi jumped on Rick's back without any warning, no noise, nothing at all between the moment when Rick was talking confidently about escape and the moment he was thrashing around trying to pull the cord away from his neck, trying to *breathe.* Harry grabbed for his pistol and the Iraqi kicked him with impossible accuracy in the groin, then went back to strangling Rick. Harry took a deep breath, tried to will away the pain. I am not, he thought clearly, going to lie here and watch my troop be killed with a piece of string. He brought his head up and down like a snake, fastened his teeth into the Iraqi's shoulder.

Taste of dust, of dirty cloth, of sweat and skin—he bit down as hard as he could, and was rewarded by the taste of blood and a muffled scream. The pain between his legs was fading now, and with renewed strength he grappled for the Iraqi's face, trying to find the eyes.

Rick heaved, threw the Iraqi off, and rolled away, trying to pull the cord away from his neck. Harry found an eye and pressed his thumb into it. The Iraqi screamed louder and pulled away from Harry's teeth. Then his body jerked as Rick, the cord hanging loosely, plunged a bayonet into his belly.

Rick had put all his weight into the thrust. In the glare of a starlight shell, Harry saw Rick's hand go into the Iraqi's body up to the knuckles. Rick coughed blood, screamed, pulled his hand away and thrust again. The stench of ruptured intestines filled the air. Rick stabbed the twitching Iraqi over and over, drew in the fouled air and kept screaming, a ragged banshee wail that had no right to come from a human mouth. Harry crawled away and watched Rick butcher the corpse.

"Alpha Charlie Zero One to all units, break contact, over."

"What the hell?" Tom was out past the Iraqis now, still very low, flying on instruments and instinct as he brought the Kiowa around for another pass. He and the other scouts could pepper them with fifty-cal fire, the Apaches could finish snuffing out the armor and AA, the Blackhawks could come down and do the pickup—it wasn't a perfect operation by any means, not with Squadron Command and who knew how many other birds knocked out of the air, but they could still accomplish the mission. Now they were supposed to break contact?

"Alpha Kilo Two Seven to Alpha Charlie Zero One, I have multiple targets in my sights waiting for the heavies. We can fry these fuckers in five mikes, over."

The voice that came back was equal parts fury and fear. "Zero One to Two Seven, this is Lieutenant Sawyer. Command's down and I'm in charge. Break contact and return to base."

No one was supposed to argue with orders, pilots least of all, but this was insane. "Zero One, I have targets in my sights, they've got good fire on the ground, the ragheads are starting to break and run. We can do this, over."

"Two Seven, we are breaking contact and heading home, do you hear me? Do you fucking hear me?"

"Tom, you have to do what he says," Langston said. "You know that" If you don't do what he says, Langston wasn't saying, I'll be the first witness at your court–martial.

"Langston," Tom said in a voice utterly lacking in emotion, "let me tell you something." He banked hard, emptied the last of the ammunition at the Iraqis, and put the Kiowa into a long climb toward the rest of the formation. "You really are an asshole."

The Iraqis were gone. Harry could see that now, by the dawn's early light. Just before the sky began to lighten, they and the American helicopters had left in opposite directions. There are these two kids, he thought: one of them's about to smash an anthill and the other one walks up and tells him not to do that. So they get into a fight, throw a few punches back and forth, wrestle around, until they both get tired. They walk away and don't worry about what happens to the ants.

Rick was a few feet away, stripped to the waist, scrubbing himself compulsively with sand. After a while he opened up a water bottle and used it to rinse himself off, then went back to scrubbing. Harry looked at him, then at the bloody mess that was all that was left of the Iraqi, and said nothing.

Got a few bites in, though, he thought, looking at the bodies scattered over the ground as far as he could see. We did that. Fire ants is what we are, I guess. Hope those bites sting for days. Thinking harder about it, he found he didn't much care if the Iraqis or the Americans stung harder. The thought saddened him, but it was no surprise.

He left Rick to his improvised bath and walked over to the next troop he could see, a Marine who was sitting cross–legged on the ground, staring out at the carnage. "Come on," Harry told him, "get up. It's a long way home."

Four

March 1991

It was almost over.

Lieutenant Commander Michael MacDonald took a good look around, trying to fix this place in his memory. He knew he wouldn't be making landfall here again for a very long time, if ever. Which was a shame, because it was a very good port—even better after the Seabees had worked their patented brand of magic, bringing it up to the best US Navy standards in less than a week—and it had been a pretty good assignment all in all, given that there was a war on. The *Altair* had sailed up the Gulf, seeing no Iraqi craft whatsoever, and sailed back down to Dammam. From there it was mostly R&R. The locals were friendly, they had great food, and the women were nice to look at even if you *definitely* couldn't touch. A nice way to spend a war.

Then everything went to shit, and Michael found himself, a supply officer whose main concern throughout his career had been ordering enough pairs of shoes, down here in Qatar running the biggest evacuation-by-sea in American history. There were captains and even an admiral putatively in charge, but it was

Michael who made everything work right, who kept everyone clothed and sheltered and fed, who dealt with the routine needs of a mass of humanity the size of a moving city and the not-so-routine ones as well. And things did get weird out here. At one point he'd had to get the *Mercy* to send over an incubator, for God's sake.

"Your troops are going to have to dismount their vehicles, turn the motors off, and push them on," he told a disbelieving Army captain. "Would we let you drive them off the ship? Yes, we would. But we're not going to let you drive them *on,* because there are a lot of other people who would really like to do the same thing, and if everyone's driving around inside the ship looking for a parking space then you'll all die of carbon monoxide poisoning, which would render the whole point of an evacuation kind of moot, wouldn't it? So get your soldiers to *push the fucking Hummers up the ramp and on the ship."*

He couldn't blame the brass for their lack of involvement. There weren't as many of them to go around as there had been, after all. So many of them, American and Qatari, had had their throats cut or their staff cars bombed, or they'd just somehow managed to disappear. And the revenge-purges afterward...

He shook his head at the memory. All the Saudis within range had been rounded up, the Americans hadn't even had to do that, the Qataris were more than happy to do it themselves. Lined them up along a freshly bulldozed trench, all of them, the ones who were yelling obscenities and the ones who were standing silent and the ones who were screaming their innocence, begging someone to believe them, and no one believed them and the machine guns started to chatter and after that none of them said anything at all. Then the bulldozer scooped the dirt back into the trench and everyone went back to packing up.

But that was long over now and the whole thing was finally coming to an end; the moving city had, by and large, made its move out to sea. For the first time he could see the perimeter, an eclectic mix of armored vehicles and infantry moving back as the evacuation proceeded. No one knew or even claimed to know where the Iraqis and their allies might be, or what sort of battle they'd have to fight if attacked, but that solid wall of mostly American–made steel gave Michael at least a little comfort.

What the Arabs had going for them was numbers and geography and fanatical determination, but in a one–on–one fight, American technology would kick their asses every time. Especially with the *Missouri* standing a little way off shore with its sixteen–inch guns, and the *Eisenhower* a little farther out with its F–14's, F/A–18's, and A–6's ready to pound the shit out of anything in the area, land, sea, or air. If Saddam Hussein poked his face in here, some Marine colonel had recently told some reporter, he'd get a hell of a bloody nose.

Michael thought Saddam Hussein, or whoever was really in charge in Baghdad these days, knew that perfectly well. He wasn't going to try to crush them here at the water's edge, historically a very bad thing to try do to Americans anyway. He was just going to let them slink away with their tails between their legs, and then walk in and take Qatar in a day or two.

The obvious historical comparison for this evacuation was Dunkirk, and that was something the brass from Washington on down found encouraging; it strongly implied that in a couple of years the good guys would come *back,* ready to fight and win. Michael didn't think so. He'd been an ensign on the *Midway* when they brought in the last choppers from Saigon, evacuating the US embassy personnel and some very lucky South Vietnamese before the NVA rolled into the city, and to him this looked a hell of a lot more like Vietnam than France.

And now it was almost over. This was nearly the last load of the last day, the moving city having shrunk to a village, and when they were gone it would be as though they had never been here. Most of the Qataris were planning to leave with the Americans, but some would stay and fight. Michael hoped for their sakes that they were killed in action rather than taken prisoner.

Something was happening out on the perimeter. He strained his eyes to see, gave up and took a pair of binoculars from a sailor. Three of the big Army M1's were moving forward in a rough triangle, infantry flanking them, darting in and out of cover. Two Marine Cobras hovered nearby.

Michael took three deep breaths, made himself relax as much as possible, ready to move *fast* if he had to. The combination of land and air power out there was enough to beat back any kind of Iraqi probe, but a full-scale attack would turn the whole evacuation staging area into a killing zone. The big-ship power out at sea suddenly seemed far away.

What was coming toward the M1's, apparently unconcerned by the massive cannon pointed straight at them, was a ragged line of desert rats in uniforms indistinguishable from the dusty ground. Michael twisted the focus wheel on the binoculars to bring them into sharper view. Yes, those were American uniforms, and some Saudi—he sensed the Qatari troops spreading out, bringing up their weapons—but they were more tattered and filthy than any he'd seen throughout the whole evacuation. And a weird mix, most of them Marine BDU's without visible insignia, but many with garish sleeve stripes he took a minute to place as Air Force.

What the hell? he thought. If this is an infiltration attempt, it's a really bad one. So they must be for real.

After some conversation, the infantry let the desert rats pass between the M1's to head for Michael's position. The Marines and Qataris around him were *very* ready now, ready and even eager to open fire at the first sign of trouble. But the infantry at the perimeter didn't seem alarmed, and the rats weren't moving like people looking for a fight. They were moving, in fact, like people who would much rather not be moving at all. Michael was very tired, everyone here was tired, but he thought he had never before seen any human beings who looked as exhausted as these.

In the lead was an Air Force NCO of considerable rank, Michael wasn't exactly sure what—E-7? E-8?—with an M16 in one hand, a radio in the other, and, weirdly, a bag marked with a faded Red Cross over his shoulder. He was a short guy, had probably been a bit chubby before he got himself stuck wandering out in the desert, was now gaunt and drawn, but he drew himself up as he approached the dock and Michael could see why he was in the lead. There was something in his face that spoke of the kind of iron will mixed with compassion that would have been needed for leadership in this crew's recent walk through Hell.

Michael read the name tag on the NCO's uniform as he approached: ELKINS. He acknowledged the man's slow Present Arms with an Annapolis-perfect salute, and leaned forward to hear his ragged words: "Master Sergeant Harry Elkins, sir, with the survivors of Khafji. Permission to come aboard?"

"Be nice if someone would really *talk* to us, know what I mean?"

Sharon muttered as they walked through the corridor, flanked by cookie-cutter Marines.

Harry nodded. The trip back had been heaven on Earth. The ship was cramped but they had plenty to eat and beds to sleep on and showers, oh God, that first shower had been like an orgasm, and of course no one was trying to kill them. The layover at RAF Mildenhall and the flight home had been better. MAC charter all the way, a Federal Express plane—which everyone thought was pretty damned funny, but it had seats and windows and pretty stewardesses just like a regular airliner—and when they landed in Washington, Uncle Sam had paid for a four-star hotel. The Marines escorting them around were REMFs but they kept the reporters away, and treated the survivors with awe. Beautiful.

But the awe of the Stateside troops and the deference of the civilians seemed to substitute for any kind of real communication, and that wasn't heavenly at all. No one would tell them anything about the big picture, how the rest of the evacuation was going, what was going to happen next, not even how many other small units like theirs had made it out alive. There was no one else around them who had been as far out in the sand as they had, which Harry didn't take as a good sign. The sailors on the *Altair* and the other ships in that convoy had done their share of fighting, no one denied that, but it wasn't exactly the same kind.... The other evacuees had all come from much farther south. And there were big gaps even there: it seemed that no one anywhere near Riyadh, for example, had made it to Qatar.

Back home they were all split up, segregated into airmen and soldiers and Marines and then further into little units that never saw each other. Most of the survivors of Harry's original flight were together, at least, but as far as he could tell that was for the simple reason that there weren't enough of them left to make it worth splitting them up. Now, here somewhere in the bowels of the Pentagon, almost everyone was gone, it was just him and Sharon and Rick and ... oh, shit.

A guy in a suit materialized on their right. "Master Sergeant Elkins," he said, "in here, please. Senior Airman Alcazar, Airman First Class Welton, Lance Corporal Perkins will take you to your debriefing area." Harry and Sharon locked eyes for a moment before the gentle but irresistible pressure of the Marine's hand on his shoulder steered him through the open door.

The door closed softly behind him, with the Marine still outside. The only people besides Harry left in the room were all wearing civilian suits. Harry felt as though he was in a suit too, newly issued Class A's which had replaced the new sterile fatigues he'd got on the *Altair,* which had in turn replaced the filthy uniform he'd worn out of the desert. That had probably been burned. If clothes make the man, he thought, the guy who was at Khafji doesn't exist anymore. Is that what they wanted?

These people, two men and a woman, were all precisely tailored, whispering of quality. Harry suddenly wanted his Marine guard back. He didn't much like either the Marine dress uniforms or the people wearing them—surely they couldn't be the same breed who had fought by his side across the desert, part of him thought, hell, they weren't even the same species—but they seemed infinitely more a part of his world than *this.*

Everyone was standing as he entered. He stood across the desk from two of them, the third by his side. They stood like that for several heartbeats until he realized they were waiting for him to sit. He did. Nice chair, firm with just enough give.

The two of them on the other side of the desk sat too, though the one who'd ushered him in remained standing. Guess we know who's in charge now, he thought. But it's not me, even if they waited for me. One of these two. Which one?

They were both about Harry's age. The man was a perfect medium: average height and weight, medium complexion, sandy brown hair thinning just a bit on top but not enough to be called balding, a face neither ugly nor handsome. Harry knew that if he looked away for five seconds he'd have no idea how to describe the guy. The woman was a lot more memorable. She was close to six feet tall, smooth blonde hair falling evenly to her shoulders, a body that spoke of both good genes and plenty of exercise, and her face was... not just beautiful, though certainly that, but... elegant, that was it. When I was a child, Harry thought, that's the way fairy-tale queens looked in my mind.

"Master Sergeant Elkins," she said, "welcome home."

"Thank you, ma'am. Um, not that I don't appreciate it, but I've been welcomed home quite a bit already. This wasn't really what I expected."

She smiled. Her teeth were, of course, perfectly even. "No, I don't suppose it was." She extended her hand across the desk, and he took it: cool skin, even pressure applied for three precise shakes. "I'm Rebecca Norman, and this is David Petrie." He knew she was referring to the man on her side of the desk, and not to the other one, whose presence he still felt but didn't see. Behind me, he thought, not moving, just waiting for something. A thug of some kind. "We're with the State Department."

Normally he would have wanted to hold on to her hand for quite a while; now he was just as glad to release it. "I didn't know the State Department operated out of the Pentagon. Ma'am."

Petrie spread his hands. "State's quite a big organization,

Master Sergeant Elkins, and we work closely with many others. Our department has always been closely associated with the DoD."

"Right. You know, you don't have to call me by my full rank all the time. 'Sergeant' is usually enough." But no way in hell do I want you calling me "Harry," he thought. Only people I like get to do that. Actually, only *people* get to do that.

"Whatever you like, Sergeant," Norman replied quickly. "Well, in any case, we brought you here because we want to discuss your future role in the service of your country."

Harry stared at her. "Ma'am, I'm a medic. I mean, that's what I do. You have someone injured, point me at him, I'll patch him up. What else did you have in mind?"

Petrie ruffled some papers on the desk in front of him. "Sergeant, not too many medics do what you did. In fact, not too many of our troops in the Gulf, regardless of specialty—or service, or rank, or anything else—managed to do anything even close to what you did, which is why you and your subordinates are here today. You're capable of a lot more than 'patching up.'"

"Okay, so how many other—"

"That's really not important right—"

"Shut up." Harry sensed the other man moving slightly behind him, decided to ignore it for now. Fuck with me, kiddo, and I'll turn around and reach down your throat and rip your lungs out, no matter what thug school you went to. Other than that, you don't exist. He leaned forward across the desk. "If you don't answer me, I won't *discuss* a Goddamned thing with you. In fact, the only people I'll be *discussing* anything with are reporters. I'll tell them all about how the spooks dragged me in here like I was a war criminal instead of letting me have my R'n'R."

Norman glanced at the stack of papers in front of Petrie, nodded, and looked back at Harry. "Our best estimates are that about one hundred and eighty–five thousand American personnel are on their way back to the US and Europe right now. Another one hundred and sixty thousand or so are holding positions in the Middle East, primarily in Israel and Turkey. We also, believe it or not, have acknowledged a request to station some naval forces along the southern coast of Iran." For the first time, Harry thought she looked like a human being. "I'm sorry to tell you that very few other American or allied units made it out from anywhere near Iraq or Kuwait, or from the Saudi interior."

Harry sat back in the chair. "Oh." Those were bad numbers. A shitload of dead... how many? A hundred thousand, a hundred and fifty? Huge numbers. Worse than Korea and Vietnam combined, in the space of weeks, not years. "Oh, Jesus Christ."

"I see that you understand why we have a lot to talk about," Petrie said. "With you in particular, I mean. You did something really quite unique." He picked up the papers. "You might be interested to know that your Medal of Honor citation is in here."

"Is that so?" Harry glanced at the papers, then looked at the floor, the wall, anywhere but at the suits. He felt very old. "All right, tell me what I need to do."

Five

April 1991

It was a time of unsettling official announcements from various world capitals. An edgy world listened to a broadcast from Moscow and grew edgier. Kremlin-watchers in Washington wept as they thanked God for the revitalization of their profession.

The television screen showed Alexander Slonimsky sitting behind a desk that the Kremlin-watchers recognized immediately as having been Gorbachev's. Perhaps now the other shoe would finally drop.

"I am General Aleksander Vassilievich Slonimsky," he said into the camera. He sat straight and proud, looking very much the heroic young savior of his country that he considered himself to be. His adoring followers had already taken to calling him Aleksander the Great—behind his back, as they thought, except that nothing was said in the Kremlin that Slonimsky didn't hear about eventually. He had no objection to the title, though. He had even briefly considered opening his speech by announcing himself to the world as Aleksander the Great, but discretion had prevailed. He was sometimes capable of discretion.

He spoke in Russian, of course. The speech went out over multiple voice channels in various major languages. Slonimsky had chosen each of the interpreters himself—not for their linguistic abilities, for he wasn't qualified to judge that, but rather for their strong, deep voices. His words mattered very much, but he knew that the impression made by the voice delivering the words mattered even more.

"As you may know, following the unfortunate death of Comrade Mikhail Sergeevich Gorbachev, I was implored to restore order to our nation by assuming the offices of President, General Secretary of the Central Committee of the Communist Party of the Soviet Union, and Chairman of the Presidium of the Supreme Soviet. This is a daunting task, and at first I doubted my ability to perform it. But I realized that my country needs a strong hand at the helm. I am a soldier, I serve the Soviet Union, and I saw it as my duty to answer this call to leadership just as I would answer a call to charge across a battlefield in the face of enemy fire."

The Kremlin-watchers nodded happily and toasted each other with strong drinks. Whatever titles and ranks this Slonimsky might give himself, in their eyes he had only one that counted: Job Security.

Surrounded by nervous advisers, the President of the United States watched the speech on a television in the Oval Office. President, Chair of the Republican National Committee, Speaker of the House, *and* Majority Leader of the Senate, Bush thought. Lucky bastard!

"I offer greetings to the world from the peaceloving workers of the USSR," Slonimsky said. "To our many friends, I offer the warm hand of socialist brotherhood. To those who are contemplating being our enemies, I give this warning.

"Our time of weakness is over. The days during which we retreated when enemies challenged us are gone, never to return. Our nation is once again strong, united, and determined—once again the hope of workers everywhere."

Much effort had been required to make the room suitable for showing on television. Slonimsky had felt it important that he be shown in the office which in the West, he knew, symbolized the center of power in the USSR. The spatters of human blood and flesh on the walls had been washed away. That had been relatively easy. More time-consuming had been the repairs required to eliminate the bullet holes. They were everywhere. Slonimsky had perhaps fired rather more bullets than were entirely necessary. When it came to pulling a trigger, he was an enthusiast.

"The peoples of the Baltic nations are eternally united in socialist brotherhood with the people of the Soviet Union," Slonimsky continued. "Any threat against the voluntary association of the Baltic states with the USSR will be resisted with every weapon at our disposal.

"At the same time, let me assure the world that the people of the Soviet Union, showing great restraint, will not endanger peace unnecessarily. Thus we will do nothing to reverse the current situation in Poland or the German Democratic Republic, unless the workers of those countries ask for our help."

"Ah hah!" said the Kremlin-watchers. "He's accepting reality and establishing the new reality. Hey, we like this guy! This is so cool!" They toasted each other again and poured each other another round.

"What the Hell is he talking about, Jim?" the President asked the Secretary of State.

Baker thought for a moment before answering. "Mr. President, I believe he's establishing a new line of demarcation to replace the old Iron Curtain. He's admitting that East Germany and Poland are lost, but he's drawing the line at the Baltics, and he's warning us about just how far he can be pushed."

"So what is this guy?" Bush asked. "I mean, if you had to say, is he a new Gorbachev or a new Khruschev?"

To himself, Baker said that he wished either were likely. "I'm afraid, Mr. President, that he may be a new Stalin."

On the screen, Slonimsky, warming to his speech and looking ever more confident and strong, expanded his horizons. "Now, comrades, I would like to talk about our southern borders. Let us be frank. Let us not engage in the sort of diplomatic circumlocutions so loved by reactionaries and counterrevolutionaries. The simple fact is that, thanks to the war the capitalist powers have recently waged against anti-colonialism in the Middle East, turmoil has engulfed a broad swath of land. Atavistic impulses have been encouraged, religious warfare is alive again, and false prophets walk the land. Let me assure you that the interests of the workers of Afghanistan and all related areas will be protected."

"Afghanistan!" James Baker leaned forward and listened intently. He silenced a confused question from the President with a wave of his hand. Then he leaned back in his chair and muttered, "Good God."

After a long moment of thought, Baker responded to the questions the President should have asked. "I think he means that he'll be sending troops back into Afghanistan. He's going to try to undo the loss of that region. He wants to reestablish control there.

He wants to reestablish that as his southern border."

"So, what does this mean?" Bush asked. "We should start sending money and arms to those ragheads again? Humiliate the Soviets again? Stick it to 'em again? Like last time. Make 'em hurt!"

Baker shook his head. "This time, it's in our interest to let them establish a strong defensible border against the Moslems. Consider the alternative. Someone has to hold the line against this new man, this Rashid. Better the Russians than us."

The phone rang while Harry was tying his tie for the third time. It still didn't look right. With a curse, he gave up on it, strode across the room and picked up the phone as it began its second ring. "Elkins."

A woman's voice said, "Mab*rook!*"

It took Harry a moment to shift mental gears and understand. Then he laughed. "English, please, Airman, or the CIA will think I'm an Arab spy."

"Think they're listening?"

"Oh, yeah. Oh, what the hell. *Shuk*ran."

Congratulations, Sharon had said in Arabic. *Thank you,* he had replied. He was pleased by how easily it came to him. As a way to keep both their minds off their probable fate and also to improve his ability to communicate with the mixed force he commanded, Sharon had tried teaching Harry elementary Arabic during the march to the sea. They had both been surprised by the quickness of his learning and the completeness of his retention and by how far he had progressed.

"Sorry I can't be there to congratulate you in person and watch your speech," Sharon said. "I really wanted to."

Harry groaned. "I'm going to make a fool of myself."

"I bet you've never done that in your life. Anyway, we're on our way to OCS in the morning, so all I could do is call."

"'We'?"

"Yeah, Rick and me."

"No kidding? Where is Rick?"

"Um, he's asleep. I didn't want to wake him. We've... We've been having a pushup contest again."

Harry was confused for a moment. Then he understood and burst out laughing. "That's great! Mab*rook!* Mab*rook* to both of you!"

Sharon laughed too. *"Shuk*ran, for sure."

There was a knock on the door. Harry asked Sharon to pass his congratulations to Rick ("Tell him it's congratulations for making OCS."), hung up, and opened the door.

Two men in similar dark suits—uniforms, Harry thought immediately—stood in the hallway. Somehow, they seemed to fill the space between his door and the wall opposite. "Sir," one of them said, "we're here to escort you to the ceremony."

They filled the elevator, too. Harry was glad he was smaller than average, or he'd have been unable to squeeze in between them, even though it had seemed an unusually large elevator when he'd ridden up in it by himself the night before. Escorts or bodyguards? he wondered. Maybe they're here to keep me from escaping if I chicken out.

He didn't mind. For a few minutes, he even managed to forget about the upcoming ordeal because of his almost paternal happiness about Sharon and Rick. Maybe they'd get married and have beautiful, very muscular children. At least something good had come out of the horror of the Gulf.

Then he was distracted by the drive along a few miles of

busy Washington streets. Cold, dry air had moved in with a front from the northwest. The sky was brilliantly blue, and a wind whipped along the streets, driving last autumn's leaves before it and plucking at the coats of the pedestrians. It was miserable if you were out in it, but it was lovely to look at from inside the car. Harry looked his full—at the bare but plentiful trees, the magnificent historical buildings, the fresh young things hurrying along the sidewalks. He felt old but happy. He wondered how long the feeling would last.

For years, Harry had wanted to do Washington as a tourist. This drive made him want it all the more. Early spring, he thought, would be just the right time for it.

The trip ended in an underground garage. His escorts ferried him into an elevator and then along a confusing series of hallways, down a long, narrow staircase, and through a doorway.

And he found himself facing a combined session of the House and Senate of the United States and being introduced to the world by the President, who called him a true American hero.

Harry's feet were glued to the floor. His stomach lurched. A few days earlier, when he had been told about the medal, he had assumed the ceremony would be held in the Hall of Heroes at the Pentagon, as it usually was—a nice, quiet ceremony with few attendees.

For a moment, he wished he had died in the desert and that someone else—anyone else—was enduring this in his place.

The President finished his introduction, turned toward Harry, and began clapping. Behind Bush, Speaker Foley and the Vice President rose from their chairs and joined in the applause. Then assembled Representatives and Senators and all the guests in the gallery rose to their feet, clapping and cheering.

Jesus Christ, Harry thought, I didn't do anything. It's those kids you should be applauding.

But he was the visible symbol of America's survival of a military catastrophe. He was necessary for the recovery of America's self-respect. He had had that explained to him already, although not in quite such honest terms.

He had also been given an acceptance speech and had been told to read it precisely as written and not to change a word. He had spent the previous evening reading it over and over, at first trying to memorize it, then just trying to make sense of it. The individual words meant something, and so did the phrases and even the shorter sentences, but he had been too distracted to understand the thing as a whole. He had resolved finally to simply read it when the time came, to just get through it.

The applause finally died down, and the members and guests sat down again. The time had come! Harry reached into his uniform jacket for the folded sheet of paper containing his speech, but then he caught sight of the red lights of television cameras trained on him, and he froze again.

Which was a fortunate thing, because the time hadn't come. He had forgotten that the citation had to be read first.

An Air Force lieutenant general Harry had never seen before stepped to the podium. No one in Harry's old chain of command; if they wanted someone with stars on his shoulders, the Surgeon General of the Air Force would have been the logical choice, but this wasn't he. The general took out a sheet of paper of his own and read from it:

"For conspicuous gallantry and intrepidity at the risk of his life above and beyond the call of duty. While leading his team of medics at the Battle of Khafji, Master Sergeant Elkins discovered that all superior officers had been killed and he was the highest-ranking man in the field. Immediately assuming command, Master Sergeant Elkins efficiently organized the surviving men and women, including soldiers and Marines and Allied troops as well as his own Air Force medics. He then successfully led his small force of American and Allied troops both in fighting off continuing attacks by numerically far superior and more heavily armed enemy forces and in a long march through dangerous terrain to a point on the coast where they could all be extracted. On more than one occasion during the march, Master Sergeant Elkins personally and directly engaged the enemy. At the extraction point, he remained on shore to provide covering fire until all under his command were safely onboard. He was thus the last to board the landing craft. Without Master Sergeant Elkins's extraordinary heroism and superb and inspirational leadership, many, perhaps all, of the men and women under his command would surely have been killed or captured. His actions are in keeping with the highest traditions of the military service and reflect great credit upon himself, his unit, and the United States Air Force."

None of what was happening seemed real to Harry. Nor did the actions described by the general. They seemed to have to do with someone else. That other man had the same name and rank as Harry, but Harry's memory of the events in the desert, even the most awful and graphically remembered moments, were like a story that other Harry Elkins had told him.

He was aware that the members of Congress and the spectators in the gallery were again standing and applauding him. The general handed him a small, rectangular box, shook his hand, smiled broadly, congratulated him.

Harry mumbled his thanks. He wanted to get the hell out of the building and into the open air.

But first he had to give the speech someone had written for him.

He wasn't entirely aware that he was walking to the podium. It was as though he were floating. He could see the audience still clapping their hands, but he could hear nothing. His thoughts drifted off in weird tangents, the way they did in dreams. Images of the desert overwhelmed him suddenly. Sand, explosions, eviscerated men. A helicopter blossoming into orange flame overhead. Linda Lewis gasping out blood.

He frowned, concentrated on the here and now, tried to bring himself back to reality. He put the pages of the typed speech on the wooden lectern, gripped the lectern's hard edges, and then made himself look up at the audience and around the great hall. My God, he thought, I'm really here! Not long before, he had watched the President on television, standing on this spot, giving the State of the Union Address. Now he, Harry Elkins, was standing here, about to speak to the world, and the President was standing off to one side and applauding him.

Too bad it was only because America so badly needed a hero, and Harry had been chosen for the role.

Damn, Harry thought, they should have chosen Sharon or Rick for this. They sure look the part more than I do.

The same thought had belatedly struck the President. He's a little guy! Bush thought. No one told me he was so tiny. And dark! He looks like a Goddamned Arab. Oh, this is just great.

"My fellow citizens," Harry read, "I come to you delivered from the desert of despair." Jesus Christ, Harry thought. How can I say this crap? Seeing no way to back out now that he had begun, he kept going. "When we were cut off and surrounded by enemy forces, the heroism of the brave men and women under my command demonstrated to the world what the American fighting man and woman are made of." And our abandonment by our own government proved to the world what it's made of, too. The temptation to add that sentence was almost overwhelming.

Harry took a deep breath and continued. He picked the sheet of paper up from the lectern so that the audience would see he was reading a speech and would, he hoped, realize that he hadn't composed it. "Thanks to American courage, American technology, and the grace of God, we were able to make our way through the desert of despair to the ocean." Where I parted the waters, thanks to the power of American self–deception. What the hell is this? We lost that fucking war!

Not according to what he had to read aloud next. The next paragraph made that desperate rush to the coast sound like a triumphal conquering march. Rather than Moses, Harry was now Sherman. A listener who hadn't been watching the news could have believed that America had won the war in the Middle East and the troops still fighting there were engaged in a simple mopping–up operation.

Yeah, right, Harry thought. I guess we won in Vietnam, too.

Until that moment, Harry hadn't understood what his role was to be. He had thought he would make a speech, get a medal, and then retreat into the anonymity of a job he knew well and did well but that the world at large never noticed. Now he realized that he was to be a propaganda tool. And not even a tool deployed to help the airmen he was trained to help. Instead, he would be used to help save the careers of the politicians and generals who had created the disaster that had cost the lives of so many of those airmen.

He made it through the rest of the absurd speech, endured the questions and handshakes and photographs, and finally asked—begged—to be taken back to his hotel room.

The same two enormous men drove him back to his hotel and escorted him to his door. "Do you know anything about when I'll be able to go back to my unit?" he asked them.

"Just wait here," one of them said.

"Stay in your room," the other one said. "You'll be contacted."

"Your schedule is being drawn up," the first one said.

They left, marching in lockstep down the hallway, their shoulders brushing the walls.

Harry could imagine what the schedule would consist of. Speeches to veterans' groups and businessmen's lunches and school assemblies. Need a hero? We can deliver one; just give us the time and place. Comes equipped with a Congressional Medal of Honor and a canned speech.

Harry realized that he was drenched with sweat. The Washington air might be unusually cold and dry, but his tension and nervousness had made him sweat profusely throughout his speech.

He pulled off his uniform and underwear and took a long, hot shower.

When he had dried himself off, he dressed in the one set of civilian clothes he had with him—jeans, t-shirt, running shoes, lined windbreaker—and headed out. He needed a long, powerful drink.

He looked in the hotel bar first, but it seemed to be full of baggy-eyed middleaged men wearing suits and fake smiles. Harry preferred honest drunks.

He didn't know the city at all, but he was sure there must be a bar within walking distance. There always was, he thought, on the East Coast. It was still daylight, so he should have no trouble finding one. As for finding his way back, right now, he didn't care.

Harry stood on the sidewalk in front of the hotel for a while, watching the traffic roar by. A peaceful, busy American city. Politically, *the* American city. The political capital of the world, some would say. Going about its important business as though men weren't slogging through the sand, killing each other, only a few thousand miles away. That was all happening in another world. Or maybe this was the other world, the unreal one.

Left or right? Harry shrugged, chose at random, turned left, and strolled down the sidewalk.

From somewhere ahead of him, he heard a rhythmic chanting. It sounded vaguely familiar, but he couldn't place it at first. Then it struck him, and he laughed. It sounded very much like the anti-war protestors he had watched marching a few times during his brief stint in college. He walked faster, hoping to catch sight of whatever this was before it broke up.

Three blocks further along, he reached a plaza where a small group of young people—college and high-school kids, he thought—with hair and clothing that could have come right out of the Sixties were holding up signs and chanting: "Hey, hey, ho, ho! Killer Bush has gotta go!"

Their voices were young, energetic, and filled with idealism.

For a moment, Harry felt twenty years old again. He was tempted to join them.

The chants turned to screams. The young protestors were dropping their signs and running in all directions, fear in their faces. Some of them rushed past Harry, almost knocking him off his feet.

Now Harry could see that they were being chased by policemen. The police wore flak jackets and helmets with visors, and they carried clear plastic shields in front of them with one hand. With their free hands, they swung riot sticks at the fleeing protestors. Harry saw one young man trip and fall. He was immediately surrounded by four policemen who began to hit him with their riot sticks. The protestor curled into a ball and tried to protect his head and neck with his arms.

Harry could hear the blows falling on the boy's back and sides. Ribs! Harry thought. Kidneys!

"Hey!" he yelled. He sprinted toward the group of policemen and their prey. One of them stopped hitting the fallen protestor and looked up at Harry.

All Harry could see was the blank facemask attached to the man's helmet. It was like confronting a man-sized mechanical insect. Harry shouted at him, "Leave that kid alone!"

The policeman stepped over the now-motionless protestor and came slowly toward Harry, raising his stick.

Suddenly, both of Harry's arms were being held in unbreakable grips. He was lifted from the ground and carried swiftly backward. He struggled and yelled and scraped his shoes against the concrete, but it did no good. He twisted around and recognized his two huge escorts from earlier in the day. One was on each side of him, and they were carrying him effortlessly through the confusion.

They threw him in the back seat of a waiting limousine. They sat on either side of him, trapping him, and the limousine accelerated away from the curb and merged into the traffic.

"You've already been a hero, you shithead," one of them said, glaring at Harry. "Now you're valuable property, so you stay out of danger."

"We told you to stay in your hotel room," the other one said.

Harry still couldn't tell them apart. "You're not in my chain of command," he said.

"The fuck we aren't," the first one said.

They were silent for the rest of the trip. The driver was another young man with enormous shoulders, indistinguishable from the first two. He didn't speak, either.

Harry assumed they were taking him back to his hotel. The trip seemed to be taking too long for that, however.

Eventually, the car pulled into an underground parking garage. His escorts pulled him from the back seat with more roughness than they'd shown toward him before and hustled him at a quick march to an elevator. They remained silent, ignoring his questions.

The elevator had no buttons, just a numeric keypad. One of the escorts punched in a code, and the elevator began a smooth ascent. The ride went on for quite a while. Harry tried to judge from the acceleration how many floors they were going up, but he couldn't tell. He thought the elevator was actually moving quite slowly, so it was possible that they were going up no more than four or five stories.

The elevator opened into a sterile hallway, blank walls and closed doors. His escorts knocked on one of the doors, then opened it and pushed Harry inside.

"Sit down." A man sat behind a desk facing the door. A nameplate on his desk gave his name as Hugh Walsh. He pointed at a chair in front of his desk, right in front of Harry. He was about

Harry's age, Harry judged, but healthier. Much more self–satisfied, too.

Harry remained standing and looked around. A standard midlevel manager's office. Not too big and not too small. Inoffensive and unremarkable abstract art on the walls. An American flag on a pole behind the seated man; that was unusual. So was the large portrait photograph one one wall, a jarring note amidst the inept abstractions. It was a picture of William Webster, the Director of Central Intelligence.

"Oh, great," Harry muttered. His suspicions about where he was were confirmed. He took the indicated chair. "I thought I was reporting to the State Department."

"Norman and Petrie? Well, yeah, they're basically State. It's complex. Responsibilities have been realigned in the Cabinet. You've been transferred to us."

Meaning what? Harry wondered. That the situation in the Middle East had deteriorated so badly that diplomacy was finished, and now all the emphasis would be on the soldiers in the field and the knife behind the scenes? "And what do you spooks want?"

"Politeness, to begin with." The voice was smooth, well produced, well controlled. There were no rough edges, as though the voice had never been raised in anger or fear, the vocal cords never damaged. "Would you like something to drink?"

"Beer. Even better, bourbon."

Walsh assumed a look of disapproval. "I meant coffee. Or a soda."

"That stuff's bad for you. That's my professional opinion. I repeat, what do you want?"

"We want you to behave yourself. You know what your

duties are now. Just do them, and don't step over the line, they way you did this afternoon at that demonstration."

"Or what? You'll draft me and send me to Vietnam?"

Walsh shook his head in disgust. "I told them we needed someone younger."

"Great. I agree. Get someone younger. I can give you a couple of names. Send me back to the desert. There's still fighting going on there, American soldiers are getting wounded, I can help them. I can still do some good there. I'm still a medic!"

"No. You're a hero. You're our designated hero for this war. The country really needs a hero right now, and you're it. We've already explained that to you. Just go where you're told and give the speeches you're told to give. And stay away from anti-war demonstrations."

"Or?"

"Or next time, the boys will wait a bit longer before they pull you out of harm's way."

"I can defend myself. I don't need them."

Walsh sneered. "Look at yourself. You're a worn-out old man. Anyway, you can do your country more good on the lecture circuit than on the battlefield."

Harry's pugnacity deserted him like air escaping a deflating balloon. The sad thing was that he knew Walsh was right. He could do a lot of good on the battlefield, but healing the nation's spirit and stiffening its spine were more important. Any good medic could do the job at the front, but while Harry's moment of fame and adulation lasted, he could do a lot more spirit-healing and spine-stiffening than anyone else could. "How long do I have to be your hero on a leash?"

"For as long as we tell you."

"What if I give a very negative interview to some local television station and then blow my brains out?"

Walsh thought for a moment. "We'd say that you were briefly captured before your heroic desert odyssey, and the Arabs brainwashed you. That you were able to lead your people to safety anyway showed just what a hero you were. We'd give you a hell of a funeral. And then we'd find someone younger and more stable—someone who appreciated the opportunity that you seem to scorn."

Harry sighed. "Okay, you've got the winning hand. But, come on, give me a time limit! Tell me I won't have to read stupid speeches to businessmen and school kids for the rest of my life."

"Let's try this," Walsh said. "Do your best at this job, give it your heroic all, and after three months we'll be willing to discuss sending you back to the Middle East."

Walsh didn't need to add that Harry probably would be old news well before three months were up.

Three months, Harry thought. A career military man could put up with anything for three months.

Six

April–July 1991

Harry soon discovered how long three months could be. There were even moments when he missed the desert. Sometimes, briefly, he wished he were back there.

Sometimes, briefly, he was.

At least once a week, he delivered the same speech to a Chamber of Commerce meeting or to a gathering of aging veterans or to a church group. About as often, he spoke to school assemblies, where he gave a shortened version of the speech. The deference, approaching awe, of the grownups unnerved him. The energy and eagerness of the kids enchanted him. The bloodthirstiness of both groups disturbed him.

At least the kids have an excuse, he thought. It's a game to them, or an athletic contest. And it's morally black and white, pure right vs. wrong. They only know what they've heard from their parents. They haven't started thinking about bigger questions yet.

The businessmen who'd never worn a uniform but who gloried in enemy death tolls and thought they were all John

Wayne—for them Harry had only contempt. It didn't help that they always seemed disturbed that he was quite so short and dark. Harry was sure that they'd have preferred someone more like Rick Welton. At least the kids didn't care about that.

The aging veterans...

Harry suspected that the ones who spoke up and talked with such enthusiasm about killing Arabs were the ones who hadn't actually been at the front. The quiet ones who listened soberly to his speech and rarely asked questions, but when they did the questions were thoughtful and worthwhile—maybe those were the ones who had been forced to kill.

Whatever his feelings were about a particular audience, he couldn't reveal them. That was part of the deal. That was why, for the first month or so, he repeated the speech that had been written for him, refraining from inserting his own thoughts. After the first couple of weeks, he could fall into a trance and let his mind drift while his mouth repeated the canned sentences.

That was when the desert would call him back.

He would be saying something about the indomitable American spirit or the superiority of American technology or the favored nature of the American system. The rapt faces before him would fade away and he would see the endless rolling sands and hear the breathing of the exhausted men and women marching with him. And he would know that it had been the best, the most important, the most fulfilling time of his life.

The Jordanian officer to his right grunted and crumpled to the ground. Blood gushed from his neck. Around Harry, there were yells to take cover. A small group of Marines headed for one of the nearby dunes at a run to take out the sniper.

Calmly and methodically, Harry tended to the fallen man.

The officer survived.

This wasn't the kind of flashback other men had told him about from other wars. This was Harry in his element, doing what he did best—doing it even better than in real life. This was where he belonged. This was the work he should be doing.

In reality, the Jordanian had died despite everything Harry had tried to do. The supplies had been too limited, the wound too severe.

"Didn't you ever feel we shouldn't be there at all?"

The question brought him back to weary reality. He was once again in the small room in the VFW post. The room was filled with long tables and folding chairs. Every chair was occupied and men stood along the walls. They crowded into the doorway from the hall beyond.

Near the back wall, there was a row of wheelchairs. The question had come from one of the men in the wheelchairs, a vet with both legs missing above the knee.

"Didn't you ever feel we shouldn't be there at all?"

It was a question he had been ordered never to answer directly. His CIA handlers had anticipated this question and others and had provided him with answers for all of them. The canned answer to this question was that Harry had concentrated on the task at hand and had left all policy questions to the Commander–in–Chief.

Harry looked at the man in the wheelchair for a long moment and then said, "You know, I was so fully occupied with keeping my people together and alive and getting us to the extraction point that I didn't have time to think about that kind of thing. I just trusted that the Commander–in–Chief knew what he was doing. Obviously, he was a hell of a bright guy."

The other man grinned and nodded.

The man next to him, missing both legs and part of one arm and with a grotesquely disfigured face, said, "The medics who were with us in Nam fired at the enemy when they had to. I remember one of them, it really bothered him afterwards. You must have killed some of the enemy. What do you think about that?"

"You do what you have to," Harry said. "Like you said. Yeah, it bothered me. I prefer to think about the ones I saved after the shooting was over."

The vet frowned. At least Harry thought he was frowning. It was hard to be sure. "You saved the enemy?" There was surprise in the man's voice, and anger.

"At that point, they weren't the enemy. They were my patients. I did what I could for them." He was completely off the script by now. He didn't care. These were things he had to say. "Mostly, they were just scared kids, hurt, surrounded by an enemy they'd heard terrible stories about, afraid they'd never see their families again. Sound familiar?"

A few of the vets nodded.

"Anyway," Harry said, trying to lighten the mood, "whether they were our allies or from the other side, I couldn't understand a word they were saying, so I just assumed it was, 'Thanks, Doc. I'll name my first kid after you.'" He got the chuckles he'd hoped for.

It was a lie, though. Sharon's lessons had kept paying off. By the time they'd reached the extraction point, Harry had understood completely what the patients were saying—whether they were thanking him or cursing him, whether they were praying or promising retribution. He'd even understood when wounded soldiers from supposedly allied armies had muttered their hopes for the coming of the Grand Master.

He thought he'd gained some cultural understanding along with his surprising linguistic skill. It occurred to him that he should be able to use that knowledge to do more good than he was doing with these speeches.

The familiar limousine was waiting outside the VFW hall to take him to his next speaking engagement. The inevitable two goons in suits were also waiting for him. They didn't bother saying who they were or what their purpose was. They never did. It was clear enough to Harry that they were simultaneously his bodyguards and his custodians. He supposed he should feel flattered that the CIA thought it might take two such enormous men to subdue him if he tried to bolt.

These weren't the same two who had rescued him from the riot police in Washington. The faces kept changing, although there always two of them, and they were always huge. Usually not very friendly, either.

These two were acting very unfriendly. "You were told to stick to the script," one of them growled.

"You were listening?" Harry said. "I'm flattered."

He hadn't seen them inside the hall, though. That meant they'd managed to plant a bug on him at some point. For a national hero, he was being treated remarkably like a prisoner.

"Listen, it doesn't really make any difference if I stick to the script or not. The public's all fired up, and I'm not going to change that by throwing in a few remarks of my own. They don't come to listen, they come to look at the hero in his uniform. Anyone else could do this, and the effect would be the same. Hell, the effect would be better if you had someone more heroic looking doing this."

Someone less Arab looking, he wanted to say. He'd heard that muttered comment often enough recently to understand that some people in his audiences wondered just what he really was. Before the war, people had tended to assume that his ancestry was Mediterranean or Spanish. If so, those genes had probably come to Britain with the Celts. Now, with awareness of things Middle Eastern so heightened, some assumed that he was an Arab.

It was not a good time to be an Arab in America. Americans were smug winners, but they were also generous ones. But they were extremely bad losers, and Arab-Americans, no matter what their political sympathies, were bearing the brunt of American rage for the Gulf disaster.

An idea struck Harry. "But I'll tell you something I can do that some taller and blonder hero can't. I can speak to Arab-American groups. In Arabic. Someone needs to heal the breach. And keep those people loyal to this country."

"Fucking ragheads have never been loyal to this country," one of the two goons said. "They're not real Americans."

Harry sighed. German-Americans during World War One, Japanese-Americans during World War Two, and now this. How could he fight that attitude? He couldn't, not with these two men. But maybe their superiors could see matters more objectively. "Just pass the suggestion back up your chain of command," he told them. "See what happens."

"Yeah, sure, Elkins. What makes you think we give a shit what happens to you?"

"Gee, I dunno. Maybe because I won a medal and you didn't?"

"Oh, fuck you. All right, we'll pass your suggestion up the

line. Now get in the car, or you'll be late for your next speech. And this time, stick to the Goddamned script!"

Harry might have felt a bit better about his situation if he'd known how trapped the President was feeling—trapped, and more than a bit frightened.

While Harry was being chauffeured by two goons to his next speaking engagement, George Bush was entertaining an important visitor in the Oval Office. It would be more accurate to say that Bush was warily listening to and watching his visitor. The visitor, Arthur Lang, had no formal title and held no official office. He was small, slender, and unprepossessing. He dressed conservatively and spoke quietly. But the President quailed before him and hung upon his words. It was clear which man was the superior.

Lang was one of the party's behind-the-scenes powerbrokers, a Republican gray eminence.

More like a black eminence, Bush thought. Black cloud. Cloud on the horizon. My horizon. He makes that whole damned part of the room dark. Sucking in all the light.

"This won't do, George," Lang said quietly. "We're getting very worried about the election. We could lose the White House and Congress, thanks to your disastrous little war. My friends and I can't afford that."

"Horses," Bush interrupted quickly, feeling his panic rise. "Middle of the stream."

Lang nodded. "The voters don't like to change horses in the middle of the stream. You're right about that. But Lincoln was using the metaphor of a rider guiding his horse successfully across the stream. I'm afraid the American people see our current situation rather differently. They see a horse stuck in the middle, the water at his shoulders and rising, and the rider about to fall out of the saddle and drown. That's not an inspiring image, George. A new horseman might be advisable."

"It's getting better," the President blurted. "Over there. Tide's turning."

Lang held up a hand. "For Heaven's sake, don't tell me you can see a light at the end of the tunnel. The country is fragmenting more and more along ethnic and class lines. That's worked to our advantage in the past, but I'm beginning to think it won't work much longer and that we need not only a new direction but also a new image, a new front man, someone who can appeal to a broader cross-section of the voters." He looked at his watch and rose to his feet. "I have a meeting with Judge Webster in a few minutes. I'll be in contact with you again on Friday. In the meantime, I want you to think about how you can inspire me with confidence in your leadership."

After Lang had left, Bush sat for a long time drumming his fingers on the huge desk.

Darn it, he thought. *I'm* the President! Poor Gorby. This must be how he felt at the end.

Saddam Hussein picked up the telephone as soon as it rang. A few months ago, he never would have had to do such a thing—an aide would have brought him a description of the caller and his needs, and if Saddam decided the call was worth his time, he would take it. Sometimes the descriptions he was given were inaccurate, but no aide had the opportunity to make that mistake twice.

Most of the time, that was still how things worked, but this was a special line, installed at the request of a special ally. Saddam wasn't sure how he felt about the intrusion, about the slight but definite loss of control over his environment, but he couldn't deny that Rashid-al-Din had rendered such valuable service that refusing the request would have been unreasonable.

"Hello, Rashid," he said warmly. He regarded the leader of the Assassins as a friend as well as an ally.

"Hello, my friend." Less warmth on the other end of the line, but that was how Rashid was. No one doubted he was a man of passion, but it was part of his power that no one saw him express it. Saddam admired such self-restraint in the abstract but had no desire to try it for himself: if you couldn't enjoy the freedom power brought, what was the point? "Congratulations on the victory your forces have won over the Americans. My reports indicate that it's nearly complete."

And your reports are probably better than my own, Saddam thought, a bit chilled. "Thank you. Your assistance made much of that victory possible, as you know. You'll be rewarded."

"Rewarded?" Now there was real emotion in Rashid's voice, but it wasn't warmth. Saddam wasn't quite sure what it was. Greed, maybe. That would be good. Saddam was an old hand at manipulating others' greed.

"Well, yes, of course. Once we've consolidated our gains—there's still quite a bit of resistance, you know—perhaps you and your people would be interested in having Syria and Lebanon as semi-autonomous territories. Lebanon is beautiful, you know."

"Yes, I know."

"Well, and the next step will be the damned Persians. They're not really like us, after all. They call themselves Muslims, but they're still heathens underneath it all. It would be nice for you to have Alamut again. Really, I intend to give you quite a bit of

... hello?"

The line was dead.

Another day, another speech. Another meeting hall. Another polite, interested crowd staring with curiosity at the hero of the Desert March.

But this time there was a difference. This time, the crowd wasn't mostly blond. Almost everyone in the room had hair and skin as dark as Harry's, or even darker. And their expressions combined curiosity and wariness. Their feelings toward him must be ambiguous, he felt sure. He was an American hero, but he was also a man who had killed many of their distant relatives.

"Es salaam alekum," Harry said.

The middleaged and older members of the audience smiled and nodded. Ahmed Miro, a man of about Harry's age, who had greeted Harry when he arrived, had made a brief speech in English introducing Harry to the crowd, and now sat beside Harry at the main table, said loudly, *"Ahlan wa sahlan!"*

Looking at the younger members of the audience, boys and girls in their teens, young men and women in their twenties, many of them frowning with concentration and looking unhappy, Harry said, *"Fee hadd hina biyitkalim ingileezee?"* Does anyone here speak English?

Miro and the other older listeners chuckled. The younger members of the audience relaxed.

Harry continued in a mixture of English and Arabic. This was a speech he had written entirely by himself, and to Hell with the CIA.

"Please forgive my grammar, my pronunciation, my vocabulary, and my inappropriate usages. I want to be courteous by trying to speak Arabic to you, and yet I fear that I will insult you by the poor quality of my Arabic."

"Your Arabic is better than my children's!" an older man called out. There was laughter from the older people, annoyance evident on the faces of the younger ones.

"Nor is it my wish to cause an intergenerational war in this room," Harry said with a smile. There was laughter. After it died down, he added, "Surely we've seen enough killing and war and destruction already in the lands you came from. Isn't it time for peace?"

Beside him, Miro muttered *"Inshallah."* Harry thought that others in the audience were saying the same thing.

"I am a medic," Harry said, "a man who binds the wounds of those who have been injured in the fighting. My friends, I can't tell you how I wish I could bind the wounds of the injured world. Clearly, that's beyond my power. I can't even bind the wounds that divide Americans from each other, that make one American hate another because of his color or his religion or his language. I know that you are Americans, that you love this country as much as I do. I know that you also love the lands you came from, where your relatives still live, countries that are being devastated by a terrible war even as we meet here in peace and brotherhood. Your hearts are torn within you, your souls are divided. I can't bind those wounds, either. I can only tell you that I am your brother. I can assure you that most Americans, even though they keep silent in the face of hatred, also call you brother. My voice is a small one, but I promise you I'll speak for you whenever I can."

There was more to his speech, but he didn't get the chance to deliver it. The audience rose to its feet at that point and began applauding and calling out his name. Ahmed Miro and the others at the head table crowded around Harry, clapping his shoulders, embracing him.

The CIA seemed willing to put him up in expensive hotel rooms. Harry had to give them that much credit. Or maybe this was just the way spooks lived all the time—James Bond on the Côte d'Azur rather than some guy freezing in a Moscow alley. The rooms usually didn't come equipped with any kind of alcohol, though; maybe that was one of the CIA's requirements. And on the rare occasions when the rooms did have some kind of bar, there was never any beer, never any bourbon. Instead, there'd be small bottles of expensive Scotch, sometimes single malts. Having lots of money must do awful things to your taste buds, Harry thought. So normally he did without an evening drink.

Tonight, he felt so relaxed and happy that he was willing to try some of the single-malt Scotch in the room's small drinks cabinet. He was celebrating alone, but he was celebrating.

Not only had the speech gone well, not only had he done some real good for a change, it had also felt good to him. Damned good.

He had felt relaxed in a way he almost never had before while making his speeches. He had felt... It seemed odd to even think the thought: He had felt at home.

He filled the glass most of the way with ice and poured some of the single malt over it and sipped. Almost drinkable, he decided. It would have been improved by the addition of Coke or Pepsi, but he couldn't find any in the room.

Harry settled down in one of the room's two armchairs, pointed the remote control at the TV set on the table at the opposite end of the room, and flicked through the channels until he found CNN. Any chance his speech earlier in the evening would be covered? Not much, he decided.

The first story summarized the day's depressing news from the Middle East and ended with a short clip of a dazed President Bush insisting that matters were well in hand. The second story showed a mob attacking a store in Indianapolis owned by an Arab–American. From there on, it got more depressing.

Harry swallowed his drink and poured himself another. This time, he dumped the remaining ice and filled the glass with Scotch.

He sat down again to watch the rest of the news.

Something was nagging at his mind, something he'd seen on the screen. The Scotch was making it hard for him to pinpoint what it was. He swallowed more anyway.

And then he thought he knew what it was. He sat holding the glass, not drinking from it, forgetting it was in his hand, while he waited through interminable sports stories and weather reports for the scene with the President to be repeated when the half-hour news broadcast cycle began again on the hour.

Once again, there was bad news from the Middle East, this time with some additional depressing details added. Then came Bush's press briefing, shown at greater length this time.

It was a formal, scripted affair, presented in the Rose Garden, with the President backed by various Cabinet members and General Powell. It had been held that afternoon, and the fresh foliage glowed in the April sunshine. Bush and the others squinted at the crowd of reporters, too manly, Harry supposed, to stand in the shade.

Bush opened the proceedings with a brief speech. It had something to with the courage and professionalism of American forces in the Middle East, who were helping to keep our brave ally Israel safe and secure despite the dangerous forces in the area. Harry would have said "despite the deteriorating situation in the area," but he didn't have a roomful of speechwriters and advisers, so what did he know? On second thought, he realized that he *did* have a roomful of speechwriters—an insight that made him start drinking his Scotch again.

Bush moved aside and Powell stepped up to the microphone-encrusted lectern. He reminded everyone how proud he was of his kids now standing watch on the front lines in the desert.

"Thin red line," Harry muttered. "But here come the Zulus."

"And I know I speak for every American," Powell added. "I know you all share my feelings. I know that if General Schwarzkopf were here today, he'd say the same thing. General, if you can hear me today, we're coming. Hold on."

Where was Norman "the Bear"? All Harry knew was that contact had been lost with him and his staff early in the game. The official word was that Schwarzkopf was believed to be operating somewhere behind enemy lines. Harry had heard a rumor about a scream picked up by a ham radio operator in Turkey, which made Harry wonder if in fact Schwarzkopf was being operated on behind enemy lines.

"And finally," Powell said, "let me say this to the new opposing forces in the Middle East: Our brave men and women have established their lines, and they—and America—will not give another inch!"

"Right," Harry said, raising his glass to the screen. "They'll be measuring the give in miles."

And then he saw what he was sure he had glimpsed before,

only now it was clear and obvious to him.

Three tall, broad-shouldered young men stood with George Bush, one behind him and one on either side. They were even taller than the President, and two of them kept their eyes roaming over the crowd in a characteristic Secret Service way. But the third man was concentrating on Bush. He was bending slightly and whispering in the President's ear, and the President was nodding. Harry had received and given orders often enough in his career to recognize the body language. The man was giving an order to Bush, and the President was nodding his understanding and acquiescence.

And there was more. Harry knew this young man. Only a few days earlier, he had sat beside Harry in the limousine taking him from one speaking engagement to another.

He was not Secret Service. He was CIA.

When the three months finally ended, Harry couldn't quite believe he had finally made it. He had become used to thinking of the time as his sentence, and it had often seemed that it was a life sentence. The bright spots—speaking to children or veterans' groups or Arab-American organizations—had been far too rare.

Now at last the sentence was over.

It caught him by surprise. The usual pair of unemotional escorts showed up early one morning before Harry had showered and considerably before he was fully awake. "What is it this time?" he asked them. "Businessmen's breakfast meeting?" He headed for the bathroom, still in his robe. "Get me some coffee from room service, will you? I'll be showered and dressed in a few minutes."

And don't touch anything he thought, although he suspected

they'd be efficiently searching the room while he showered, looking for evidence of disloyalty. "Disloyalty" had become a popular word on the news lately.

"No more speeches," one of the escorts said. "You're finished with that. We're taking you back to Washington. Mr. Walsh wants to talk to you."

"No shit?" Harry said. "Well, I'll be damned. Where am I now?"

The escorts looked at each other in disgust. "You're in Des Moines," one of them told Harry. "You should try drinking less. Save the few brain cells you have left."

Inside the shower with the water running, Harry muttered, "Fuck you." Des Moines, Topeka, Indianapolis... they all looked much the same when all you saw were airports and meeting halls. And as for alcohol, wasn't the right to drink one of the things they were fighting for in the Middle East?

By the time he got out of the shower, the coffee was there and the two goons had packed his few belongings for him. A freshly pressed dress uniform lay across his bed. He was so used to one being available for him every day that he no longer thought twice about it. He stood in the steam-filled bathroom doorway in his robe and looked at the two hostile goons for a moment, then said, "Take the luggage downstairs and wait for me in the lobby. I'll be there eventually."

They glowered at him but did as he said. He dressed and drank the coffee, taking his time with everything. It was a small victory, but he relished it.

For three months, Harry had been flown around the country on commercial flights. Now he was brought back to Washington on a Learjet with only the two escorts for company. He didn't really mind. He was content to stare out the window and watch the cloud cover crawl by.

They passed over the leading edge of the front somewhere over Pennsylvania, and the carpet of clouds below them thinned and then disappeared. Harry saw quite a few rivers and lakes before the descent began. All the water made him think of the desert. He realized with surprise that he missed it.

By noon, he was back in Hugh Walsh's office. Nothing had changed during the three months, including Walsh's look of self–satisfaction. "Still no beer or bourbon?" Harry asked. He thought of using his line about the fighting in the Middle East being about the right to drink, but he decided not to bother.

"Good God, man!" Walsh said, scandalized. "It's just barely afternoon! I can get you some coffee, if you want."

"Never mind. What I want is what you promised. You said if I was a good boy for three months, you guys would send me back to the Middle East front as a medic."

Walsh shook his head. "I didn't say we'd send you back to the front. I said we'd be willing to discuss it."

"Shouldn't take long. There's nothing to discuss. Send me back."

Walsh smiled. "You're right. It didn't take long. We've already discussed it. Now, I have a different proposition for you."

Harry began to rise from his chair and opened his mouth to object.

Walsh held up his hand. "Wait a moment. You might as well hear me out. You have no choice, you know."

Harry knew. He shut his mouth and sat down again.

Walsh smiled. No, he smirked. "Good. Now, Elkins, we've been going over the videotapes of your speech to that group of

Arabs in Cincinnati. What were they called?"

Videotapes? Okay, he had realized early on that he was bugged; probably they'd hidden a microphone in his uniform. But video cameras? Where had they hidden those? Recreating the scene in his mind, he couldn't see a place where they could have been hidden. These people obviously had expertise in areas his own experience didn't cover.

"The Southern Ohio Arab–American Friendship League."

"Christ," Walsh said. "Sounds like something the Soviets could have made up. Anyway, we had some of our Arab language people watch the tape, and they said good things about your ability to speak the language. Very elementary Arabic, they said. Very basic. But you have a talent for it."

What about my rapport with the group, Harry wondered. Didn't you guys notice how they responded to me? And how I responded to them?

"Yeah, I know I have a talent for Arabic. While we were in the desert, trying to reach Qatar, I asked one of my people who knew Arabic to teach me a bit so that I could communicate more easily with the Arab refugees who were with us. It came to me pretty easily. I don't know where that talent came from, but it was handy."

"It came from a childhood friend of yours, a boy named Chaim Abramovich," Walsh said. He was reading something on his desk. Harry could see a stack of papers but couldn't make out what they were. "His parents were Israelis," Walsh continued. "They lived next door to you in Philadelphia, and you spent more time in their house than in yours. Chaim's parents spoke mostly Hebrew at home, so you listened to it constantly. You were young enough that you probably absorbed something, and it showed up in adulthood as a talent for a related Semitic language. That's our people's theory, anyway."

Until now, Harry had forgotten about Chaim. He saw him again, now, a small, dark, intellectual boy with curly black hair. Harry felt a flood of warm childhood happiness. Then he felt a chill down his spine. "Does it have my blood type in there, too?"

"Of course. A positive. The subordinate who gave you Arabic lessons in the desert was Sharon Alcazar. We're interested in her, too."

Who isn't? Harry thought. "All right. So you're spooks. I already knew that. What's your point?"

"Also, you look like an Arab."

"So I've been told."

"During the last three months, we've been discussing what to do with you when your time was up. This talent for Arabic was a pleasant surprise. In fact, it's a godsend. Look, medics are a dime a dozen." Noticing Harry's reaction, Walsh said, "Okay, maybe they're not that common, but the point is we can train almost anyone to be a passable medic. But your combination of language talent and appearance is something special. After a few weeks of our language and cultural training, we think you'd make one hell of an in–country agent.

"There's some kind of weird new Arab empire growing out there. We don't know enough about it, but we need to know everything. You could do a lot more good behind the lines than you ever could as a medic on the front lines. You want danger? What I'm talking about is a lot more dangerous than being a medic. You want service to your country? This is it. This is big time and long term. As a medic, you'd probably save a few lives. As an agent, you could help save the world."

Harry sat staring at him, openmouthed.

Walsh waited for a few seconds and then added, "Some of those Arab refugees who were with you in the desert, *whom you rescued,* are doing that kind of work for us now. They're out there as agents, our agents. They want to help us, they want to overthrow this new tyranny and liberate their homelands, but of course they're scared. You can imagine what would happen to them if they were exposed. Now, they respect you enormously because of what you did for them in the desert. It would give them a tremendous boost, a lot of confidence, if you were there on the scene helping them. Supervising them. It would be kind of like what you did during your desert march."

Harry was surprised—almost disappointed—at the crudity of Walsh's attempt to push his buttons. He'd expected much greater sophistication and subtlety from the CIA.

And yet, the man had said the right things, damn him.

"I don't know anything about being a spy," Harry said. "Anyway, I've been on TV a lot. I'd have to live among people who'd recognize me immediately. It wouldn't work at all."

"You've been on TV a lot in this country," Walsh said. "You haven't been on TV a lot in the other Allied countries. They're all building up their own heroes. More to the point, you haven't been seen on TV on the other side. They don't seem to think very highly of TV or other modern media, and they control them very tightly. I doubt if there's anyone in the entire Arab world who knows who you are other than the people you'll be working with, your fellow agents. Anyway, you'll grow a beard, have longer hair—you'll be unrecognizable.

"Now, as for knowing the job, you can trust us to teach it to you. That's one of the things we do. By the time we're done with you, you'll speak the language fluently, you'll know the culture backwards and forwards, and you'll know a whole lot of other stuff you can't even imagine right now. You can trust us on this. We're the experts."

You haven't been very expert so far, Harry thought. Why didn't you see this Arab uprising coming?

He certainly didn't trust them.

But, by God, the man was right. The idea of being an agent behind Arab lines excited him. It was like the kind of adventure he had daydreamed about as a boy. The adult Harry knew it would be terribly dangerous, but it excited him anyway.

And then there was the good he could do. Walsh and his CIA cronies would want him to deliver reams of information, and he would try to do that. At the same time, though, he could be trying to understand just what had happened, what changes were taking place in that mysterious new other world, and what it meant for the rest of the world.

And what Harry Elkins' role in all of this might be.

In the version of the story prepared by the government for public consumption, Harry had led his people on a perilous but ultimately triumphant march through the desert to salvation. That had been the end of the tale. But for Harry, the tale hadn't yet ended. During the march, he had been focused, had had a purpose: get as many of his group as possible alive to the departure point in Qatar. He had done that, and then the focus had disappeared. He had been drifting ever since Qatar. He now realized that unconsciously he had been looking for some new purpose, something as thrilling and focusing and all–consuming as that desert command had been.

Now he had been offered exactly that new purpose.

Harry nodded. "It's a deal."

Major Halif Said had been commissioned at the height of the war with Iran. He was a young man from a good family then, used to a comfortable life, thrown into battle and charged with leading men even younger than he, boys really, who had mostly grown up poor and without the comforts to which he was accustomed; but on the battlefield they were all equally deprived. The confines of his tank were ferociously hot and stank of fuel and hot metal and smoke and unwashed human bodies, and when the gas came and they had to fight in masks and rubber suits, the choking heat was enough to kill a man without the enemy firing a shot.

It could have been worse, of course. He could have been in the infantry.

Both sides paid for tiny breakthroughs with huge slaughter, until the ground was lined with corpses. The tank offered the only chance of significant movement, and sometimes it bogged down, the treads choked with a cement composed of dirt and human flesh and blood. Gas could turn entire battalions of fighting men into twitching, puking, helpless animals, like drowning rats in a cage. Halif's tank ground through the bodies of infantrymen of both sides who lay dead in their trenches. And the Iranians had it worse. At the end of the war they were truly children, emaciated thirteen-year-olds dressed in rags, charging, firing wildly with rifles as big as they were, and they would never have had a chance of accomplishing anything except that there were so many of them and they never stopped. Machine guns scythed them down, main tank guns blasted holes in their lines, and they would not stop.

Halif had never, during the entire four years of his service against the Iranians, been as frightened as he was now.

The Caliph's forces were drawing steadily closer. This body had launched from Syria, from a base at Abu Kamal just over the border. Rumor said that Rashid al-Din Sinan himself was with them, that the warlords running wild through Jordan and Egypt and Saudi Arabia were imitators and lackeys. That made sense to Halif. The Syrians themselves wouldn't have many men to spare—they'd be too worried about Israeli armor rolling down from the Golan straight into Damascus—but Syria was perhaps the only truly stable country in the entire Arab world right now, and the one most firmly under the Caliph's control. And the bulk of the soldiers who were about to meet Halif's men were Iraqis.

He wondered if he knew any of them. Were they his friends, the men with whom he had fought the Iraqis and later the Americans? If he saw any of their faces—which he could not help fearing, as unlikely as he knew it to be—would he hesitate before firing, and perhaps give them a chance to kill him first? No, he decided, he wouldn't. They were Iraqis only by the country of their births. They were traitors, no longer really his countrymen and definitely no longer his friends. And he knew they would kill him eventually, probably in the next few hours, but he would take as many as he could with him. The survivors of this battle would wake up in screaming nightmares for the rest of their lives, nightmares of the sort Halif knew from too much experience. There was a certain weird comfort in that thought: after today, he would never again hesitate to sleep for fear of his dreams.

"What the hell *is* that, Bill?"

Staff Sergeant William Petrucci had no answer for Captain Harwood's question. No one had any answers, which was a problem for intelligence troops whose job it was to answer questions. The satellite feeds were not nearly as reliable as Colonel Rowe made them out to be at the press conferences, and the TR-1 and SR-71 overflights were spotty at best at a time when half of Europe and Asia were priority areas. This little clump of antenna-studded buildings in the middle of Fort Meade was where everyone from the President on down expected to get their answers from, and there just weren't any.

"I can tell you what it's not, Captain," Bill said. "It's not routine maneuvers, like we thought at first." He pointed at the screen in front of him, where the image was becoming steadily more clear as the image-processing computers did their magic. The satellite feeding them these images was over the Red Sea right now; as it drew closer to its target area, it sent out microburst transmissions of steadily improving images, and the computer fed Bill's monitor the best it could come up with via interferometry and deconvolution.

Terrain features and buildings, augmented by the computers' database of stored images, were sharp, but anything moving fast—such as an armored force—was of necessity indistinct. Only when the satellite was right over southern Iraq would they get the best images, and then only for a minute or so. Ten minutes after that, the satellite would be over central Iran, and there would be no more images of the area around Baghdad at all. The satellites had high-inclination orbits, which meant that they gave their best images of any one spot on only about one out of eight orbits. The next satellite which would give them images even this good was almost three hours away.

A day from now, more intense analysis by both computers and human beings would give a clearer picture. But whatever was happening would be long over by then.

Three hours ago, these tanks had been southwest of Ar Ramadi, about sixty miles from Baghdad. Now they were approaching the Iraqi capital's western suburbs. That was a pace well within the reach of any decent armored force, as long as they were not facing armed opposition. Now the force was slowing, spreading out, unmistakably ready to engage an opponent. Bill leaned closer to the screen. There was something there, something fuzzy in among the razor-sharp buildings at the railroad fork between Batrah and Shaykh Hamid. Not emplaced artillery, but something like it, that had not been there the day before.

"Is that Syrian armor?" Captain Harwood mused, looking at the readouts on their radio transmissions. "Doesn't seem right."

"Some of them are," Bill said, "but you're right—look there." One wing of the force was now completely halted.

"Jesus Christ, that's an Iraqi formation!"

Bill glanced at his superior, feeling his eyebrows rise. Harwood laughed. "They do teach us officers something, you know."

"Yessir." In peacetime, Intelligence was as rank-conscious as any other part of the service, maybe a little more so than most. Officers ran the show, enlisted did the shit work, and the line was clearly drawn. For the last few months, there had been too much of both types of work for such distinctions to be maintained. Harwood was a good boss, he paid attention to what his troops thought about him, and Bill knew he did plenty of thinking of his own.

"So why are Iraqi tanks getting ready to fight a battle outside their own capital?" The obvious question, and once again, Bill felt helpless to give an answer.

"Oh, shit." The computers had finished processing their next chunk of information, and now the image was slightly better—the satellite would be at the best possible point in its orbit right now, over a spot fifty miles south of An Naiaf—but obscured by clouds of dust or smoke. One thing that did stand out clearly was scattered points of light.

Bill tapped at some keys and brought the images into realtime. The clarity dropped by orders of magnitude, buildings and terrain becoming as fuzzy as the maneuvering tanks, but now he and Harwood could see the battle forming on the ground. Static clouds became roiling smoke plumes, and lights winked in and out across the entire field of view like lethal fireflies. Soon they could see, even at this poor resolution, the unmistakable flicker of burning vehicles.

That answered the question of what had been partially concealed among the buildings: the mysterious opposing force. They were moving now, their concealment gone, lining up for a battle that would be clearly a matter of numbers, strength against strength. That had crippled the Iraqis in the early stages of Desert Storm, their stubborn reliance on massed firepower against the infinitely more sophisticated American tactics, at least until the mass of the Caliphate became overwhelming. Here were Iraqis fighting Iraqis, the Syrians and the Jordanians little more than sideshow participants, and it would be brutal.

The images were getting worse again. Bill took the display back to pre-processed stills, one new image every thirty seconds. For a few more minutes the men watched the battle, little movement other than small units jockeying for position, and then Baghdad was out of the satellite's reach. Fort Meade, and therefore the United States, was once again in the dark.

Communications had disappeared in the first minutes of the battle. The Syrians might have few men to spare, but they had ample jamming equipment, less than a decade older than the best the Soviets could manufacture; Iraqi electronics were a generation older. Halif could communicate by flashing his tank lights in pre–arranged codes, but that was all that was left of his contact with the over two hundred tanks and almost a thousand men of whom he was supposedly in command.

It hardly mattered. No one had any doubt about what to do.

"Fire!" he screamed, hoarse with heat and dust and the smoke of previous rounds loosed from the tank's 125mm main gun. The gunner pulled the trigger and the tank rocked back, huge noise filling the fighting compartment, as another round went downrange. The T62 which had been Halif's target jerked, slewed a quarter of the way around, and stopped moving. His own T72 was a far superior fighting platform, could chew up the older tanks without putting itself in much danger, much as the American M1's had done to the T72's before sabotage and chaos cut off the supply lines on which all modern armored forces depended. A core force of a hundred or so T72's in the midst of just over three hundred T62's and having their backs to their base of supply was the best hope the defenders of Baghdad had.

The T62 disappeared in a flash and a cloud of dust. Halif's round must have started a fire inside the tank which had cooked off the ammunition in the magazine. Bits of metal rained against the body of the T72, almost unnoticed in the roar of battle around them. As the smoke began to clear Halif saw the lean shapes of two T72's steering around the wreckage, their center–mounted turrets easy to identify even through the haze. They sent their expendables in first, he thought.

"Get us behind some cover," he told the driver, trying to keep calm. He thought the loyal Iraqis still had more modern tanks than the Caliph's men, across the entire battlefield, though the Caliph's forces were larger overall. Right here, all that mattered was that his tank was outnumbered two to one. If the Caliph's vehicles had not yet realized that it was a T72 that had destroyed their comrades, if they expected to be able to charge ahead, if both tank commanders tried to go in for the kill instead of offering each other proper support, Halif might be able to beat them both. If, if, if...

The driver had also fought the Iranians, and drove the massive tank as easily as another men might have handled a small car. Halif braced himself as they reversed, swerved around a wrecked mobile artillery piece, and slid behind a warehouse. This was really concealment, not cover, but it would do for now.

The gunner knew his job as well. He depressed the main gun slightly, aiming at a point just beyond the edge of the warehouse. Halif took a deep breath and forced himself to pop the hatch and raise himself out of the tank. He blinked in the sunlight and sneezed as his nose caught the pervasive battlefield stench of fuel, gunsmoke, and burned meat. His testicles tried to crawl up into his belly and for a moment his heart simply refused to beat, but he forced himself to remain outside the tank. The safety of the fighting compartment was largely an illusion anyway, and he wanted to see what was happening with his own eyes.

The enemy tank's main gun appeared beyond the warehouse, and then its bow. Halif gripped the machine gun in front of him, not to fire it but to brace himself against what he knew was coming. Then the main gun roared again and the tank rocked under him, throwing his ribs painfully against the hatch.

It was a perfect shot, taking the other T72 in the deck just under the front of the turret. The turret and main gun lifted away from the main body of the tank, flying over the warehouse and landing somewhere on the other side. Halif prayed it would crush more of the Caliph's men when it fell, unlikely as he knew that to be. What was left of the tank was a smoking ruin.

He dropped back into the fighting compartment. "Beautiful!" he told the gunner, then turned to the driver. "Turn us around, do it now." The mark of a good commander was that he rarely had to give orders; the tank was already wheeling to meet the other tank. Halif had expected them to come around the other side of the building—it was what he himself would have done—but like the first tank, this tank's crew had underestimated how close Halif's tank would be to the building. Its main gun was aimed fifty meters farther back, threatening bare dirt. Bullets from its bow machine gun bounced off the T72 and left bright marks on the dull metal of the still-open hatch, as harmless as raindrops.

But it was in the open, moving fast to present a more difficult target, wheeling both body and turret to bring the main gun to bear. "Aim for the rear deck!" Halif yelled. There was no time for the perfect shot. The best thing to do was simply hammer their opponent, keep the enemy off balance until—

—the enemy commander had the same thought, and his gunner fired first. The shell hit the very end of Halif's tank, expended its shaped charge in the wrong direction and did no significant damage, but the force was tremendous. The tank lifted onto its left side and came down again with bone-jarring impact. Metal ground against metal in a way Halif could not precisely identify but knew was *wrong* as the driver continued to turn the tank. The gunner swore, moved the gun, and fired back.

Baghdad was coming back into view. Bill knew what to look for now and had left the display in realtime. His and Captain Harwood's experience would substitute for computer enhancement, at least for now. And both of them wanted to see what was happening as soon as they could.

The change was subtle but profound. An untrained observer would have seen little difference. The dark blobs representing tanks and other vehicles were less organized now, formations shattered in the first minutes, but both sides were still firing and maneuvering. It still looked, at first glance, like a fairly even fight.

Bill could see the larger pattern, order out of chaos. Although their line as such had disappeared, the attackers still had an overall momentum, driving steadily if slowly east toward Baghdad proper. And the defenders could not stop them. Their concealment among the railyard buildings had been a good plan, but it had not been enough for the kind of surprise that would have won the battle—and neither was their now desperate stand in the open. In three hours, the battle had been decided.

There was plenty of killing to go before it was truly over.

Captain Harwood was at a desk a few feet away, talking on the phone. When he hung up, his face was grim. "CIA is pretty sure it's Saddam's loyalists trying to hold Baghdad against this Rashid guy. But they don't have any idea why, as usual. I mean, they didn't tell me that, but it's pretty obvious."

Suddenly Bill felt very calm. "Well, that's their problem." He pointed at the screen, where the way to Baghdad was becoming clearer by the minute. "Anyone has any questions, we may not be able to tell them why, but we can sure tell them who won."

The shot took the Caliph's T72 in the treads, and the tank spun wildly as the good treads on the other side bit while the side facing Halif's tank slid. The net effect was overcorrection, with the main gun now pointing at the warehouse and the enemy gunner unable to swing the gun back fast enough. Pieces of tread flew away, each one the size of a man's arm and moving fast enough to be lethal as a bullet, punching holes in the warehouse wall.

"Fire," Halif said in what seemed to him to be sudden quiet, and this round punched into the enemy tank just under the turret. The gun continued to spin for a moment, pointing at them and then away, but did not fire. Inside the tank would be a hell of molten metal and burned flesh.

He pulled himself back up out of the hatch and looked around. It took very little time to realize that no matter how successful he and his crew had been, things had not gone well for Saddam's men as a whole. His tank's relative shelter next to the warehouse had probably been the only thing that had saved them from being blasted into oblivion at a safe distance from the wolfpacks of the Caliph's tanks that now controlled the battlefield. He dropped back into the tank and pulled the hatch shut.

"Get us back toward the city," he ordered. In Baghdad itself there might be a chance at more effective resistance. If he stayed away from the main body, the Caliph's men might take his tank for one of their own long enough for him to get back in contact with headquarters. The tank pulled away from the warehouse, metal still grinding unpleasantly inside it; they would be lucky if it reached Baghdad.

The voice of God roared in his ears, and he could not see. In a moment, hearing returned, but sight did not. Someone was screaming. He put his hand to his face and felt something wet and cold where his eyes should have been.

The next round hit the tank a moment later and sent a jet of vaporized metal through his brain.

Seven

June–July 1991

Baghdad was screaming.

Rashid stood erect, much of his body exposed through the tank hatch. He made his bodyguards very nervous by doing that. Baghdad was largely subdued, but the popping and chattering of small-arms fire were clearly audible not far away, and in some parts of the city there was still even the rumble of artillery. The war was over, but innumerable small battles still waited to take the lives of faithful Hashashim. And cities *ate* soldiers.

Rashid didn't worry. He wanted to hear the screaming.

Over a thousand of his faithful, and God alone knew how many of their allies, had died overcoming the last-ditch defense outside the city. They had left behind a field of shattered metal and smoking flesh such as the world had not seen since El Alamein, twenty thousand Republican Guard soldiers dead in a matter of hours, but still... And pushed into a corner, even the conscripts of the regular Iraqi Army, those who had not already gone over to Rashid, could fight. In this city, with plentiful buildings for cover and almost unlimited ammunition and streets many of them had known since childhood, they could fight quite well. Many more of the faithful would die here.

Which was why the screaming had begun, and would last for weeks, perhaps months: Rashid wanted payment.

His tank faced down Haifa Street toward the Presidential Palace. In this part of Baghdad, it had proven fairly easy to deal with resistance; the streets were broad and straight, designed to showcase the magnificence of whatever despot occupied the Palace at the moment, the absolute power of the state embodied in a single man. In other parts of the city, where ancient streets and buildings had been left in their original states, the remnants of the Iraqi army could hold on. Here they had been almost obliterated, except in the Palace.

Rashid appreciated the glory of the building and its surroundings, and so had decided not to simply knock it down. Foolish men, the largely secular rulers of Iraq, to glorify themselves to the point that they seemed to forsake God's favor which had elevated them to that state; but the Koran did not condemn beauty. He would keep the Palace for his own, somewhat altered to reflect his own tastes.

Once it was subdued, and it was time and past time for that.

Some of the beauty would have to be destroyed, he thought; no way around it. "You may fire when ready," he told his gunner, and the man grinned and disappeared inside the tank for a moment. Then the tank rocked underneath him, and a noise so huge it went beyond sound into pain assaulted his ears. He did not clap his hands over his ears as the infantrymen nearby were doing, did not even allow himself to blink. God had chosen Rashid for this moment, and nothing made by man could overcome His will. The sound of the tank's main gun was a whispered echo of

His voice.

The tools of man could be impressive enough in their own way, though. The huge doors of the Palace simply disappeared, and through the hole Rashid saw pieces of the men who had stood behind them. Before the echoes of the shot died away, his picked force surged forward. Several hundred men, each of them known to him since they were boys, not assassins but the finest battlefield killers in the world. Strength and speed and marksmanship, they had those in abundance, but more importantly they had silence. For well over a decade this battalion had trained for moments just like these, times when they must fight together as a single being without having to speak. No shouted orders, no battle cries; the loudest sounds they would make would be with their rifles. Even the clatter of their boots on pavement seemed soft, subtle, a hint of the movement of armed men rather than the thing itself.

Inside the Palace, they would overwhelm the numerically superior force defending the building before their enemies fully comprehended that they were there.

Rashid heard the small-arms fire from inside the Palace, muffled and echoing compared to the clear sounds of shots in the open air, almost as soon as the last of his men were inside. Without looking at his watch, he counted the minutes. Three... seven... ten... and before a quarter of an hour had gone by, the shooting stopped. Then he allowed himself to smile. It had been even faster than he had hoped.

A squad came out of the hole where the doors had been, a whole squad although one of its members was limping and had a dressing tied around his calf, and another had blood running down his face. The defenders had been brave enough. It was skill they were lacking, and without skill courage was useless in the end. That was a lesson Rashid had learned long ago and had spent most of his adult life passing on to his recruits.

His attention went to the man his soldiers were dragging with them. The Iraqi uniform was gaudy next to the unadorned fatigues of the Hashashim, but now it was filthy and torn. The face above the uniform collar was equally filthy, and bruised, and as pale as a European's. The mustache, once neatly brushed, was now tousled and crusted with blood from the crooked, swollen nose.

So Saddam had fought at the end. Rashid was glad to see that, the visible signs of struggle. This man had once been his ally and Rashid did not want to send him to God a coward.

Rashid reached into the tank and picked up two items. One, a bag such as a doctor might carry, he kept in his hand; the other he slung over his shoulder. Then he leapt from the hatch and landed perfectly straight on the ground. His legs, no longer a young man's, burned at the impact, but he kept his stride measured as he walked toward where Saddam slumped in the arms of two Hashashim. As he walked, he opened the bag and reached inside.

Saddam didn't look up as Rashid reached him. His eyes swept back and forth along the ground, and his face was slack. This is a man, Rashid thought, who has seen something so unbelievable he cannot accept it. Rashid pulled the item from inside the bag and reached out with his other hand to pull Saddam's face up.

"Why?" the Iraqi asked, his voice dull.

Rashid held the item he had pulled from the bag up in front of Saddam's eyes. Dead, lidless eyes stared back at the Iraqi. Rashid's fingers kept a tight grip on the short hair, turning the head side by side so Saddam could see the burns and gashes. The lips were burned away, and the ears had been removed with the same jagged blade as the eyelids. The expression on what was left of the face left no doubt that these injuries had been inflicted while the head was still attached to the body. The only clean wound was the cut through the neck, a single perpendicular slice of great precision, which had severed bone and tendon and flesh as neatly as any surgeon might have done.

"Schwarzkopf," Rashid said. "The fearless leader of the defilers of the House of God. The infidel, the invader, the Crusader, the *Frank."* He felt real wonder as he spoke those words, heard it in his voice. "After seven centuries, they still haven't learned. I tried to teach this one. You can see that I tried to teach him. When I saw that he would not learn, I ended the lesson." He let the head fall to the ground, leaned close to Saddam. "Do you know why God allowed this to happen?"

"Because we defeated him," Saddam whispered.

Rashad straightened, took one step back, and kicked Hussein in the stomach. The Iraqi doubled over, and the men who had been holding him let him fall to his knees. He vomited, barely missing Schwarzkopf's head.

"God defeated him," Rashad said. "And God chose me as the instrument through which He would bring about that defeat. 'We' did not defeat him. You had your job to do, and you did it well, and if you'd been content with that I would have rewarded you. Instead, you forgot your place, Saddam. You started talking about rewarding me, as though you had such a thing in your power. You forgot that although to rule Iraq is a great thing, to serve God in the ruling of His house is greater."

Saddam looked at the American's ruined head, then at

Rashid. The dullness of his face had now been replaced by fear.

"No," Rashid said, "I won't do that to you." He reached over his shoulder and grasped the other thing he had taken from the tank. "I think you, at least, have grasped your lesson well enough not to require further teaching."

The ancient Damascus scimitar flashed out from its scabbard in a wide arc, gaining speed as Rashid put his shoulders into the stroke, a perfect cut, so flat and straight a blow that he hardly felt any resistance as metal passed through flesh, and he had to put almost as much effort into stopping the swing as he had into starting it. Hussein's head rolled away some distance. His body remained kneeling for several seconds, the heart's last beats pumping blood high into the air, before collapsing forward.

Rashid lowered the sword and spoke without bothering to wipe the blood away. "I want two poles, very high, to stand in front of the doors of the Palace. Put Saddam's head on one and the infidel general's on the other. Have them face each other. They should find plenty to talk about." Then he strode forward, trailing blood as he went, into his new home.

Hidden in a shattered doorway, unnoticed by Rashid's Holy Guard, a trembling Ali ibn Daoud watched the display of Schwarzkopf's head and the beheading of Saddam.

Unnoticed by the Guard, or noticed and dismissed as unimportant? The distinction no longer mattered to Ali. Being an eyewitness to the second great Rape of Baghdad had made him understand that what mattered was not ego or recognition, but survival.

Sprawled in the street before him, covered with the dust of the city's death, stark in the brilliant sunlight, were the bodies of two women. They were dressed in black cloth from head to foot, visible sign of Saddam's belated attempt to gain the support of the religious by turning from his old secularism to devout Islam. Much good it had done him. Much good it had done them. Rashid's cannon shells and Rashid's Holy Guard alike distinguished only between what and who stood between them and their target and what and who didn't.

There were times, and this was one of them, when Ali wished he could revert to the devout certainties of his youth—not artificially, like Saddam after his invasion of Kuwait, during the preparations for his war against the American-led coalition. No, genuinely. Ali wished he could believe in a militantly protective divine power as he once had, the way Rashid and his growing army of followers did. Cynical and worldly, Ali knew that there was nothing out there in the void but the void itself. There was no divine authority that favored one people or civilization over another. Those nations with the most arms and soldiers, the best generals, and the greatest willingness to shed blood would prevail over the others, and that was all there was to it.

But, oh, how he wished right now that he could believe!

Dressed in black himself, Ali stood motionless in the shadows cast by a broken arch, breathing shallowly, eyes closed to slits, hoping that not even a chance reflection of light from his eyes would reveal his presence.

He could hear gunfire in the distance, and screams. The ground trembled under his feet. Dust filtered down from the stones above him. He feared the archway would collapse upon him, but he dared not move.

The dust of the street was soaked with the blood of the two dead women. Ali could smell the blood. Flies buzzed about the two bodies, unconcerned with the violent doings of human beings, thinking only of laying their eggs.

Would that he could be as unconcerned!

With the impeccable timing of the unfortunate, Ali had come here on business, leaving behind him the safety of Tunis. He had arrived in Baghdad just in time for the beginning of Rashid's siege, well in time to see the unstoppable, grinding assault by Rashid's Holy Guard.

He had known Rashid as a frightening figure but one as much in the shadows as Ali was now—Rashid as a potential conqueror, as a tyrant over his fairly small group of followers. Now he saw him out in the sunshine, leader of a host, captain of the multitudes, conqueror of Baghdad, scourge of his enemies.

Rashid, master of the world?

Ali would worry about that later. Right now, he had to get out of the city alive.

Moving by the millimeter, Ali eased himself from the safety of the ruined arch and out of sight of the activity in front of the Presidential Palace. He needn't have worried. Now that that archway, that building were no longer impediments, the Holy Guard were not interested in it or in whoever might be standing in it. If they had deemed him a threat, it would of course have been a different matter. But they could tell that he was just another terrified survivor trying to escape with his life.

Once out of sight of Rashid and the Presidential Palace, Ali moved more swiftly. Still he kept to whatever shadows he could find.

Baghdad had become a city of horror. The Holy Guard, core of Rashid's forces, weren't the only ones Ali feared. Their followers and hangers-on were less disciplined and less driven by ideology and therefore, Ali thought, even more dangerous. The ancient city was in the hands of men who paid lip service to Rashid's cause but whose real cause was pleasure and gain. All around him, fires burned and people cried out in terror and agony. Men screamed, children died, women wept. It was as in ancient times. Once again, Ali thought, there would be a Pyramid of Skulls. Once again, Baghdad would become a city of corpses, an object lesson to the Arab world.

Like the refugees of thousands of years before, Ali made for the desert.

The Middle East was in turmoil. It took Ali three weeks to reach home.

He arrived to find his wife packing.

He stood in the bedroom, dusty, exhausted, his clothes stinking of his own stale sweat, and watched Leyla for a few minutes. She seemed to be pretending he wasn't there. Finally, he spoke. "I was looking forward to my cool house. Instead, it's hot. Is the airconditioning not working?"

"I had it removed. You know I never approved of it."

He digested this for a while, trying to remember her expressing disapproval of the airconditioning and failing. The barrier around her was almost palpable. He tried a different tack. "You're going on a trip?"

"I'm going home."

"You *are* home."

"I used to think so." She continued packing. She had two suitcases lying open on the bed. Under his silent gaze, her movements became quicker, her folding less precise, her packing less careful.

"You pose a riddle. I thought you never liked riddles."

"Oh, be silent."

Astonished, Ali was silent.

Leyla paused for a few moments, a towel draped over one arm, arrested in mid-motion. She kept her back to him. Then she resumed both her packing and her talking. "The world is changing," she said. "The Caliph says that he is restoring the world to the way it was, the way it should always have been. You've always rejected that message. I can't live with your hypocrisy any longer. I'm going home."

Still puzzled, Ali said, "Home?"

"To my village. To my parents."

"Ah! How Western of you," Ali said with a sneer. "How secular."

Leyla said nothing and continued packing. Ali stared at her back. She was a shapeless figure muffled in layers of black cloth. How could this be the slender, intense young revolutionary he had fallen in love with and had enjoyed nights of furious passion with? She had been secular enough in her revolutionary zeal and Western enough in her sexual enthusiasm. After their marriage, she had made it clear that she would not tolerate his taking a second wife, even when his business had prospered enough so that he could easily afford one. Oh, yes, she had been secular and Western enough when it had suited her.

And yet she had been changing, bit by bit, along with the world around them. How could he have missed the signs? Because I wanted to, he realized. To Ali, Rashid's revolution had always been a means to an end. To Leyla, it had always been an end in itself. Her commitment to Rashid's pan-Arabism was nothing new. The concealing black clothing was, though. When Ali had left for Iraq a month earlier, she had still been wearing blue jeans and an ordinary blouse. Surely, he thought, under all that covering, the lovely body was unchanged! Surely!

"Packing up and going home to mother," he said mildly. "Didn't we see this scene a few months ago? Yes, I remember. It was in an old movie we were watching on Italian television."

"In my father's house, there is no television." She continued packing.

Or other entertainment or diversion in that dark, gloomy place, Ali remembered. Or much joy in any form, for that matter. It was a house where all lived in fear of the grim patriarch who ruled it.

Not all that different from the one I grew up in, Ali thought. How he had longed to escape it, chafing at the restrictions and impositions, scarcely able to endure it until he was at last old enough to leave and make his own way in the world.

Which, he knew quite well, made it all the stranger that in allying himself with Rashid, he had in fact subjugated himself to a powerful father figure. Ali's inner turmoil over this very matter had only grown where he had hoped it would diminish and fade away.

"There's no longer any television in this house, either," Leyla said with satisfaction.

Ali groaned. "You're assuming they'll welcome you back with loving, open arms. Perhaps they'll beat you instead. Or even worse."

"If they beat me, or even worse, it will be because I deserve it."

"You're mad. Perhaps it's the heat."

The wall around her grew thicker, became impenetrable. He

felt that she would no longer hear him even if he screamed, and he lacked the energy or will to scream.

Ali finally admitted defeat. He watched her complete her packing. When she was done—taking little with her, in the end, as though eager to show how little of their home really had to do with her—he offered to help her carry her two suitcases to the taxi he assumed would be waiting outside. She ignored him.

As though they had been waiting for a cue, three large young men entered the house unannounced. Ali stiffened in alarm.

Then he recognized them: cousins of Leyla. They had been much smaller when he'd last seen them. He nodded and greeted them by name. They didn't reply.

Two of them picked up the two suitcases and headed for the front door. Leyla followed them. The third cousin followed her. He turned around and stood quietly watching Ali.

Ali held his arms out to show his lack of hostile intent. "This isn't how I imagined it would end," Ali said mildly.

The third cousin sneered and left the house. Moments later, Ali heard a car engine start. It moved away, fading in the distance. He wished he had gone outside so that he could have said something sarcastic about using camels instead of a car. Not that it would have mattered if he had done so.

Ali sighed and relaxed at last. In all this time, he had not moved from the place where he had been standing and watching his wife's packing and departure. He had referred to a movie, and indeed the entire scene might have been a movie, or a woodenly acted play, for all the personal involvement he had felt. He felt guilty at his lack of distress and his feelings of relief.

Now he could divest himself of his sweaty clothes and bathe.

And after that, he thought, time for a drink. Assuming Leyla hadn't discovered and destroyed his secret supply of brandy.

The telephone rang. Thank God she didn't have that removed, too, he thought. He hoped it wasn't a call from yet another member of his wife's family. He suspected that a conversation with any of them wouldn't be pleasant.

He stepped over to the small table beside the bed and picked up the receiver. "Allo?"

"Ali ibn Daoud?"

Despite the heat of the day and the heavy dampness of his clothing, Ali felt a chill. He didn't recognize the voice, but he recognized the type of voice, sensed the type of man at the other end of the line. One of Rashid's agents? He hadn't done anything yet, only thought treasonous thoughts, but his legs felt weak anyway, and he sat down heavily on the bed.

"Ali ibn Daoud?" the voice repeated.

"Yes, this is Ali."

"This is Abdelhalim. It didn't sound like you at first."

Ali felt lightheaded with relief. It was, after all, a friend, a business contact. "I'm still myself," he said with a laugh. "I've been through some difficult experiences, though. I just got home ... " He paused, then said, "From Baghdad."

"Ah, Baghdad. We've been hearing stories."

"I could tell you more stories. Travel is very difficult. It took me weeks to get back."

"The world is falling apart," Abdelhalim said sadly. "My business is terrible. There are refugees flooding into Tunis with awful stories of their own. Everything is in chaos. At least the telephone's working today. We were supposed to have a meeting last week, but now I understand why you weren't there. I don't know if there's any point in rescheduling it. As I said, there's no business now. We could talk about trying to sell things to all the foreigners, though."

"The refugees?" Ali said. "I don't think they'd be good customers at the moment."

"No, no, not them. The city is suddenly full of Americans and British and French. Germans, too. They say they're here on business, but I think it has more to do with the war against the Caliph. I know they're not buying anything from *me."*

"So you've spoken to these people?"

"I've tried to. They aren't very talkative."

No, Ali thought, they don't sound like a business opportunity. Abdelhalim was right about that. But they might mean another kind of opportunity. It was one Ali was reluctant to grasp, but he feared he had no alternative if he didn't want to become an irrelevant bystander.

"Perhaps I should give them a try," he said. "Do you know any of the Americans well enough to introduce me to them?"

"It won't do you any good," Abdelhalim warned him. "But if you insist, I could probably do that."

The meeting, when it was finally arranged, was to take place on a Saturday morning on Habib Bourguiba Avenue. He had been instructed to walk down toward the lake. His contact would join him, and they would look like two men strolling casually along the tree-lined street.

Ali did as instructed. Ten o'clock found him walking down the street in the direction of the lake. He tried to look like a casual stroller, but he was terrified. He kept imagining a bullet crashing into his back. His shoulders tensed and he held his head rigidly, as though that would enable him to withstand the shot he was sure was coming at any moment. Outside in the street? They were crazy! They would be instant and obvious targets for the Hashashim, who had become as skilled at assassination as their namesakes of old. He should have insisted on meeting in one of the hotels, perhaps the El Hana, which he had just passed and where he had often held business meetings in quiet, secluded rooms.

The sun was warm on his shoulders, and he drifted to the side of the street, seeking the shade of the giant trees that lined the avenue. He tried to delight in the song of the birds that filled the trees, but he failed. No shade was deep or dark enough to protect him from the hostile eyes he was convinced were watching him, no song was beautiful enough to keep his thoughts from the danger he was sure surrounded him.

The avenue had been popular with tourists in normal times, but these weren't normal times.

Everywhere, there were refugees. Individuals, couples, families, they lay beneath the trees or sat against the fronts of the shops and hotels lining the once-elegant street. They had the look of refugees everywhere and in every age—expression stunned or wary, clothes ragged, belongings piled around them. If not for what he saw in their faces, Ali might have thought they were beggars already into their daily work. Their faces and the fact that these shattered people avoided his gaze, shrank away from him in fear, instead of asking him for money.

They were silent, too, unlike beggars. They huddled together, seeking safety against an outside world that had changed suddenly, inexplicably into horror. They said nothing, not even to each other. Even the children among them were silent.

What had they seen, Ali wondered. Horrors even greater

than those he had witnessed in Baghdad? Terrible as those sights had been, the victims had been strangers to him. These people, he knew, had seen their friends and family members slaughtered.

They were reenacting an ancient tragedy that Ali suspected would never end. There had always been pyramids of skulls and always would be, until the end of time.

But these were real people, not abstract concepts. What would happen to them now? He suspected the government would try to make them keep moving, would prefer them to be someone else's problem.

There must be many more behind them, though, a great and terrible river of despair, vast numbers of desperate people trying to escape the devastation wrought by Rashid's expanding empire.

What did I help bring upon the world? Ali asked himself.

The streets were also filled with foreigners. Not tourists, these hard and purposeful men, but military men from many Western countries, taking advantage of the government's terror of Rashid to assert power over Tunisia and the rest of North Africa. They were tall, a head taller than the Arabs they moved among, their skin and hair were light, and they looked about arrogantly, as though they already ruled. They were the new Crusaders, and Ali had helped bring them here. He had worked to force them out, but what he had done in Rashid's service had had the opposite effect.

Perhaps I deserve to die for this sin, he thought.

He walked slowly, continuing down the street toward the lake, his hands clasped behind him, his head bowed. He was no longer aware of the sun or the birds or the refugees or the foreigners. He no longer feared the bullet in the back. Instead, he welcomed it as his proper punishment.

This mission he was on was a foolish one. Not just foolish: it compounded his sin. These Crusaders, how could they help him or his crumbling world? They had no interest in saving the Arab world from Rashid. They only wanted to save themselves and their allies in Tel Aviv. Worse than that, they wanted an excuse to extend their own power over the Middle East. He had helped to bring them here, and now he was proposing to help them again!

He stopped walking and looked at the Crusaders. It was a hard look, an angry look. He stood unmoving, letting the pedestrian traffic flow around him, while he glared at the tall, arrogant men.

His contact was one of them, of course. He was daring the man to approach him. Did they have to courage to expose themselves, or were they cowards after all, as he suspected, hiding behind their technology and advanced weapons?

"Es salaam alekum."

Ali glanced sideways. It was a fellow Arab, a man shorter and even darker than he was, and dressed much the same way. An Egyptian, by his accent.

"Wa alekum es salaam," Ali muttered, hoping the man would go away. Whatever the other man wanted, he was endangering himself by talking to Ali, and Ali had no wish to draw an innocent fellow Arab into the trap he had foolishly set for himself.

"Ali ibn Daoud?" the other man said.

Ali felt breathless. His earlier feelings of calm acceptance had fled. This small, mild man—this was Death.

"You are Ali ibn Daoud, I believe?"

Ali forced himself to breathe. He became aware again of the birds and glanced at the trees. It would be a shame to leave all of this so soon, he thought. "Yes. I am Ali."

"Good. You were walking that way." He nodded in the direction of the lake. "Let's continue." He strolled off.

Ali followed. Another man might have thought he had the freedom not to follow, to run for his life instead, but Ali knew better. He was sure he was already surrounded, that others in the crowd were also Rashid's men.

He caught up with the other man. "I know I have no right to ask you a favor," Ali said, "but I feel I must do so anyway. Would you please use some quick method and not the garrote. I have always had a terror of choking." It was a gamble that this man would not sadistically choose the garrote precisely because of what Ali had said. Rashid had always emphasized pragmatism and the surest path to the goal. A quick death for Ali would therefore be better. Or so Ali hoped.

But the other man stopped for a moment and looked at him in amazement. "Garrote? What are you talking about?"

Now Ali was the one who walked, forcing the other man to catch up with him. "You were sent by Rashid to kill me. The Hashashim often favored the garrote. Therefore, I made my request. I assumed you would be honest and straightforward with me and not play games. Now, we need to find a quiet place for you to do it."

The other man laughed. "How eager you are to die! But I hope you won't die for a long time. We need you. Let's just keep walking along this crowded street, as you were instructed, so that we won't be too conspicuous."

"You're with them!" Ali gasped. "You're working for the Crusaders, not for Rashid! How can you betray your people this way?"

The other man said in an annoyed tone, "Please stop using

that silly word. I'm certainly not a Crusader. I'm an American. We didn't even exist at the time of the Crusades. My name is Harry. Call me that."

"You're an American? I was sure you were an Arab! An Egyptian."

"Good. Very good." His pleasure was almost smugness. "I'm very happy you thought so, and I hope everyone around us thinks so, too."

They walked in silence for a while. Ali was trying to readjust. The world kept shifting around him. He didn't know what to make of this Crusader who called himself Harry and looked and sounded as fully an Arab as Ali himself. Or as Rashid himself, Ali thought suddenly—a thought that made the world seem to shift all the more.

"We have business to discuss," Harry said, "but I think we should talk about something else first. When you thought I was an Arab working for the West, you called me a traitor. So I assume you think of yourself as a traitor?"

Ali nodded. "Yes, I'm a traitor. I mustn't help you. I don't even deserve to live."

"Everyone deserves to live," Harry said forcefully. "I've seen too many people die to think that anyone deserves death. Listen to me, Ali ibn Daoud. The Arabic-speaking peoples built one of the world's great civilizations. Your ancestors were cultured and tolerant when mine were brutal savages who murdered anyone who didn't think or look like them. You even preserved our own culture for us, Greek culture, when my ancestors tried to eliminate it. You gave us a great part of our science and medicine and mathematics long ago. You have survived great turmoil and fearsome invasions, including from my ancestors. Your civilization has persevered, and the world still has much to learn from it. Now it's threatened. Truly threatened. Not by a few foreign ideas, but by the sword." He paused, then gestured at the crowded street. "And not by them, by those... Crusaders. You know where the real threat comes from, don't you?"

He had echoed Ali's own thoughts to an eerie degree. Ali said reluctantly, "From Rashid."

"Yes. From Rashid. You contacted us to say that you had worked for Rashid but that now you wanted us to help you work against him. I have to tell you that some of our people were reluctant to respond. How do we know that we can trust you? That's what they said. I tend to go by my instincts, and they tell me to trust you. But perhaps I'm being foolish. Perhaps I should leave and we'll never contact you again."

Ali tilted his head toward a small café nearby. "Come. They have excellent coffee."

"I'd prefer a beer," Harry said, "but never mind."

After they had each been served a small cup of intensely strong coffee along with a plate of sugar cubes, and after the waiter had left, Ali leaned forward and began to speak softly. He was finally putting into words the thoughts that had been boiling in him since the moment of Saddam's beheading in Baghdad.

"At the start, I supported the Grand Master and worked to further his ends because I thought that would further my own ends. For a very long time, I have resented the subjugation of Arab interests to those of the West. I thought that a revival of Arab nationalism and culture would be a counterweight to the rapacity of the American and British oil companies."

"Fighting one evil with another?"

Ali shrugged. "Just a tool, a means to an end."

"The means shape the end."

"Perhaps. But I was convinced that the Grand Master and the revival of the Hashashim and their methods of assassination would lead to something much finer, the revival of the great Arab civilization of the Middle Ages, but this time secular, and far more inclusive. That was my great hope."

"Then Rashid proclaimed himself Caliph, and you changed your mind about him."

Ali shook his head. "No, I thought that was even better for my hopes. I managed to convince myself that Rashid's new title would mean greater inclusiveness in the new Empire. Yes, the title has very non-secular significance, but it also has wider Islamic connotations."

Briefly, Ali wondered not only why he was being quite so open and forthright with this man, but also why it was so important to him to win his trust and liking. After all, one of the most terrifying characteristics of the Hashashim of old had been their ability to infiltrate to the very center of the organizations and armies opposed to them, and the new Hashashim were reputed to have done the same thing. So this man, this Harry, might actually be one of Rashid's men! Who knew whether Rashid's tendrils reached deep into the intelligence agencies of the West?

What if Harry was in truth an assassin sent by Rashid? Even so, Ali would tell him his true feelings, and perhaps Harry would carry those back to Rashid. Perhaps that would do some good. And if Harry was just what he claimed to be—well, perhaps that would do some good, too. Ali had become fatalistic lately to a degree that surprised him.

"What has been happening all over the region has

disillusioned me," Ali continued. "What started, I thought, as a drive to knit all Arabs together into a single nation no other nation would be able to exploit or impose its will upon has become instead a drive to build an empire for Rashid. What I saw in Baghdad... The residents of Baghdad ceased being fellow Arabs. They became merely obstacles between Rashid and a tactical goal."

"So now you see him as a danger? So do we. That's why you offered your help to us."

For a while, Ali didn't answer. Then he said, "Yes, I see him as a danger. I decided that I had to tell the world the truth about him. If nothing else, I had to tell the story of the fall and death of Baghdad.

"But I see you as a danger, too. You Westerners, along with the Soviets, you're trying to encircle and contain Rashid. You must know you won't succeed. Might as well try to encircle and contain a volcano. That's what he represents, you know—something that's been bubbling underneath the surface for decades. You think in terms of oil interests and spheres of power, you and the Soviets. And the Arab leaders who are your puppets are thinking only about holding onto power. They're autocrats, tyrants, they think only about themselves, so they're willing to sell our countries to you in return for being kept on their thrones.

"You have to understand that to millions of Arabs, no matter what he does along the way, Rashid is the great liberator, the man who will drive the Crusaders out and humble them, the man who will depose and kill the tyrants and replace their rule with something purer, something ordained by Heaven, something that cares about the welfare of the masses."

His voice had risen. By the end, it shook with passion. Harry looked at him in alarm. "You said you see Rashid as the real danger. Are you sure which side you're on?"

Ali slapped the table in frustration. "Can't you understand? I'm on both sides! I'm on neither side. Who is the greater danger to the future I want to see? You, or Rashid? For the moment, I think it's Rashid. But what if you succeed in defeating him? Then we'll be back to where we were before, and you'll be the real danger. How am I supposed to know what is the best thing to do?"

Harry smiled. It was quite disarming. "Of course, my advice isn't objective, but I'll give it to you anyway. I've been in the position of having to deal with more than one danger at a time. I chose to concentrate on the most dangerous opponent, the force I thought most likely to destroy me and the people under my command, and put the rest off—while keeping an eye on those other dangers, of course. But you have to be careful about dividing your energies. You run the danger of putting insufficient energy into any one task. In this case, I advise you to concentrate on defeating Rashid and returning the Middle East to some kind of stability and peace. End the current bloodshed and conquest. The sooner that happens, the less our influence in this area will grow. Then, when Rashid is out of the picture, you can turn your attention to us. I promise you, this conversation is private. Only you and I know what we've discussed, and that's the way it will remain."

To his own surprise, Ali found himself believing Harry. This was a man you had to believe, or at any rate wanted to believe. Nor did he still suspect him of being an agent of Rashid.

Despite all of that, Ali wondered what he was letting himself in for. "I'll take your advice, Harry. What's my next step?"

Harry pursed his lips and thought for a moment. Then he

said, "Next, we smuggle you to Washington, D.C. in a diplomatic box so that you can be trained to kill with hands, feet, knives, and poisons."

Ali stared at him openmouthed.

Harry grinned. "Joke."

Ali burst into loud laughter. It was a release of tension as much as anything else. "Thank you, Harry. Now, what's the truth?"

"There'll be people snooping into your background for a while, I'm afraid." Harry was utterly serious now, and a bit sad. "The people I work for aren't great respecters of your privacy. Or of mine."

"I agree with them," Ali said. "They have to know they can trust me. They have to convince themselves that my approaching you wasn't a trick by the Grand Master to insert one of his people into your organization."

It was Harry's turn to be surprised. "You really don't mind their investigating you? Well, well. Perhaps you should be the controller, not me. Okay, so once they've finished their investigation—and they might already have finished it, because it's probably actually been underway for a while—then we'll get together again, you and I, and we'll start making up lists of everyone you know and everything you know about them. You see, this is one of those businesses in which who you know really is more important than what you know. And then we'll start recruiting some of them. We're still in the early stages of building our network. You'll help me build the network, and then you'll help me run it. In fact, you'll probably end up doing most of the work running the network."

"And what will you be doing while I'm running your network?"

"Our network," Harry said. He put a fresh sugar cube in his mouth, then picked up the small cup of coffee and sipped it appreciatively. "I'll sit in outdoor cafés and drink coffee and watch the world flow by," he said around the sugar cube. He smiled. "You mustn't ask questions."

"A lot of new habits to learn," Ali said. He too put a sugar cube in his mouth and sipped coffee.

And then they sat silently, exchanging an occasional smile, sipping their coffee, and watched the world flow by.

Eight

July 1991

The great building was a beehive, Farouk sometimes thought. Workers rushed to and fro constantly, frowning, concentrating on their missions, oblivious to everything around them. He even fancied he could hear a constant buzzing everywhere.

They were all men, of course, the worker bees in this particular hive. Farouk had no objection to that, although he did miss seeing the occasional pretty young secretary or file clerk. Ah, well, even if there had been women there, they'd have been covered head to foot.

He hurried down a long hallway and up the broad staircase at the end of it. Three flights to climb! Why did they refuse to install elevators? Did they think Allah would object to that? Almost, he shook his head in impatience, but he caught himself in time. The men rushing past him in the hallway, the ones going down the stairs while he was going up or pushing their way around him in order to go up faster than he was, might all seem preoccupied, and surely most of them were, but he had no doubt there were spies among them. There were guardian bees disguised as workers, and their stings were deadly.

And television cameras, of course. Concessions were made constantly to Western technology. Telephones. Radios. Television sets. Airconditioning, thank God. In this building more than any other, computers. Most visible to the outside world were the very modern weapons for the Caliph's armies and police forces. All of that, certainly. Pragmatic arguments could be made for each one, and where a pragmatic argument could be made, a theological argument in support of the pragmatic one was sure to follow. Farouk had no doubt that another element of Western technology permeated the building: surveillance cameras.

And more than the building. He was sure that the cameras and the undercover guards—secret police, that was the right name for them—were everywhere in the city beyond the walls of this building, probably everywhere in every city and large town of the Caliphate. People he knew and worked with had disappeared, and after they had vanished, no one would talk about them.

How quickly people learn those habits! Farouk thought. His own people had learned them well in the preceding seventy-plus years, but these people seemed to have reached the same level of self-preservation in mere months.

It wasn't that he disapproved in principle. In principle, he thought the Caliphate was doing just what it had to do. But that didn't mean he wanted to be caught and eliminated by the Caliph's policemen.

Three flights up, and then down another long hallway filled with hurrying men. At the end of it was a door that was almost precisely above the one by which he had entered the building.

Once again, Farouk silently cursed the absence of elevators.

The door at the end of the hallway was the holy of holies, the seat of the Caliphate's power, the office where Rashid-al-Din Sinan spent his days, the room from which he ruled his growing empire.

The door opened as Farouk approached it. Inside the door stood two huge men in green dress uniforms. They stood aside for Farouk to pass. It was a routine he was used to by now. At first, he had had some difficulty hiding his trepidation, but by now he could pass between the two mountains of muscle and deadly competence with only the slightest tremor, only a small sense of relief—carefully hidden—when he had moved beyond their reach.

A faint smell of something as he passed them. A drug? He thought so but couldn't put his finger on it. Not hasheesh, as would have been appropriate with the original Hashasheem. Perhaps some subtler modern equivalent.

It was a small room. It might have been the office of some minor functionary. The only furniture was a few chairs around a small, round table, and the only visible modern technology was a television set in an alcove in the far wall. The wall and ceiling hangings that had given the house in Damascus the appearance of a giant desert tent were not in evidence. What Farouk saw was plain and unadorned, not the movie set that had so amused Ali ibn Daoud many years before.

Had Ali still been in Rashid's favor and in his inner circle, had he been in this room with Farouk, he might at first have thought that the man who stood at the center of a circle of advisers, towering over them, had changed little since those early days of their revolution. Rashid still looked far more the scholar than the warrior. He still looked like an ascetic, as indeed he still was. What had changed was the great strength of will, the steel at his center. That was now even greater, and it grew as his empire expanded.

Rashid raised his glance from the face of the adviser he had been listening to and caught sight of the waiting Farouk. He stared into Farouk's eyes, and Farouk felt the look almost as a physical blow, sapping his own strength and self–control.

Farouk gritted his teeth and straightened to his full height, unconsciously asserting himself.

Rashid smiled slightly, pleased both at his own strength and at the strength of this valued subordinate. He waved aside the men surrounding him and stepped forward to Farouk. "What news have you brought me, Farouk?"

"More confirmation, Master. The Soviets have decided that the civil war in Afghanistan works in their favor. They'll keep their own forces along the border, in Tajikistan for example, to make sure the fighting doesn't spread into their territory. But in general they're concentrating on a defensive posture for the moment."

"This is from your people in Moscow, of course."

"Of course."

Rashid nodded in satisfaction. "Good. This corresponds to other information I've received recently."

Meaning from some parallel spy network you've had someone else set up, Farouk thought. You're double checking the information for accuracy, and you're verifying my loyalty.

None of which made Farouk uneasy. Of course whatever other agents Rashid had planted in Moscow would pick up the same information as Farouk's people had.

"Please join us, Farouk," the Caliph said. "We're trying to work out the details and timing for our eastward expansion."

Farouk bowed his head. "I am honored, Master."

And indeed he was. This group of men was the Caliph's most inner circle. Never before had he been asked to stay after delivering his latest information. Certainly Rashid had never solicited his opinion about diplomatic or domestic policy before. It was not only an honor, it was also an amazing opportunity, and not one he could afford to pass up despite the time pressures he felt.

He went back across the room in Rashid's wake and joined the group of advisers. For the next few hours, he mostly listened. When he spoke, it was sparingly, in a few carefully prepared sentences. His judicious speech earned him growing respect from the others, he could tell. This amused him.

Much later, long after dark, Rashid walked slowly home through the brilliantly lit streets. The light of the Caliph's countenance shone everywhere, it was said. It was also said that there were no more dark places in Baghdad. That wasn't quite true. The electric lights might seem ubiquitous, but there were still some unilluminated nooks and crannies.

Or so Farouk had to assume. It was possible that even those places were watched by spy cameras equipped to see human movement in the dark. He could only assume—hope—that that was not the case.

Farouk walked slowly. The air was mild and fragrant and the way was pleasant. The streets—safer now than ever before in the city's history—were alive with strolling crowds even this late at night. People gathered in small, friendly groups, chatting. Chatting carefully, it's true, choosing their words deliberately and with forethought, but still the nighttime city was alive and warm.

Farouk smiled occasionally at those he passed, greeted someone by name from time to time, but he didn't stop for conversation. He moved steadily through the city toward his home. He seemed to be thinking, perhaps about the meeting he had just participated in. His head was bowed, his brow wrinkled, his hands buried deep in his robes. He looked mostly at the ground and seemed much of the time to be unaware of the beautiful, newly recreated city he walked through.

His hands met in a pocket that lay against his stomach. He had sewn the pocket himself, not trusting anyone else to alter his clothing. Slowly, carefully, painstakingly, moving his hands as little as possible so that no one passing him might guess what he was doing, he wrote words on a small piece of paper. Not daring to take the paper out to see what he was doing, not daring to do this in his own home, which he was sure was saturated with spy devices, Farouk held the paper in one hand, the pen in the other, and visualized the shapes he was making.

He had been trained to do this and he had spent much time during the last few months using the skill, so he was fairly confident that he wrote legibly. Still, of necessity the paper was small, and he had a lot of information to condense into as few words as possible.

He was finished with the task by the time he reached the mouth of the dimly lit alleyway he always used as a shortcut to his house.

This was the ultimate risk. This was the moment when everything could come crashing down on him.

Breathing regularly, trying to keep his heartbeat steady as a matter of pride, Farouk walked down the alley. He maintained his previous pace, walking neither more slowly nor more rapidly than before.

The alley was part of the old city, left over from before Rashid's armies had invaded and leveled most of Baghdad. It predated even Saddam's oil- and ego-fueled building programs. Perhaps that was why it was so dark, Farouk thought. The only light was what was reflected from the white walls of the tall, new buildings nearby. Rashid stepped carefully. He knew the way well, but the ground was uneven and littered with rocks, only dimly visible in the reflected light.

Halfway down the alley, midway between the brightly lighted streets at either end, was an abandoned garage. Farouk had passed it occasionally during the day and had glanced in through the shattered windows at the two dust-covered old cars parked inside. Sometimes he wondered why there was never any sign of the owners. Had they been victims of Saddam? Was that why the building and the cars had remained untouched, from some primitive fear of being infected? Whatever the story, Farouk was happy to take advantage of the opportunity the building gave him.

As he passed, he stepped close to the garage door. In one quick, smooth, practiced movement, he drew the paper from under his robes, crumpled it into a ball, and threw it through the broken windows.

He continued on his way and reached his house unharmed, untouched, as safe as anyone could be in the capital city of Rashid-al-Din Sinan.

An hour later, a figure moved within the garage, almost invisible in the murk. It collected the crumpled ball of paper and left with it. Before dawn, it would deliver Farouk's message to the next station on its journey.

Two days later, the piece of paper, now carefully smoothed and pressed inside a leather folder, reached Khodinka Airfield and the men eagerly waiting for it.

They read it, discussed it briefly, and then passed it up the line with alacrity. These were not the old days, when they might have delayed the message, those days when the GRU considered its own judgment better than that of the men in the Kremlin. They might still feel that way, but under the rule of Aleksander Slonimsky, they kept those feelings to themselves. Nothing was immune from the power of Aleksander the Great, not even the men who ran the GRU.

The message sent in by Farouk Haidar, whose real name was Andrey Danielovich Ostrokhov—for the spymaster was a spy himself, a double agent, a mole—made its way to Slonimsky's desk within hours.

The Soviet ruler read the few sentences and smiled. The agent had reported what he wanted to hear.

Briefly, he wondered about the man's safety. What would happen to him if one of his messages ended up on the Caliph's desk instead of on Slonimsky's? Then he shrugged and put the matter aside. If anyone were to ask this agent, he would probably say that he served the Soviet Union, and if he had to give his life in that service, then so be it. In fact, he and all his fellows served Aleksander Slonimsky. But that was as it should be, Slonimsky knew. Strong men made nations and history, and weaker men served them. That was the way it had always been and always would be.

Slonimsky pressed a button on his desk. A voice answered deferentially. "I want to dictate a letter," Slonimsky said.

Minutes later, a timid young man entered the office. He held a spiral notebook in one hand and a pen in the other. His face was pale and tense. Slonimsky knew that look well: it was fear. That too was as it should be.

Slonimsky gestured to the chair in front of his desk, waited till the young man had sat down and opened his notebook, and then began dictating. "Send this to General Secretary Jiang Zemin in Peking. Dear Comrade Jiang, etc. Add the usual salutation. You probably know it better than I do. Here's the text.

"One of our agents in Baghdad reports that the Caliphate has decided to turn its attention eastward. As its armies move steadily through Iran, fifth columnists will be used to foment rebellions ahead of the moving frontier to make the work of conquest easier. The goal of course is to create a mighty new Moslem empire. For now, its western border will be the Mediterranean Sea, what is now the coastline of Israel, Lebanon, and Turkey. Eventually, Rashid intends to spread his control over all of North Africa, as well. None of this will be a surprise to you. What will perhaps be new, what our agent reported, is that for the immediate future, North Africa and possibly the Arabian peninsula will be largely ignored while the Caliphate seeks to extend and consolidate to the east. I must warn you in the name of Socialist brotherhood that Rashid does not plan to stop the eastward expansion until he has invaded and conquered what he refers to as Eastern Turkestan—that is, the Xinjiang Uygur Autonomous Region.

"I am of course concerned about the threat this poses to the southern regions of my own country, and I am already deploying significant defensive forces along my southern borders—"

Slonimsky paused, then said, "Change that to 'our southern

borders.' To continue. We must also maintain our forces in Europe to discourage NATO from taking advantage of any confrontation between us and the Caliphate. That is, we must keep forces stationed both to the south and the west, forces of such intimidating power that neither of our two great enemies will try to invade us. But let me emphasize that all our forces are defensive, or at least the southern ones are. I especially don't want you to misinterpret any of our troop movements as a threat to your own security. We face a great and growing threat from this fanatical new enemy, and only by cooperating in the true spirit of Socialist brotherhood can we hope to keep these barbaric forces at bay.

"Add the proper formalities to the end. I'm sure you know that part well, too."

The young man sprang to his feet. "I'll have this ready for you to proofread in fifteen minutes, Comrade General."

Slonimsky waved his hand dismissively. "I trust you to type well and proofread carefully. Transmit it through the proper channels as soon as it's ready."

The young man stared at him in amazement for a moment. Then he straightened and threw back his shoulders. "Thank you, Comrade!" He rushed from the room, proud now rather than timid.

Why, this is even easier than shooting them! Slonimsky thought. It still surprised him, each time this happened. Control of weaker personalities was really such a simple thing.

Not as pleasurable as shooting them, though.

Thinking of pleasure, he stood up and walked from his office. On the other side of the door, guards snapped to attention. They were the only people in the anteroom. There were six of them.

Each wore a blue-and-gold dress uniform of a new kind, designed by Slonimsky himself. They were members of his growing personal guard, selected from the finest men in the Soviet armed forces. Each uniform was crisply pressed. Each carried an AK-74 at perfect vertical.

Slonimsky smiled with pleasure. He saluted them with an enthusiasm that was renewed each time he saw them. He walked through the anteroom to the corridor beyond. The six guards fell into formation behind him, three on the right and three on the left.

Briefly, Slonimsky wondered if he should have made the uniforms all black, in imitation of Ivan the Terrible's Oprichniki. But, no, he didn't want to draw too many comparisons to Ivan. What about Peter, that even greater Czar? Perhaps he should have changed his name to Peter before taking power, or shortly after. Then he could be another Peter the Great instead of Alexander the Great. Why be compared to a Macedonian instead of to one of the greatest of Russians? Should he build a new capital, like Peter, and name it after himself, thus making the comparison clear to everyone? A Russian Alexandria, perhaps.

Slonimsky shrugged. Time enough for such matters later, after he had surpassed the great Macedonian in empire building. There were vast territories awaiting him before he must face the lack of new worlds to conquer.

He walked steadily but without hurrying through the great, rambling building. His guards followed him closely, their eyes moving steadily from side to side.

At last Slonimsky reached a certain door. Beyond it lay an apartment, a large and well-appointed suite of rooms that he was using for the same purpose other rulers of Russia had used it for:

to house the ruler's current mistress.

Slonimsky produced a key, unlocked the door, entered, and closed it behind him. The guards remained behind, taking stations beside the door and along the corridor. No orders were necessary from the General. They knew their roles, and they had performed this particular maneuver many times before.

Time moved slowly by in the hallway. No people moved by. The guards were alone. They stood quietly, stolidly, only their eyes moving, but those were in constant motion. If there had been someone watching them, he would have been unable to tell if they envied their master his pleasures, or even if they felt the urge toward such pleasures themselves.

But there was no one there to watch them. No one would have dared to do so.

Two hours passed before Aleksander Slonimsky emerged from the apartment. He looked tired and satisfied. Not sparing a glance for his guards, he walked back toward his office. The guards fell in behind him.

Her name was Maria Gorova, and she was a spy.

Slonimsky had no idea who her masters were, and he didn't care. When had she been recruited? He did wonder about that sometimes. He hoped it had happened during one of her periods of study abroad, not here at home in Russia, for that would signify security problems he didn't want to have to deal with now.

Perhaps she reported to the Germans, perhaps to the Chinese, perhaps to the Americans. Whoever it was, he was grateful to them for training her so well in the sexual arts. What mattered to him was that the secrets she thought she was extracting from him so skillfully would end up in the right ears. Those confidences whispered on the pillow would confirm,

Maria's foreign masters would think, what they were also hearing from other agents.

Right now, he hoped those confidences were ending up in Peking. But even if not, Maria would still be serving a useful purpose.

Some day, Slonimsky knew, her usefulness would end. He would be sad when that day came, but he would be as ruthless as his position required. When her usefulness ended, Maria would die. It would be quick and painless. He owed her that much for the pleasure she had given him. But it would still be final.

Slonimsky slowed. For a few seconds, he felt immersed in sadness, as though all the tortured souls whose deaths this building had seen were surrounding him, begging for his pity. Some day, Maria's soul would be among them.

Then it occurred to him that once Maria had been eliminated, another much like her would probably show up to make herself available to him. Perhaps Maria's successor would be even more skillful.

The moment of sadness passed and Slonimsky walked with a bounce again. Like the other great conquerors of history, he thought, he had a sex drive that was far greater than that of the common man. Maria Gorova was his due.

"You wanted to see me?"

Sharon had known the reporting protocol ever since Basic, and OCS had drilled it into her even more thoroughly: an officer who expected proper respect from her subordinates should show that respect to her superiors, and that meant when you reported to someone's office you didn't just push the door open and say hello. Most of her fellow newbie lieutenants were a bit nuts when it came to getting all the rituals right. And she had been too, when she'd actually been in OCS, especially since most soldiers didn't believe anyone in the Air Force knew how to salute or come to attention right anyway.

But most of her classmates had been fresh out of college with no prior service at all, and even among her fellow vets, none of them had come back from Khafji.

She wasn't sure how these people fit into the protocol, anyway. Soldiers were supposed to treat civilian coworkers with the same respect as superior officers, whether they were chow hall cooks or GS–17 administrators with as much pull as the average full–bird colonel. It was part of the principle of civilian control. State Department big shots surely merited the same treatment.

"Lieutenant Alcazar," the woman said, extending a hand which had never field–stripped an M16. But her grip was firm and Sharon thought there was a lot more strength waiting behind the control. A very tall woman, slender but broad–shouldered, smooth glossy blonde hair framing a pale face and hard, penetrating eyes. The man at the desk was outwardly different, with slightly scruffy brown hair, shorter and less obviously in shape, nondescript all in all, but the eyes were exactly the same.

"That's me," Sharon agreed, returning the controlled handshake and reaching over the desk to give the man the same. "As of eight weeks and three days ago." After OCS graduation, a staff car to take her to the MAC terminal when most of her classmates had gone in a shuttle bus, a day of travel time and eight weeks of accelerated training at Monterey. Then graduation there, and another day to get to Washington. One day of recovery and now this. In the last four months she'd had two and a half days entirely to herself.

"I'm Rebecca Norman, and this is David Petrie."

"I know."

They had the grace to look surprised. "Did someone tell you it was us you were coming to see?" Petrie asked.

"No. I just, um, heard your names somewhere." From Harry, in the middle of a conversation laced with rapid switches between Arabic and English, but these two didn't need to know that. If they *didn't* know that, then if there did exist an intelligence network monitoring the survivors of Khafji, these two weren't tied into it. But someone probably knows, she thought, someone I've never seen.

The look they gave her said they had a pretty good idea who "someone" was, even so. Well, hell with it. Career military meant a lot of people were going to know things about you, even if you were a cook or a supply clerk. Or a cop. Being a spook was worse, maybe, but how much worse could it really get?

"Have a seat, Lieutenant." Petrie.

"Thank you."

"Your orders are for Fort Meade, is that right?" Norman.

"That's right." Like you don't already know.

"Running a SIGINT so-called platoon, which means you and a couple of NCO's doing the translating, a few junior enlisted for the scutwork." Petrie. "A few years, you do a good job, you get your railroad tracks, get to do some actual analysis. A few years after that, oak leaves, and you finally get to command a unit that's actually the same size in reality as the platoon you once had on paper. At twenty-five years, maybe you have a bird, you retire and don't talk to your husband or your kids or your priest or God himself about what you did, ever. When what you did was listening to the radio."

"All this, after Khafji." Norman.

"If that's what you want." Petrie.

Sharon leaned back in her chair and studied them. This is a reverse interrogation, she decided; you're trying to put something into my head instead of get it out. It would have worked well on anyone but a cop. Probably worked on Harry, the poor bastard, except these two didn't have time to do it to him—the CIA did it first. So they're not holding back with me.

Everything they had said was, of course, true.

"What I want," she said, "is to die at age one hundred and three surrounded by my great-grandchildren. If some of what I do along the way helps keep more American kids from dying in a desert shithole, that's fine with me."

Norman and Petrie glanced at each other, then looked back at her. What did I say? she wondered. There was a tension in the room that hadn't been there before. It seemed entirely possible that one or more of the people here was going to die in the next minute. She considered the possibility that one of them might be her. If so... well, that would mean the desert had finally caught up with her, was all.

"Some of what you do," Petrie said, "may help keep Americans from dying in a variety of locations."

Not murderous tension, then. Damn it, the road back from Khafji was too long, you're still thinking the way you did then. Different ways of fighting battles here.

"That sounds good," she replied. "In and of itself."

"You'll be working with both the CIA and the NSA," Norman said. "Probably half the people around you won't be in uniform. What do you think about that?"

Sharon shrugged. "I work with whoever gets the job done."

"Good, that's good.... So maybe you could work with us."

"Whoever."

Norman walked slowly around the desk toward Sharon's chair. Sharon had a good idea of her own physical presence, knew she intimidated many other women and inspired a mix of lust and intimidation in a lot of men; it was an ability she had earned with hard work and found useful throughout her SP career. But Norman would cause these reactions to a much greater degree. No matter how tough or pretty Sharon was, she couldn't match the tall blonde's presence, the *impact* of her height and icy beauty. Sharon kept herself upright in her chair by an effort of will.

"You could work with us," Norman said, *"while* you're working with everyone else."

"That's a lot of work." Both Norman and Petrie scared the hell out of her, she had to admit that to herself, but she wouldn't back down from them. You're not as bad as the Caliph's men, she thought. And they tried to kill me, and I'm still breathing, and a lot of them are skeletons in the sand.

"It depends on how the workload is arranged," Petrie said. "Here's the deal, Lieutenant. You go to Meade, do your job, write letters to your boyfriend, whatever. And once every couple of weeks you have dinner in D.C. with a friend of yours." He nodded in Norman's direction. "Hell, your friend's a civilian with a nice job at State, she makes the money, she pays for your dinners. That's all we ask. Just some regular conversation."

Sharon laughed. "Mr. Petrie, you've *got* to know what kind of background checks I went through to get this job. Now, not having reported for duty yet, I don't really know, but I kind of imagine my bosses will be keeping a pretty close eye on me when

I'm permanent party at Meade."

"Yes they will," Norman said. "If you were meeting someone from, oh, the Soviet embassy, that would be a problem." She spread her hands. "But no one will even raise an eyebrow. We've known each other for years."

"What?"

"John F. Kennedy High School, Denver. You went to Lincoln, but your older brother graduated from JFK." Norman smiled, the first genuine expression Sharon had seen from her. "We called it 'Jail For Kids.'... Anyway. So did I. Same year. He and I had a year-long relationship. Very serious for high school kids. I was over at your house all the time. You and I got along very well, a big-sister-little-sister kind of thing. I'm delighted to run into you now that we're both adults."

Is this true? Sharon wondered. No, no way in hell. Tommy could never stay with one girl for more than a month—hell, he's still not married. I'd remember this.

Norman shrugged, obviously reading Sharon's thoughts from her face. "That's what your background check says. And mine. I saw your brother's picture. Nice looking. I wish I had known him when we were both at JFK, actually, but it's a big school."

"No you don't," Sharon muttered. "He treated his girlfriends like shit." It was the only thing she could think of to say.

Petrie laughed. "I don't think anyone's background check ever mentioned that."

"How long have you been planning this?" Sharon asked.

"Since right about the time we talked to Master Sergeant Elkins," Petrie said without hesitation, which improved Sharon's estimation of him. "Or shortly afterward, when it became clear that our colleagues in the CIA had their own plans for him. I hope you won't be insulted that you were our second choice."

All right, then, they want to be honest. "I don't think I can be insulted by any comparison to Harry, not even second place. But stop beating around the President. You want me to spy on the people I'll be working with." Sharon took a deep breath. "Let's assume for the moment that I'm willing to do this—what then? If I fuck up, you fuck up, someone in your organization somewhere fucks up, well, in case you didn't notice, I'm going to be working with some very dangerous people. I know because, in fact, I'm one of them. And I don't want them pissed off at me."

"There's no perfect intelligence operation," Norman said, "but some are better than others. And safer. We've put the machinery in place for this one, and we believe it will work." She moved a little closer to Sharon, looking down into her eyes. Stagey, Sharon thought, but effective all the same. "And this one may be more important than anything you'll be doing at Meade. There are some very ugly things going on right now at the highest levels of the United States government. The same government, the same *people,* that left you and a lot of other GI's out there in the desert to die. We need to know what the hell they're doing, and you can find out."

Sharon suddenly felt weirdly calm. She'd never really wanted to be stuck behind a desk for the rest of her career, they were right about that... and if this was what it took to be a field agent, well, there were places to go from here. And worse ways to make a living, she knew that very well.

"Deal." She rose from the chair, shook Norman's hand, then leaned across the desk for Petrie's. "I'm sure you'll know where I'm billeted before I do. Give me a call."

Nine

July–August 1991

"Tonight we're debating, 'Who lost the Middle East?'"

The screen went blank, cutting off the debate before it could get started. Arthur Lang put the remote control down carefully on the coffee table and leaned back against the white leather of the couch. "Well, George," he said. "Who do you think lost it? More to the point, who do you think the American people think lost the Middle East?"

Bush felt like an unprepared schoolboy facing a humorless, narrowminded teacher, and like a schoolboy who would have preferred to be outside playing, he was tempted to give a sarcastic, impertinent reply. "You did," he wanted to say. "Margaret Thatcher did. Saddam Hussein did. Boy, talk about losing! That guy really lost, didn't he? Who says we've lost it? We haven't lost it yet! Not all of it, anyway!" Instead, he said nothing.

"Well, I'll tell you, then, George," Lang said.

I knew you would, Bush thought.

"They feel that you did. You lost the Middle East."

"Les Aspin," Bush said. "Foley. Gephardt. Mitchell.

Democrats."

Lang nodded. "Yes, they all supported you in sending in the troops to push Saddam out of Kuwait."

"Quick victory. Aspin."

Lang nodded again. "Yes, that's right. Les Aspin predicted a quick victory. He's not running for reelection this year. He's already announced that. We expect his seat to remain Democratic, but it'll probably be some younger, anti–war Democrat. Do you understand what he did? He took the blame for supporting you, and he threw himself on his sword for the sake of his party. I've always disagreed with the man's politics, but I have to say I admire his action, the nobility with which he's ended his career, this selfless act of sacrifice for the sake of his party. Surely you agree."

Bush considered saying something about the American people not wanting to change horses in the middle of the stream, but he remembered in time that he had tried that approach unsuccessfully with Lang once before.

Lang didn't give him a chance to think of a defense. He bored in. "It's probably already too late to salvage the Congressional elections next November. We expect to lose big. You'll be more isolated and more powerless than ever. We expect the Democrats to win a huge majority, and you know what that means: they'll be cockier and even more the stooges of Moscow than they already are."

"Stooges of Moscow?" Bush repeated. He hadn't heard this kind of political language in a long time, and never from Arthur Lang.

"Yes." Lang nodded. "That's what they really want, Soviet dominance. We all know that. Why pretend? They love this

Slonimsky fellow. They'll block everything, and then two years later, they'll win the Presidency as well. If you're running, that is."

"I'll fight. You'll see. Rally the people. Commander–in–Chief."

Lang looked at him with contempt. "You're the laughingstock–in–chief. Do you really not understand that? Well, we do."

"Who's we? You're just money men. I know about you."

"You don't know anything about me. I'm working for a higher purpose nowadays, and you're standing in the way."

"So? I'm supposed to fall on my sword?"

"Fall or be pushed, George. We're not giving you a choice. You have to understand that."

"To Hell with all of you. I'm the President. I'm the guy they elected. Get out, Arthur."

Lang smiled. "I know you're not naïve or stupid, George, but you have an elevated idea of your privileges." He stood. "Don't take too long. We need to start laying the groundwork for '92, and you've become an insurmountable liability." He walked out of the Oval Office in his usual swift but unhurried manner, a man in control of the world around him.

The door shut behind him and then opened again immediately. It was one of the Secret Service men normally stationed in the corridor outside.

Bush smiled at him. He liked these strong, alert, loyal young men. They seemed so much more truly American than a scheming little wimp like Arthur Lang. "Yes?"

"Mr. President," the strong, alert, loyal young man said, "I think you should give serious consideration to what Mr. Lang was saying. We'd prefer it if you left willingly and walking."

He left, closing the door behind him, leaving Bush frozen in place at his desk.

Arthur Lang drove from the White House to an office building in suburban Virginia where the Vice President was waiting for him.

Here, he knew, his tactics would have to change.

Lang thought about it while he parked his car in the only shade available, that cast by the building itself. He mulled over his tactics while he walked swiftly through the gleaming lobby, oblivious to the greeting of the security guard. He pushed the elevator button and waited patiently until the elevator arrived. He got in and pushed the button for the fifth floor. Fortunately, he was alone in the car. He didn't feel like making small talk.

With Bush, browbeating was the best tactic. But while it was possible to browbeat a man out of the White House, it was next to impossible to browbeat one into it.

It had long been clear that Quayle's family envisioned him as President eventually, and it was inherent in the nature of the man that one of his limitations was his inability to see how limited he was. What must be made clear to him, however, was that he could be President, but he could not be in charge. Browbeating at this stage might simply make him bolt, and then Lang and the people he now worked for would have to go through the procedure of having the President nominate a replacement, which would be followed by hearings run by Soviet stooges.... No, far better to cajole the younger man, jolly him along, make him think he'd be sufficiently in charge, let him delude himself that he could control the men who'd really be controlling him.

The door opened on the fifth floor, and Lang walked down the short hallway, feeling properly prepared and quite satisfied with himself.

He knocked on an unnumbered door. Invisible eyes examined him briefly, and the door was opened by yet another strong, alert, loyal young man. Lang nodded at him, trying to hide from himself a moment of nervousness, even of fear. They were so large, these young men. And so cold. And so capable, he thought, of anything.

"He's here?" Lang asked.

The younger man nodded and gestured with his head toward a closed door.

Men of few words, Lang thought. Just as well. He had no interest in exchanging pleasantries with goons. He opened the door and entered the inner office. It was large, paneled in dark wood, outfitted with heavy furniture, including a huge desk. One wall, behind the desk, was mostly window; through it he could see the rolling hills of Virginia.

Hugh Walsh sat behind the desk. He nodded a greeting to Lang. The Vice President was standing in front of a world map on the wall to Lang's right, frowning in puzzlement.

"Mr. Vice President," Lang said.

Quayle turned, the frown still on his face. After a moment, it faded. "Oh. Yeah. Hi, Art."

Lang gritted his teeth. He hated being called Art. "Thank you for making time for us, sir. I'm glad you could come here."

"Well, the Secret Service said it would be okay." He pointed at Walsh. "Personal assurance from this guy here."

Lang looked at Walsh, who looked back expressionlessly. This all seemed a bit premature to Lang. He himself had come onboard only days before, and he realized there was a great deal of history and many hidden arrangements that he knew nothing about, but still it seemed advisable to him to keep up the appearance of an independent Secret Service for a while longer.

Ah, well, he told himself, I'd better stick to what I'm best at and leave the other stuff to these people. They seem to enjoy it.

"But I don't know why I'm here," Quayle said. "Or why I wasn't supposed to tell the President about it. I'm happy being the Vice President. I really want you to know that, Art. I know I've made a few mistakes. Is that the problem?"

"No, no, we have no problems with your performance, Dan. Mr. Vice President." He sighed and wished he were elsewhere.

There were two chairs before the desk. He gestured toward one of them. "Sit down, please." He waited till Quayle was seated, then sat in the other chair and leaned forward, holding Quayle's gaze with his own and putting all the earnestness he could into his voice.

"Dan," Lang said, "as I'm sure you know, the President has been under a lot of strain because of events in the Middle East. We're not entirely sure he'll want to run for reelection."

"Oh, that's really sad. The poor guy."

Lang and Walsh watched him quietly until understanding began to penetrate.

"Hey, what about me?"

Lang managed to keep his contempt hidden. "That's why we wanted to meet you here, sir. We think you'd be the natural one, the right man to become the party's candidate in '92."

"Really?" Quayle swelled visibly. "That's great!"

Lang hesitated, trying to choose his next words carefully. He wanted to say that they realized that Quayle was lacking in experience, but they had planned for that and they intended to bring him up to speed in time for the election. Before he could utter the sentences he had finally constructed in his mind, Quayle spoke.

"You know what? I'm ready right now. Everyone hates Bush. He's gonna hurt us in the Congressional elections. Maybe it would be better if we put a new man in the White House right now. What do you guys think?"

Lang was speechless. The party's welfare was almost as important to him as the continued success and supremacy of his class, and for that reason he was willing to sacrifice the President if he felt it was the best path, but nonetheless he retained some shreds of personal loyalty, and he had assumed that the Vice President retained even more. This degree of cold-bloodedness astonished him.

Walsh cut in, his voice as smooth and well-modulated as ever, as though he had expected nothing else from the Vice President and had known ahead of time what he should say in response. "It's an intriguing idea, sir. We've certainly discussed it from time to time. We were waiting for the right time to bring it up with you."

Now Lang stared at Walsh in amazement. He believed the CIA man: Walsh—and whoever the others were he was referring to when he said "we"—had indeed been discussing dumping Bush right away.

It might be the only way to save the party, though, he told himself. It had to be considered.

But who was Walsh to be considering it? The deal was supposed to be that Lang was in charge, as he had always been. Walsh and his people were to remain in the background, to provide support and help when Lang asked for it. But Lang was still the boss! That was the deal, damn it!

Walsh continued. "We weren't sure if you'd want to take on

the negative feelings now being directed at the presidency, along with its burdens. Perhaps it would be wiser to wait for a while, to establish yourself with the public as an independent figure, a man with positions and policies of his own."

"Hmm," Quayle said, "good point. I could make a few speeches. Explain how I spoke up in Cabinet meetings in opposition to sending in the troops."

"The people supported sending in the troops," Walsh reminded him gently. "However, as I remember, you were the leading voice of caution during those heady early days when everyone else thought not only that victory was assured but that it would be easy."

Quayle was nodding in agreement. "You're right," he said. "I did say what you said. Yeah, that's right!"

Not only was Lang speechless, he decided he'd better stay that way. He hated to admit it, but Walsh was doing a better job than he could have. The CIA man seemed to know just what buttons to push. The guy should be running for office, Lang thought. Or writing speeches for those who are.

"Of course, it was understandable," Walsh said, "that the country was gripped by optimism and enthusiasm in those early days of the war, when most of the Cabinet and the Pentagon thought we were facing only the Iraqi army. Of course."

"Uh, of course," Quayle said. "But they were wrong?"

"Exactly!" Walsh said enthusiastically. "You're right now, and you were right then. You cautioned that there might be—probably was—something more dangerous concealed in the background in the Middle East. You didn't know what it was, but you sensed its presence."

He paused for effect. After a while, Quayle said vaguely, "Uh, right."

Walsh said, "Now, the American people aren't aware of these facts. We need to explain all of this to them. I gather you're willing to speak out now and explain matters to the voters?"

"You bet! When do I start?"

Lang jumped in. It was time for him to reassert control of this meeting. "We need a year at least to make the public fully and properly understand your role in the conduct of the war."

"A year!" Quayle and Walsh spoke together.

"Yes. That way, at the beginning of the primary season, you can announce your intention to seek the nomination, and the public will be ready for it. That will also give us time to persuade the President that it's in the best interests of the country and the party that he not run for reelection, so that the way will be clear for you to step in."

Quayle deflated. Walsh looked down at the desk, then looked up again, his face as smooth and composed as before. He turned to Quayle. "Sir, perhaps you'd better return to your office now. Mr. Lang and I will discuss the details of the next few months. This is the sort of thing you shouldn't have to be bothered with."

He waited until Quayle had left the room, and then he said mildly to Lang, "I really don't think we should wait that long. It would be best if he ran in '92 as the incumbent President. He'd be sufficiently disconnected from the Gulf disaster so that wouldn't hurt him, and that way there'd be no opposition to his nomination from within the party. Nothing we'd need to worry about, anyway."

Lang shook his head. "I still think we need a year. Opposition from within the party is my area. My people can take care of that."

"I thought we had an arrangement."

"We did. We do. I take care of all internal party matters. That's my bailiwick, that's where my influence and contacts are. Of course, I include in that all contacts with the President. If there's anything external that needs to be taken care of, that's where you come in."

Walsh drummed his fingers on the desk for a second or two. He saw no reason to tell Lang that his people were already in very close contact with the President, nor that Bush had lately been displaying a surprising streak of independence. Quite soon, Walsh could see, that annoying independence might become dangerous to Walsh, his people, and his plans. He said, "The President knows how we operate, of course, because of his past service as Director of the agency. That might present difficulties in the matter of our taking care of anything external, as you term it. You know that I and my people are operating without authorization."

Lang shrugged, an elaborate display of disinterest. He felt back in control of things now, and he wanted to impress Walsh with who was in charge. "That's all supposed to be your area of competence. I'm relying on you to do your job properly."

"I see. Speaking of which, a year from now, how are you going to convince your man to step aside?"

"I meant what I said about it being for the good of the party and the country. I'll explain that to him."

"And if that isn't sufficient? This is a man who fought for a long time to get to the top. He won't relinquish his position easily."

"If it comes to that," Lang said reluctantly, "it might be necessary to show him that no one is indispensable and that no one is safe."

"I see. To frighten him, you mean?"

"To show him that no one is indispensable and that no one is safe," Lang repeated.

Walsh smiled. "I see," he repeated.

Joe Grant had been at the White House for almost eight years, having been assigned there early in the first Reagan administration. He was in his early thirties, tall, handsome, strong, serious, with close-cropped hair, and a well-tailored suit that hid perfectly the heavy-duty automatic strapped to his side. In short, he was a fine example of the Secret Service breed, and George Bush had always been happy to see him, first as part of the contingent protecting Reagan, and now as one of his own protectors. Fine young man, Bush thought. Credit to his service. And so, when Grant asked to speak to him about a private matter, Bush closed the door to the Oval Office and gestured toward the white couch.

The fine young man sat down, sinking into the couch.

Bush sat in one of the chairs and leaned forward attentively.

"Mr. President, I know you recently ordered the Service to fire a few of the men who were guarding you. And I realize that you probably feel I shouldn't be asking you about this."

"That's right," Bush said in surprise. "I dumped 'em, and you shouldn't."

"And of course you haven't seen a sign of them since you gave that order."

"You're damned right!"

"Well, Mr. President, in fact, they were temporarily reassigned to other duties until their presence here at the White House wouldn't be an issue."

"What the hell are you talking about?"

"I mean, sir, that they were assigned elsewhere so as not to upset you. Soon, that won't matter, and they'll be back."

"Joe, I still don't know what you're talking about. I'll tell you something. Probably shouldn't. Do it anyway. Those men tried to give me orders. Me! I'm the President, damn it. I'm the one who gives the orders. Told 'em off. Threw 'em out."

"Yes, sir. They gave you orders because they were following their instructions."

"From who?"

Grant ignored the question. "And now, Mr. President, I'm going to follow my instructions. We'd like you to resign immediately. Leave office, leave the city, leave the public eye. It's best that way. It's safest that way."

Bush stared at him openmouthed. Finally he said, "Are you nuts?"

"Oh, no, sir. We're tested regularly. Sir, I like you. I always have. Really. I honor you for your service. But now you can do your best service to the nation by resigning."

Bush stood up and stalked angrily back to his desk. "Well, hell with that. Not gonna do it. Wouldn't be prudent. Wouldn't be right."

Grant stood too. "But it would be safe, sir. Mr. President, if you insist on trying to remain in office, you'll be putting yourself in danger."

"From who?" Bush demanded again. Getting no answer from the stoical younger man, he continued, "Don't know what's happened to you, Joe. Sold out to the Arabs or something, maybe. The Secret Service is loyal, though. They'll protect me. Got nothing to worry about. Now you get out of here. And you're fired."

Grant sighed. "I'm sorry, sir. I'll have to discuss this with my superiors at Langley." He left unhurriedly.

Langley? Bush thought. What the hell? Must have misheard. He must've said "Lang." Lang's involved in this.

Nonetheless, he picked up his telephone and told the man who answered to get hold of William Webster immediately. "Get to the bottom of this," Bush muttered.

Less than a minute later, the phone rang. Bush snatched the receiver from the cradle. "Judge?"

"Sorry, Mr. President. Judge Webster is unavailable. No one seems to know where he is or when he'll be back in his office."

Bush put the receiver down again, and then he leaned back in his chair, feeling suddenly weak. His arms slid off the arms of the chair and dangled with the fingertips almost brushing the floor. He found himself thinking again about Gorbachev.

The heat and humidity had returned. Washington was stifling. It was close to midnight, but the lateness of the hour had brought little relief. The Langs complained to each other as they stood waiting for the valet to bring the Mercedes around.

"At least the restaurant was comfortable," Harriet Lang said, trying to change the tone. She was always the peacemaker, the one who strove to convert disastrous family outings into happy ones. As usual, her husband and daughter didn't cooperate. And Jean's latest possibility, a likable young man named Fred or Frank or something like that, was very obviously wishing he was somewhere far away from the entire Lang family.

"Yeah, the restaurant was comfortable, but the food was lousy," Jean said. "Didn't you think it was awful, Fred?"

Fred. That was it. "Did you say your family is in Illinois, Fred?" Harriet asked brightly.

"Yes, that's right." He looked at Harriet with gratitude, thankful that he didn't have to answer Jean's question in front of her parents, who had paid for the expensive meal. "Downstate Illinois."

"Isn't that nice. You must miss them."

Not usually, Fred thought. But right now, I sure do.

Their car drew up to the curb with a squeal of brakes. In the light from streetlight and the restaurant, you could just make out the car's rich golden color. The three–rayed star emblem atop the hood gleamed.

A young man wearing a white, long–sleeved shirt and khaki pants leaped from behind the wheel and dashed around the car opening the doors.

"Thank God," Jean said. "I hope the airconditioning's already on." She got into the back seat, and Fred joined her. Harriet sat in front, in the passenger seat. Arthur Lang stood by the driver's door, studying the bills in his wallet, deeply concerned that he might make a mistake in the dim light and give the valet a higher denomination bill than he intended. Finally, satisfied that he held in his hand just one five–dollar bill, he handed it to the valet, climbed in, and closed the door behind him.

Lang was a cautious driver, as he was cautious in all things. He pulled away from the curb slowly, merging carefully into the meager traffic. He drove, still slowly, in the right–hand lane, glancing nervously at the occasional car catching up and passing him in the lane to his left.

As the Mercedes approached the next intersection, a car drew even on his left. It paced the Mercedes for a few seconds, staying even with it through the intersection. A man in the passenger seat stared at Lang intently and then turned and said something to the driver. The car sped up, cut in front of Lang, and slowed.

Lang slowed as well.

The car in front stopped. Its brake lights filled the interior of the Mercedes with a blood–red glow.

Lang stopped. Grunting in annoyance, he looked at his side mirror. He hated changing lanes, but he'd have to get around this car.

But another car was in that lane, blocking his way. It too had stopped. Two men got out it and walked to Lang's side of the car. Two other men got out of the car in front and came up to the passenger side of the Mercedes.

One of the men on Lang's side tapped on his window. Lang hesitated for a moment, then lowered it.

The man who had tapped on the window bent over, bringing his face level with Lang's. "Good evening, Mr. Lang."

"What's going on here?" Lang asked. He spoke loudly, angrily, but he couldn't keep the tremor from his voice. The man looking in the window was vaguely familiar. Could he be the one who had opened the door at the office building in Virginia? "Who are you men?" Lang asked. "What do you want?"

The other man smiled. "Don't worry, sir. This will only take a minute."

His hand appeared at the window. He held a large semiautomatic pistol.

Lang sat frozen in shock. Behind him, his daughter screamed.

The man pushed the muzzle of his gun against Lang's temple and fired.

The right side of Lang's head exploded, showering the other three occupants of the car with blood and brains and slivers of bone.

Harriet Lang slumped forward. The bullet that had killed her husband had struck her in the neck. It had had enough force left to snap her spine and embed itself in the upholstery of her door. She was already unconscious and would die without immediate emergency care.

In the back seat, Jean was still screaming. Fred sat frozen in place, his mouth open. Crazily, detachedly, he was telling himself that he had been wrong earlier when he had thought that the evening couldn't get any worse.

The assassin stepped away from the window. One of the other men took his place. This one poked the barrel of a submachine gun through the open window.

Jean screamed louder.

Fred said, "I'm not really with them."

The man outside the car laughed and pulled the trigger, holding it down while he sprayed the inside of the car. He was careful to include Harriet in the front seat. The noise inside would have been deafening if any of the car's occupants had been alive to hear it.

"Christ, what a mess," the second shooter said in disgust. "I got blood all over me."

"I told you to stand further back," one of the others said.

They got back into their two cars and drove away. Despite the heat, every window within hearing was now locked. No sirens sounded.

Joe Grant was back in the Oval Office.

"Thought I fired you," Bush said. He had wanted it to sound forceful, brusque, dismissive—perhaps nothing more than a gesture of defiance against the inevitable, but an impressive and admirable gesture, at any rate. Instead, it was a whine.

Grant didn't even bother responding to Bush's words. "Mr. President." He emphasized the title slightly, making it something ironic, sarcastic. "I've been sent to urge you again, strongly, to resign immediately. This city has become a dangerous place. Consider what happened to Arthur Lang last night."

Bush shifted nervously in his chair. "It was—They—Who?"

"That's irrelevant, isn't it?"

Faceless, competent men, that's who, Bush thought. I should know. I used to have people like that working for me at CIA. Christ, maybe the same people!

"Why Lang?" he asked plaintively.

Grant stared back at him impassively.

As an example, Bush thought. An example to me. Lang meant nothing. Killed him, his family. Just to show me what could happen to me. Rather not kill me if they don't have to. Better for them if I go away quietly. Same way I used to arrange things when I ran CIA. Playing my own game with me. Bastards.

And he knew that he no choice in the matter, could not do otherwise than go away quietly. He'd fought so hard, for so many years, to get here, to this preeminent position in the country, in the world. And now, after such a short time to enjoy his place at the top, he had to give it all up. "Not fair," he muttered.

"Life isn't fair," Joe Grant said, echoing a line John Kennedy had spoken in very different circumstances.

If Bush had had any resistance left in him, the image that suddenly dominated his imagination, of President Kennedy's head exploding like Art Lang's, would have eliminated it. "I'll draft a letter," Bush said.

Grant reached inside his suit jacket and drew out a folded sheet of paper. He unfolded it and spread it on the desk in front of Bush. "That's already been done. Here it is. Just sign it."

"What about a speech? Gotta make a speech. Explain it. To the American people."

Grant shook his head. "Just sign the letter. Then go pack an overnight bag. We'll send everything else after you."

Bush sighed. Every moment, every sigh, every breath meant a few more seconds as President.

He looked at the sheet of paper before him. It was on standard presidential stationery: the presidential seal at the top, beneath that "THE WHITE HOUSE," underneath that "WASHINGTON," and then the date below that. The text was simple:

Dear Mr. Secretary:
I hereby resign the Office of President of the United States.
Sincerely,

Then came the space for his signature. Finally, below that, was the address:

The Honorable James Baker
The Secretary of State
Washington, D.C. 20520

"Gee, this looks familiar," Bush said.

"Just sign the damned thing."

It was the profanity, mild though it was, that jerked Bush into action at last. He signed the resignation letter and picked it up and held it out to Grant. As the Secret Service man—or whatever he really was now—was folding it again and putting it back inside his jacket, Bush asked, "I guess you've arranged something with Danny boy?"

"You can find out by watching the news, just like everyone else. We'll give you a couple of hours to get packed. Better get moving." He left the office, not bothering to close the door behind him.

Bush stood up slowly and looked around the office, the seat of power, the center of the world, for what he knew would be the last time. Not even three years, he thought bitterly.

Then another calculation struck him. "Damn," he said aloud. "Kennedy beat me by four months!"

Ten

August 1991

The newly sworn-in President faced the cameras, cleared his throat, swallowed, saw the light blink red, caught the producer's signal, and said, "My fellow Americans, this is an hour of history that troubles our minds and hurts our hearts. Nonetheless, our long national nightmare is over. Our constitution works. Our great republic is a government of laws and not of men."

What the Hell does that mean? Quayle wondered. Who wrote this crap? This is, like, a historic moment. Boy, I'm gonna fire all these guys and write my own speeches from now on.

For now, though, he had no choice but to read the words scrolling across the teleprompter.

"As we bind up the terrible wounds of recent events in the Persian Gulf, as we regroup and reorganize and prepare to take the offensive against a barbaric enemy who has no respect for God or family or traditional values, let us at the same time remember the Golden Rule and brotherhood and the eternal requirement that we seek the approval and guidance of that higher Power, by whatever name we honor Him, who ordains righteousness, justice, and victory."

What the fuck does *that* mean? the President wondered. Jesus Christ, do these guys think I'm Shakespeare, or something?

"And we will have victory. We will never surrender, we will never give up. We will fight in the desert sands. We will fight on the coastlines of the Persian Gulf. Even if the United States should last for a thousand years, nonetheless future generations will say that this was our finest hour."

I've read that before somewhere, Quayle thought. I've gotta get Walsh to explain this stuff to me. I can't trust anyone else, but I can trust him.

"I ask you to pray for me. I ask you to pray for America. Above all, I ask you to pray for our brave men and women who are fighting for our way of life in the desert sands right now, this very minute. Pray for victory, pray for the triumph of the American way, for democracy, for free-market capitalism. God helping me, I will not let you down. God bless America. Good night."

Not bad, Quayle thought. Maybe these guys are okay, after all. That speech was okay. And short, too.

The red light faded away. The crew and their equipment departed. The room returned to normal.

Hugh Walsh pushed himself out of the embrace of the white leather couch and rose to his feet. "Excellent job, Mr. President. There are phrases in that speech that will be in all the history books."

"You really think so?"

"I'm sure of it."

"Because I wrote parts of that myself, you know."

"Why, no, I didn't. Now I'm even more impressed."

"So what's next? I'm really eager to wade into it."

"It's been a very stressful few days, Mr. President. I think you and your wife should go to Camp David for a break. You want to conserve your strength, build it back up before you get into the really heavy lifting of the office, if you see what I mean."

"Oh. Well, sure. Okay, Hugh. Whatever you say."

"By the way, sir, we still haven't settled the issue of whom you'll nominate as Vice President."

"I guess I really have to have one, huh?"

"Oh yes, I think so."

"Who was that guy you suggested?"

"Joe Grant. He's one of your Secret Service guards. Solid man, good name, good background. Just turned 35, so he's qualified."

"Has he ever been elected to anything?"

"No. That makes him an outsider. Just what the country wants nowadays."

"Gee, I dunno. You think the Senate would approve him?"

"Oh, I think I can guarantee that."

Rashid–al–Din turned off the television and smiled. Quayle had just finished his acceptance speech, and Rashid knew that America was in even worse political trouble than he had realized.

Rashid stood and walked to a window, looking out over the city that was now his capital.

The sun was rising. The city streets were still in shadow. After the rebuilding, there were no tall office buildings remaining. Those that had survived the final assault from Rashid's forces had been torn down during the reconstruction. Across the skyline, he could see the minarets of rebuilt mosques, far more visible than they had been before his advent and the city's destruction and rebirth. The crescents atop them glowed golden in the early light. The muzzeins' calls to prayer echoed across the city.

He had always loved the dawn for its symbolism and possibilities. And today's dawn he loved especially, for today would see the great ceremonial dedication of this city as his capital. The speech he had just watched, broadcast live from Washington, was like a special gift to him from Heaven on this special day.

"What have you learned?" he asked.

Behind him, his secretary said, "Master, one of our men within the CIA reports that the new American President is completely under the CIA's control. Or at least that's what the people within that agency believe."

Rashid nodded. "May it be so. How is the city?"

"Calm. Even the nights are always calm now. We have no more problems."

Rashid turned around, frowning in annoyance, and his secretary trembled. "That wasn't what I was asking about. I assumed that much. I wanted to know about preparations for the celebrations later today."

"The people are gathering, Master," the young man stammered. "They've been gathering since the middle of the night. Everyone wants to be in a good position to see and hear you."

Rashid's frown deepened. "Everyone? We're not the world's only assassins. Does 'everyone' include those who are here to kill me? There are surely some such among the crowds."

"No, Master! Your security people are everywhere, watching, checking. As you instructed, all entry points to the great square were blocked off, so that every member of the crowd had to pass through a checkpoint and be searched. All high points with a view of the platform are occupied by your own men. I assure you, you will be safe!"

"Will you stake your life on it?"

The secretary stood speechless, his mouth open, his face pale. He could think of nothing to say. Everything he had already said had apparently, somehow, been the wrong thing.

Suddenly, Rashid smiled. "Never mind. You've done well, Sayyed. You may go now."

Rashid watched the young man practically run from the room, and he smiled again. Not only was keeping his underlings on their toes, afraid for their lives, a wise technique of rule, it also gave him considerable pleasure.

The ceremonies were to begin at nine o'clock. Harry Elkins arrived before dawn. He passed through a checkpoint without trouble, outwardly calm and innocent, his heart pounding rapidly.

The open space was immense, a rough semicircle almost a mile across, with its arc formed, on the east, by the curve of the Tigris. The buildings and streets that had filled much of that space in earlier days were long gone, and the surface of the open space was perfectly smooth, perfectly flat concrete. Saddam's last palace, his last stronghold, shattered by the guns of Rashid's Holy Guard at the end of the fall of Baghdad, had been swept away. Now the new capitol of the Caliphate stood in the curve of the river, a huge building, vast, extending as much underground as it did above. The building—the complex—retained the beautiful style of the public buildings erected under Saddam's rule, but they had been built on a far greater scale.

Harry had seen the Capitol glowing in Baghdad's brilliant

sunlight, and he had seen it lit by powerful floodlamps at night. He thought that the result of the months of reconstruction was magnificent.

It was still dark when Harry arrived, and the floodlamps were lit, but the front of the building was obscured by a high wooden platform built during the preceding week. This stage was lit by spotlights; the ceremonies would take place there. The upper levels of the building behind the stage formed the backdrop. Harry took up a position with the river to his left, so that he was looking southeast toward the capitol. The rising crescent moon hung above the building, brilliant in the clear air.

Later, as the eastern horizon began to glow, the muzzein's call floated across the city. Harry thought that he was hearing it amplified by hidden speakers somewhere atop the capitol. Had that been done in Saddam's day? Harry didn't know, but he doubted it.

The swelling crowd stopped moving. All around Harry, people lowered themselves to the concrete for the *Salat-al-Fajr,* the morning prayer. Still not quite used to this, not as quick as he knew he should be, Harry stood for a moment. Here and there about the square, in the dim light, he could see other figures standing for a moment while the crowd knelt. As he emulated those around him, Harry wondered how many of those others who were slow to act where non-Muslim spies like him—and whether all of this was being watched by the Caliphate's security services.

His heart was hammering again. I'm really not cut out for this, he thought. I need a beer and a smoke.

He knelt and placed his forehead against the concrete and willed himself to blend into the crowd. He muttered the words of the prayer, not because he believed them, but as a way to calm himself.

Why was he putting himself in danger this way, so unnecessarily? There was no need for him to be here. He had come to the ceremony because he wanted to see and hear this historic moment, to be a part of it. He could not have said exactly what it was that drove him, why he wanted to participate. These were his enemies, after all. His whole mission was to work for their destruction. Being here in the square was unlikely to contribute to that mission. The ceremony was no doubt carefully planned and would be carefully executed. Harry would see and hear nothing of any value.

But today's event was momentous, it was pivotal, it was the end of one world and the beginning of another. Harry was driven to be here, and it was pointless to try to analyze why.

Not far away from Harry, one of the figures who stood for a moment too long was Ali ibn Daoud. He stood for yet a moment longer, staring around. He had noticed Harry in particular, recognizing him by his size and how he moved. Harry Elkins, he had thought, and then corrected himself: No, Haroun al Kindi. He must be careful to refer to Harry by that name even in his thoughts. He must never slip up. Bad enough if he endangered himself, but he must never bring disaster upon these other men.

Ali was there to prove something. Not to Harry or to Harry's superiors, but to himself. He had to feel sure that he was truly free of the Grand Master's spell.

After the prayer, Ali stood again and looked around. He was trying to reconcile the way the area looked now with the way it had looked when he was last in Baghdad. Wasn't he standing in almost the same spot now as when he witnessed the beheading of

Saddam? But the ruined buildings were gone, swept away by the might of the victorious Grand Master, now the Caliph. The wall he had hidden behind, the arch that had sheltered him—all gone.

Those two women over there, whispering to each other. Didn't they stand where the bodies of two other women had lain silently, bloating in the sunlight, infested with buzzing flies, their blood soaking the ground around them? Now the blood was as hidden as the ground itself beneath layers of concrete. All was clean and pure, orderly and controlled. He couldn't quite reconcile this splendid new city, this glorious capital of a mighty new empire, with the shattered towers, the columns of smoke, the shrieks and groans, the cries for help from beneath fallen walls, the sounds of gunfire and explosions... the lidless head of an American general dangling from Rashid's grasp, the whistling sweep of the sword slicing Saddam's head from his body.

All of that horror was gone, banished from existence, replaced by a shining new city that was an ancient one reborn.

But there, above the wooden platform, at the top of the capitol building's walls... Ali squinted. Yes, it was as he had been told. The great doorway to the building was hidden by the platform, but he could see the tops of the two poles that stood to either side of the door. Each was topped with a small, dark, roundish object: heads, shriveled and blackened in the sun, surely little more than shreds of leathery skin stretched over whitening bone.

The American general, his name turned into a gruesome prediction, looked sightlessly out over the evidence of his last and greatest defeat, at the manifestation of his enemy's growing power.

Saddam, just as sightlessly, gazed at the expanding size and strength of his own onetime capital city, now the capital of an empire he might have imagined but could never have achieved.

Ali shivered and felt a touch of the fear whose existence he had come here to disprove. He didn't belong here. He never had.

Time passed. The temperature rose as the sun climbed higher. The square was flooded with daylight. The concrete grew hotter. The crowd kept swelling, flowing into the square, the people pressing ever more densely against each other.

At nine, figures appeared on the platform. Speakers set on posts along the encircling arms of the river crackled to life with the first of a series of speeches.

The amplified voices echoed from the buildings across the river, booming, unintelligible, cacophonous. Harry frowned and concentrated but could understand only a word here, a phrase there. He looked at the faces of the crowd around him—the men's faces, the only ones visible. They were covered with sweat already, as was his own, but they seemed oblivious to physical discomfort. All conversation in the crowd had stopped. They stared, strained, toward the raised platform, focused entirely on it, oblivious to him and to each other.

What were they feeling? What were they hearing?

What was he missing?

Even now, even here, he stood apart.

The heat grew intense. The sun baked down, and the reflected heat radiated up from the concrete. His dark clothes clung to him, soaked with his sweat. The booming, echoing speeches reverberated in his head, making him dizzy. The crowd pressed in even more tightly. Soon, Harry thought, it would become impossible to escape.

Harry could hardly breathe. He was suffocating in the heat, the stench of close-packed, sweating bodies, the airlessness, the miasma of human breath. He felt faint, lightheaded. Unconsciously, he leaned against one of his neighbors. The other man seemed not to notice. Harry felt detached from himself, from his body, from his past and his world. He was part of a great ocean of human feeling, carried along by history's tides.

A vast moan arose from the crowd. The Grand Master, now the Caliph Rashid, had appeared on the stage.

Ali listened carefully, but Rashid's words, like those of the other speakers before him, were almost unintelligible. Somehow, despite that, the great force of his personality came through. Ali was glad he could understand so little of the speech. He feared that if he could hear all of it clearly, he might fall under Rashid's spell again.

As far as Ali could tell, the speech was a mixture of history as interpreted by the Hashashim, stories of oppression of the Arabic peoples by Westerners, a promise of total victory over those oppressors, and a description of the glorious future for all citizens of the Caliphate that would follow that victory.

This went on for almost an hour. When it ended, Ali realized he was disappointed. He had expected—feared—something new, stirring, not this rehash of old ideas and announcements. If this was the best Rashid could do, and on such an important occasion, then perhaps there was little to fear from the Grand Master after all!

Then he looked around at the crowd, at the adoration in the men's faces and the women's postures, sensed their transport, and he understood that Rashid was even more dangerous than he had thought.

Rashid left the stage, followed by the other officials. The ceremony was apparently over. By now, the sun was at its zenith, hanging directly above the massive structure of Rashid's capitol. The heat and airlessness were unbearable. Very soon, it would be time for *Salat-al-Zuhr,* the long noon prayer.

Ali was panting for breath and having trouble concentrating. Must get out of here before the prayer begins, he thought, or it will be impossible to move. I won't make it.

Fortunately, others had had the same thought. The crowd began to drain sluggishly away. Second by second, the crush diminished. Ali could breathe properly again.

But not everyone left. All about, Ali could see silent figures lying on the concrete. It might have been adoration, but Ali suspected it was unconsciousness because of the heat, the crush of the crowd, the dead air. He wondered how many of them would die.

Ali moved with the crowd toward the exits. As the mass of humanity thinned, he looked toward the place where he had last seen Harry. The crowd parted momentarily, and Ali glimpsed a heap of bodies lying on the concrete. There was a space around them as though the departing crowd feared contamination.

Ali frowned in worry. Slowly, determinedly, he pushed his way through the crowd in that direction.

A mixed group of men and women lay together unmoving. Ali tugged at arms and legs, growing desperate. A couple of other men came from the crowd to help him. At last, near the center of the group, under all the others, he found Harry.

At first, he was sure Harry was dead. But then Harry's eyes flickered. His lips moved, and he mumbled something Ali couldn't make out.

Terror struck Ali. What if Harry, in his semi–conscious state, said something in English?

Ali began speaking loudly, drowning out Harry's mumbling. "Haroun! Oh, my brother, thank Allah you are alive! I so feared for your life." He tried to pull Harry to his feet but, weakened as he was himself, lacked the strength. "Please," he said to the other men, "can you help me? Get him to his feet, and then I'll be able to support him. I must get him home to our parents' house. Please!"

Others came to his aid, pulling Harry up, talking excitedly, helping to cover up Harry's muttering. They half–carried Harry away.

When they were free of the crowd at last and through a now–abandoned checkpoint, one of the men offered to help Ali carry his brother to their parents' house.

"No, no," Ali said. He forced himself to stand up straight, holding Harry up by an arm around his waist and with Harry's other arm around his shoulder. "I'm all right now. We'll both be all right. See—he's really quite light, a small man. Thank you for your help." He hurried away down the nearest street, walking as quickly as he could.

Once out of sight of his would–be helper, Ali let Harry drop to the ground and sank down beside him, gasping for air, his heart pounding.

When he had recovered a bit, Ali said in a low voice, "Harry, you'll have to wake up. You have to walk under your own power."

Harry muttered something again.

What was he saying? Ali leaned closer, trying to make out the words. Then he understood, and he froze in horror.

"Rashid," Harry said. "Glorious. Glorious."

"Ready." The word passed back through the chopper, from Rick to the platoon sergeant back through the men. "Ready." "Ready." No one said it loudly, but even over the rotor and engine noise Rick could hear it working its way through the crowded Blackhawk. "Ready." It was a significant word.

The pilot was very, very good. He brought the chopper down to hover six inches above the clearing, the only decent landing zone in hundreds of square miles of jungle–covered mountain, and held it there as steady as though he'd landed. Rick looked over his shoulder briefly at the faces of his men, First and Third Squads here, Second and Fourth in another Blackhawk fifty meters away.

Every single man of Second Platoon, Alpha Company, Second of the Three–Thirty–Third, trusted him. That felt good. They trusted him because he led from the front, because despite his Air Force background he'd proven ever since OCS that he was as good an infantryman as any of them, because of his Air Force Cross that he *hadn't* earned riding multimillion–dollar hardware through the sky at Mach 2, but most of all because he had come back from Khafji, and to every GI in the world that was known as a synonym for Hell.

He grabbed hold of the door and threw himself forward, hit the ground running or he would have fallen on his face, kept running until he saw a likely–looking hole in the ground, and threw himself into it. His pack drove the breath out of his body and made his ribs creak, but he ignored it and brought his rifle up to scan the jungle through its sights. Behind him the others were doing the same. In minutes the platoon had formed a defensive perimeter that would stop anything short of an armored assault. And the 'Dogs were tough, but they didn't have tanks. Yet.

Behind him the choppers roared away. Very soon there were only infantry and jungle sounds: breathing, muttering, the rattle of unsecured equipment, and about ten million different kinds of insects. You could go completely insane in the jungle listening to the bugs. Spend long enough listening to them and you became convinced they were communicating with you instead of each other, telling you things, warning you that you were going to die, and very soon. Like you didn't know that already.

Rick thought he still preferred the bugs to rifle fire.

He lay there for several minutes, Colombia's ever–present groundwater soaking into the front of his BDU's, listening to the jungle. Not just bugs, now; the birds and mammals that had been scared away by the choppers were coming back. Caws and grunts and somewhere, far away, a growling cough. His skin crawled, as it hadn't when he'd launched himself from the chopper into what might have been a firefight. Jaguars scared the hell out of him, worse than bullets. But the cats were smart, and by now they knew that the smell of human sweat and gun oil meant *stay clear.* Maybe they were smarter than people in that regard.

Cats and 'Dogs, they'd both try to kill you if they could.

He was just about to move when Corporal Martin hissed through his teeth. Martin was a Mississippi swamp boy, had grown up hunting in terrain that was as near to Colombia as anything in the continental US, and he had very sharp eyes besides. Rick trusted the Southerner's judgment of the jungle much more than his own. Now, he thought, if we were fighting in a big, cold city... His home in Eden Prairie, outside Minneapolis, felt very far away at that moment, farther even than when he'd been in the Gulf.

"What is it?" he muttered. They'd taught him that at the

jungle warfare school in Panama, never to whisper, just to speak as softly as he could. That sound died away in the jungle, but a human whisper would carry, and it sounded like nothing else.

"Not 'Dawgs," Martin replied. "Don't think so. Too big. But people, sure enough."

Rick exhaled very slowly and sighted in on the jungle. Damn it, as far as his own eyes were concerned there was just nothing *there.* In the desert you could at least see them coming—

—except when they jumped on you from behind in the middle of a firefight and wrapped a cord around your neck and—

—oh Jesus Christ I can't breathe Harry help me get this motherfucker off me I need air please I need air—

—sucked in dry cold desert air burned his throat burned his lungs but it felt so much better than dying—

—shove the bayonet in right there in the gut die you son of a bitch you tried to kill me die die die—

Lieutenant Rick Welton shook himself and focused back in on what was, not what had been. He swallowed hard against remembered agony in his throat and watched three figures coalesce out of the trees like gathering mist.

Not 'Dogs, as Martin had said. Americans, he thought. Surely they were Americans. Two white, one black, all of them tall and healthy and with all their teeth. The part of his mind that was still a medic made the evaluation automatically: these men might have been living hard recently, but they'd had lives of good nutrition and carefully planned exercise instead of the killing labor most of the 'Dogs had known. A lot like Rick himself, although he thought these guys had been living a lot rougher than Second Platoon. At least until now.

But their uniforms were very worn. It took him a while to

make out the Pathfinder flashes on their breast pockets, the Ranger tabs on their shoulders. Spooks, he thought, though they were demonstrably infantrymen as well. Still spooks. There were special ops units operating throughout South America, nebulously defined groups of Rangers and Green Beanies and Recon and SEALs and Combat Controllers and God knew what else, taking their orders from the CIA and NSA and DIS and the whole rest of the alphabet.

They weren't carrying packs, and even their LBE's were incomplete. Mostly they seemed to have stuffed everything into their BDU pockets. Ammunition, plenty of that, and demolition equipment and field dressings and some big–ass knives on all their belts. What Rick didn't see was food. They probably drank the muddy river water around here like it was champagne, and what they ate, Rick didn't want to know.

"Halt," Rick said. His tone was flat and conversational. "Advance and be recognized." Martin and a couple of the other guys nearby looked at him like he was nuts, but fuck it, he was going to do this by the book. Spooks made him nervous.

The spooks glided toward him. They made no noise and didn't seem to have to move the underbrush aside as they moved. Rick thought that if he looked very closely, he'd see that their feet weren't actually touching the ground. "Third Pathfinders, Cauca Valley Group. You guys Two–Triple–Three?"

"That's us."

One of the guys, a staff sergeant little older than the other two, nodded and said, "Figured you must be. *Los Perros* don't fly in the daytime, and you did all that too fast to be Colombian gov." He shook his head. "Noisy, though."

Rick stood up carefully. Around him, some of his men were

doing the same. There was no need to get themselves soaked even further while having a friendly conversation. A lot of them stayed down, though, in case someone not so friendly decided to break in. That could change the tone of the conversation fast.

"Choppers make noise," he said. "Not my fault."

"True." The sergeant held out his hand to the corporal next to him. "Map." He took the plastic-coated document and unfolded it as carefully as if it were a holy relic. Out here, maybe it was. Rick thought about huddled conferences in the desert night, over maps that showed current topography but a political layout unlike any the mapmakers had imagined.

"Okay," the sergeant said. Apparently the other team members, the corporal and a Spec-4, weren't going to speak. That was okay with Rick. The sergeant looked like a pretty normal guy if you ignored the grime, but the other two had impassive killers' stares that bothered Rick in exactly the same way as a jaguar's cough. "Right now we're here," pointing at the map, "which is about seven klicks from here," another spot, on lower and flatter ground, "which is the village the *Perros* use as their local HQ."

"Who says that's so?" Rick asked. "CIA?"

"We say so," the sergeant replied, and now his eyes had the same expression in them as his subordinates'. Rick consciously restrained himself from taking a step back. "We've been watching comings and goings down there for months. We know what goes in, what goes out, and what goes on inside. They can't take a shit there without us knowing it. Sir."

"Okay," Rick said.

"Place is called Roldanillo Norte." He pointed his thumb over his shoulder. "Roldanillo is a good-size town about twenty klicks south, southeast. River between here and there—more of a creek, really—doesn't have a name, but the locals call it the Riachuelo Orina." A couple of guys in the platoon snickered.

"What?"

"Means 'Piss Creek,' el–tee," said PFC Pabón. The Puerto Rican had a loathing for the locals that most of the Anglo troops couldn't hope to match. "Must be what they do in it."

"Piss, shit, fish, drink, wash clothes, bathe, irrigate, you name it," the Pathfinder sergeant agreed. "Which isn't as bad as it might be, because it's very fast–moving, washes everything downstream pretty quick. Be careful when you try to cross it. It's little but it can still pull you down and drown you. Anyway, not a problem there since *Los Perros* moved in. This bunch probably got trained by FARC, or *Sendero Luminoso* down in Peru. They've got good camp discipline. Everything stays clean." He shook his head. "All over the Goddamned place, *Perros* are getting smarter. Turning into a real army."

The enemy—this enemy, in this particular place—called themselves *Los Perros Colombianos Guerreros,* the Colombian Dogs of War. To most GI's in the theater they were therefore Collie–Dogs, or just 'Dogs. To these guys, who had been living in some Latin jungle or another since long before Rick had gone to OCS, it was probably easier to name them in Spanish than in English.

"So what do they have in the way of defenses?" Rick asked. "Bunkers, barbed wire, what?"

The sergeant shook his head. "Nothing that elaborate. They don't think any GI's or Colombian gov are going to get in here. They're more worried about paramilitaries, and the growers who haven't gone *Perro.* So you've got a shitload of sentries on a tight rotation schedule, all with rifles and bricks, and a little CP in the middle of the village with mortars. More flexible than a real firebase." His tone, Rick thought, was admiring.

The job of Second Platoon was to go in, kill ninety-five percent of the 'Dogs, and bring back a couple of survivors for interrogation, all without "excessive" civilian casualties. Winning hearts and minds, as the Pentagon had said a quarter of a century ago, and apparently still thought they could. Of course, they'd won too few hearts and minds in Vietnam, and just about none at all in what was now the Caliphate. Was it supposed to work better now just because they were in the same hemisphere?

Rick would still try not to leave too many civilian bodies behind. He didn't give a shit about hearts and minds. But the part of him that had been a medic recoiled from the thought of killing people just because they were in the way.

"How tight is the rotation?" he asked.

"Pairs at ten, fifteen meters, walking pace. Four-hour shifts, three a day, with half an hour off between. They stagger them throughout twenty-four hours, so you never have a real shift change where no one knows what's going on, and you don't have everyone tired at the same time." The sergeant shook his head. "El-tee, these guys are living well and they know their shit. It's like an easy bivouac back in the States, not a war. They get just enough shooting to keep them sharp, not wear them out."

"So how do you suggest we take them?"

The spook grinned. "That's your problem, sir. They pay us to watch and report, not solve platoon-level field problems."

Rick nodded. The guy might be a bit of an asshole about the way he was saying it, but he was right. It was Rick's responsibility to figure it out, and that was what the Army had spent its precious time and money training him to do. The sergeant and his men had

had much more training than Rick, when you came right down to it—Pathfinder plus Ranger school was almost a year—and God knew how much more experience in the jungle, but theirs was a specialized job and Uncle Sam wasn't going to waste them on a regular infantry job.

Uncle Sam had Second Platoon for that.

"All right. Thank you, Sergeant."

The spook nodded and rose, and he and his men drifted back into the jungle as silently as they had arrived. Spooks in more ways than one, Rick thought as he watched them melt back into the bush. Ghosts. Walking corpses who don't know they're dead yet, or just don't care. A hundred years from now, they'll still be here, alongside the jaguars.

He stood, feeling his Doc Martens take the weight of his body and equipment. The civvie boots weren't nearly as thick or heavy as Army issue, which meant they didn't last as long in the field, but they were still durable and a lot more comfortable in this environment. That was something Sharon had taught him. One of many things Sharon had taught him, he thought, and forced his face to relax before anyone could ask him what he was smiling about.

He circled his hand over his head briefly to signal the squad leaders to form up around him. "We'll take it slow, three meters per man, six per fire team, ten per squad. Think everyone can hold together with that?"

SFC Villarial, the platoon sergeant, said, "I'll make sure of it." Rick nodded. Villarial would be trailing the platoon a few meters back, weaving back and forth along its line of march to get any stragglers back in the main body. He wasn't the yelling, strutting type of NCO, Villarial wasn't. He enforced order with muttered reproofs that were scarier than any parade–ground bellow, and when he threatened to cut out a private's heart and slow–cook it over a campfire, he was instantly believed.

The NCO had lived in Panama, and had his family there. Rick had been a guest at barbecues at Villarial's home a few times, and watched him playing and giggling with his nine–year–old daughter.

Second Platoon peeled itself off the ground and into traveling overwatch a fire team at a time, the defensive perimeter melting away until the platoon had formed itself into a moving bubble of violence roughly the size and shape of a football field. Rick thought briefly of his high school team. They'd thought they were tough, back then. They had simply had no *idea.*

A healthy soldier could have covered the distance to Roldanillo Norte in a little over an hour, at a brisk walk over a good road. Getting there through the jungle inevitably took longer, and getting there with the cautious movement required when people might be trying to kill them at any minute took longer still. The march was a five–hour–long green blur for Rick, discomfort turning to pain but never anything he couldn't manage but God damn he wished those fucking mosquitoes would just leave him alone, that the jungle would break into another clearing just for a klick or so, that there was at least a little bit of a breeze instead of dead saturated air that made every step feel like swimming through piss. Crossing the Riachuelo Orina went quickly and barely seemed to make a difference to how soaked he felt. He could see the men to either side of him, and dimly make out those beyond *them,* and that was just it. The jungle sounds masked even the reassuring human sounds, the harsh breaths and muttered curses as another troop stepped in a sinkhole or got tangled up in a monster spider web.

At least they didn't meet any jaguars.

Then it ended. Like most such villages, Roldanillo Norte was hacked out the jungle that constantly threatened to overwhelm it, and except for the space reserved for farmers' fields, the wild growth would normally have formed a green wall around its edge. Here, though, the 'Dogs showed the discipline the spook had described: fallow fields had been kept trimmed down to provide a field of fire out to about fifty meters. Rick sensed the abrupt thinning in the jungle well before he actually saw it, and raised his rifle just above his head, barrel pointed downrange.

Second Platoon knew how to handle this. The jungle was an enemy bigger than any of them, and all anyone could do was endure it. But people to kill, that was something they could control.

There were sentries, as the spooks had said. Rick saw three pairs pass by, moving shapes behind the thin screen of jungle brush separating him from them, while he stayed as still as he could and willed himself to look like a plant. Fifteen meters was a long way in the jungle, but it wouldn't be much at all in the cleared area; the pairs of sentries would have visual contact the whole time. Subtlety was right out. And fuck it, his men were good at sneaking around, but he wasn't going to get them all in there without anybody noticing anyway.

Somebody took the decision out of his hands. About thirty meters down the line, in First Squad's territory, he heard the dull rattle of an AK-47 followed by the high-pitched chatter of an M16, and then the whole line opened up. He shed his rucksack and propelled his body forward like he was going for a sack, breaking through the tree line into the open, one of the sentries *there* just to his left, wide eyes very white in the dark Indian face as he tried to bring his rifle to bear but Rick was faster, a burst from the M16 to cut him down as his partner's face disappeared under a line of tracer from a SAW, found a depression to take cover in and hit the ground so he could look around and take stock.

It was, he decided almost as soon as he was down, no time to take a break. There were a hundred and fifty meters of clear ground between the tree line and the rough border of the village. The entire platoon could die in that space.

His troops knew what they were doing even if he'd lost track. They leapfrogged forward by fire teams, dashes of thirty meters or so before they went down and sent covering fire downrange. So far it seemed to be working. Whatever other sentries had been present along the tree line were dead or gone, and there was only sporadic return fire from the village. Rick envisioned civilians flattened on the floors of their houses, arms over their heads, praying that the next bullet to come through the walls would miss them. He pushed the image out of his mind as he sprinted forward. Second Platoon could worry about that when they'd *won.*

They were almost into the village when the mortar shells started coming down.

Rick had no warning to speak of. Later his mind would reconstruct the whistling that had preceded in the impact, but in that moment he was only aware of being lifted off his feet by an impact like one huge slap all over his body, and then he was lying on the ground. His hearing started to come back and he managed to get his hands over his ears before the second wave of shells landed. When he took his hands away, he almost wished he hadn't. Now he could hear the screams.

Second Platoon's textbook assault had been stopped as surely as if it had run into a wall. Wounded and dead and pieces of dead were randomly strewn out across the clearing, as though they had been dropped carelessly from a helicopter. But ten meters away were the first buildings of the village, 'Dogs starting to filter out with rifles in their hands. If Rick could get his troops in there among the buildings, they would still have to deal with fighting building-to-building, but they would have a chance. Out here they had none at all.

He put his M16 on full auto and hosed down the approaching 'Dogs with the whole clip. They went to ground immediately, not panicking, taking good cover. Disciplined troops. Rick slapped in another magazine, fired again more briefly, and made himself get up and start to move. He stumbled on someone's arm, kept his balance, kept moving, let loose with the rifle at anything he saw move. What was left of his platoon was, thank God, doing the same. The fine order of their attack had been broken but they still had firepower and training on their side.

In among the buildings, 'Dogs coming back up now, firing from inside houses and around corners. There was not and could not be any order to this sort of fighting; in seconds the battle had gone from a platoon-level assault to ten different two- or three-man street fights. "Don't get hung up!" he shouted to anyone who could hear him. They had to keep moving forward, to get to the mortars at the CP. In front of him a 'Dog officer took a shot with a .45, missed. Rick squeezed his M16 trigger and nothing happened. Jammed, out of ammunition? It didn't matter. The 'Dog had clearly expected Rick to go down, and frozen when he didn't, but that wouldn't last long.

Rick kept running forward, swung the rifle butt up into the 'Dog's jaw, put all his weight into the blow the way he had when he was clearing away offensive linemen. The 'Dog sagged away from the blow, his face a red ruin, and fell twitching. Rick dropped the magazine from his rifle, fished in his LBE's for another and realized he was out of ammunition. Jesus Christ. He kicked the 'Dog in the head to make sure he was really down, dropped the M16, stooped and picked up the .45.

Then, at last, they were in the center of the village. Small and poor as it was, it had a paved European-style public square, which had made a perfect command post for *Los Perros.* The mortar crews scrambled around, still sending shells downrange, but it was over and as soon as they saw the Americans they knew it. Most of them put their hands up. Those who didn't were cut down.

The silence was almost as deafening as the noise of battle had been. Rick was suddenly very aware of how tired he was, of the smell of blood and shit permeating the air, of the weight of the dead man's pistol in his hand. He looked around to try to get an idea of how much of his platoon had made it in. Eighteen, nineteen guys: about half. Occasional rifle shots told him some of the platoon was still out there. Figure two-thirds are either okay or walking wounded, he thought. The worst battle of their entire time in Colombia had taken maybe five minutes.

Pabón limped forward. Rick looked him over with a medic's eye, trying to see the wound. There was nothing wrong with the private's leg that he could see. Maybe a twisted ankle? That could happen easily enough, running through what passed for roads here. Then he saw how Pabón was clamping his arm to his side, how that part of his uniform was darkly stained. Jesus Christ, Rick thought, he got shot in the gut.

His *left* side, which meant the private could still use the rifle dangling from his right hand. The M16 was a light weapon; it was just barely possible to hold it up like a pistol. Pabón approached one of the 'Dogs, an older man in a uniform cleaner than most, and swung the weapon up toward the man's head.

They spoke briefly in Spanish. Rick knew very little of the language, mostly obscenities and wartime slang, but he thought their tone was oddly neutral, almost friendly. Then Pabón's rifle cracked twice, and the *Perro*'s brains sprayed back across the flagstones of the square.

"*¡Pendejos!*" Pabón screamed, and dropped to his knees. The rifle dropped from his hand and clattered on the ground. He fell sideways and lay curled into a ball beside the corpse.

"Shit," Rick said, and ran forward. The shooting might have set off a general massacre, and that wasn't what they were—supposed to be—here for, but he couldn't let one of his men die right in front of him. He pulled Pabón's hands away and gently lifted up the BDU shirt. It was a decent wound, as such things went: through and through, fairly well forward so it probably hadn't done more than nick the kidney, and there was none of the overpowering fecal stink that would have accompanied a serious intestinal wound. The bleeding was steady but manageable, though of course there was no way to know how much might have emptied into the abdomen. Pabón had had the strength to make it this far and to kill a man before he collapsed.... Rick felt his wrist for a pulse. 130, 140 beats per minute, something like that, and the fact that it was still present in the wrist meant the blood pressure wasn't too bad. Respirations were probably in the high twenties, also a bit too fast but acceptable. Medevac him out within an hour and he'll make it for sure, Rick thought. He started feeling Pabón's hand and wrist for a vein.

"Sir," someone was saying. "El–tee!"

Rick looked up irritably. It was Culligan, one of the medics. He had an IV rig in one hand and an oxygen bottle in the other. Rick reached for the IV and then looked at Culligan, confused, as the medic pulled it away from him.

"I'll deal with this, el–tee," Culligan said.

"No, I think I got a vein," Rick said. "Hand me some betadine and a cath. Good veins, I can get a sixteen in."

"I'll *deal* with it," the medic said again. Rick heard the emphasis in his voice, realized how quiet it had become, looked around. Everyone was standing there, Americans and 'Dogs and civilians alike, looking at them.

"Oh. Right." Rick stood. "All right, then."

Second Platoon had done its job without having to be told, which Rick supposed said something good about his leadership. Or maybe it just meant that his men were smarter than he was, remembering where and what they were while he lost track and snapped back to being a medic. The prisoners stood in small groups, well away from vehicles or buildings or other possible cover. The American troops who weren't directly guarding groups of prisoners had formed a loose perimeter; the civs wandering around at the edges of the square were probably either friendly or too scared to try anything, but a few GI's waving M16's in their direction would provide added incentive to stay peaceful. Villarial and a couple of Spec–4's were going through 'Dog bodies, frisking them for intelligence materials—and, probably, anything valuable—before stacking them in neat piles. A small hog sniffed at the bodies and started to chew on a hand before Villarial kicked it away.

Rick called out, "RTO up!" There were more prisoners and a shitload more wounded than he'd expected. The original plan had been for them to go back up to the LZ where they'd come in—some CIA bullshit about keeping local disturbances to a minimum, as though that made any sense at all after a firefight—but no way in hell was he going to march this group back there. The evac choppers could come right down in the middle of the square and if the REMF's and spooks didn't like the big show, they could do it themselves next time.

He took the offered PRC-77 handset. "This thing on the battalion push?" The radioman nodded and Rick clicked the button. "Foxtrot actual to Oscar one, Foxtrot actual to Oscar one, request dustoff soonest, with two Bravo Romeo and two Bravo Mike at Point Sierra, over."

A moment later, the radio crackled back, "Oscar to Foxtrot, say again, Point Sierra? Over."

"Foxtrot to Oscar, roger, dustoff at Point Sierra with two Bravo Romeo and two Bravo Mike. Foxtrot actual out." The two helicopters that had brought them in, plus two more fitted out for medevac; it might be excessive, but it would give them room to get both the whole and the wounded home, and the prisoners to wherever they were going. Not home, that was for sure.

It would be a while before the choppers arrived. That should give Second Platoon time to comb Roldanillo Norte for stragglers and wounded. And dead, of course. Plenty of those.

"Lieutenant?" Villarial, still over there with the corpses.

"Yeah, what is it?"

"Come take a look at this."

He walked over to the piles of bodies. Scrawny, most of

them—it hadn't been hard work for Villarial and the Spec-4's to stack them like that. Typical Colombian peasants, a lifetime of hard work and poor nutrition until they'd decided to become *Perros,* and even harder work afterward. But give a kid a choice between a powerless life in the coca fields and a potentially shorter but infinitely more rewarding one carrying a rifle, and it wasn't hard to predict which he'd choose.

Two bodies had been set apart. They were both white, for one thing, in sharp contrast to their largely dark, Indian-featured comrades in arms. But that wasn't what had attracted Villarial's attention. Like the spooks who'd met them at the LZ, like the men of Second Platoon, they had clearly been well-fed their whole lives. Their uniforms were, well, *uniform* as well, not the patchwork of various countries' fatigues most of the 'Dogs wore.

"These must have been some really big 'Dogs," Rick said. "Cool. Too bad they didn't make it—Intelligence would love having a little chat with them."

Villarial shook his head. "That's not it, el-tee. This one here?" He nudged one of the bodies, a middle-aged man with silver hair and features that would have been distinguished if not for his missing jaw and throat. "I know him."

"Huh?"

"Yeah." The platoon sergeant, whom Rick had never before seen have trouble saying anything to anybody, seemed to struggle to get the words out. "Used to see him at the NCO club sometimes, up in Panama. Intel. Nice guy. But never talked shop."

Rick stared at the two dead men. Not big 'Dogs at all. American soldiers, in the middle of a pile of enemy dead.

What the fuck?

Eleven

August–September 1991

On a ledge on a rocky outcropping near Kariz–e Elyas, Gul Aman looked out over the darkening plain and laid his hand gently, possessively on his RPG–7.

He was fond of this weapon, attached to it. It was one the Mujahidin had captured from the Soviets early in war. Unfortunately, it had been manufactured in Russia and was inferior to his team's other RPG–7, which came from Bulgaria by way of China by way of Pakistan. It had done its job, though. It was rugged enough and reliable enough, and it seemed a wonder compared to, say, the one–hundred–year–old Enfield that had been Gul's sole weapon at the start of the war. Enfields against Soviet tanks and helicopter gunships! It had been a slaughter. "But we evened up the odds," Gul said in satisfaction, patting the grenade launcher.

"Yes. Certainly. Wonderful." Ahmet was too young to have seen any of the early fighting. The stories some of the older men told about killing Russians fascinated and excited him, made him wish he had been old enough to be part of it. Gul, though, seemed mainly to want to talk about the technical specifications of his damned RPG–7. Now Ahmet pointed northwards with his chin, toward the frontier, toward Turkmenistan. "They're our brothers over there. They're waiting for us. Why aren't we invading, instead of sitting here, waiting in case the Russians invade us again?"

"Politics," Abdul said. He sat a few feet away, also watching the plain, but he had been listening to the conversation between Gul and Ahmet. "It's all a lot more complicated than that."

Ahmet shook his head. "It's not complicated at all. It's very simple. Especially now, because of the Caliph in Baghdad. If we moved over the frontier, the people all over the area would rise up to support us. Perhaps the Caliph would send his own forces to help us. But even without that, the Russians would run away, just as they ran away before when we attacked them. Allah was with us."

Gul sighed. "They didn't run. They retreated. It was a sensible decision on their part. But it was hard for us, it was very hard. We lost a lot of men. Women and children, too," he added. "Whole villages, whole regions devastated. Allah was with us, but He required that we do the actual work."

Abdul laughed. "Allah's like that," he said.

"You shouldn't talk that way!" Ahmet said.

"Will you report us to someone?" Abdul asked sarcastically. There were parts of the country—the south, near the Pakistani border—where such talk might indeed be dangerous. But not here, facing the real enemy, in the company of true brother warriors. "You shouldn't interrupt Gul when he talks about his grenade launcher," Abdul told Ahmet. "You might learn something. Besides, it's his woman. I remember a time, near the end of the war, when we were crossing a river under enemy fire, and Gul nearly drowned because he refused to let his RPG–7 go and save himself."

Gul smiled. "And you see, I was right." He remembered the incident clearly—and with some sadness. In those days, a group of ten men, like the present one guarding this border crossing, might have had as many as five RPG–7's. Now they were down to two.

All too obviously, the men Gul reported to no longer took the Soviet threat seriously. When the new Soviet leader, whatever his unpronounceable name was, had made his bellicose speech implying that he planned to reoccupy Afghanistan, these border posts had been beefed up. But then the Soviets had done nothing and the feeling had arisen that the menacing speech was just a pose for domestic political purposes, that there was no actual new Soviet threat. The Jamiat–e Islami, the Hezb–e Islami, the Hezb–e Wahdat, and all of the rest of them, nominally still allies, were increasingly concerned with preparing their forces and positions for the coming struggle with each other for control of the country. None of them could afford to tie up their men and weapons pointlessly on this frontier. The force along the frontier was being reduced to a token, while weapons and men were concentrated elsewhere, in the interior.

Gul feared that the coming struggle would be long and bloody. Young Ahmet would lose his naïveté and his eagerness in it, if he were lucky enough not to lose his life.

Gul patted his weapon again. "This is worth more to us than any woman."

"I wouldn't go that far," Abdul said. "Especially now that the sun's going down and it's getting cold." He watched Ahmet for the expression of disgust he knew the younger man would not be able to hide. When he saw it, he laughed. Gul tried not to laugh along with him but couldn't quite manage not to.

Begench watched the three men on the ledge. He lay on a shallow slope, his head poking above the crest of the low ridge. He rested his weight on his elbows and gazed steadily through binoculars. Despite his excellent eyesight and the fine lenses, it was getting harder to see the men as the light faded. For now, that didn't matter. He knew just where they were, and he doubted they'd move in the next hour. When the time came, he and his comrades would use night-vision glasses.

He had no idea what the men on the ledge were saying, and he didn't care. Their conversation was a low, distant murmuring, scarcely distinguishable from the night breeze even to Begench's ears. If he had been able to make out the words, he would have been highly amused by Ahmet's claim that they were brothers.

Begench, a native Turkman, had been recruited into the Spetsnatz from the regular army during the war in Afghanistan. He suspected it was his enthusiasm in pacification activities as much as his linguistic talents and his ability to blend into the local population that had attracted someone's attention. He might look like those Afghans on the ledge and speak their language with near fluency, but he felt nothing in common with them. He considered himself a Soviet first and foremost and only second a Turkman. For that matter, he wasn't a true Turkman, for his grandfather had been a Ukrainian. "Moslem" didn't figure into his self-image at all. To him, those three Mujahedeen were obstacles to the Soviet reconquest, and he'd be happy to remove them.

He lowered his binoculars and crept back down the slope,

making no noise, raising no dust. He moved in a crouch, keeping himself hidden from the Mujahedeen on the hillside.

Not that they'll be watching as carefully as I would be, if I were in their position, he thought. They're good, but they're not Spetsnaz.

Nonetheless, he took no chances. Even when he was fairly sure he was hidden from them by nightfall and the lie of the land, he moved with care. And silently: the Mujahedeen's ears were sharp, as many a Soviet soldier had found to his regret during the war.

Finally, he reached the camp. He announced himself with a low whistle, the tune a prearranged signal, and was allowed to pass. He noted with approval that he had not been able to see the man standing guard.

Inside the perimeter, things were more relaxed. Captain Pyotr Rodzhinsky was sitting cross-legged on the ground. In his right hand, he held a piece of the bread that had been their main rations for the past two days. It was dark, hard, chewy stuff, and it was getting harder by the day. In his left hand, he held a small glass. Because of the fading light, Begench couldn't see what was in the glass, but he doubted it was water. Rodzhinsky looked back and forth, from hand to hand, from bread to glass, from the legal and proper to the severely frowned upon, as if unable to choose between the two.

Begench stepped up to him and saluted. "Comrade Captain."

Rodzhinksy gestured with the piece of bread. "Begench."

Begench pointed at the bread and the glass, which he could now see contained a small amount of pale, brown liquid. "A metaphor for life, Captain?" It was the sort of joke no one else would dare with Pyotr Rodzhinksy.

The captain smiled. "No, just bread and brandy. You've worked with Russians for too long! What's the situation?"

"I saw three of them on the ledge. They're sitting there, watching for our tanks. They think it'll be a repetition of the last time."

"Good. They're underestimating us. Weapons?"

Begench shrugged. "All I could see was one RPG–7. The same ratio we used to see."

Rodzhinksy smiled again. "Also like last time. Of course, the same is true of us. Except that this time, *we* aren't underestimating *them.*" He tilted his head back and drained the last of the brandy from the glass, then set the glass on the ground. He set the bread next to it. He leaned over and held his left arm against his chest while he pressed the button on the side of his watch. The watch face glowed with a faint green light, which he was shielding from view with his body as best he could. He let the light glow for only an instant. Then he said to Begench, "Time to move out, Sergeant. Get all the teams in motion. I want each of them in place well before dawn."

Begench straightened and saluted again. The gesture was virtually invisible in the swiftly deepening darkness, but it felt right to him. It was a transition from an almost casual conversation with a man who had been a friend as well as his commander for years into something more formal, something strong and active with nothing casual about it.

He hurried off to get the teams assembled and under way.

It was all real now, Begench thought, as real as the last time but better, for this time they had a real leader. With General Slonimsky in command, the days of weakness were over. Slonimsky would not accept a withdrawal, he would not countenance defeat.

Begench approved thoroughly. He knew that his captain did, too.

Pyotr Rodzhinsky did approve—both of Slonimsky's style of leadership and of the plan to reinvade and, this time, properly subdue Afghanistan. No one had told Pyotr that this was the intention, of course. He was of far too low a rank to be included in larger-scale planning. It had been easy enough for him to put two and two together, though.

What came next? Was control of Afghanistan an end in itself? From what he had heard so far of Slonimsky, and from what he had seen of the men who had taken over control of the armed forces since Slonimsky had taken control of the government, Rodzhinsky felt sure that Afghanistan was just the first step. If Slonimsky wanted to spread Soviet power even further, well, Pyotr approved wholeheartedly of that, too.

But he didn't like splitting up his team.

He had nine men in his Spetsnaz unit. Besides Begench, there were a radio operator and men who specialized in demolitions, sniping, and reconnaissance. They had all received some cross-training, so that if one of the specialists were lost in action, one of the other men could assume his duties, but they were scarcely experts in each other's fields. Begench was the only real exception: officially, his duty was to serve as Rodzhinsky's second-in-command, but he was a better sniper and recon man than anyone else on the team. But he was just one man. Spetsnaz units were designed to act as just that, units. Having to separate them into three-man teams was making Pyotr jumpy. He saw each three-man team as much less than a third of the whole. More like a limb cut from a healthy man.

And he hated like hell to think of losing any of them.

What choice was there? None. Orders had come down, and he would obey them. "I serve the Soviet Union," he muttered. Besides which, the orders made sense.

At least it wasn't quite the old days. Back then, during the attempt to hold onto Afghanistan, the Spetsnaz troops had been supplied only with RPG-16's and -22's. In range and power, they were inferior to the RPG-7's of the Mujahedeen, so that the Spetsnaz had had to capture the superior rocket-propelled grenade launchers from the Mujahedeen. Those weapons were mostly of Chinese and Pakistani manufacture—not bad, but not as good as the three brand-new, high-quality, Soviet-made ones Pyotr's unit had brought across the border with them. And that, of course, was thanks to General Slonimsky. According to what Pyotr had heard through the grapevine, someone high up in the GRU who had served in a Spetsnaz brigade in Afghanistan had dared to speak his mind to Slonimsky about the equipment situation. Slonimsky's immediate reaction had been to promote the man and put him in charge of equipping all the troops—Spetsnaz and regular army—for this new invasion.

The grapevine was generally pretty reliable, in Pyotr's long experience. The story was certainly consistent with everything else he had heard about Slonimsky. Pyotr had never met the new Soviet ruler and doubted that he ever would, but he approved of everything the man had done so far and was happy to serve him, for it was clear that Slonimsky, more than any of his predecessors, truly served the Soviet Union himself, just as Pyotr and his fellow soldiers did.

Well, perhaps Pyotr didn't approve of absolutely everything Slonimsky had done. Surely he could have taken control and then consolidated his power with less bloodshed. Pyotr would have had no objection, for example, to letting Gorbachev go into exile in the West.

But that was water under the bridge, and the excellence of the results of Slonimsky's actions was beyond dispute. There are no doubt ramifications and complications I know nothing about, Pyotr thought. If I had been in his position, perhaps I would have been forced to act the same way.

Begench appeared, saluting again. "We're ready to move out, Comrade Captain."

In the gloom, Pyotr felt the salute from the movement of the air and his long association with Begench more than he saw it. He sprang to his feet and returned the salute crisply. "Good. Action at last." Too much thinking, he could have added, but he kept that to himself.

He could see the men moving past him only as indistinct shapes, but he knew that, thanks to Begench and the two other sergeants, everything would be in fine order. He was sure each man had every piece of his equipment, that everything was in prime condition, and that each soldier could find his way even in the dark. The Soviet forces had had to withdraw from Afghanistan once, and the Spetsnaz had had to go with them despite the wish of some to remain and fight on behind the enemy's lines, but Pyotr and his fellows had taken with them the knowledge of how to fight the Mujahedeen, and they were going to use that knowledge now. They had also taken with them a burning hatred of the Mujahedeen and a devouring need to avenge their country's defeat, and that would drive them in this new war, drive them fiercely, make them unstoppable this time.

Begench led the way for the three-man team Pyotr had

assigned himself to. Pyotr had no problem letting the senior sergeant lead the team. Begench had proved himself repeatedly during the last Afghan war, and Pyotr trusted the man implicitly on a mission like this.

Yuri, a private, came next, carrying the RPG-7 by its handle.

Pyotr brought up the rear. He carried nothing. Just my immense authority, he thought, suddenly amused that the sergeant and the private led the way while the captain followed them and, unlike them, had nothing important to do.

They moved silently. Pyotr trusted—and hoped—that the other two teams were also moving silently as they headed toward their targets. He had been assured that the Mujahedeen had not issued any kind of night-vision equipment to their men in the field. Nor did they have airplanes to spare for this almost forgotten frontier. In this dry terrain, he knew they were raising dust as they moved, but small dust clouds would be invisible in the dark. No, sound was the danger. The sharp hearing of the Mujahedeen was legendary among Soviet troops, so much so that the average Soviet soldier attributed almost supernatural hearing to the enemy.

Supernatural hearing and supernatural silence. The Mujahedeen had won the last war partly by being able to move without the Soviets detecting them, not even with all their technological advantages.

Spetsnaz, though, were different. We outdid them at their own game, Pyotr remembered. We move even more silently than they do. He was suffused with justified pride.

There would have been no point in remaining behind to keep on fighting after the Soviet withdrawal, Pyotr knew. The function of the Spetsnaz during a war was to go in first, ahead of a general attack, and soften up the enemy. Sometimes, Spetsnaz sleeper agents would be stationed in a country years ahead of a planned invasion, their sole function to perform a specific act of sabotage before Soviet troops crossed the frontier. Others would be stationed in foreign countries to gather intelligence—spies, in other words, a job Pyotr knew was important but thought would probably be boring. But the real job of the Spetsnaz, in Pyotr's view, was to enter ahead of the main Soviet forces and clear the way.

As they would be doing tonight.

Gul Aman awoke an hour before dawn. Despite the blanket he was wrapped in, he shivered in the cold. He curled up and tried to ignore the cold and go back to sleep. He knew he had only been asleep for a few—too few—hours since being relieved by Abdul.

A faint memory intruded. A sound. Or had he dreamed it?

It was the cold that woke you up, he told himself. Abdul will hear any sounds, and he'll know what they are. If it's something to worry about, he'll alert us.

For a while, Gul dozed uneasily. The cold and a growing discomfort in his bladder kept him from sleeping properly. At the same time, he was too sleepy and the blanket, inadequate though it was, was too warm. He couldn't rouse himself enough to emerge into the cold air and walk away to relieve himself.

He opened his eyes slightly and watched the eastern horizon slowly appear in silhouette against the faint glow of the predawn sky.

He lay for some moments in a drifting, detached state. It was pleasant, watching the sky lighten. He could almost forget why they were there.

Then he heard someone snoring. It was a familiar sound.

It was Abdul.

Instantly, Gul was fully awake. He leapt to his feet. The blanket slipped to the ground. He was oblivious to the cold.

Furious, he strode over to the dark pile he knew was Abdul and kicked the man awake.

"What? What?" Abdul's sleepy face emerged from under his own blanket, just visible in the growing light. "Something wrong?"

"You were supposed to be on guard!"

Abdul groaned and pulled the blanket back over his face. "Nothing happening. No more war. Go away."

Gul was almost paralyzed by his anger. This was impossible! Abdul had never behaved this way in the old days. What had happened to him?

Still furious, Gul turned away and paced around the ledge they had chosen as their watch place.

They were alone on it, he and Abdul and Ahmet, the latter still sleeping soundly nearby. Dreaming dreams of conquest, no doubt. Their weapons were untouched, just as he had seen them at last light at the end of the previous day. He stared out into the distance, squinting, trying to penetrate the deep shadows that lay in the folds of the landscape.

Nothing moved. Nothing had changed.

Slowly, Gul relaxed. Perhaps Abdul was right, after all, and he was the foolish one. This wasn't the war. As Abdul had said, there was no more war. Maybe they weren't really needed here.

Gul sighed and stepped away from the others. He walked behind a large rock so that he would partly hidden, parted his robes, and began to urinate onto the ground.

For a moment, he reveled unthinkingly in the pleasure of

release. Then his thoughts began again, annoyingly. This was all so silly. What were they doing here? Playing soldiers!

He finished urinating, shook himself to get rid of the last drops, and decided to apologize to Abdul for the kicks. He'd let the other sleep until he woke up naturally, though.

The hillside above him exploded.

The concussion knocked Gul from his feet and slammed him against the rock he had been hiding behind. He was stunned by the impact, drifting, unaware of his crushed left shoulder. He slid helplessly to the ground.

Confused, unable to understand what was happening, Gul heard Abdul yell something. Then everything was drowned in an immense roar as the hillside collapsed.

Gul died almost instantly as tons of dirt and rock fell on him. The other two died in the same instant, Ahmet while he dreamed of conquest.

From just over 350 meters away, Pyotr Rodzhinsky watched the hillside roar down onto the ledge and the three Mujahedeen, and he smiled in satisfaction. The rockslide filled the narrow ledge and spilled over it, shooting dust and small stones into the air.

"Get down until it's over!" Begench shouted at him. Begench and Yuri huddled lower down, in the minimal shelter of the small rise.

The roar and rumble of the falling rocks almost drowned Begench out, but Pyotr heard him. He shook his head. He didn't want to miss an instant of this. He stayed in position, lying on his stomach at the top of the rise, his elbows resting almost where Begench's had the day before, holding his binoculars in front of him and watching the mountain bury the Mujahedeen. A stone hit the ground near his right elbow and bounced away. Something grazed his temple. He ignored it and watched, straining to see through the rising curtain of dust.

Satisfied at last, Pyotr slid down to where the other two men lay. "Good shot," he said to Yuri.

The sergeant and the private looked up cautiously. The noise had finally stopped. Begench rose to his feet and looked at their target. "Looks safe," he said. "Yes, good shot. I thought it would take two or even three to finish the job. Very unstable rock."

"It's an unstable country," Pyotr said. "Come on, let's get back to the rendezvous point and find out if the other teams had as much luck as we did."

Yuri folded the RPG–7's tripod and picked the weapon up by its handle. He stood obediently, waiting for the next order.

For the first time, Pyotr noticed the layer of dust over everything, including Begench and Yuri. He stood up, looked down at his uniform. He was surprised at how much dust there was on him. There were also tears in his clothing.

"You're bleeding, Comrade Captain," Begench said, pointing at Pyotr's face.

Pyotr rubbed a hand across his forehead. It came away covered with a smeared mixture of dust and blood. He felt no pain at all. All he felt was elation. "This is nothing," he said. "There'll be much more blood. But this time, thanks to Comrade Slonimsky, very little of it will be ours."

It was a coordinated attack of exquisite precision and paralyzing impact.

During the Soviet Union's previous attempt to conquer and hold Afghanistan, troop strength barely got above 100,000 men.

This time, Slonimsky was in charge, and he was not given to half—or one-tenth—measures. This time, one million men crossed the frontier.

Pyotr's team was just one of many advance units. Each had a similar mission. They attacked simultaneously, eliminating what little border defense there was. At the very instant Yuri fired his RPG-7, tanks began rolling across Afghanistan's long northern border with the Soviet Union. Just as in 1979, airborne troops landed in Kabul, and Spetsnaz troops appeared suddenly at airfields and government and communications sites.

Afghan government troops were disarmed and government officials were arrested and immediately shot—except for those who were actually Soviet plants.

In other parts of the country, the surprise attack was of a different type. Sometimes it's best to blind the enemy before attacking. Other times, it's best to go for the heart first.

Gulbuddin Hekmatyar bent over a map spread on a table. He was in the north, but his attention was focused on the south, on Kabul. He stroked his long, black beard. Founder of Hezbi Islami, still in his forties, recipient of millions in aid and armaments from the United States, he had spent years fighting the government with little effect other than to weaken it so that it could not resist attacks from the south by the Taliban. Now he wondered whether another rocket attack on Kabul would have any worthwhile effect. The approach he had pursued until now had begun to look pointless. Something new was called for.

Hekmatyar straightened and gestured. Abdelhalim Khairi, who had been standing patiently a few feet away while Hekmatyar pondered strategy, approached the table. "You have reached a decision?" Abdelhalim asked. "Shall I send the order for the bombardment?" Shall we impose more pointless misery on the people of Kabul, those who still remain? Shall your rockets rain down on the miserable, making them still more miserable?

Hekmatyar shook his head. "Not yet. There are other factors to consider." He smiled at his faithful and reliable aide. "Did you know that I've been approached by Dostum and the Hezbi Wahdat? They're interested in an alliance."

"You would ally with a Communist?"

"Former Communist." Hekmatyar shrugged. "Why not? It might be a faster route to power. We would rule jointly, but I would be the Prime Minister."

"Ruling over a pure Islamic state?" Abdelhalim hoped he had kept the sarcasm from his voice. None of this should matter to him, but he had begun lately to feel emotionally involved. That was dangerous. He was glad the schedule was what it was.

"How long have you been with me?"

"Almost two years," Abdelhalim said.

"Yes." Hekmatyar nodded. "And in that time, you've become my right hand. You know my thoughts and my deliberations, my strategies, my maneuverings. Your counsel has been invaluable. But sometimes you're surprisingly naïve. We have to deal with the world as it is, not as we think it should be." He walked to a window and leaned on the sill. "Look." He beckoned again.

Abdelhalim joined him at the window. Even through the thick glass of the closed window, he could see the carpet of brilliant stars that filled the northern night sky. He could also feel the cold radiating from the glass, and he could imagine the thin, dry air out there. There were hills to the north and west, but the eastern horizon was flat, and it was now dimly outlined against the first, faint glow of dawn. It was a beautiful country, in its stark, arid way, and he was coming to love it.

"This is my country," Hekmatyar said. "No one else is entitled to rule it the way I am. I will remake it in my own image. You have to understand that compromises are necessary. Often, one must appear to be something other than one really is for the sake of greater benefit in the long run. You can even say that one must tell lies in the service of a greater truth."

"You put my mind at ease."

Hekmatyar looked at him sharply, stared at him for a moment, then decided that he had spoken sincerely. "Good."

"You are the true Lion of the North," Abdelhalim said. This time, even greater sincerity and fervor resonated in his voice. "The Soviet Union knows that. At the moment, you concentrate on Kabul and your quest for power there, but even so you and your forces are the main barrier between the Soviets and the reconquest they long for."

"Very true," Hekmatyar said. He was flattered and made no effort to hide that. "Lion of the North. I like that! Yes, I'm what stands in their way. And once I control the government, they'll have to give up all thought of invading us ever again."

"Quite so," Abdelhalim said.

For a few minutes, both men were silent. They watched the eastern horizon grow more distinct, a sharp line against the glowing sky. Then at last the first red rays touched the tops of the western hills.

"So," Abdelhalim said. "It is time."

Hekmatyar turned to him with a questioning look. "Time for what?"

Abdelhalim drew a small automatic pistol from the folds of his robes and shot Hekmatyar between the eyes.

Leaving behind the body, with its frozen look of surprise, Abdelhalim walked calmly from the room, from the building, and from the town. No one else would enter that room for a couple of hours at least, he estimated. He would have all the time he needed.

He was a true native Afghan, but his loyalty was to a cause he considered greater than nationalism, greater than Islam. He served history, he served the proletariat, and for the last ten years, he had served the Soviet Union.

Pyotr Rodzhinksy was an optimist by nature, and his prediction that very little of the blood shed during the reconquest would be Soviet proved to be overly optimistic. In fact, a good deal of the blood was Soviet. But it was far less than half, and that was a small enough quantity to occasion rejoicing and not grief in Moscow.

Rather, there was grief, in Moscow and elsewhere, but not in official circles.

Pyotr knew too well how that grief would be initiated in many a family. A letter would arrive from Army headquarters, impersonal, written by some overworked and uninterested clerk, virtually a boilerplate with appropriate names inserted. "From the Ministry of Defense to so and so. Your son killed in action at such and such a date serving in such and such a regiment with our forces in Afghanistan." Some time later, a metal coffin, a "zinc," would arrive for burial. A sealed coffin, which the parents were forbidden to open. No last sight of the lost son would be permitted, no details about his death would be forthcoming. Some parents would wonder if the coffin truly contained their son, or someone else's. Some would even wonder if it contained a body at all or if it was being used to smuggle drugs back home.

The boy had served the Soviet Union and now his usefulness was at an end. His parents' grief would last their lifetimes.

Years earlier, a friend had passed to Pyotr copies of some letters written to the families of young American soldiers who had died during their country's foolish involvement in Vietnam. Those letters had been personal, individual, written by the boys' commanding officers in the field. Pyotr had been touched by the letters, moved by the genuine pain that shone through them, the sense of loss those officers had felt. That was something he understood quite well. Nothing could make up for the loss of a child, Pyotr knew, but surely those letters were better than the cold, formal one that was all Yuri's parents could expect—better both for the parents and for the officers who wrote them. Pyotr could never suggest that he be allowed to write a letter like those American ones he remembered. Such a letter would violate endless layers of secrecy. Such a suggestion on his part would raise suspicions about his loyalty. He could only write that letter in his imagination.

Encamped on a hillside above the smoking remains of a farming village, Pyotr formulated the letter in his mind. He tried to think of words that would comfort Yuri's parents, imagined himself writing the words on a sheet of lined paper, but the words and the paper vanished and he saw Yuri instead—Yuri as he had looked at that last moment of his life.

The image was a horror and a shame.

Now he had lost two of the ten men he had started with. The Pacification March, as it was being called, was far from over, and he feared there would be more deaths along the way. Twenty percent fatalities in his unit already! And he had been told not to expect reinforcements.

Every death hurt, and would hurt, but Yuri's had hit Pyotr particularly hard.

The action had been over, so they had thought. Every inhabitant of the village lay dead. A quarter of them had died in the initial assault—sudden, deadly, unexpected, unprovoked. Afterwards, Pyotr's men had lined up the terrified survivors in the open space at the center of the town and shot them in the back of the head, one by one. Children, women, men—old men, only, for unsurprisingly there were no young men there. Then they had shot the animals. Nothing was to be left to dilute the terror or lighten the countryside's sense of hopelessness. That was the whole point of the Pacification March. Villages were chosen at random and eliminated. No cruelty, no rape, no torture. Nothing stolen. But total destruction of human and animal life. Nothing was left. You see, was the message to the villages that survived, we are unstoppable, we are remorseless, we are a terrible force of nature. Cease all resistance, do our bidding instantly and completely, betray any of your countrymen who don't do the same, and perhaps you will survive. Perhaps.

Pyotr had put Begench in charge of the last part, the killing of the survivors and then the animals. He could handle the initial assault. Pretend the objective was a military target, an enemy stronghold, not a village of unarmed farmers. That was all right. That he could do. But when he faced the captives, bewildered and frightened civilians, and not even a young man of military age among them, when he actually looked into their eyes, saw their pleading looks, understood their delusion that his men were acting on their own accord and that he, an officer, would surely stop them, that was when Pyotr turned away from the task in revulsion and told Begench to finish it.

When the last shot had been fired, Begench had reported to his captain the job was done, and then Begench had shrugged, an eloquent gesture that said, These people don't count, they were just in the way.

It was an attitude Pyotr wished with all his heart he could adopt.

As Pytor's unit had marched away from the supposedly dead village, he had heard a distant popping sound. Yuri, marching just in front of him, carrying his RPG–7 as always, had slumped lifelessly to the ground, the left side of his head missing. Blood sprayed as Yuri fell. He fell on his left side. Red brain tissue spilled onto the dirt.

Pyotr forced that image away. He tried to summon again the image of a sheet of paper and his own hand writing on it.

My dear friends. I write to you as your son's commanding officer to express my deepest sympathy for your loss. Yuri was a fine young man and a fine soldier. I hope it gives you some comfort to know that he died in the service of the Soviet Union, while displaying great courage in the face of enemy fire. His comrades admired him and many owe their lives to him. They share my feelings and join me in extending condolences.

In the face of enemy fire? His back was to the enemy when he died! He had no chance to display courage or its opposite. For that matter, how much courage does it take to shoot a group of terrified, unarmed civilians?

The enemy fire that had killed Yuri had turned out to come from one of the burning buildings, a barn. Who was in there, and how he had managed to elude the seemingly thorough search

Pyotr's men had carried out after they'd captured the village, Pyotr had no idea. Nor did such details really matter, except as an object lesson to Yuri's surviving comrades about the value of thoroughness. In that sense, perhaps some of them might indeed owe their lives to Yuri some day, or at least to the way he had died.

Pyotr had let his men take out their fury at the treacherous enemy by firing into the burning barn until the building had collapsed entirely, sending up a geyser of flames and sparks.

Something had begun screaming within the fire at that moment. Begench had given the order to cease fire. The men had stood quietly, listening to the screams. It had gone on for what seemed like many minutes but surely, Pyotr thought later, could not have been. Surely it had been over in seconds. Surely, he told himself. Surely!

Satisfied at last, the unit had marched from the village a second time. This time, nothing fired at them. The only sound now was the crackling of the flames they left behind.

My deepest sympathies for your loss.

My deepest shame for the action which led to that loss. I no longer understand why we're doing this. No, I understand it, but I fear I can't tolerate it.

"Comrade Captain."

Pyotr looked up. Begench stood before him, calm and efficient, at attention but looking relaxed, subordinate but never subservient. Did the man ever feel moral qualms? Pyotr suspected not. But that was what made him so valuable, so indispensible, so much a rock. That's why he should be in command of this unit, not I, Pyotr thought.

"A good day's work, Captain," Begench said. "We've come 50 kilometers from Kariz–e Elyas Herat. I calculate that we've killed more than 600 of the enemy so far. That's more than twelve per kilometer. A good rate."

Pyotr laughed despite himself. "Other people measure a march in kilometers per day, but you measure it in enemy dead per kilometer."

"Of course, Comrade Captain. If kilometers per day were all that counted, we could have been transported by air. Deaths per kilometer is the whole point of this march, isn't it?"

Pyotr nodded and sighed. "Indeed it is. You're quite right about that."

Automatically, he looked around to make sure that they were alone. He had always trusted Begench with his secret thoughts. As for the others, he would trust them to cover his back in a firefight, he would trust them with his life in a desperate situation, but he didn't know which of them he could trust with knowledge of his political views. He was quite sure that there were one or two whom he must never trust with anything that could be used against him politically, but he had no idea which of his men those one or two were.

"What's the point of all of this?" Pyotr asked. He gestured toward the smoke rising from the village into the darkening sky. He kept his voice low. "This terror. This horror. It has no military value. We've been doing grim and dirty work over the last fifty kilometers. For what? We've already won this war. We won it in the first 100 hours. All that was left after that was mopping up, and our unit isn't even part of that. They're calling this the Pacification March." He shook his head. "I call it pointless terrorism."

For once, Begench looked worried. He lowered himself to the ground, sitting cross-legged like Pyotr, and he dropped all pretense of military formality. "You know why we're doing this, Pyotr. We made the mistake last time, thinking we'd won the war when we smashed what organized defense there was. The guerillas simply established themselves all over the countryside, thanks to the support of the people, the villagers like those ones." He, too, gestured toward the burning village. "But this time, they'll be too terrified to offer the guerillas any support, thanks to what we're doing on this march. Us and the other groups like us."

"That's the theory," Pyotr agreed, "but the reasoning is misguided. The guerillas will appear again, and if the villagers don't support them willingly, then the guerillas will take what they want by force. That's always the way it works, everywhere, in every guerilla war. It doesn't matter how much terror the government uses, or the conqueror in this case. The guerillas simply use more. And then we'll respond with still more terror. And they'll respond with even more yet. There'll be no end to it. This country will simply be destroyed. That's what it will mean to the people of Afghanistan. To us, guerilla warfare will mean a slow attrition of men and equipment. We'll be bleeding again, just like the last time. We had a brilliant victory, sudden and total. But in the long run, I'm afraid we'll be defeated again, just the same way we were before."

"No. We lost the last time because we were half-hearted. The men in Moscow have taken the lesson to heart. They've learned from what happened before. Slonimsky is strong. He knows what must be done. Because of him, we're strong, too."

Pyotr grunted. "I too approve of Slonimsky's strength and what he's done for our country. He is the indispensable man. But he's not infallible. I think he's wrong this time."

"So you're not sure your orders are the best ones possible. What will you do? Disobey them?"

"Of course not! I'm a soldier. I serve the Soviet Union. But my thoughts are my own."

"Always." Begench nodded his agreement. "Still, I'm glad to hear you intend to follow orders no matter what, Pyotr. That's what I told them when they asked me. 'You can depend on Comrade Rodzhinsky to follow orders to the letter and in an exemplary fashion and to keep any doubts to himself.' They don't want men who never question the wisdom of those above them, you know. They just want men who follow orders thoroughly and well regardless."

Pyotr was bewildered by this sudden change of tack. "'They'? What are you talking about? Who are 'they'?"

Begench smiled. "Why, the men at Khodinka, of course. My superiors."

Khodinka Airfield. Headquarters of the GRU. Pyotr was stunned and for a moment couldn't speak. His skin crawled. He wanted to scratch himself, to brush at whatever it was that seemed to be creeping around on him. With an effort he suppressed the urge and sat still. Then he said cautiously, "We're Spetsnaz. The men at Khodinka are our superiors, of course."

Begench smiled again. "Don't pretend to be naïve, Pyotr. I'm talking about my direct line of report. Through one chain of command, you're my superior. Through another, I report directly to Khodinka. I've been ordered to observe your behavior carefully and to report regularly."

Pyotr breathed slowly, deeply. Once. Twice. Then he said, "And what have you reported, if I may ask?" My friend, the man I trusted. What have you told them about me?

"You may ask, but I'm not allowed to tell you. However, I can tell you to rest easy. You have nothing to fear. In fact, very soon you will receive orders to return to Moscow and to go to Khodinka, where you will be given new training and a new assignment."

"What? But the march, the men. . . !"

"Both will be handled appropriately. I'm to replace you in command of this unit. I might even be made a lieutenant. Imagine me as a junior officer." For the first time, Begench looked uncertain. "You don't doubt that I can do it, do you, Pyotr?"

"I think you will do it frighteningly well. So what's this new assignment?"

Begench shook his finger. "Sorry. I can't tell you that, either. Just wait until you reach Moscow. Everything will be explained to you." He rose. He stood silently for a moment, looking down at Pyotr. Then he added, "The new training will be very difficult. Don't fail it."

Twelve

September 1991

Yegor Duridanov stood quietly, patiently, his AK-74 on his shoulder, waiting for his master to appear.

He tried to take pleasure in the quality of his weapon, which he kept perfectly cleaned and oiled, and in his new blue-and-gold uniform, which he kept spotlessly clean and perfectly pressed, and in his erect, military bearing, and in the company of his impressive, heroic comrades, and most of all in the surpassing importance of his assignment, which was to protect the life of the USSR's ruler, a man so many wanted to eliminate. But his feet hurt. His lower back hurt. And he was bored.

He had no idea how completely all of that was about to change.

Especially the boredom.

The door of the inner office opened noisily and Aleksander Slonimsky appeared. Tall, handsome, his back straight, his shoulders broad. If anything marred his heroic appearance, perhaps it was the trace of a self-satisfied smirk on his face. Yegor ignored that, for he was filled with admiration and something approaching worship for the man who had saved his country. Yegor and the other guards straightened to even stiffer attention, if that were possible.

Slonimsky saluted them. He marched through the anteroom to the corridor beyond. Yegor and his comrades fell in behind him and followed.

Through corridors and down stairways, the guards followed Slonimsky. Yegor's eyes roved steadily from side to side, looking for danger, for a threat, for an assassin. The hallways and staircases were empty, and that was a good thing for any would-be attacker, for Yegor and his fellows would have torn limb from limb anyone who threatened this man, this leader they protected and worshiped.

When they reached their destination, Slonimsky unlocked a door and entered, leaving Yegor and the others to guard the corridor while he took his pleasure within.

Yegor stood to the right of the door. Another guard stood to the left. The rest of them spaced themselves down the hallway in both directions. They remained still, silent, unmoving—except for their eyes, which moved constantly. No one would be allowed to endanger their master while he played.

Yegor had no idea what his comrades thought of all of this: it wasn't something he had discussed with them, and he would never raise the subject in the guard barracks. For himself, he felt no resentment, not even any moral disapproval. What applied to other men didn't apply to Aleksander Slonimsky. There was something about the man that made you feel that way. He was so sure of his special stature, special needs, special rights that you accepted his own opinion of that specialness without thinking twice about it.

But there was more to it than that. Yegor felt that Slonimsky deserved such rewards for what he had done for the country. Virtually singlehandedly, Slonimsky had saved the Soviet Union from collapse, from succumbing to the power of the West, which meant the military and economic power of America.

Now the USSR was once again a great power. Once again, the world listened respectfully to words issuing from Moscow. Once again, the other powers—even the Americans!—thought carefully and long about Moscow's reaction before planning any new military adventures.

What was even more, the disaster in the desert, the ongoing military catastrophe the West was suffering at the hands of the newly arisen Caliphate, was opening many new doors for the expansion of Soviet influence and rule.

The evening television news readers were circumspect about all of this. They beat about the bush. But Yegor could read between the lines. He understood that the Soviet empire was on the verge of sudden and astonishing expansion. His heart swelled at the thought of it. And he knew that there was one man who deserved the credit for the great change of national fortune. That man was Aleksander Slonimsky. Yegor was convinced that history would regard Slonimsky as the greatest leader Russia had ever had.

So of course such a man deserved recreation, relaxation, recuperation. For some men, that might take the form of playing cards, or drinking heavily, or watching a sporting event. For Slonimsky, apparently, it took the form of hours of sex with a beautiful woman. Well, so be it.

Not that Yegor would have minded a few hours of sex with a beautiful woman. With any woman, he reminded himself. Even half an hour.

Almost, he sighed. But he caught himself in time and managed to hold onto the stiff, stolid attentiveness that the other guards were demonstrating. Silence. Alert silence. That was what was required of him. And he would do it: he owed at least that much to Aleksander Slonimsky.

Yegor's feet and lower back began to hurt again.

Time passed. The guards were alone in the corridor. The walls and doors were thick, and no sounds came from the apartment.

Eventually there was a click, and the door through which Slonimsky had vanished earlier opened again. The General stepped through the doorway.

This time, Yegor noticed the smug look on his face and felt just a tickle of annoyance. Yegor might feel privileged to stand guard, and he understood that Slonimsky needed and deserved such release, but that smirk seemed to be rubbing Yegor's face in what Slonimsky had and he didn't.

Duty, Yegor reminded himself.

He turned to his left and stepped out into the hallway, ready to lead the detail in step behind Slonimsky. He stood at attention, waiting.

Holding the door open, Slonimsky turned to say goodbye to the woman inside the apartment.

Yegor turned his head unthinkingly to his left.

Maria Gorova stood just inside the apartment. She wore shorts, athletic shoes, and a tank top, as if she were a runner competing on a track somewhere, outside in the summertime.

Yegor stared, unable to tear his eyes away. His heart skipped a beat. Two beats. Three.

He gasped, filled his lungs.

And hoped Slonimsky had not heard him.

Fortunately, the General was occupied with his farewells.

For no real reason, and despite her name, Yegor had assumed that Gorova was Asiatic, perhaps from Mongolia. Small and dark, he had thought. Exotic. And certainly weak and submissive—that would be Slonimsky's preference in a mistress.

But this woman standing in the doorway, embracing Slonimsky briefly as though she were his equal, why, she was muscular, robust, blonde and blue eyed, a true Slavic heroine. She might be a descendant of one of the northern goddesses the ancient Slavs had brought south with them.

Yegor had spent many happy hours as a boy reading the *Povest vremennykh let,* despite his schoolmaster's disapproval of the version of early Slavic history that ancient document contained. From that, he had progressed to a variety of Scandinavian and Icelandic tales. Yegor's imagination and his budding desires had both been fired by the stories of powerful blonde heroines, warrior women, fully a match for the mighty men of their times. He had dreamed of such women. They had figured in his daydreams of adventure and his erotic fantasies. No real woman, no matter how classically blonde and Slavic, or tall, or athletic, had matched those fantasies. He would glance at them and dismiss them.

But now he was transfixed. Here she was: his dream.

And then Gorova looked at him over Slonimsky's shoulder, caught and held his gaze, and looked into his soul.

Slonimsky released her, stepped back. He came between them, blocking Gorova from Yegor's view.

The door closed. She was gone.

Yegor felt it like a physical blow, a tearing loss.

This is absurd! he told himself. A woman you don't know, a woman it would endanger your life to try to know, a woman who doesn't know you and surely has no wish to know you—how can you let yourself fall into this adolescent trap?

But she's the one! he thought. She's the one I've waited for all my life. Longed for. She's the only one in the world! How can I turn away and forget what just happened?

And then he had to turn away, for Slonimsky had begun walking briskly down the corridor. Yegor had to almost jump forward to catch up with him and take his proper place just behind him—guardian of the General, leader for the moment of the General's other guards.

All the way back to the General's office, the marching tramp of their boots became the cadence of his thoughts: *She's real! She's real! She's real! She's real!*

Yegor was off duty the following morning, when Slonimsky next went to visit Gorova. One of the other guards mentioned the visit casually in passing in the barracks, saying that he had happened to glimpse the General's current mistress and couldn't understand why a man who could have his pick of beautiful women would choose someone so large, so ordinary, so very Russian.

"If I was Slonimsky," he confided to Yegor, after looking around carefully to make sure no one else could hear him, "I'd write to my friends in Peking and ask them to send me a girl from there. Chinese women! Ahh!" He licked his lips. "But this one," he added, "why, she's as tall as I am! Almost as broad across the shoulders, too, I swear it. You should have seen her."

Yes, Yegor thought, I should have. "Valya, you've never even been to China," he said.

"Mongolia. Close enough." Kikorov licked his lips. "What a time that was."

"You've already told me about it," Yegor said curtly. He couldn't bear another telling of Kikorov's awful stories of the things he had done in Mongolia. "Enough."

Yegor began pulling double duty, taking on others' shifts, so that he could be sure to be on station whenever Slonimsky was in his Kremlin office. He made sure he was always the one standing to the right of the doorway while Slonimsky was in Gorova's apartment. That way, when Slonimsky emerged, Yegor could, without anyone suspecting anything, step away from the wall, execute a left face, and turn his head slightly and look through the open door.

Only rarely was Gorova there, bidding Slonimsky farewell, dressed as she had been that first time. Often, she wasn't visible at all. But he thought—assured himself it wasn't his imagination—that she started to come to the door more frequently to say her goodbyes, and that she looked for him deliberately. Looked at him whenever she could do so without Slonimsky noticing. Stared at him for a long moment. Daring him, challenging him? Mocking him? Yegor had no idea which it was. All he knew was that he wanted to be there to see her whenever it was possible, to see her and to hold her gaze for that precious instant.

When the General left the city for one of his rare trips to the provinces or his even rarer trips to foreign capitals, then Yegor caught up on sleep. Or tried to. No matter how exhausted he was, Maria Gorova haunted his thoughts. He developed a strange and disturbing physical condition that caused him to visit a military doctor, who told him, in a scandalized tone, to stop masturbating so much or at least to do it more gently.

He could see in the mirror how gaunt he was becoming, how dark the shadows under his eyes were. He told himself how silly this was—to lose sleep, to endanger his health over a woman he had seen, really, only a handful of times, who was at best amusing herself with his reaction, and worst of all who was the property of one of the most dangerous men in the world. Then he would immediately tell himself that she wasn't just amusing herself. No, she was as drawn to him as he was to her! She wanted something from him—sex, love, rescue. Whatever it was, he was ready to provide it.

What did she do in that apartment the rest of the time, when Slonimsky wasn't with her? Yegor never saw her outside the apartment. He made cautious—very cautious—inquiries, satisfying himself that she spent her life in there. She ate in there. She obviously exercised in there. And of course she slept in there, both alone and with Slonimsky.

At that last image, Yegor ground his teeth. His adulation for the General who had saved his country and restored it to a place of strength and respect in the world began to give way to something darker. Yegor's love for and desire to serve the Soviet Union was just as strong as ever, but he found himself wondering if General Slonimsky's way was the only way to govern the country. Perhaps his methods had been necessary at first, when the country was so weak, so capitulatory, when it was in the hands of men who were little better than traitors. But the necessary but nasty work had been done—by Slonimsky, admittedly—so wasn't it time to change tactics and make the country a more pleasant place to live? Or at least a safer place for women like Maria Gorova?

For Yegor was sure now that Gorova hadn't taken on the job of being Slonimsky's mistress. How could she? No, impossible! Threats, blackmail: it must have been something like that. She was trapped and needed rescuing. That was the meaning of her desperate, pleading look!

But what could he do about it? He knew that there were other guards stationed in that hallway even when Slonimsky wasn't there. Not Slonimsky's personal guards, but armed and alert men, nonetheless. He couldn't just walk up to the door, knock, and ask to be let in. He wouldn't even reach the door, and he probably wouldn't live for long after trying.

At least she's not in serious physical danger, he told himself. As long as she stays on the General's good side, she'll be safe.

I'm in much more danger than she is, because of my thoughts.

Yegor's diligence and his seemingly eternal presence guarding Slonimsky had not gone unnoticed. He rose swiftly through the ranks of the guards. He had been a junior sergeant when he was recruited into Slonimsky's guards. Within three months, he had been promoted twice and had attained the rank of senior sergeant.

This was an even more impressive feat than it would havc been in the regular army. There, the total number of men under arms was growing rapidly because of the aggressive draft system, thereby creating a growing need for officers of all ranks, even while the steady drain of battlefield losses kept opening up new slots. By contrast, Slonimsky's personal guard was fairly small and stable, although members of it did disappear occasionally with no explanation ever being given to their comrades. As it happened, both a sergeant and a senior sergeant had been among those who disappeared during Yegor's three months.

So it was Senior Sergeant Yegor Duridanov whom General Slonimsky turned to when he needed a delicate task performed yet again. The last time, Yegor's predecessor had done the job and had done it well. But that man was gone. Slonimsky sighed at the thought. He had been a good man, in most respects. What a shame he had betrayed Slonimsky's trust. On a fairly minor matter, to be sure, but Slonimsky felt that in his position he couldn't afford to ignore even slight infractions. It was necessary to make examples of transgressors in order to keep would-be transgressors terrified. An example had certainly made of that guard. Slonimsky smiled at the memory.

But what a loss to the guard!

Four months ago! he thought in wonder. That long! It seemed like yesterday. It was in the time of Gorova's predecessor.

Gorova had been living in that apartment for close to three months already. Slonimsky shook his head in amazement. It was too long, far too long. Dangerously long. Well past time to end it. She had lasted far longer than any of the others, and he would miss her for longer than he had missed any of the others. It would be difficult at first. He would be lonely for a while.

Slonimsky forced his moment of self-pity away and stepped to the door of his office. He opened it and called out, "Senior Sergeant Duridanov, please come here."

It was useful to single men out occasionally. They and their fellows would be filled with fear and uncertainty for a moment. Those not called upon would experience both envy and a hope that the man who had been singled out was about to be removed, perhaps opening up the chance of a promotion. And then the man himself, once he realized that he was not to be punished but instead honored with a personal mission from Slonimsky, would be filled with pride and with even stronger devotion to his General.

Subduing and controlling men without breaking them was a fine art, Slonimsky thought. All the great conquerors of history had mastered that art, and so had he.

Yegor marched into the room, stopped in front of Slonimsky, and saluted. He stood stiffly at attention, the ever-present weapon at his shoulder.

Slonimsky considered telling him to stand at ease but then decided not to. He wanted to see how long the young man could hold that brace without trembling.

Slonimsky stepped away from Yegor and examined him. The guardsman looked worn and tired. Slonimsky frowned and wondered for a moment if he had chosen the right man for this mission. Perhaps this sergeant's nerve wasn't as strong as Slonimsky had assumed? But then he saw how still and straight the young man stood, how strong his self-control was, and he knew had made the right choice.

Leaving Yegor standing at attention, Slonimsky closed the door and then went behind his desk and sat down. He leaned forward, his elbows on his desk, his fingers laced. "This is such an historic room," he said. "Dmitri Yazov was standing just about where you are when he died. I'm sure you didn't know that." He nodded gravely. "Important history has been made here. And now I have a mission for you, Senior Sergeant, that will also be part of our history. Oh, it won't be in the textbooks. In fact no one but you and me and a very few others will ever know about it all. But it's very important to the security of the nation nonetheless. There will be no physical danger to you, although you might find it ... well, 'distasteful' would be the right word. Which I would certainly understand and for which no one would blame you. After all of that, are you willing to do this job for me?"

Whatever it was, if it would keep Yegor close to this dangerous tyrant and therefore close to Maria Gorova, Yegor would do it. "Certainly, General. I serve the Soviet Union."

Slonimsky waited for a few seconds. When Yegor said nothing, Slonimsky prompted, "And?"

"Oh, and you, General. I serve you above all."

Slonimsky smiled. He was a bit annoyed, though. Even though this man hadn't been taught to say that he served General Slonimsky, he should have understood what he was supposed to say. Perhaps it was time to issue an edict changing the standard phrase appropriately. "I serve General Slonimsky and the Soviet Union." Yes, that had the right tone. For that matter, Slonimsky thought, it was probably also time to award himself the rank of Generalissimo. Only Stalin had ever held that rank before in the Soviet Union, and Slonimsky was already well on his way to surpassing Stalin both in territorial gains and in domestic power. And with fewer deaths and far less damage to the economy and infrastructure.

Time enough later for self-congratulation, Slonimsky thought.

So he explained to Senior Sergeant Duridanov what had happened to Maria Gorova's predecessors, what must happen to her now, and what role Yegor was to play in all of this.

"In just a few minutes," Slonimsky said, "I'll be going to that apartment for one last visit. As usual, you and your comrades will stand guard. When I leave, the other guards will leave with me, but you will stay behind. Don't worry, no one will challenge you. This time, I will have left the door unlocked."

For the first time, Yegor realized that Gorova had no control over whether her door was locked. That was done entirely from the outside. He found this particularly shocking—but not as shocking as what he heard next.

"You will enter the apartment and lock the door behind you. You will then kill Maria Gorova. Don't worry about noise. That suite of rooms is extremely well soundproofed. You may use a gun or a knife if you must, but I would prefer that you strangled her. I'll want those rooms ready for use again fairly soon, and blood and bullet damage can take quite a while to clean up and repair properly." He looked around his office with an expression of distaste. "I don't think it can ever be done properly.

"Now, when all of that is taken care of, you will carry her body to the following location." He described carefully an area of the building where Yegor had been taken once on an orientation tour, right after joining the guard. "You can find that?"

"Yes, General." The words came automatically. My God! he was thinking. My God!

"You were shown a staircase there but you weren't taken down it. Correct?"

"Yes. General."

"Take the body down that staircase. At the bottom, there is a furnace room. A man will be waiting for you down there. He will help you put the body into the furnace. Watch him and make sure he does his job right away, which is to turn up the flames so that the body is destroyed. You don't have to wait for the process to be complete," Slonimsky added reassuringly. "It takes quite a while, and that's the distasteful part I mentioned. When you're sure the process is underway, you can leave and return to your barracks. Take a day or two of leave. No more will be said about any of this, but I assure you I will remember your faithful service in this difficult and important matter. Do you understand everything?"

"Yes, General. May I make a request?"

Slonimsky frowned. "What is it?"

"I'd like to have Junior Sergeant Valentin Kikorov accompany me on this mission. I feel that two men would be preferable, both for the initial action and for the transport of the body."

"Hmm." Slonimsky looked Yegor up and down. "She's certainly very strong." He smiled in reminiscence. "I have good reason to know that. Yes, perhaps two men would be better for the initial action, as you called it. And for carrying the body, which will be quite heavy. All right, Sergeant. I grant that request. I'll be ready to leave in a few minutes. You're dismissed."

Yegor saluted, about faced, marched to the office door, opened it, and left. He was the picture of the disciplined, controlled Soviet soldier, but his mind was in turmoil.

A plan to save Maria Gorova had sprung full–blown into his mind, instantaneously. Could he pull it off? How could he not!

He closed the door behind him as he left the office. He kept marching through the outer room, gesturing to Kikorov to follow.

Yegor went into the hallway beyond the outer office, where there was a degree of privacy, and stopped. He looked Kikorov up and down. Yes, it would work. It would have to! There would be only one chance. "Valya, the General has a special assignment for us. For you and me."

"For me? Really?" Kikorov swelled with pride. "I'm ready! Whatever it is, I'm ready!"

He really is, Yegor thought. He'll have no compunction, whatever the orders are. Unlike me.

"The General will be visiting Maria Gorova in a few minutes. We'll accompany him and guard the door while he's inside her apartment, as usual."

"Ah, if only I were the General!"

"Pay attention, Valya!" Yegor went on to describe what was supposed to happen to Gorova after Slonismky left. He said only the minimum, but Kikorov understood everything immediately.

"He's tired of her," Kikorov said. "Good. Maybe he'll replace her with a Chinese woman."

"Say nothing to the others. The General was insistent about this. This is a special, secret duty assigned to the two of us. He's depending on us to be discreet, silent, and efficient."

Kikorov stood even straighter. "He can depend on me!"

"Yes. We'll both do what is required of us. Now we'll rejoin the others. Do everything as usual, but when the General leaves the woman's apartment to return to his office, stay behind with me."

They returned to their stations in the outer office and waited.

Shortly afterward, Slonimsky came out of his office and started off on his usual walk through the ancient building toward Gorova's apartment.

The apartment currently and temporarily occupied by Gorova, Yegor reminded himself. Was the smirk more pronounced than usual, the smugness greater, the swagger more noticeable? Yegor told himself he was imagining things. How could a man smirk or swagger even more than usual when he knew he was on his way to his last assignation with his mistress, and he had given orders that she was to be killed afterwards? Why, such a man would be a true monster! But then, surely Slonimsky was a monster just for wanting this last assignation, this last chance to use the woman's body before her murder.

A monster, yes, Yegor told himself. He is a monster. Any betrayal—no, any act of resistance, of defiance, anything that interferes with his life—is an act of patriotism.

Slonimsky reached his mistress's apartment, entered it, did whatever he did within it. Yegor stood on guard outside, his face impassive, his bearing erect, his stomach churning.

It seemed like hours before Slonimsky emerged again.

Gorova wasn't visible in the open doorway. The General pulled the door to behind him, caught Yegor's eye and nodded slightly, then strode away. This time, Yegor was sure that the smirk, the smugness, the swagger were all more pronounced.

Yegor and Kikorov remained behind. If the other guards were surprised, they were also too well trained, not to mention too well cowed, to say anything. They marched away behind Slonimsky, filling in the two spaces without the need for orders. Yegor imagined he could read their minds: If it's okay with the General, then I'm not going to be the one who makes waves.

The tramp of the guards' boots echoed away into silence. The hallway seemed to be empty except for the two of them.

Yegor put his hand against the door timidly, paused, then pushed on it. It was heavy, difficult to move. He pushed harder, and it swung open silently on its heavy, well-oiled hinges.

The two of them stepped quietly into the apartment. They could hear the sound of a shower running in another room.

The floor was covered in thick carpets that silenced their

footsteps—something Yegor had never noticed before, thanks to his obsession with Gorova, but for which he was now glad. He pushed the door closed behind them. He wished there were some way of locking the door from the inside.

Kikorov looked around at the expensive furniture and whistled. "Nice!"

Maria Gorova came into the room suddenly. She was dressed as she had been every other time Yegor had seen her. "What are you men doing here?" she demanded. "Get out immediately, or I'll call the General!"

Yegor's heart lurched. He wanted to say something reassuring, but before he could think of anything, Kikorov laughed and said, "You silly bitch! The General sent us. We're here to kill you. Maybe we'll have some fun with you first, though."

Gorova looked at Yegor. She said nothing.

"Be silent, Valya," Yegor ordered.

Kikorov shrugged. He continued to stare at Gorova, though. "Strong," he whispered. "She'll put up a good fight, eh, Yegor?"

Yegor swung his AK-74 suddenly. The barrel smashed into Kikorov's forehead. Kikorov collapsed onto the carpet and lay motionless.

Gorova stepped toward Yegor, her hands coming up. He pointed his weapon at her. "Stay back! Take off your clothes."

Startled, she stopped moving. Then she laughed. "My God, you're going to rape me and then murder me?"

"Don't be a fool. I want you to switch clothes with him." He gestured with his chin toward Kikorov. "You're about the same size and coloring."

Gorova understood immediately. "Clever," she said. "I always knew you'd help me when the time came." She reached behind herself to undo her top.

She was naked in seconds. She stood still, letting Yegor stare at her. He thought, Truly, she's a goddess!

Kikorov stirred and moaned.

Gorova reached out a long, muscular leg and prodded Kikorov. "Were you told to shoot me?"

"No. Too messy. We were supposed to strangle you."

Gorova nodded. "Good idea. Sasha is a clever man, too. Well, then." She stepped over to Kikorov, stood over him with one foot on either side of his chest, leaned forward, and placed her hands carefully around his neck. "You probably would have made a mess of it anyway," she said. "This is the way it's done."

Kikorov opened his eyes. He winced and looked around in confusion. "What. . . ?"

Gorova leaned forward, putting her weight on her hands. She grunted with effort. The muscles of her forearms bulged.

Yegor heard something crack. Kikorov's back arched. His eyes bulged. Veins stood out on his forehead. He clawed desperately at Gorova's wrists. Then his arms fell loosely to the floor, his eyes rolled back in their sockets, his face grew slack.

Gorova straightened. "You see? It's easy. You could learn to do that, too."

She was a warrior maiden bestriding the vanquished foe, Yegor thought. Terrible, terrifyingly desirable.

"Help me undress him," Gorova said. "Be careful, though. His body might relieve itself. I don't want that in the clothing."

Yegor roused himself. He couldn't stand there, frozen with a mixture of desire and fear. How could she respect him if she saw his reaction? He had to be businesslike, efficient, calm. Like her.

"Do you have other clothing?" he said. "I was wrong. We

can't use those skimpy clothes of yours. We have to cover him up. The size and coloring are right, but that's all."

She bent forward and stroked her victim's face. The gesture seemed almost tender. "A good shave, fortunately. Yes, you're right. Wait here."

She went into one of the interior rooms and came out a few seconds later with some clothing over her arm. She laid it out on the floor next to the body. Heavy trousers, long boots, a thick sweatshirt with a hood. Suitable clothing for the outside, the way the weather was this year, or for the colder parts of the building. Also loose, bulky, and disguising—sufficiently so, Yegor hoped.

"Good, all right," he said. He hoped his voice was calm and emotionless. He could no longer tell.

Dressed in the heavy, bulky clothing, Kikorov's body could easily be mistaken for Gorova's. Or so Yegor hoped.

Certainly Gorova, dressed in Kikorov's uniform and with the cap pulled low over her brow, looked like a male guard—a powerful, dangerous one.

A Valkyrie, Yegor thought.

My God, I'm completely infatuated with her! I'm lost, utterly lost.

Gorova slid her hand downward over Kikorov's face, pulling his eyelids down over his bulging eyes. The eyes wouldn't close entirely, but their strange appearance was less noticeable at first glance. She frowned, then pulled the sweatshirt collar up over Kikorov's nose. Still not good enough. She shook her head and muttered in annoyance. She bent the body's head forward, then pushed sharply. Yegor heard another crack, a much louder one this time. The head stayed in its forward position. Gorova nodded. "Okay, let's go."

Yegor lifted the shoulders and she took the feet. It was surprisingly easy to touch the body, to think of it as an object and not something that had once been a living comrade in arms.

Together, they carried the body out of the apartment and in the direction Slonimsky had described. By the time they reached the staircase, Yegor was panting and sweating. Gorova seemed unaffected. She moved and breathed as easily as she had at the beginning.

Yegor tried to hide from her that he was out of breath. He nodded toward the staircase. "Down there. This is the hard part."

"Yes. I'd better go first."

Yegor started to protest, but he could see that she was right. She clearly had more stamina than he did, and he had begun to think that she was probably stronger, too.

They went down the stairs carefully, carrying Kikorov's body. The staircase turned to the left at a right angle every ten steps. They seemed to be in a shaft, with gray concrete walls on all four sides and a dim light at each landing. Yegor tried to estimate how deep they were going, but he soon lost count. He could think of little besides the growing ache in his shoulders and knees, and of his weakening fingers.

And of Maria Gorova.

He couldn't let go of the body, though. He couldn't let himself so much as slow down, and certainly he couldn't complain. Gorova kept moving downward steadily, easily, showing no effects of the exertion. She did most of the work of maneuvering the body around each right-angle turn.

It's just because I've been getting so little sleep, he told himself. That's my problem.

But truly, she is a goddess!

It grew hotter as they went down. The air was thick with humidity and the smell of something burning—wood, he thought, but he couldn't be certain. He could hear the furnace now, the muted roar of its flames, the clanging of metal. He was drenched with sweat. His arms trembled. He could even see sweat on the back of Gorova's neck. He felt surprised at that.

At last the descent ended and they found themselves in a gloomy cavern, its far walls and ceiling lost in the darkness. Directly ahead was the furnace. Orange-white flames showed through the small, thick round window set into the metal door. "Let's put him down here," Yegor said. He barely managed to set the upper part of Kikorov's body on the concrete floor before it slipped from his grasp. Gorova set her end down carefully.

A tall, slender man stepped from the shadows. He ignored both of them. His eyes were fixed on the corpse lying on the concrete floor. Yegor stiffened in alarm. In the dim light, it was even harder to tell whether the corpse was that of a man or a woman, but he remembered that he had referred to it as "him." Surely this man had heard him.

The tall man prodded the body with his shoe. "Ah, the General's latest." His voice was soft, a baritone murmur, almost lost in the background noise. "I was told to expect her. She's large. I'd heard that." His face was long, lined, gray. He looked up suddenly and stared at Yegor. "You can go away now. You've done your duty, soldier. Just leave her to me. I'll take care of everything." He licked his lips, a gesture so like Kikorov's characteristic one that Yegor jumped.

From the corner of his eye, he saw Gorova stiffen. He sensed that she was infuriated and about to attack the man. "No!" Yegor said loudly, startling both of them. "I have my orders. Direct from

General Slonimsky himself. We're to wait here until you've placed the body in the furnace and begun to burn it up. We're going to watch until you do that."

The man glared at him. "After all my faithful service, you're claiming the General still doesn't trust me? Is that what you're saying, soldier?"

"I'm saying that I have my orders. And that it was General Slonimsky who gave me those orders, in person. Would you like me to report back to him that you refused to do as he ordered?"

"It's usually this way," the other man muttered. "And why? What a waste! They're still young and beautiful when they reach me. He has no more use for them." He sighed. "Ah, well. Maybe next time. All right, then. You two will have to do the lifting. I'm not well."

He stepped over to the furnace door, wrenched the big handle downward, and swung the door open. It moved slowly, massively.

The basement lit up with the glow of the flames. Heat washed over them.

"Hurry up!" the man shouted. "I don't like having this door open!"

Yegor and Gorova picked up the body. Again, she carried the feet.

Kikorov's body seemed heavier, as though it was fighting against its fate now that it had seen the flames.

Just a foretaste, Valya, Yegor thought.

They carried the body to the open door. The bottom of the door was waist high. Gorova held the ankles in one hand and placed her other under the body's thighs. She heaved the lower half of the body over the ledge of the door and set it down on the ledge. Then she helped Yegor shove the body in the rest of the way. They gave it a final push so that it rolled onto the glowing bed of the furnace. The burning coals shifted beneath the weight. The body turned over slowly in the flames. The head tilted back, and the sweatshirt slid down to a normal position. Kikorov's face looked out at them impassively. The eyes were still almost closed.

The tall man pushed them away and slammed the door shut. "At last," he said. His breath wheezed. "It's done. Now go away."

"Just a moment." Yegor steeled himself and peered through the small window. He wanted to be sure, before he left, that the flames had done enough to erase the corpse's true identity.

He stood so that neither of the other two could see into the furnace. He looked through the small window, staring into Kikorov's face.

The clothing was afire. Flames flickered around the dead man's face. Kikorov's hair flared and then quickly vanished, reduced to a black stubble. His eyelids slid up, and his bulging eyes started back at Yegor. His mouth opened. The body moved, twisted slightly, repeating in a subdued way how Kikorov had arched his back and struggled when Gorova had killed him.

Horrible fear clutched at Yegor. Valya was still alive! He was being burned to death!

But he told himself that couldn't be. It was just some strange reaction of the dead skin and muscles to the awful heat.

Still Kikorov stared at him. How do you like this? he seemed to be saying. Eh, comrade? Your handiwork! His eyes bulged even more.

His left eye burst. Then the right.

At last the skin and flesh darkened and began to fall away. The charred remnants of the clothing were indistinguishable from what was left of the body itself. The legs began to fold up, the knees drawing up to the chest, the arms tucking against the sides. Kikorov seemed to be shriveling, returning to fetal form.

Yegor sighed with relief. No one could identify him now. Soon only bones would be left. A careful examination of those would reveal that it was a man's body that had been burned here, not a woman's, but how likely was such an examination?

Yegor turned away from the furnace. "What do you do about the bones?" he asked. "And the teeth." He had just remembered that teeth often survived fires. Those would make identification easier than the bones would.

"We leave them in there, of course," the tall man said. "What else should we do with them? They don't take up much room." He laughed. "Why, that furnace contains a record of the General's love life! Well, the part of it that he's conducted in the Kremlin, anyway."

The man's frankness was astonishing. Perhaps the heat down here and seeing the furnace used this way had affected his mind.

"Thank you," Yegor said. "We have to leave now. I'll be sure to tell the General how helpful you were."

"Why so fast? You've done your job. Now you can relax. No one visits me down here. I have some interesting ... mementos. I'd like to show them to you."

Yegor shivered. Once again, he sensed violence building in Gorova. "We have another assignment to take care of right away. Come, Valya!"

As they were climbing the stairs side by side, she leaned toward him and muttered, "No one would have known for days. You should have let me—"

Yegor put his finger to his lips.

Gorova said nothing.

They walked in silence until Yegor had led them out of the building.

As they were crossing Ivanovskaya Square, Yegor tried to break through the ice that seemed to have formed around her. "You used to see civilians here, in the old days. Before the General took over, I mean. I came here as a boy myself, a few times, when I was a Young Communist."

"No," Gorova said thoughtfully, "Sasha wouldn't want civilians wondering around loose inside these walls. Not even Young Communists. Where are we headed?"

"To the barracks. That's where we'd be expected to go. Valya and I, I mean."

"So I'm to spend the rest of my life wearing this uniform and living in a barracks surrounded by young men? Interesting."

"No, of course not! I just have to sign us both out there. We have leave coming. The General said to take some leave as a ... " He stopped himself in time.

"As a reward." She nodded. "Yes, I'd have done the same thing, in his place."

"Good God! How can you talk that way? Don't you realize that I've given up my entire career for you?"

Gorova smiled. "Don't be angry. Once we get out of this place, I'll reward you."

"I don't want a reward! I want... I don't know what I want." I want to follow you to the ends of the earth, he thought. I want to be by your side for the rest of my life.

"We'll see what we can do," she said. "By the way, what's your name? I know I'm Valya, but I don't know who you are."

"Yegor Duridanov. And your name is Valentin Kikorov. I know your real name, though. Can I call you Masha?"

She shrugged. "If you like."

"Ah, there!" The entrance to the barracks lay ahead. He found that he welcomed it. The conversation, such as it was, had been more unpleasant than the silence which had preceded it.

The barracks were new, less than six months old. They were set into the corner where the southern and eastern walls met, just below the Beklemishevskaya Tower.

Despite being so new, the barracks building itself was small, cramped, and uncomfortable, and normally Yegor hated being inside it. But there was a way to get on the roof, and from there one could look over the wall and have a fine view of the river and down the Ordynka. He was sure Gorova would love it after being confined within her apartment for so long. But as they approached the small, dark entrance to the barracks, with a soldier standing guard beside it, she stopped.

"Yegor," she said in a low voice, "do I have to go in there with you? People who knew Kikorov will be looking at me close up. They'll know right away I'm an impostor."

She was right, of course. "No, you don't have to." He tried to keep the disappointment from his voice. "I can sign us both out. After all, I'm a senior sergeant." He hoped that would impress her, at least.

"Good. Fine. Hurry up, then." She looked around and shivered—the first sign of nervousness Yegor had seen in her. "I really want to get out of this place as soon as possible."

Despite his bravado about his rank, Yegor had feared that there might be difficulties—especially if Major Luzhkov was on duty, for he enjoyed making life difficult for the men under him.

Major Luzhkov was indeed on duty, but he was obsequious, as though Yegor held the higher rank. "Leave authorizations and passes for both you and Junior Sergeant Kikorov? Of course! I have them ready for you. Here they are."

"You had them ready? Comrade Major, how did you know—"

"Oh, I received a call from the General's office a while ago. I'm to congratulate you and Kikorov on the fine work you did on that special assignment. Whatever it was," he added hurriedly, obviously eager to assure Yegor that he wasn't prying. "Where is the junior sergeant? I wanted to congratulate him, too."

"He's waiting outside. He's really eager to get going and enjoy his leave."

Luzhkov laughed heartily. "I should think so! After pulling off a difficult task, of course you both want to go and enjoy yourselves. I hope you'll do me the favor of letting the General know that the papers were ready and waiting for you. And that I congratulated you on the successful completion of your mission."

"Your concern for your men is legendary throughout the Kremlin, Comrade Major." Yegor took the papers and escaped as quickly as he could.

Later, as they walked side by side down Bolshaya Ordynka, Yegor told Gorova about his encounter with Luzhkov. He tried to make it a humorous anecdote, something that would make her laugh or at least smile. Something that would make her like him. He also wished that she weren't still disguised as a fellow soldier. If she had been dressed in women's clothing instead, he would have been able to argue that, to avoid suspicion, they should act like a soldier and his girlfriend. I should put my arm around your waist, he would say. But in truth, even if she had been wearing a dress, he wasn't sure he would have the courage to make such a suggestion. So he concentrated instead on aping Luzhkov's mannerisms.

"He sounds like a typical thickheaded uniformed dolt," she said impatiently. Then she smiled to soften the insult and added, "You're one of the rare exceptions. We're walking south, aren't we?"

"Yes, we are."

"Why? Did you have a specific destination in mind?"

He had to admit that he didn't. "I just wanted to get as far away from the Kremlin as possible, as quickly as possible. We should probably get out of the city, too."

Gorova nodded. "Oh, yes. That was my intention all along. However, I wanted to go the Leningrad railway station. Which," she added, gesturing over her shoulder with her thumb, "is back that way."

He stopped. "Oh, I didn't—I should have asked you. I didn't realize you had plans other than surviving." He turned around.

Gorova grabbed his arm and then quickly released it. "No! We'll keep heading south. We'll take a circular route back to the Leningrad station. I don't want to go past that place again." She shivered, quickly controlled it. "That would arouse suspicion. We're supposed to have known where we were going when we left."

They resumed walking south. "Why Leningrad?"

"Because I want to get a train to Helsinki."

"Helsinki!" Yegor laughed. "I don't think our papers will let us go there!"

"No, of course not. I'll be picking up other papers along the way."

"I don't understand."

"I'm going to teach you a thing or two, Yegor Duridanov. Just stay by my side for a while."

Forever! "All right."

They walked silently for a while. Then Yegor said, "We'll take a train to Leningrad, then. That's where you'll get us our next set of papers?"

"You're learning things already!"

"We don't really have to hurry to the station, you know. The way I arranged everything, no one has any suspicions. They assume it's your body in the furnace, and we have two days of leave. So they're not even expecting us back in the barracks until the day after tomorrow."

"What are you trying to say, Yegor? What would you rather do right now?"

"We could walk around the city. Look at the sights."

"Is that what you and Kikorov would be doing, if you and he were on leave right now?"

"Well, no," he admitted. "We wouldn't even be walking together. He'd be heading for the nearest place where he could get a drink and... well, other types of relaxation. As for me, I'd probably go home."

"Where is home?"

"Just outside Kalinin."

"Ah, so you'd probably be headed for the Leningrad station yourself, then."

"I suppose so."

"And you and Kikorov certainly wouldn't be strolling around the city looking at the sights, wasting home time and drinking time and screwing time."

"I didn't say that he—"

"You can speak frankly in front of me, Yegor. There's nothing about the world I don't know. Anyway, my point is that it would look believable if we turned left here and started walking back toward the Leningrad station. It will look like I'm just accompanying you that far. If anyone's following us, and someone probably is—don't turn around! keep walking!—then it will all look quite natural. They'll be surprised when I get on the train, too, but I'm hoping that they'll assume you've invited me to come home and see your family." After a few seconds, she said, "Tell me about your family."

It was a subject he was always happy to talk about. He told her about his parents and his younger brother and sister. He described the house he had grown up in. He talked about the small town in great detail. His enthusiasm grew, his voice rose, and he was unaware of her growing sadness.

"You love it all very much," Gorova said.

"Oh, yes. I love all of them. I miss them whenever I'm away from them. You know, we could get off the train in Kalinin and take a bus to my home. I know you'd love all of them, too."

"And how would you explain your comrade-in-arms being a woman? You've planned so carefully to avoid drawing attention to us, you've managed to get us this far, and now you want us to go to a small town and undo all of your hard work!" She sighed. "Anyway, it's not your parents and brother and sister we have to fool, it's the people who'll be coming along later to question them, when you don't return to your post. Just think of the danger you'd be putting all of those people you love in."

After a long silence, she added, "Really, it would be best if you did get off at Kalinin. You could say that Kikorov stayed on the train, and you don't know where he was planning to go. Eventually, he'll be considered a deserter."

"What do you mean? What would you do?"

"Continue to Helsinki, as I originally planned."

"I'm not leaving you."

Gorova turned to look at him for a long moment. Then she muttered something, turned her face forward again, and was silent. Finally she said, "It's all your choice."

"Anyway, you'll need someone to protect you. After what that monster did to you, it won't be easy for you to start again. Some day, when he's overthrown, we'll be able to come back. I'll see my family again then."

Gorova looked at him again for a while, then looked away without saying anything. She pointed ahead: Leningrad station.

The train stopped briefly in Kalinin. Yegor made a show of reading the magazine he had bought while they waited for the train to leave Moscow. As the train began to move, pulling out of Kalinin, he looked up briefly, stared out the window, then looked down at his magazine again and continued pretending to read. Gorova watched him but said nothing. Had he looked at her, he would have seen the sadness and pity in her face.

Later, Yegor put down the magazine and looked out the window at the passing countryside, villages, small towns. "My father took me to Leningrad once, when I was a boy," he said. "I don't remember the details, but I do remember that I thought it was beautiful, like a fairytale. I'm looking forward to seeing it again. Will we be able to spend some time there?"

Gorova smiled at him. "We'll see."

Still later, after the sun had set and the horizon was lost in gray murk, she asked, "From that childhood trip, do you remember the approach by train into the city?"

Yegor shook his head.

"It's an interesting sight. Especially when we cross the river just before we get to Chudovo. Come. Follow me."

"How do you know this area?"

"Yegor, I didn't spring into existence in that damned suite of rooms! I had a life before that."

She left the compartment and led the way down the corridor to the door at the end of the coach. A sign in red letters next to the door handle said AUTHORIZED PERSONNEL ONLY BEYOND THIS POINT! Gorova ignored the sign and opened the door. She stepped through, held the door open, and looked back at Yegor, her eyebrows raised.

His first instinct had been to obey the sign. He always had obeyed the rules, whether they were spoken or written.

After what you've already done, he told himself, and considering what you're planning to do, breaking this silly rule is very minor.

He followed her.

They stood together on the platform connecting the two cars. It was formed by two overlapping metal plates, each an extension of the frame of one of the cars. The plates moved constantly relative to each other as the cars moved separately. The whole platform swayed from side to with the motion of the train. Yegor grabbed the short railing that extended from the body of one of the cars and gripped it tightly.

The moving air was a cold wind, the clacking of the wheels drummed through his legs, the rattling roaring of the train surrounded them.

Gorova stood with her legs apart, knees bent, moving easily with the train. She laughed at him. He couldn't hear the sound she made. She leaned close and shouted, "Look! Look out there!"

He looked where she was pointing. In the distance, he could see the wide, sinuous course of the Volchov River, silver against the dark countryside in the fading light. "Beautiful!" he whispered, and he forgot the sounds and the wind.

They passed under a highway, rolling along even faster, lurching from side to side. Yegor gripped the railing and watched the river and felt Gorova's presence beside him and thought he was close to paradise.

The train rolled over the river on a narrow bridge. Yegor stared down at the water far below in wonder.

He heard Gorova say, "Sorry!" And then something sharp, long, agonizing, burning erupted into his chest, into his heart.

He felt himself being lifted up, flung out into space. He drifted down through the darkness, down toward the river. He had no control over his arms, his legs, his voice. He couldn't breathe. He glimpsed Gorova far above him, staring down at him, an arm stretched toward him.

He understood. In the final instant, he thought it had all been worth it, and he had no regrets.

The water embraced him like the arms of Mother Russia herself, and he ceased thinking forever.

Sloppy.

Sharon examined the printout spread out on her kitchen table. Her training had taught her that even printing this stuff out without explicit authorization would get her reassigned to commanding a chow hall unit at Fort Dix. Taking it home with her would be good for ten years at Leavenworth in peacetime and a firing squad in the current state of quasi-war.

But training and reality could be very different things. Her platoon and their NSA counterparts were working triple overtime trying to make sense of the mass of information, give the Pentagon and the White House something they could use. Trusted people—which in the current state of desperation meant pretty much all officers, especially those with medals, and suits above a certain level in their own mysterious rank structure—were *encouraged* to bring their work home with them, just so the shit would get shoveled. And nobody was checking too carefully as to what that shit actually was as it left the building.

"Trusted" being a relative term, of course, Sharon thought. To the Echelons Beyond Reality, what with her medals and all, she was gold. On the ground, plenty of her coworkers wondered, sometimes aloud, about her last name and features that could have made her Moammar Gadhafi's illegitimate daughter. Her facility with Arabic, valuable as it was for the job, was a liability in a lot of people's eyes. She'd never thought she'd prefer the opinions of the EBR's to those of the people around her, but...

She could get *this,* and that was what mattered.

No one item by itself told her what she wanted to know. The papers contained intelligence reports from Pakistan to Argentina. Some were transcriptions of compressed burst transmissions a few words long, written by high-risk field agents who would disappear if anyone around them had any idea who they were. Others were innocuous diplomatic messages, written by embassy personnel, with their real content buried in paragraphs of officialese. Every item was interesting to someone in Washington, but it was Sharon's job to put it all together, to find some larger meaning. She had, perhaps, performed her assignment too well.

Actually, there was no doubt of that at all.

She stretched, looked around her small apartment, took another sip of coffee. She didn't pay much for the place, but the coffee was by God the best she could get. Have to spend my money where it counts, she thought. Coffee was one of the three great sensual pleasures according to the Book of Sharon, sex and Vietnamese food being the other two. There was a great Vietnamese restaurant down the street, but after seeing Rick off she'd discovered in herself a new tendency toward fidelity. She was spending a lot of money at Kinh Do and specialty coffee shops.

The computer? she wondered. No, she wouldn't commit this to disk, however useful the machine's indexing and cross-referencing abilities might be. It was the property of her employers. By their orders, she left it on all the time, and once a day it dialed its latest-and-greatest 9600 baud modem on its own and talked with the mainframes at Meade. She had no idea what those conversations were about and had been instructed not to try to find out. What she was about to do was legitimate work, but she already had an idea that her conclusions would really piss someone off.

So she did it the old-fashioned way. She started with ten sheets of blank paper, and after a few hours of work added another fifty, covering them with scrawled notes and boxes and lines connecting information from the reports. She made no marks on the reports at all, though at work she would have had no reason not to do so, and it would have saved her quite a bit of tedious copying. When she was done, she had already decided, she would open all the windows and burn the papers one by one in the sink, then rinse the ashes down the drain. An extra hour of work to avoid most of a lifetime in prison seemed like a good trade to her.

She drank the expensive coffee like a trucker slamming down the cheap stuff in an all-night diner. One corner of her mind, the part that was always observing and calculating—money, the desert night, satellite photos of troop movements, whatever—kept a running total and reminded her that she could save a lot of money by leaving for a few minutes to get a white can marked COFFEE at the grocery store; she ignored it. After the fourth pot, or maybe the fifth, she realized that her hand was shaking so badly her writing was becoming illegible. She switched to water until she almost fell asleep, then went back to the caffeine.

Finally she had what she'd known she'd find all along.

The sky was beginning to lighten. No point in trying to sleep, she thought. I'll just start getting ready for work in half an hour or so. And tonight was her dinner date with Norman. That was good. She'd been feeding State with information, not getting anything in return but a few good meals, for long enough. They *owed* her, and it was time to collect a fraction of that debt.

Uncle Sam knew there was another big war coming in the Middle East, sooner or later—maybe a month, maybe a year, maybe a decade—and he didn't want to lose this one. So the thing to do was to keep the troops sharp, get something better to toughen them up than the stateside training bases. Which was why, she was now certain, Rick was in Colombia fighting a war financed, on both sides, by US government money.

The State Department spooks could find something better for him to do. Sharon was going to make sure of it.

Thirteen

September 1991

When Major Stepan Luzhkov was given the news, his first thought was how it would affect him. His second thought was also how it would affect him, as was his third.

His fourth thought was how he would tell Aleksander Slominsky about it.

Very briefly, he entertained the idea of not telling the general at all. Not face to face, at any rate. Let someone else tell him. Send some junior officer to do it. But he gave up on that, albeit reluctantly. Telling Slonimsky this disturbing news would be dangerous anyway. Making it appear that he, Luzhkov, had something to hide, some reason to stay away, would make it that much more dangerous. Or what if Slonimsky interpreted his sending someone else as meaning that Luzhkov didn't take the matter seriously? That might not be dangerous to his life, but it would certainly be fatal to his career.

So he went himself.

The anteroom was of course filled with Slonimsky's guards, Luzhkov's own men. In the barracks, he was used to being the big man, the one all of these men kowtowed to. Now he was nervous about facing Slonimsky, especially with such news. He felt like an outsider, an intruder. And these men, his men, struck him very much as Slonimsky's guards and dangerous.

He was accustomed to inspecting their uniforms and their weapons and finding fault. It was one of Luzhkov's techniques for reminding them that he was their superior, that he even had the authority to throw them out of this elite and privileged unit. Now, even though he wore a uniform just like theirs, their uniforms cowed him. And their weapons terrified him.

Oh, they had all snapped properly to attention when Luzhkov entered the room. He could find no fault there. He had let them stand that way while he asked one of them to tell the General that he had to see him on urgent business. He had relished for an instant the return of a feeling of power over them.

Then he had made the mistake of telling them to be as they were.

They resumed standing or sitting casually at various places around the room. They stared at him impassively, disinterestedly. They were unimpressed by his need to see the General. After all, they saw the General a few times each day. Their attitudes, their expressions seemed to say: You're on our turf now, Major. Watch your step.

The guard who had gone in to announce him came out of Slonimsky's office and said, "Please enter, Major. The General will see you now."

Perfectly polite. Nothing to complain about. Nonetheless, his voice set Luzhkov's teeth on edge.

His heart beating faster, Luzhkov marched into the office, came to a halt in front of the massive desk, and saluted.

Slonimsky looked up at him and frowned in annoyance. "What is it, Luzhkov? Be quick."

"One of your guards, Comrade General."

"Yes? Yes?"

"Dead. Murdered."

"That's very unfortunate. But surely this is the sort of thing you've handled before. It's your responsibility. Make sure you replace him with a good man."

"Comrade General, of course I wouldn't bother you with such a detail normally. It's just that the man involved, the victim, was Senior Sergeant Yegor Duridanov."

He waited for Slonimsky's reaction, but it was another annoyed frown. "That name means nothing to me, Luzhkov. You're wasting my time."

"Comrade General, he was the guard you gave that very special assignment to a few days ago. You also ordered me to reward him with extra leave. Moreover, he was last seen with another guard, Junior Sergeant Valentin Kikorov, who was his assistant on that special assignment, and Kikorov is missing."

The frown deepened, but this time Luzhkov sensed with relief that it had nothing to do with him. "Interesting," Slonimsky said. "Details?"

"After Senior Sergeant Duridanov had signed both of them out for leave, they were seen exiting through the Spasskaya Tower gate and walking south on Bolshaya Ordynka together. However, somewhat later they were both observed at Leningrad Station, boarding a train for Leningrad."

"These men were friends and had gone on leave together before?"

"Well, I have no idea if they were friends, Comrade General."

Luzhkov forced out a laugh. "I don't concern myself with which of my men like each other and which of them don't. After all—"

"After all," Slonimsky interrupted him angrily, "that's exactly something a commander in your position should be concerning himself with."

Luzhkov paled and took a step backward.

Slonimsky waved a hand. "Continue."

"Er, yes. As I said, they boarded a train for Leningrad together. Duridanov's body was discovered on the banks of the Volchov River just south of Chudovo, right around where the train crosses the river during the approach to Leningrad. He had been stabbed. We think he was stabbed on the train and then thrown off. We've found blood on one of the platforms between two of the train cars."

"And the other man? What was his name?"

"Junior Sergeant Valentin Kikorov."

"Yes. Kikorov. Was he followed after he got off the train in Leningrad? Presumably they had a falling out, fought, one man killed the other, and then the killer went into hiding."

"Er, well, Comrade General, Kikorov never did get off the train."

"What?" Slonimsky half rose, then sat down again. "Good God! Luzhkov, this is very disturbing."

Because of the special mission, whatever it had been, Luzhkov had assumed Slonimsky would be unsettled, but his reaction seemed out of proportion to the loss of two replaceable men. "We'll bring the guard unit back up to strength right away, Comrade General! You won't even notice anything."

"Good God!" Slonimsky repeated. "You fool, there's much more to this. The second man, Kikorov, he must have been murdered on the train as well. Someone killed both of them and threw both of their bodies off the train. The second body will turn up, you mark my words. The important questions are: Who killed them, why, and what connection does this have with the task they performed for me? It can't be coincidence that they were both killed." Suddenly he stopped and sat frozen for an instant. "Second body," he repeated in a low tone. For just an instant, he became a frightened man and not the all-powerful ruler of a mighty nation.

Then Slonimsky shook himself and became as he had been before. "Major, return to your post," he snapped. "Replace those two men. Think no more of this. Go now."

Luzhkov saluted and marched from the office. He walked through the outer room, his head high, his shoulders back, his stomach held in. He hoped none of the guards noticed that he was trembling and drenched with sweat.

It took three days after the flow of gas into the furnace was turned off—over the strenuous objections of the man tending it—before the ashes were cool enough to be shoveled out and examined. The results were reported to Slonimsky immediately.

He sat at his desk for an hour reading, rereading, then reading for a third time the five closely typed pages from the pathologist. At last, he sighed and ordered that the furnace be restarted.

Down in the basement, the tall, slender man received that order with a grunt of wounded satisfaction. He turned dials, relit flames, and listened with a growing smile to the roaring sound he could just hear through the thick metal walls. He looked through the small window in the door and nodded. He felt the growing heat on his face and smiled even more.

When he was sure that all was as it had been before, he moved back into the shadows. The old amusement waited for him in the dark reaches of the old room.

It was hours later and he was asleep when the room began to echo with the tramp of many booted feet.

He barely managed to get his trousers and shirt pulled on and to pad barefooted to the front before the platoon of men in blue-and-gold uniforms reached the bottom of the staircase.

"What do you want?" he said angrily. There was scarcely room for all of them in the space between the foot of the stairs and the door of the furnace. Or possibly it just seemed that way because they were so big. "Get out of here!" he blustered. "Go on, all of you, back up the stairs!"

They ignored him and stood at attention, two rows of them, AK-74's on their shoulders.

Then he heard more bootsteps coming down the staircase. Just one pair of boots, this time. Walking casually, easily, not marching.

Aleksander Slonimsky came into view. He stopped a few steps up from the bottom and looked down at all of them. "Hello, Vitya," he said conversationally.

"Sasha! Why, what a surprise! You've never come to visit me here before."

Slonimsky came down the remaining few steps and stood facing the other man. "I've never needed to before. You've always taken care of your business down here properly, haven't you?"

"I don't understand. What do you mean? I'm still taking care of my business properly—the business you've entrusted to me, Sasha."

"Really? Is that why there was a man's skeleton in your furnace?"

"A man's—A man's—But how can that be? The only bodies that ever went in there were..." He looked at the men standing unmoving to either side of them. He lowered his voice. "The ones you had sent to me, Sasha."

"So I had been assuming. But I begin to wonder. You see, Vitya, that man's teeth survived along with his skull, and we've identified him as Junior Sergeant Valentin Kikorov. He was one of two men who brought a body down here for you not too long ago. That was the last time I had a body delivered to you. And to make matters more interesting, there were a few scraps of clothing adhering to his bones, and instead of a guard's uniform like these—" he gestured at the armed men around them and began shouting "—THEY WERE FROM CLOTHING LAST WORN BY THE WOMAN I HAD SENT TO YOU!"

"They were the same size," the tall man whispered. "Oh, heavens, they were the same size!"

"What are you talking about?"

He gestured wildly. "The body and one of the guards. They were the same size! And the bigger guard, he wouldn't let me have the body. I mean, he wouldn't let me handle the business. He kept me away and insisted on putting it in the furnace himself. And then he stood in front of the window and blocked my view! I remember all of that! Don't you see, Sasha? He betrayed you! It's nothing to do with me!"

"Vitya, Vitya," Slonimsky said softly, "if I can't trust you implicitly, then what good are you to me?"

The tall man licked his lips quickly. "You need me. I know things. Not just about what happens down here. I know things from before, too."

Slonimsky nodded. "Yes, you do. I remember things about you, for that matter." He turned to the guards. "Search the basement. Tell me what you find."

"No! You can't—!" Before the man could say more, Slonimsky backhanded him. Slonimsky's heavy fist crashed into the side of the tall man's head, knocking him sliding across the floor. He lay stunned, silent.

The guards disappeared into the darkness.

Slonimsky waited patiently, legs slightly apart, hands clasped behind his back.

The tall man forced himself to a cross-legged sitting position on the floor and put his head in his hands. He moaned in pain.

Slonimsky ignored him.

The guards began to return. Even in the dim, red light, Slonimsky could see that their faces were pale. One of them said, "Comrade General, there are... there are body parts back there. Lying on army cots and on blankets on the floor."

"Male or female?" Slonimsky asked. "Which parts?"

The guardsman closed his eyes for a moment and held his breath as though he were trying not to throw up. After a moment, he said, "Legs and lower torsos. I think. They're ... they're decomposed, Comrade General. I can't even tell if they're male or female."

Slonimsky nodded. He glanced at the man on the floor, who had stopped moaning and was watching them silently. "Nothing has changed, has it, Vitya? You promised me it would be different this time. I told you the bodies had to disappear entirely. Well, now they will." He turned back to the guardsman. "You and your comrades will gather up all those parts and bring them here and throw them into the furnace, where they were supposed to go in the first place."

The man on the floor shrieked, "They're mine! They're mine, Sasha! I need them! I have to have them! I can't live without them!"

Slonimsky gestured with his head and the guards hurried away into the darkness. They returned carrying bundles wrapped in blankets. "Good," Slonimsky said, nodding approvingly. "That's clever. Don't touch any of it yourself. But don't worry: they can't really be decomposed, or the smell would be far worse. He probably dried them in the heat."

"Yes, Comrade General," one of the guardsman said. He looked like he was about to faint.

Slonimsky walked over to the furnace door and yanked it open himself. Bright red light and fierce heat filled the space. "Quickly now," he said. "Throw them in."

The guards obeyed eagerly. Slonimsky nodded again in approval. "Good. Excellent. That takes care of that."

Slonimsky closed the furnace door and turned to the man sitting on the floor. He was sobbing as though his heart had been broken. "Vitya, Vitya, come on, be a man! You were never this weak and soft in the old days. Come, look, watch them all burn up. You'll feel better for it."

"I can't, Sasha! I can't watch!"

Slonimsky strode over to him, grasped the back of his shirt with his left hand, and yanked him to his feet. "Oh yes, you can. I'm ordering you to watch." He forced him over to the window in the furnace door and held him with his face pressed against the hot glass of the window. Slonimsky ignored his struggles and cries of pain. He held him in place easily with one hand. "Ah, look, there goes another one. Nothing but bone left of it. Isn't it wonderful? Isn't this a fine way to eliminate evidence of all kinds, Vitya? Don't you see how important the job was I had entrusted you with? But you betrayed me, Vitya. That soldier betrayed me, and he's paid for it. You haven't paid yet, have you?"

At last, Slonimsky pulled him away from the glass. One side of his face was red and blistered.

"You used to be one of the best, Vitya. But now I fear you're one of the weakest and poorest of the lot. And dangerous to me. The things you know ... "

"No, Sasha," he moaned, "I don't know anything. I've forgotten everything. I've always served you."

"One last service then, Vitya."

"Anything, Sasha!"

"Silence. That's your last service, Vitya: eternal silence."

Suddenly, Slonimsky punched him in the stomach. He let go, let the man fall to the ground, where he curled into a ball, clutching his stomach and trying to breathe.

Slonimsky opened the furnace door again. He opened it wide. "In you go. Goodbye, Vitya." He bent, picked the man up as though he weighed nothing, and threw him into the furnace. Then he slammed the door shut.

Slonimsky watched intently through the window. Vitya writhed on the red–hot exposed floor of the furnace, writhed among the remnants of his beloved body parts as though he were copulating with them for the last time. He reached out to Slonimsky. His mouth moved, forming the word "Sasha!"

"What? Louder, Vitya. I can't hear you." Slonimsky laughed.

Very soon, the man stopped moving and lay still on the metal floor. Slonimsky stood watching as the clothes flared up and disappeared, as the flesh smoked and cracked and peeled away.

"Good," Slonimsky said. "Very good. Well done, Vitya." He turned and strode away and marched up the stairs. His guards followed obediently.

Now I'll need to find a replacement for old Vitya, Slonimsky thought. One of these men would probably be good for the job. They've acquitted themselves well. But none of them would volunteer, of course. Not after what they've just seen. Ah, well, at least it won't become an urgent matter for another month or so yet.

Too bad that was necessary, he thought. Ah, but it felt good to do some actual work with his own hands again! He had been trapped behind that desk for what seemed like years although it had actually been less than half a year. He felt invigorated, rejuvenated. I must find some way of feeling like this more of the time, he told himself. Vitya's last service to me was a good one. Thank you, Vitya.

Rick didn't turn around to look at the ship he had just left. He had three days, and he didn't intend to spend a minute of that time being a soldier. Desert to jungle and now back to the desert, and he had a not entirely irrational fear that he wouldn't be so lucky this second time around. So cram in the sights and experiences while you can. Ancient buildings, ancient neighborhoods, views from Mount Carmel, and most of all beaches and the Mediterranean and beer and with luck women. He intended to savor it all.

Behind him, the requisitioned cruise ship was moored at Quay 5 of Haifa's main port, rolling slightly, slowly in the swells. Men still walked down the gangplank, carrying their heavy packs, already sweating and cursing the heat.

Low, black shapes dotted the horizon. They were ships from MPSRON Three, shifted from Somewhere Near Guam to the eastern Mediterranean. They were loaded with tanks, ammunition, engines, spare parts, food, fuel, other supplies—enough to sustain up to 17,000 Marine air and ground forces for up to 30 days. Rick had no doubt that more of the same were already on the way.

From here, some of the ships looked like barges. The days of civilian freight transportation in these waters were over, though. Launches churned the water between the harbor and the distant shapes. Helicopters whirred high overhead, ferrying troops inland, bypassing the harbor entirely, carrying men from the safety and routine of the sea directly to front–line camps.

No passes for them. Some of them would be dead before they saw anything of this ancient land.

Not that I saw all that much when I was here before, Rick thought. Mostly, I saw sand.

Not this time.

He settled his pack more firmly on his shoulder, straightened, and marched determinedly into the city.

The harbor was cordoned off from the city by the Israeli Defense Forces. He passed through a checkpoint manned by three slight, dark young men who could have been mistaken for Arabs. Rick assumed they wouldn't appreciate being told that. They were friendly, though. They looked at his military papers and tried to make conversation, although their accents were so heavy that Rick couldn't understand them. They waved him through, smiling.

A broad street led away from the harbor. "Away" was the direction he wanted. Maybe it would take him up to the mountain.

More likely he'd find a restaurant or bar along the way, which would be even better.

Just beyond the checkpoint, where anyone coming from the harbor couldn't miss it, a huge banner hung high across the street. Most of it was taken up by a photograph of a beefy, middleaged man in an Israeli army uniform. His jaw was clenched and he stared determinedly off to the right. To the right of the photograph was a word in Hebrew. Below that, one in Arabic. Beneath that, in English, "Sharon."

Startled, Rick stopped and stared at the banner. What the hell? Why was Sharon's name on a banner across a street in Haifa? He felt dizzy and disoriented for a moment.

Then he understood. Accent on the last syllable. Not his Sharon but instead the former Housing Minister, onetime soldier, wealthy cattle farmer, now Prime Minister of Israel. Rick had read a bit about him in a brochure handed out on the ship during the voyage to Haifa, an attempt to familiarize the GI's with their new host country. Rick had read a few paragraphs about the man and quickly decided he didn't want to know any more. The size of the banner and the pose confirmed his immediate negative impression.

Yes, "away" was indeed the direction he wanted to go in.

He walked along the sidewalk, fascinated by the whiteness of the buildings and the greenness of the trees and bushes. It was marred by the endless roar of traffic, the smell of exhaust and diesel oil, the haze and the dust. He had read in that brochure that Haifa was a busy port and a bustling commercial city. The harbor had certainly been crowded, and out here so were the sidewalks and the street, but the traffic in the harbor was warships and troop carriers, and the vehicles in the street were trucks of every size, some standard olive drab, some painted in desert camouflage, deuce-and-a-halfs shaking the sidewalk with their passage, gamma goats, Humvees, and the people on the sidewalk were all in uniform.

Most of the uniforms were from various American services. He also recognized the insignia of various NATO nations. There were some he couldn't even identify.

The whole damned world's here, he thought. Armageddon. Jesus, the religious crazies were right, after all! We *are* going to have the final battle here! And Saddam was right about the Mother of All Battles, he was just off in the timing and location.

One of the Humvees passing by had a red cross painted on its side. Rick stood and watched it for long seconds, feeling its tug. Then he resumed walking.

Rick held tight to his pack as he pushed his way through the crowd. He suspected that not everyone pressing past him was wearing a legitimate uniform. This would be a fine place for a professional pickpocket to put on an invented uniform and ply his trade.

His senses kept twitching. Ever since he'd passed through the IDF checkpoint, he'd had the feeling that someone was following him. Maybe one of those pickpockets, a very persistent one. But why stick with one American soldier, with all those other targets around? If someone was following him, then it was probably specifically Rick they were after.

The idea made the skin of his back tighten, as if in unconscious preparation for an attack. Every now and then, Rick stopped walking, put down his pack, and stretched, hoping he looked like he was resting, and tried to look around casually. All he saw was the milling crowd.

Christ, he thought, this is even better territory for an assassin than a pickpocket. Especially one of the Hashashim, if what they say about those guys is true. Bump against you in the crowd, slide something long and sharp into you, and vanish back into the crowd before you even fall down.

He shouldered his pack and walked on.

Someone grabbed his free arm from behind.

Rick spun around, dropping his pack, swiping the clutching hand away, falling into a defensive crouch.

Then he straightened. "Jesus Christ! Where'd you come from?"

"Hey, Rick. I wasn't sure it was you at first. I've been following you, trying to make sure."

They shook hands vigorously, grinning at each other. "Jerry Talbott!" Rick said. "What the fuck are you doing here?"

Talbott was a small, wiry, intense man. He wore glasses with heavy dark frames. He had tightly curled light-brown hair. He was wearing jeans, running shoes, and gray t-shirt, making him one of the few people on the street not in a uniform. He seemed to be covered in dust. On closer inspection, Rick realized the t-shirt was actually white.

"I work here," Talbott said. "When I can get work. The rest of the time, I drink coffee, argue politics, and try to get laid. Obviously, you're here to save the Free World from—Oops, I almost said 'godless atheistic communism.' Gotta learn to change the spiel, right?"

Rick shook his head. "You haven't changed at all. Yeah, you're right. I'm here to save people like you from"—he nodded in what he thought was an easterly direction—"people like them." He picked up his pack again. "Come on."

"Where are you going?"

"I've got a three-day pass, so I wanted to do the tourist thing until the last possible moment."

"Okay, but where are you going?"

Rick paused. "Truth is, I don't know. I'm just walking. There must be lots to see here."

Talbott nodded. "Oh, yes, there is. But you'll need a guide. I'm tired, I'm hot, I need a beer. Let's catch up."

Talbott led the way to a sidewalk café. He left Rick at a table, watching the crowds swarm by, while he went inside and bought them each a beer. He came back to the table with two uncapped bottles. "No glasses," he said. "They told me all the soldiers keep getting drunk and breaking them, so from now on, we have to drink from the bottles." He handed one of the bottles to Rick, set the other one on the table, and sat down.

Rick ran his fingers up and down the side of the bottle, clearing away the condensation and watching it form again. He put his hands around the bottle, cooling them, feeling cooler all over. He sighed. "Damn, I could have used this the last time I was here."

Talbott drank greedily for a few seconds. He put his bottle down and said, "I saw your name in the stories about that Elkins guy. He seemed a bit too good to be true. That whole thing did."

"Harry Elkins," Rick said quietly, "is one of the finest men I know. It wasn't too good to be true, it was too terrible to be truly reported."

Talbott grinned. "Uh oh, he's speaking in a low, steady voice. It's the doughty farmer of the Northern Plains. Gotta be serious now."

Rick laughed. "Shithead." His bottle rattled on the table, and he grabbed it just in time to keep it from falling over. The heavy vehicles passing by on the street were shaking everything. He could feel the vibrations in his bones, and he wondered what they were doing to the buildings in the older parts of the city. "So what kind of work are you doing here, Jerry? I thought you were going into teaching."

"Yeah, I thought so, too. But I didn't have the patience for a Ph.D., so I drifted into journalism. See, we're both crusaders!"

Rick grimaced. "Jesus. Calling us Crusaders, that's enemy propaganda."

"That's what the locals call you, too."

"The locals?" Rick looked around. "You mean the Israelis? That's ridiculous."

"Not the Israelis. Of course not. They're delighted you're here. They're happy to have you use their whole damned country as a staging point for the war. Without all of you, all of this," he gestured at the passing uniformed crowd, "they'd have gone under long ago. This would be just another part of the Caliphate, and there probably wouldn't be a Jew left living. No, I mean the, er, other locals. The Arabs."

"There are Arabs here?" Rick looked alarmed.

Talbott laughed. "There were Arabs here long before Israel existed. And even after. Almost half the population of Haifa was Arab before the war began. Now, of course, they're being driven out one way or another. Security risks, what with the Caliphate prowling around just beyond the border. You still didn't tell me how you ended up in uniform, Welton."

"I wasn't cut out for the scholarly life."

Talbott laughed again, even louder. "No shit, Dick Tracy. That was pretty obvious."

"I guess it was pretty obvious to the fine people who ran the University of Minnesota, too. They sort of invited me to go away. Which was fine with me. I only went there because that's kind of what you did after high school. I was a hot shit football player in high school, and I had this idea that I'd become a famous football player in college, and then I'd slide right over into the NFL for mucho bucks, and everything would be fine."

"You'd already given up on that by the time I met you."

"Yeah. It didn't take long. It's easier to be a hot shit jock in high school than on a big college campus. I wasn't big enough or fast enough. And I really didn't care about it enough. So college was pretty boring for me. Unlike you. You always had causes. You always wanted to save the world."

"You just wanted to get laid."

"Well, the place was good for that. But you know, I even got tired of that. It was too easy."

"Bastard."

Rick grinned at him. "I tried to help you out a few times, but you'd start making political speeches to the girls I fixed you up with. You just never learned. Anyway, I never even bothered declaring a major. I spent three semesters there and got lower grades each semester. So one morning I woke up in my dorm room thinking, What I need in my life is a little adventure. So I walked down the street to the nearest recruiting station. The recruiter asked me what I wanted to do in the military. I don't know, maybe kill people, I said. He said, This is the Air Force, son, not the Army. If you want to kill people, go next door. So I said, Oh, okay. In that case, how about healing people? He said, Medic. Yeah, we can do that. And that's how I ended up with Harry Elkins in the desert. So what's your story? I got sent here by the government. How'd you end up here?"

"I always wondered where you went," Talbott said. "I wrote to you a few times after you left the campus and disappeared. I wrote to your folks' home in Eden Prairie." He frowned at his beer. "When you didn't reply, I decided I shouldn't keep bugging you. I left the state the next semester anyway. Went to California. Got married. Got divorced. Got laid a lot. Got drunk a lot." He stopped talking abruptly.

"And then?"

"And then I grew up. Got serious. Got a job. There's a lot going on that people need to be told about."

Rick smiled. "You *haven't* changed."

"Neither have you."

Rick's bottle danced on the table again. This time, he wasn't fast enough, and it fell over. "Shit!" He shoved his chair back quickly, just in time to avoid the beer spilling over the edge of the table and onto the concrete. "Good thing I was almost finished with that."

Talbott said, "I'll get us both another. I don't make a lot of money, but I bet it's more than you. Try not to spill the next one."

"I didn't spill it. The table spilled it."

Talbott chuckled. "You never could hold your liquor." He stood up and went back inside.

Their friendship had seemed strange to others but natural to them, Rick remembered. They had met in freshman English. Rick was from the suburbs, Talbott was from Minneapolis. The small streetwise kid had tried to take the big naïve kid under his wing and explain to him how life really worked. That was how Talbott had seen it, anyway. At the time, Rick had thought that Jerry really knew how life really worked. Now, despite the warmth of old friendship, there was a tension and distance between them that seemed to stem as much from just how much life Rick had experienced during the last year as it did from the natural antagonism between their two professions.

He wasn't sure he could ever be close to anyone again. Except Sharon. And Harry. But they'd been through Hell with him.

Still, it was nice to see someone from long ago. He'd be friendly to Jerry Talbott for old times' sake. The old friendship wasn't there, really; he could admit that much easily. But he still felt some affection for the other man.

Talbott put the two new bottles down on the table. "They've raised the price since yesterday, the bastards. Some people do okay when there's a war on, and I don't mean just the people who make armaments."

"Who do you work for, Jerry? A local newspaper?"

Talbott shook his head. "I'm freelance. There's a bunch of progressive publications back home that carry my reports. You've never seen them?"

"Nope. Sorry."

For a moment, Talbott looked injured. Then he grinned and said, "Not the kind of magazines you read, right?"

"Probably not. I don't read much, nowadays, in fact."

Talbott snorted. "Why bother? The news is so filtered and controlled and censored that all you're really getting is government propaganda."

"But not in the magazines you write for, huh?"

"No, of course not! But even they're limited. We used to at least have pool reporting, which wasn't a whole lot like real reporting, but at least every now and then a real reporter would get to the front. Now your bosses have instituted what they're calling Single Point of Contact reporting, which means that they hand us a printed statement a couple of times a week, and that's all we get to send back home for the eager masses to devour.

"In the States, all our sources are drying up. Same thing has already happened here. The Shamir government wasn't exactly friendly to the foreign press, or even to their own press. Now that Sharon's taken over, it's a lot worse. My unofficial sources are disappearing, along with the local peace movement. I used to have contacts in Peace Now and B'Tselem, but a lot of those people have emigrated. The ones who're left have turned hawk, or at least they've learned to act like hawks. Or they've just clammed up. The ones who wouldn't clam up, well, they seem to have disappeared."

"Christ," Rick muttered. "At least stuff like that doesn't happen back home."

"Yet." Talbott tilted back his bottle and drank noisily for a few seconds. Then he banged the bottle down on the table and glared at Rick. "Sam Nunn just introduced a bill into the Senate. They're calling it the Support Our Forces Act."

"Good." Rick drank slowly. He wanted to put an end to this conversation and go sightseeing. His pleasure at seeing Jerry Talbott again was evaporating quickly. He had forgotten Jerry's crusading fierceness about whatever cause he happened to be currently enlisted in. Now he remembered it and also how it had annoyed him even in college.

"Bullshit! There's nothing good about it! Don't let the name fool you. That bill is a big step toward a police state. It gives the government no end of special wartime powers."

"Oh, come on, Jerry. You're getting carried away. Look, I really want to spend my time sightseeing, not arguing politics. So why don't you stay here and have another beer, and I'll start walking. Maybe we can have a drink together again before my pass expires." Like Hell.

Talbott grinned. "Man, I can see right through you, just like always. Watch it!" He grabbed at Rick's beer, which was toppling over. "Still think that's due to traffic vibration? Some soldier you are!"

"What else? Artillery fire? We're too far from the front, and I'd have heard it. And we know the other side doesn't have rockets capable of reaching here."

"Saddam had some."

"Yeah, but he used them up trying to stop the Caliphate's forces. Probably. Anyway, he's gone and there hasn't been a sign of Scuds or anything like them since the early days."

"Maybe. Well, you're right about those vibrations not being from the other side. Come on, let's go walking. I'd like another beer myself, but I can see that one more will put you under the table."

Rick snorted. "Yeah, right. I was the one who used to practically carry you back to the dorm."

"Yeah, well, I've grown up since then. But you haven't."

They left the café together and walked up the street in the direction Rick had been headed in originally. "This'll get us up above the city a bit," Talbott said. "On the flanks of Mount Carmel. Great view from up there."

They walked for some time. The crowd thinned as the road rose. "Used to be tourists here," Talbott said. He was sweating profusely and panting.

"Hike much?" Rick asked.

"I write about things. I don't do 'em. Anyway, the tourists are almost gone. Just a few locals now. No foreigners going up to look down."

"There's a war going on, Jerry."

"That's the point. You'll see."

They walked in silence for a while. Eventually, Talbott stopped and told Rick to turn around and look.

The city lay spread out before them, white buildings against green and brown. Parts of the view were blocked by palm trees, but Rick could see the shape of the peninsula the city sat upon and the dark blue of the Mediterranean straight ahead and to the left and right.

Talbott pointed down to the left. "See down there? The coastline? That's where some of the primo beaches are. You probably want to spend some time there."

"You read my mind."

"Easy thing to do." He pointed to the right. "The port. That's where you came ashore. And there," he pointed straight ahead, "that's North. You'll want to spend some time along the seaside there. Touristy stuff. Elijah's Cave is down there, or so they claim."

"It's beautiful!"

"Yeah. It's boring. Wish I was in Jerusalem right now."

"Why the hell would you want to leave all of this?"

"Because Jerusalem is more interesting. According to my sources, the Prime Minister is encouraging the Temple Mount Faithful to make their move today. Nothing like that happens here. Even before the war, the people here were focused on making money and enjoying the good life. Gotta give the fanatics in Jerusalem this much: they're not boring."

Even up here, the sun was strong and the breezes were warm. Rick stepped into the shade of an evergreen tree and looked out to sea.

To the horizon and to left and right, the Mediterranean was covered with ships. They looked small from here, but he knew they weren't. From up here, the scene was peaceful and beautiful. Down there, men and machines passed through the city in a frenzy and the world hung in the balance.

The navies of the West were gathered in every safe port along the Israeli coast, disgorging men and planes and tanks and trucks and mobile missile launchers and helicopters for the increasingly desperate fight against the armies of Rashid-al-Din Sinan. But most of all men. None of the rest mattered so much as the men, the warm bodies, the troops who carried and operated the equipment, who threw their fragile lives against the advancing iron wall. Here the West was making its stand, just as centuries earlier it had made its stand before the gates of Vienna. Now just as then, failure would mean the fall of a civilization, the triumph of madness.

This is another good war, Rick thought. We can't afford to lose this one.

"Aren't you going to ask me about the Temple Mount Faithful?" Talbott said.

"Gee, Jerry, tell me about the Temple Mount Faithful."

"Not that much to tell. They're an extremist group. Back when Shamir was Prime Minister, they tried to march on the Temple Mount in Jerusalem. They wanted to tear down a mosque up there and replace it with a synagogue."

"Why?"

Talbott shrugged. "Something about bringing the Messiah. They interpret some lines in the Bible as a prophecy that the Messiah will come when Solomon's Temple is rebuilt. Something like that. The police stopped them."

"There are madmen in every country. So what?"

"Well, see, now that Sharon's in power, rumor says he's encouraging those guys to try again, and this time, the police won't be allowed to interfere."

"Sounds like a good way to start a religious war. Sounds nuts, in fact."

Talbott nodded. "Yep. And before this Caliphate shit, no Israeli government would have allowed it to happen. But the present government is just waiting for an excuse to drive the remaining Palestinians out of Jerusalem. They even have a term for it: 'ethnic cleansing.' You like that? The rise of the Caliphate's given them all the ammunition they need. This country's government is in the hands of men who talk openly about ancient prophecies and who try to make them come true. I tell you, the madmen are in charge of the asylum. It's happening at home, too."

"You need to take a vacation, Jerry."

"Fuck you. I'm not just blowing smoke, Welton. This is all real. You don't understand. You haven't seen bodies all over the place."

"Bodies all over the place," Rick repeated softly. He couldn't tell Talbott just how many bodies he had seen, and in just how many places.

"It's just the excuse Sharon needs," Talbott said. "The Temple Mount Faithful will do some stupid thing. The Arabs will riot, and his police will shoot them. They'll kill them all. That'll be the end of any Arab presence in Jerusalem. Nice and simple. America won't protest. Europe won't. We need Israel too badly right now, and Sharon knows that. Ethnic cleansing."

"That's ridiculous," Rick said. "I can't believe it works that way."

"Remember your beer falling over? Traffic in the street, right?"

"Right. Of course."

"See that?" Talbott pointed down to their extreme right, a valley, where dust was rising above the green of orchards.

"Dust storm."

"Dynamite. Arab houses. Part of that ethnic cleansing."

"Bullshit." It couldn't be true. That wasn't what he was here to fight for.

"Sorry, kid, but it is true. Palestinian, Israeli Arab—it doesn't make any difference now. They're all potential fifth columnists or worse in the eyes of the Sharon government. They either leave the country voluntarily, or, well, they disappear. Then their houses get blown up, and there's a new Jewish settlement or suburb there. A lot of the area around Haifa was Arab villages fifty, seventy-five years ago. Now it's Jewish towns and suburbs. How do you think that happened?"

"You've bought into Arab propaganda, Jerry."

Talbott shrugged. "That's all I thought it was, too, at first. Then I saw it happen. Come with me, and I'll show you. You should know what kind of people you're risking your life for."

"So the other side's better? You were always an idealist, but you weren't naïve. Now you think that if the Jews gave up control of this country, everyone would live in peace?"

"Well, no," Talbott admitted. "Everyone's a murderous bastard out here. Or will be, if you give him half a chance. The Arabs will drive the Jews into the sea if they can. The Jews will drive the Arabs across the Jordan if they can. Right now, it's the Jews who can, because they've got the guns and our government isn't going to object. What we want is to have this country secure and stable and in the hands of our friends. That's why you and your buddies are here."

"Me and my buddies are here to stop the Caliph's armies from advancing into Europe. That's what we're here for."

"Uh huh. Are you willing to come with me?"

Rick looked up and then to the left. The sun was halfway down the sky already, declining toward the sea. On the horizon, he could make out a bank of fog moving toward the land, slowly covering the transport ships out there. "It's too late. I need to get some food and a hotel room. Then I want some night life, not political indoctrination. I've had plenty of that."

"Night life. Wine, women, and song. Good idea. Follow me."

Talbott started back down in the direction from which they'd come. Rick hesitated, then followed resignedly. The old friendship was no longer there, he couldn't deny that, but he felt guilty about the fact and felt that he ought to try a bit more to recapture it. Not to mention that Talbott knew this city and he didn't.

As they walked back down into the city, Talbott said, "All the hotels are full. Military officers, civilian military consultants, diplomats, arms dealers, even a few reporters, although God knows why they're bothering. Oh, yeah, and spies, of course, from all over the place, pretending to be diplomats or arms dealers or reporters or whatever. You don't have much chance of finding a room. I know a family that rents out rooms occasionally, though. Like me to see if they'll put you up for the night?"

"Sure. I guess."

"Good. As soon as we find a phone, I'll give them a call and get everything arranged."

They ended up back at the same café as before. While Rick

drank a beer, more grateful than ever for the brisk coldness of the liquid in his mouth, Talbott went inside to find a telephone he could use. He came out after a while, smiling. "No problem. You're all set. It's too far to walk. There's a taxicab on its way. Drink up."

"Hope the driver speaks English," Rick said. "Or you speak Hebrew."

"Won't be a problem."

Rick saw why when the cab arrived. It was an ancient, dented Chevrolet. The writing on its side was not the square letters Rick had already come to recognize as Hebrew, but flowing Arabic script.

The car stopped in the street. Other vehicles honked at it. Drivers cursed. Pedestrians turned to look.

The cab driver got out and stood looking around. He was short, slender, dark-haired, and had a moustache. Rick had already seen lots of Israelis that looked the same, and in fact Harry had that look about him, too, but from the way some of the pedestrians glared at the taxi driver, Rick had little doubt that he was an Arab.

Talbott jumped up and waved frantically. The driver saw him, grinned, waved back, and came over to them. The two men embraced, slapping each other on the back. They exchanged a few quick words, their tone too low for Rick to make anything out.

Talbott released the other man and turned to Rick. "Rick, this is my good friend Ahmet. Ahmet, Rick is a friend of mine from college. He's going to be spending the night in the spare room in Bereit's house."

Ahmet frowned and muttered something to Talbott. They talked in the same low tone as before. Rick couldn't even tell if they were speaking English. Finally, Ahmet shrugged, smiled, and held out his hand to Rick. "Welcome, Rick. My sister is a good cook. You'll be comfortable." Without being asked, he bent, picked up Rick's pack, hoisted it to his shoulder, and headed back to his taxi. Talbott followed him.

Oh, shit, Rick thought, what am I getting myself into?

Resignedly, he swallowed what was left of his beer and followed the other two. He could feel eyes boring into his back, and he knew the looks weren't friendly.

Rick got into the back seat and Talbott sat in front, beside the driver. They moved slowly through the heavy, mostly military traffic. Rick could see people on the sidewalk glancing at the car, then looking again, looking at the Arabic script on its side, and beginning to glare at them. "Heavy going around here," he muttered.

Ahmet laughed. "Don't worry. I was a private chauffeur in London for five years. This is nothing. It's just a small town."

"Did they shoot at you in London?"

The mood in the front seat grew instantly sober. "Good point," Ahmet said.

"Yeah," Talbott said. "Feels like it's just about to happen here, doesn't it? But don't you worry, Rick. You're fighting the good fight. You're on the side of light and justice."

"Lay off him, Jerry," Ahmet said.

Rick looked out the window again. "Are you taking me back to the harbor? Looks that way."

"Nah, I just need to get on the Derek Bar–Yehuda highway."

After a time, they seemed to have left the worst of the traffic behind. Now they were speeding along a highway with only a few other cars on it. In the deepening gloom, Rick glimpsed flames shooting from smokestacks off to his left. The car's headlights lit up a sign giving the distance in kilometers to Nazareth.

Great, he thought. I'm on a religious pilgrimage.

But long before they had gone that far, the car turned off the highway and onto a rutted dirt road. The only light was from the taxi's headlights.

Ahmet slowed to a crawl. He cursed at every bump. Twice he had to maneuver around small groups of black goats that seemed to feel they had more right to what road there was than he did.

Ahmet shouted angrily at the goats as he passed them. They watched him for a moment and then went back to nosing in the dry, sparse grass.

Lights showed ahead. Rick leaned forward to look through the windshield, straining his eyes against the dark. They seemed to be entering a small village. Oil lamps, and in a few cases low–wattage electric bulbs, showed through the windows of the stone buildings.

The last of the daylight was almost gone. Rick could make out little now except the buildings crowded close on either side. As his eyes adapted, he could see children running about everywhere. Dimly silhouetted against the sky, the buildings looked small and seemed almost to be settling back into the earth.

Ahmet stopped in front of one of the low buildings. Children erupted from it and surrounded the car. Ahmet and Talbott both got out, and the children surrounded them instead, hanging from their arms and legs and clothing. The noise was astonishing.

Rick climbed out more slowly. He was ignored by the crowd. They moved as a mass into the house Ahmet had parked in front of. Rick followed.

This was one of the few houses with electricity. The exterior might be ancient, but once inside, Rick could have been in a typical American house, albeit a small one. There was even the requisite television set blaring against one wall and being ignored. It wasn't showing a sitcom or cop show, though; instead, tanks rolled across the desert, sand spraying up from their treads. Rick shuddered and turned away from the set.

Talbott was embracing a pretty young woman. She was dark, Arabic looking, but dressed like Talbott in blue jeans, running shoes, and a t-shirt. Talbott released her and introduced her as Bereit. "And this is Rick Welton, my friend from college."

She held out her hand. Her grip was strong, forthright. "Welcome, Rick. We have the room ready for you."

Out of the corner of his eye, Rick noticed a group of children carrying his pack through a doorway. They were having a hard time of it. Alarmed, he moved in their direction.

"That's your room," Bereit said quickly. "This is a small house, but we make do. Ahmet will have to share the children's room tonight."

Rick almost asked Talbott where he'd be sleeping, but he saw how Talbott and Bereit were holding onto each other, and he realized that was a silly question.

He had supper with this strange family—hamburgers and French fries, to his surprise, but the kids all seemed to love it—and smiled politely at Bereit's apologies and promises of something more elaborate the next day. When he had a chance, he drew Talbott aside. "Jerry, this situation makes me nervous. What about the rest of the village?"

Talbott punched his shoulder lightly. "Shit, man, now you're the one who's listening to propaganda—Israeli propaganda. The neighbors don't mind me. I'm winning them over. Slowly but surely."

Later, though, Talbott seemed happy enough to have Ahmet drive them both back into the city. "I need some night life, too," he told Rick.

Ahmet dropped them off and went in search of his own entertainment. If there ever had been a time when Jews and Arabs socialized together in Haifa, that time was apparently past.

The rest of the evening was disappointing.

There was alcohol, there was music, there were available women. There were too many young men drinking too much—men back from the front, men on their way to it. They could have been in any city anywhere in the West near the front lines of any war in history.

Talbott drunkenly declared himself faithful to Bereit. Rick was under no obligation of faithfulness to Sharon, but he looked at the women who offered themselves to him, he remembered Sharon naked in his bed, and he sighed and politely declined.

The air grew colder after sunset. Even in the sidewalk cafés on the concrete sidewalks, next to the military traffic rumbling through the streets, the temperature fell below 60 degrees. Rick was wearing a short-sleeved shirt with no undershirt. Warmer clothing was in his backpack. He felt annoyed, but he was sober enough to know that he didn't want to go back to that village for the night.

Finally, Ahmet showed up, weaving through the crowd, seeming to magically know where they were. It was dark enough, and the crowds were drunk enough, that he was willing to take the chance of entering the undefined but understood forbidden zone. He got Talbott to his feet, his arm around Talbott's waist, Talbott's arm draped over his shoulder, and heaved the American to his feet. "Time for bed, Jerry," Ahmet told him.

Talbott moaned.

Ahmet stared at Rick, eyebrows raised.

Rick shook his head.

Ahmet shrugged and made his way back through the crowd. Talbott took an occasional uncertain step but he was being carried by Ahmet more than he was walking.

Rick sat for a while longer, a half-empty bottle of beer forgotten on the table in front of him. He watched the people around him, the men and women desperately trying to connect with each other, desperately trying to ignore what lay just kilometers to the east.

They can't ignore it, he thought. Not anymore than I can. They can't connect with each other. Neither can I. I used to be able to, though. With the people I took care of, anyway. When I used to heal people. Now here I am killing people, just like I started out wanting to do.

After a while, he gave up on it all and asked the people around him if anyone knew where he could find an officers' club. He got directions, followed those for a while, asked again, and kept repeating the process until he found himself at a rundown hotel with uniformed men and women going in and out the front door.

He was, he realized, almost back at the harbor.

He proved his identity to the corporal manning the front desk, signed himself in, and was shown a cot in a dimly lit alcove formed by the right angle between a bookcase and a wall. Thanks to the war, there were no actual rooms available.

Rick didn't care. He found the nearest men's room, relieved himself, then found the cot again, lay down on it fully dressed, and fell instantly asleep.

Hands shook him awake.

He blinked against the sunlight flooding the hotel lobby. "What? Who the fuck—?"

"Lieutenant Richard Welton, United States Army?" The man asking loomed over Rick. He was huge even compared to Rick, swarthy, with thick black hair cut short and a thick black moustache. He was in IDF uniform.

Rick frowned at the stiff epaulets. Oak leaf.

Suddenly he woke up. "Yeah, that's me." He pushed himself to his feet. "Major?"

The man was huge, solid, a bodybuilder. He might even be able to do more pushups than Sharon, Rick judged. There was an air of ruthlessness about him. The half dozen soldiers standing behind him had the same air.

"Major Shimon ben David," the officer said. "Come with us, please, Lieutenant."

I'd like to wash up, Rick thought. I'd like breakfast. I'd like coffee.

He said nothing. He followed the major. Then he realized that he wasn't exactly following. The soldiers surrounded him. It was more like he was being escorted.

They went outside. It was even brighter out here. Hotter, too. He blinked against the bright light. He wished he could shower and brush his teeth.

A dusty Land Rover was at the curb. Ben David gestured Rick in and then got in after him. One of the soldiers went around to the other side and got behind the wheel. The remaining five men climbed into the back. Large and strong though he was, Rick doubted if he'd be able to get out until this gang decided they wanted him to. He glanced down and noticed that the man on his right had a missing left little finger. They've been through it, too, Rick thought.

The vehicle started off with a roar and jerk. The driver blasted his horn until traffic made way for him. He made a U turn and began driving as fast as the traffic would allow, using his horn liberally.

"Nice morning," Rick said. No one replied. He shrugged and settled back.

Everything looked very different in daylight. But then he saw smokestacks off to his left, and he realized that they were following the same route Ahmet had taken the night before.

They turned off the highway onto a dirt road, and now Rick was sure. He sat up, tense and stiff, staring through the windshield.

Ahead was a roadblock manned by a group of Israeli soldiers. Unlike the men at the checkpoint near the harbor he'd passed through the previous day, these men weren't relaxed and smiling. The Land Rover stopped. Ben David leaned out of the window and spoke to the soldiers briefly. Rick listened, but they were speaking what he took to be Hebrew.

The soldiers pulled a wooden barrier aside and the Land Rover lurched ahead. They bounced down the dirt road for a while, and finally they pulled to a halt behind a familiar old taxicab. Everything looked different in the light, but Rick had no doubt where they were.

There were no children running around. No adult villagers, either. No sounds. The only people visible were Israeli soldiers, all standing silently, grimly fingering their weapons. They looked around alertly, nervously.

What had happened to the goats? Rick wondered. He could

see no sign of them.

Ben David got out and gestured for Rick to follow. He led the way into the house the taxi was parked in front of.

The television set was smashed. The table Rick and the family had eaten at the night before had been turned on its side and pushed back against a wall. In the space this had created, bodies lay in pools of blood.

Rick's head swam. I could have helped them if I'd been here, he thought. I'm a healer.

The body nearest him was slender, a woman's. She lay on her back in a pool of blood. She was naked. Her arms were stretched out to the sides, her legs were spread wide. Her crotch was covered with blood. Her eyes stared at Rick. Her mouth was open as though she were yelling. Then her head rolled sideways almost independent of her body. Her throat had been slashed to the spine, almost decapitating her.

"Bereit," Rick whispered.

"Say again?"

"Bereit," Rick repeated. "Her name. This was her house."

Ben David nodded. "And this one?"

A man's body. Fully clothed, but also lying on its back with the neck slashed almost through. "Ahmet. Bereit's brother. A taxi driver. That's his car outside." Rick looked around. "Christ, those are her kids! You even murdered the kids!"

"We?" Ben David was astonished. "You think we did this? It was the other villagers. Or maybe a raiding party from Lebanon. We found them like this. Come outside. There's another body I want you to identify. We know who it is, but we'd like an independent identification."

He led the way from the house. He walked between some of

the buildings to a small open space. Another body lay here, on its face in the dust. A small man. Light skin. Light-brown hair. Jeans, running shoes, t-shirt. The remnants of a pair of glasses lay on the ground near him; they had been ground into the dirt. His back was splattered with blood. There was a line of bullet holes across his t-shirt.

Ben David reached out his foot and turned the body over with the toe of his boot. The front of Talbott's chest was a smashed-open horror of exit wounds.

Rick drew a series of deep breaths. Finally he managed to say, "Jerry Talbott. American. A reporter."

Ben David nodded. "That's what we thought. He's no loss. Always prying. Trying to tell the world we're killers."

A sergeant stepped up to ben David, saluted, and said, "Kokhav!" Then he looked at Rick and said, "Major." He stepped away and ben David followed. They spoke briefly. The sergeant saluted again and walked away, vanishing behind one of the buildings.

From somewhere nearby there were the sounds of rifle fire. Rick looked around wildly for cover.

None of the Israelis seemed alarmed.

Rick tried to relax, watching the soldiers, wondering what the hell was going on.

Ben David came back. "We know you were here," he said. "You were followed last night. Is this yours?"

One of the soldiers had been standing quietly to one side holding Rick's pack.

"Yeah, that's mine." He took the pack. Someone had spray painted a swastika on it. "Thanks."

"We just needed to be sure about the identities. We've

checked up on you, and you're safe. You can go now."

"What about the villagers? There may be wounded people out there. I can help them!"

"We have to assume they're all collaborators. We'll bring bulldozers, get rid of this village." Ben David smiled. "Don't worry, it's no loss. The land will be used."

"My God," Rick said, "you can't do that. It's not their fault!"

Ben David stepped toward him, glaring. "This is our part of the war, Lieutenant. You go back and fight your part. Leave this part to us."

"I can't—"

"You go back now," ben David repeated. He gestured, and two of his men stepped up, one on either side of Rick. "It's Friday afternoon already, and we have a lot of work to do before dark. You go back now and leave all of this to us."

For a moment, Rick stood his ground. Then he hoisted his pack to his shoulder and let the two soldiers lead him back to the Land Rover.

The Israeli was right. This part of the war was theirs. Rick couldn't change the world by himself.

Starting the day after next, he would be doing plenty of his own killing.

Fourteen

October 1991

Mikhail kept the sign under his raincoat as he walked. The side with the words was against his chest. His raincoat was buttoned and belted, and he kept his arms pressed across his chest, keeping the sign in place. He hoped he looked as though he were cold. He must not draw attention to himself.

The members of Fourth of June liked to remind each other that it was essential never to draw suspicion, never to stand out, never to look unusual. That way, you could go anywhere anyone else did, and no one would pay any attention to you. You'd have time to perform your act of resistance and then leave quickly, head for home, again without arousing suspicion.

He *was* cold.

Maybe I should have worn my heavy winter coat after all, Mikhail thought.

His teeth were chattering. He clenched his jaw and hurried along.

It was almost dark. There weren't many other people walking this late, and only a few cars passed by. The other pedestrians were also all hurrying, but they were wearing heavier clothing than he was.

A fine drizzle began, almost an icy mist. Mikhail could feel it freezing on his eyebrows and hair. Soon, he was sure, it would turn to rain, and then ice, and then snow. I'll be home and warm by then, he told himself hopefully.

His head was freezing. His hair felt wet. Water ran down his cheeks and under his collar, into his clothing. Mikhail cursed his decision to wear his raincoat and no hat. He had thought that if he wore his heavy coat he'd be unable to hold the sign hidden against him. It might have slipped and fallen out onto the ground, in full view of others. Of the police. And if he was wearing his raincoat, hoping to look like a man who was warm enough that way, he couldn't very well also wear his thick fur hat. That would look silly. It would draw attention.

Finally he reached his destination. It was an abandoned shop, its windows covered with plywood. It had opened under Gorbachev and been shut down under Slonimsky. The owners had been taken away and had not been seen since. Everyone knew what must have happened to them, and no one talked about it. Mikhail gritted his teeth again, but this time it wasn't because of the cold.

It was dark here now, thanks to the time of day and the lack of working streetlights. As Mikhail had expected, the drizzle had turned to rain. A wind rose, driving the rain into his face.

He looked around quickly. The sidewalk and street were deserted. During the daytime, this spot would be in sunlight for much of the time, and the sidewalks would be crowded. It was perfect.

Mikhail looked around again. Then he opened his coat, took

out the sign, flipped it around and held the top of it against the plywood with his left hand. He dipped his right hand into his coat pocket and drew out a small hammer and two nails. He put one nail in his mouth, the other in his left hand, held it in place against the top of the sign, hammered it into the plywood quickly with three powerful blows.

The sound echoed in the empty street, only partially muffled by the rain and the rushing sound of the wind. Mikhail was shivering, and only partly because his coat was open and he was getting wet and even colder. He looked around again. Still no one. He held the second nail against the bottom of the sign and hammered it into place.

He dropped the hammer back into his pocket, turned, and hurried away, buttoning and belting his coat as he went. He was cold and he was frightened, but he felt triumphant. He had struck a blow for freedom.

Behind him, the wind blew the rain against his sign. Just barely visible, the sign read

POLAND HAS DEMOCRACY!
WHY DON'T WE?

It had taken him two hours to make it, drawing the letters and then filling them in with his fountain pen, the large sheet of paper flat on his apartment's table. Now the ink began to run. The words became distorted, blurred, indecipherable. First DEMOCRACY vanished. Then POLAND. Then finally WE. Not many minutes after Mikhail had turned a corner and set off almost at a run for home, his sign had reverted to being a blank sheet of paper. By morning, it would scarcely be recognizable even as that.

Mikhail's wife greeted him at the apartment door with a cup of hot tea and a happy message. "Guess what, Misha? Your brother's come for a visit!"

Delighted, Mikhail pushed aside the offered tea. "Get vodka! This calls for a celebration!"

He rushed into the apartment and embraced his brother, who had risen from the one armchair, laughing.

"Petya! My God, Petya!" Mikhail shouted. "What are you doing back home? I thought you were still out there somewhere killing people!"

His brother and his wife put their fingers to their lips and said "Sshh!" simultaneously. Then his brother embraced him and called him Mikhail Andreyovich.

Mikhail grinned. "Sorry! I'm just so damned glad to see you. Okay, you don't want to talk about it. Or you can't." He punched Pyotr in the stomach. "Well, wherever you've been, it's been good for you. You're as hard as nails." That word made him think of the sign he had nailed up only a little while ago, and that in turn made him think of the danger both his wife and his brother would be placed in if he were caught. The smile of delight left his face.

Pyotr seemed not to see the change in his brother's mood. He patted Mikhail's comfortable paunch and said, "Whereas you look more like our father every day." He laughed. "Maybe even like our mother! Actually, I've been behind a desk in Moscow for the last few months. This is the first chance I've had to get away." He held up his hand quickly. "But I can't talk about that, either, so don't ask me."

Mikhail frowned, once again the older brother. "Months? Of course you could have gotten away! What nonsense! Lilya, where's the—?"

Quiet and efficient, his wife had gone to the kitchen and returned with two small glasses of vodka.

"Oh. Thanks."

The two brothers threw back the vodka and embraced again.

"This stuff is piss," Mikhail said. "Come, Petya, let's go for a walk and see if we can find some place we can buy something better."

"Not at this time of night, surely," Petya said.

Mikhail gave him a hard stare. "I said, let's go for a walk," he repeated sternly.

Petya threw up his hands. "Whatever you say, brother."

"This time, wear your heavy coat," Lilya said. "And take along your hat and gloves."

"Yes, yes, of course. What about Petya? Why aren't you bossing him around, too?"

"Because I leave that up to you," Lilya said. "Petya, put your scarf on and button up your coat!"

Petya laughed. "Nothing ever changes in this apartment. I guess that's why I love coming back here. It's warm and accepting but it's also comfortingly predictable."

"Comfortingly predictable," Mikhail grumbled. "Well, we'll talk."

Properly bundled up at last, they left the apartment. Behind them, Lilya called out, "Don't be too long! I'll have supper ready in about thirty minutes."

By now, the streets were dark and empty, and there was a thin layer of ice on the sidewalks. The two brothers walked carefully, holding onto each other.

"This is the way it was when we were boys," Petya said, his voice filled with nostalgia. "Walking together in the cold and the dark, keeping each other from falling down."

Mikhail looked at him, but Petya was nothing but a vague silhouette against the distant streetlights. "The way I remember it, you used to let go of me deliberately, and then laugh when I fell."

"Nonsense! It was the other way around. Besides, you used to make such a comical sound when you hit the ground."

Mikhail laughed. "I guess I still do. Little boys still laugh at me when I fall on the ice."

There was a pause while the brothers walked silently, slowly, arm in arm.

Then Mikhail said, "I'm so glad to see you, Petya. I wish you had come earlier, though. As soon as you were in Moscow."

Petya was silent for a long moment, then said, "I've been going through a difficult time, Misha. Thinking about my future. And about what I've done in the past. I didn't want to come to see you and Lilya and impose it all on you. I wanted to work everything out first."

"Ah, you idiot! We're exactly the people you should come and see during such a time." Mikhail considered his next words carefully. "And have you worked everything out?"

"Well, not everything. But things are clearer now, and I think I can see the right direction."

"That's vague!" Mikhail said. "I was hoping you'd be more specific, now that we're out here alone."

"So that's the real reason you wanted to go for a walk in this nasty weather."

"That's most of the reason. Of course, if we do happen to find someplace still open where we can buy something to celebrate with properly, that will be fine, too."

"But you know we won't. Not a legal place."

"Then we'll go back home and drink more cheap vodka. We'll need to get warm."

"You used to share everything with Lilya."

Mikhail said nothing for a while. Then he gestured toward a side street, even darker than the street they were on. They turned down it. Finally, Mikhail stopped walking. The brothers could scarcely make out each other's faces. There were no cars, no other pedestrians, no streetlights at all on this street. Mikhail leaned toward his brother and said in a low voice, "In the old days, what I had to share wouldn't have put her in any danger."

Petya lowered his own voice to the same level. If someone was lurking in the dark, trying to listen, he would surely not be able to make out a single word. "But now there is? What are you involved in, Misha?"

"How do I know if I can trust you?"

"I'm your brother!"

"That means nothing nowadays. You know that. But that's why we're out here—so that we can both speak frankly, without upsetting Lilya or putting her in danger. No more vagueness. Where do you stand on our new ruler? His new powers, his new occupation of Afghanistan, his expansionism, his tyranny?"

There was another long pause. This time, it was Pyotr who thought about his words before speaking. "If I were planning to betray you, brother, you would already have said too much. I think you do trust me. On some level, anyway. Now I'll repay that trust. In Afghanistan, I grew sick of what we were doing, of the things I saw—no, of the things I *did.* When I was stationed back here again, I was glad that at least I wouldn't have to do such things again and that I'd have time to think about it all, try to put it in perspective. In short, rebuild my patriotic feelings. Instead, I found myself supervising men who were doing things here that I was ashamed of. I'm sorry that I'm still being vague, but believe me, you wouldn't want to hear the details and I don't want to tell them to you. And you're safer not knowing them. What I'm trying to tell you is that I lost my patriotic fervor in Afghanistan, and now I've lost my loyalty in Moscow. The things that are happening to my country ... I no longer want to be part of it."

"So you think you can atone for your deeds?"

"I don't know if I can. I don't think so. But maybe I can undo some of what I did."

Mikhail relaxed. He straightened, unaware until now that he had been bent over as if to guard against an anticipated blow. He drew his right hand from his pocket and put it on his brother's shoulder. "You always were a good boy. I knew you must still be one."

Pyotr laughed—a bit too loud, a laugh of release as much as of amusement. "Still playing the grown-up older brother! No, Misha, I don't think I'm really a very good boy at all. But I know what I have to do now."

"What you have to do now is join us."

"Us?"

"A group of friends and me. You don't know any of them. They're people I've met since we last saw each other. We call ourselves the Fourth of June."

"I don't understand—"

"The Fourth of June," Mikhail repeated. Unconsciously, he had raised his voice to a normal speaking volume. "In 1989, that was the date of the first free elections in Poland. That was the beginning of the end of Soviet domination for them, the beginning of their democracy. Our motto is, 'Poland has democracy. Why don't we?'"

"Sh! You're shouting!"

"Sorry. I can't help but be excited when I talk about this."

"So you want us to be like Poland?"

"Oh, no. I want us to be freer and richer. Our motto means that Poland was able to throw off the chains and achieve democracy. We're so much bigger and more powerful than Poland. Why can't we do at least as much as they did? In fact, I do want us to push Slonimsky out of power, but I don't want him to be allowed to retire into safety and obscurity. I want him to stand trial for what he's done. I shouldn't say 'I,'" he corrected himself. "I should say 'we,' all of us in the Fourth of June movement. We want him to stand trial and to be punished. The ultimate punishment." His voice turned harsh. "For the ultimate crimes, he deserves the ultimate punishment."

"What you're saying is a crime," Pyotr pointed out. "I don't mean that you're proposing criminal acts, I mean that just saying what you just said is against the law, and the punishment for such words is very harsh indeed."

"I suppose you have intimate knowledge of that?"

Pyotr sighed. "Unfortunately, I do know more about it than I'd like to. But come now, Misha, surely all this is just talk! It's easy to say you'll do this and that to a powerful ruler, but it's another matter to actually do anything to hurt him."

"Oh, we're doing things already! We're taking small steps, early ones, but the effect of everything is cumulative. You don't know about any of this yet, but you will. Once you've joined us."

"Are you sure you want me?"

"Are you sure you want to do real work to save this country, not just sit behind a desk and agonize over the part you've played in destroying it?"

Pyotr smiled, invisibly in the dark. "You always did like to ask the long questions. Yes, I really do want to join you."

Mikhail grabbed him and embraced him tightly. "Little brother! I always knew you'd come right in the end! All right, let's go home and finish that bottle of vodka. Tomorrow, I'll introduce you to the others."

Pyotr met most of them the next day in Mikhail and Lilya's apartment. For the first time, he wondered if Lilya was involved in what Mikhail was doing. Did she perhaps think these were just ordinary friends, or did she know more? He knew he ought to find out.

Meeting the other members of the Fourth of June made Pyotr feel sad. Why couldn't they look and act more heroic? These people thought they were working to destroy the rule of Aleksander Slonimsky. That was a huge, an immense goal. It demanded people who were correspondingly immense, larger than life. Heroic figures, that's what they should have been. Instead, they reminded him of the lowest, meekest clerical staff at Khodinka.

There were five of them, all middleaged men, and they all went by aliases, assumed names. *Noms de guerre,* Pyotr thought, and had to stifle a laugh. The aliases were simple Anglo-Saxon nicknames, as if the men had taken them from old American or British movies. Which, he thought, they probably had.

Before the others arrived, Mikhail told Pyotr that in the Fourth of June, he was known as Mike. "And you'll be Pete," he added.

Some conspiracy, Pyotr thought. He had no doubt that the man introduced to him as Jack was actually named Ivan, that Nick was Nikolai, and so on. They really do need my help, he thought. Not for planning attacks on the infrastructure but for covering their tracks. I'm the only real professional in the group. There was no point in worrying about such things for now, though.

They might be a silly, inept, laughable bunch of middleaged clerical workers with delusions of grandeur, but to Pyotr's surprise he liked them. They were sincere, and they were driven by a genuine love of country, driven by a patriotism so great that it had forced them out of their comfortable lives and roles and had led them into actions that could cost them at least their freedom, probably their lives.

One of them, the fat, constantly sweating Nick, told Pyotr that to the goal of overthrowing a tyrant and freeing their beloved Russia, "We have pledged our lives, our fortunes, and our sacred honor." It was a ringing phrase, and one Pyotr was sure he had read somewhere before although he couldn't remember where. It seemed odd, overly heroic, coming from such a very unheroic man. And yet in his own way, chubby Nikolai—"Nick," rather—was heroic for that very reason. He was the best kind of hero: a man lacking heroic stature or special training, an ordinary man, an ordinary citizen, filled with fear, even with terror, who sees what is right, what must be done, and forces himself to stand up and do the very thing that terrifies him most.

And yet, as the evening progressed in Mikhail and Lilya's overheated apartment, as the levels in the three new bottles of vodka dropped rapidly, as the protestations of heroic determination flowed thicker and faster, Pyotr couldn't help but contrast this group of men to the ones he had commanded so recently in Afghanistan. To Begench, small, slender, unwavering, ever efficient, ever deadly. To Yuri, stolid, quiet, precise, falling to the ground with his brains sliding from his blasted-away head...

Pyotr shook himself. That was different, he thought. They were different, the men of my unit. Being heroes was their job. But these men, being bus drivers or teachers or bank cashiers, those are their jobs. Being heroes and patriots is their choice.

He looked around the room, at the ordinary men, the laughable men, passing around the vodka bottles and making their brave declarations.

It terrifies them. They need alcohol to still their shaking. None of them has ever fired a gun. Not since their days in the Young Pioneers, anyway. None of them has been physically hurt since boyhood. They may not be wealthy, but they all lead comfortable, safe lives. And yet now they're all willing to risk the ultimate punishment for the sake of their country, to free Mother Russia from tyranny. The ultimate sacrifice for the ultimate cause. That's how they see it.

Unconsciously, he raised his glass to the room at large, a salute from one soldier to others. Die well and live forever in memory. Your country will never forget.

Oh yes it will, Pyotr thought. Of course it will. It will forget because it will never know.

Pyotr was jerked from his reverie by the word "bomb."

"What was that?" he asked. "A bomb?"

Mikhail laughed. "Pay attention, Petya! He never did," he told the others. "He daydreamed all the time, when he was a boy." His speech was slurred.

One of the men, Sarge (Sergei? Pyotr wondered), repeated what he had said. "At the Paveletsk railroad station. Midnight on

Thursday. Day after tomorrow. There won't be any commuters around. No one will be hurt. But we'll have an effect."

No one will be hurt but some poor babushka cleaning the station, Pyotr thought. Or a night watchman. Martyrs in the struggle, I suppose. "Why Paveletsk?" he asked.

Sarge said reluctantly, "Partly because Slava and I—"

"Stan!" Mikhail said loudly.

"Sorry. Stan and I live near the station, so it's convenient. But it's more than that. We've seen soldiers leaving from that station. We think they're headed for the southern frontier."

"Lightweight clothing," Stan mumbled. "Desert fighting." He raised his glass. "More!" It was almost empty, but he was tilting it so far that he was about to spill what was left in it.

"Yes, right," Sarge said. He and Stan were sitting beside each other on Mikhail's small, sagging couch. Rather, Sarge was sitting and Stan was leaning against him, looking on the verge of unconsciousness. Sarge reached over and straightened his friend's glass. "Desert equipment. Anyway, if we disable the station for a few days, that will slow down the war effort. That's one of our goals."

Pyotr thought, Most likely all that will happen is some commuters will be inconvenienced the next day. Maybe they'll be so upset with Slonimsky's administration that they'll start a riot which will grow into a revolution. He laughed silently at that idea. These people are fools. Why should the government even bother with them? The only real harm they can do is to themselves.

"I was a sapper," Stan said suddenly in a loud and surprisingly clear voice. Pyotr realized that the man was staring at his face, reading the doubt there. "In Afghanistan," Stan said. "The first time. Don't you worry about me. I know what I'm doing." The brief light of intelligence faded from his face again. He slid sideways. His head landed in Sarge's lap. He sighed, closed his eyes, and went to sleep.

Pyotr looked at Stan, trying to imagine him as a member of his own unit in Afghanistan, one of the sappers. He couldn't do it. It was impossible to reconcile the images he remembered from the front with this worthless sot.

"He's right," Sarge said. He acted as though nothing unusual had happened, although Pyotr could hear the embarrassment in his voice. "He does know what he's doing. He'll be fine by morning, and everything will go according to plan. Midnight tomorrow. You'll see." He laughed. "I mean, you'll hear! This whole part of the city will hear."

"The whole world will hear," Mikhail said loudly. He refilled his glass, raised it, and shouted, "Freedom!"

The others joined him in the toast. Then they all fell to serious drinking.

Pyotr sat quietly, watching the show, expecting the police to burst it any moment. When that didn't happen, he decided that the neighbors were probably just as drunk as this gang, too drunk to pay attention to treasonous shouts. Or possibly shouting of various kinds was so common in this apartment building that no one bothered to listen to the words.

The show wasn't much of a show, after all. Just a group of drunk middleaged men pretending to be freedom fighters. He had far more respect for the Mujahedeen, for all that he had worked so hard to kill so many of them. But they had been tough, they had known what they were doing, they were fearsome opponents. And they were always sober.

Pyotr's attention drifted to the worn carpet in front of him.

He tried to imagine it as it must have been when it was new. Mentally, he restored the colors, sharpened the patterns again. Suddenly, with a shock, he recognized it.

Why, this was the carpet in our parents' house! In their bedroom! I used to love to look at it when I was a boy. Misha always liked it, too.

Once, Misha tried to take it from their room and put it in ours, Pyotr remembered. He actually thought they wouldn't notice. How our father beat him! Father finally stopped only because I asked him to.

Misha, you like to play the wise, mature older brother, but you were always the one doing foolish things and getting into trouble, and I was always the rescuer. Ah, Misha, Misha, you've really done something foolish this time!

And here I am again. To set everything in order again. To tie up all the loose ends.

Mikhail had begged him to stay the night in the apartment. After all the years of separation, he had said, they should spend more time together before going off to Sarge and Stan's apartment to wait for the great act of revolution.

"No, what I don't want to do is raise suspicions by behaving unusually," Pyotr had pointed out. "I'm normally home in my own apartment by a decent hour, and I'm always at my desk at work promptly on time. I take few vacations, and I schedule them well ahead, and I never change my schedule. If you have a reputation for regularity, Misha, then irregularity attracts attention."

Misha put his finger beside his nose and waggled his head. "Aah, you're wise beyond your years, little brother. Of course you're right. I should have seen that myself. In fact, I'll emulate you. I'll be at my own desk at the factory right on schedule, as always, and I'll behave just as I always do. And then we'll meet here tomorrow at dinnertime, yes? You will have dinner with us, won't you?"

Lilya had come into the room in time to hear the last few words. "Oh, yes, Petya! You will, won't you? We haven't seen you in so long."

Pyotr smiled at her. He had always found it easy to smile at Lilya, from the first day his brother had introduced her to the family. He liked her for the good she did Misha, and he liked her for herself. She was a soft, warmhearted woman, always inoffensive, always concerned with the happiness and comfort of others. Physically, she was short, overweight, and plain, but her sweetness showed in her face, and even though she was far from the physical type Pyotr preferred, he could understand why Misha was happy with her. What had puzzled him from the first was what Lilya saw in Misha.

"Yes," he told her, "I'll be here for dinner tomorrow. It'll be a long, hard day at work, I expect, because of the anticipation, looking forward to—"

At that moment, he caught sight of Misha's warning expression and understood that Lilya knew nothing of the anti-government plotting. Well, that was something to be thankful for, anyway!

"—your fine cooking," he finished lamely.

But Lilya accepted his words at face value. She smiled happily at him.

And now here he was, bright and early the next morning, just as he had said, at his desk. Quite a few dispatches had arrived overnight from his people in the field, and now he was reading them, trying to digest and understand them all, and mentally composing his summary for General Artushev.

He was far from done when the general called him into his office. With a sigh, Pyotr put the letter he was reading into his desk drawer and locked it. It was a gripping story of assassination and escape, written rather more in the style of a popular novel than was proper in such a case, and Pyotr had let himself be drawn into it, forgetting the objectivity and speed that were necessary in this job.

When he entered Artushev's office, the general closed the door behind him, gestured him to a chair in front of the desk, and said, "So, Pyotr Andreyovich, how are you adjusting to this boring desk work? Is your behind spreading? Do you miss the sand and blood of Afghanistan?"

Uncomfortably, Pyotr said, "Comrade General, I serve—"

"—the Soviet Union." Artushev waved his hand. "Of course you do. We all do. That goes without saying. If we ever seriously doubt your loyalty, well ... "

Then we won't discuss it with you calmly like this, was the unvoiced rest of his statement. We'll just send you up the chimney. Not like the retired agents who die of old age and then their bodies are cremated and sent up the chimney. No, you'll still be alive and conscious when we shove you into the furnace.

That had been the fate of the man in the film clip they showed Pyotr on his first day as a potential member of the GRU, the Glavnoye Razvedyvatelnoye Upravlenie, Soviet military intelligence. Strapped firmly to a metal sled, the man in the film had struggled with all his might, straining against the bindings, but all to no avail. The sled had vanished into the furnace, the flames has brightened for a few seconds, and then he was gone—

up the chimney, the only way to leave the Aquarium, the GRU's headquarters. "It costs one ruble to get in, but two to get out," Pyotr had been told. "This is your last chance to say no, not to join." He had said yes, knowing it was the right thing for him to do.

Now, he sensed, he had to give Artushev a more specific answer, not the standard catchphrase he had tried a moment ago. "I admit there are times I wonder if I couldn't be doing more good if I were back with my unit at the front. I'm sure my replacement is a good and competent man," he added quickly. "What I mean is, am I personally doing as much good for my country by working behind a desk, processing papers, as I would be if I were back in the field? I really don't know."

Artushev grinned. "That was very nicely phrased," he said. "Now, as for me, I really like not having barbarians with turbans on their heads shooting at me."

They aren't turbans, Pyotr wanted to say. But of course he didn't say it.

Artushev's grin vanished and his other face showed, the face of the man who had survived a purge and exile and now had the ear of those in power. "I implied that we don't seriously doubt your loyalty, Pyotr Andreyevich, and that's quite true. Some of the men above me, though, are a bit uneasy about you, about certain things in your background and your behavior, about things you've said, let slip, now and then. I hope you'll learn to be more careful with your tongue. I also hope you will after all lay to rest their doubts in the way we've discussed."

Pyotr's mouth felt suddenly dry. For a moment, he imagined he could hear the roar of the crematorium furnace, feel the flames licking at his feet. Avoiding the temptation to lick his lips, to cough, to move about, he sat still, trying to look calm and unruffled, and said, "Yes, Comrade General, my plans are unchanged. I hope that soon there will be no more doubts about me, about my loyalty, about my fitness."

"Good!" This was again the hearty, jovial face of Artushev, the buffoonish man other men tended not to take as seriously as they should. "Wonderful. Of course, you'll understand that I never have had any doubts about you. Now, then, I was going to say before that you're a young and vigorous man, not like some of us here, so it's entirely understandable if you're getting a bit bored and restless stuck behind a desk. No, no," he held up his hand, "don't object, don't argue with me about it. I have a possible new assignment for you. It will be much more interesting than what you're doing now, it will get you out in the field, and I think it will give you the chance to, um, serve the Soviet Union much more than you're doing now. Have you ever heard the name Maria Gorova?"

"What?" Pyotr was caught off balance by the apparent sudden change of topic. "No. No, never. Should I know that name?"

Artushev chuckled. "No, you shouldn't. If you did, it would raise those doubts about you again. Until quite recently, Maria Gorova was Generalissimo Slonimsky's ... very special friend. Now, historically, such friends have not had a very good life expectancy. That's as it should be, when you think about it. After all, by the nature of their ... of their work, they tend to know quite a bit of inside information that could be dangerous in the wrong hands. And in fact, we know that they also tend not to be young innocents. They are not, for example, young girls who came to Moscow from the provinces looking for adventure and ended up going down an odd alleyway. In almost all cases, they were intelligence agents, just as much as you and I are."

"Whose agents?" Pyotr asked. "The Americans? The Germans? Someone else?"

"All of those, and many others," Artushev said with a shrug. "Don't forget the Caliphate. They all want to know what's going on inside the Kremlin, they all think they're being very original when they send a charming young woman trained in certain special skills and tell her to be sure to catch the Generalissimo's eye. So we investigate each one right away, from the moment she catches his eye, and we determine who employs her, and we make sure she's never able to send any information to her employer unless it's actually disinformation that the Generalissimo wants her employer to hear, and then when the Generalissimo tires of her special skills, we create a vacancy for the next very special friend."

Pyotr repressed a shiver. Did these young women, these young agents, know the fate of their predecessors? Did they set out on their missions anyway, each hoping she would be the one to break the pattern and get her messages out before dying? Such courage astonished him and filled him with admiration. Compared with it, the risks of being under fire in Afghanistan seemed small.

"And Maria Gorova?"

"She was different." Arushev grimaced. "For one thing, we never could find out who she was working for. We finally concluded that she wasn't working for anyone."

"So she really was an innocent young woman from the provinces?"

Artushev laughed. "Not from the provinces, and certainly not innocent! She had left a few bodies behind her, in fact. No, we decided that she must be working for herself. This isn't a profession in which you expect to find self-employed people, you know. Not outside espionage novels, that is. In the real world, that just doesn't happen. But in her case, it did. We reached that conclusion just about the time the Generalissimo grew tired of her and decided to eliminate her. And then she did something we really thought impossible. She seduced one of the Generalissimo's special security guards, and the man helped her to escape—first from the Kremlin and then from the city. And then, apparently, from the country. We have recently learned that she ended up in America, where she is apparently selling her information to the CIA."

Pyotr whistled in amazement. "I've heard about those security guards. They're supposed to be unstoppable killers and fanatically devoted to Comrade Slonimsky."

"Presumably Gorova's special skills were enough to overcome his devotion and reorient his loyalty. As for his being an unstoppable killer, we found his body on the banks of the Volchov south of Leningrad. He had been stabbed once in the heart. We're convinced Gorova did that."

Pyotr felt a chill run through him. "She's a monster!"

"Yes. How I wish she were working for us! I'm sure you wonder why I'm telling you all of this."

"I have been wondering that, yes," Pyotr admitted.

"I've been speaking to your trainers. They agree that you have acquitted yourself extremely well and are ready for the most demanding of field assignments. We're very worried about what Gorova is telling the Americans. She hasn't told them everything, fortunately. It's a good thing she *is* working for herself and for money, in fact. She's tantalizing them with minor facts and holding out for a big payoff before she tells them all about the Generalissimo's private habits and whatever else they think they can use against us. So there's still time."

"Time for what?"

Artushev's eyes twinkled. "For you to go to America and kill her."

Pyotr stared at him, eyes wide. He was unable to speak.

Artushev's expression changed. The twinkle left his eye. He scowled. "You're frightened?"

"No! I'm delighted! But, Comrade General, I'm also surprised. This is a choice assignment, a plum. From what you've told me, I understand just how important it is and how much credit the man who carries it out successfully will gain. So I wonder why someone much more senior than I hasn't taken it for himself." He hesitated for a moment. "In fact, Comrade General, I can't help wondering why you haven't taken this job yourself, instead of assigning it to me."

Artushev transformed himself to joviality again. "I don't like the idea of being shot at by men in cowboy hats, either. Unlike you, I *like* being safe behind a desk here in Moscow. I'm happy with the point my career has reached. I'm content to stay at this level. But you're young and vigorous with so much ahead of you. Adventure! Romance!" He paused, then added with undisguised relish, "Deaths. Settle those doubts first, and this assignment could be the beginning of a glorious career."

Pyotr knew perfectly well from the training he had already received that the only Americans who wore cowboy hats were genuine farmers or genuine fools. But again he didn't correct General Artushev's ideas about what the men of other nations wore on their heads. "How am I to be inserted?" he asked.

"The usual way. You'll be assigned to our embassy in Washington as some sort of diplomat or other. You'll have to do some actual work, of course—boring stuff, more paper shuffling. Do that work well, though. Some of the more daring of our senior diplomats have been complaining about the number of embassy and consulate positions occupied by our people and KGB agents. The KGB people, especially, consider actual diplomatic work beneath them, so our embassies abroad are having trouble keeping up with their workload."

He chuckled. "Did any of your trainers tell you about these subtle side issues in the great game of espionage? Probably not. But there it is. It's in our interest to keep the diplomats happy. While you're finding out exactly where Gorova is and planning how to get at her, if you can do the work the embassy gives you well, the diplomats will be that much more cooperative with the next agent we assign to them. And probably that much less cooperative the next time the KGB wants to use the embassy as a cover for one of its agents." He smiled happily. "You see? This is the kind of intrigue *I* like!"

Pyotr returned to his desk. He tried to concentrate on his work, but it seemed pointless compared to what faced him tonight and the mission that would follow. He made it to lunchtime, ate an apple at his desk, stared unseeing at the papers in front of him for another hour, and then gave up on it and left. This was unusual for him, and unusual for the office, but he had put in so many late hours during the previous two weeks that he didn't see how anyone could object.

And of course he did have an eventful evening ahead of him.

Dinner was as much liquid as solid, especially on Mikhail's part.

Pyotr couldn't tell if his brother was drinking so much in premature celebration, or to subdue his nervousness, or just because he had a weakness for alcohol. Their father had drunk far too much, too.

Lilya smiled indulgently at her husband and kept an eye out for potential accidents, catching the water glass Mikhail bumped and keeping it from toppling over, or pouring his tea for him so that he wouldn't scald himself.

A good woman, Pyotr thought. Why couldn't I have found one as good? Because you never looked for that kind of woman, he told himself. You found just the type of woman you were looking for, and you managed to avoid permanence and involvement, just as you wished. You kept yourself safe at the expense of this kind of happiness, of a home, of children.

Misha doesn't have children, either! he reminded himself. Thank God.

Pyotr drank only a little. He had always drunk sparingly, fearing loss of control, fearing loss of strength, fearing similarity to their violent father. And right now he didn't feel the need for it, as Misha apparently did. What little physical danger Pyotr might be in was nothing compared to Afghanistan. The danger tonight was not to his body.

He ate little, too, despite Lilya's urging him to eat more. The three of them were alone around the small table, and yet Lilya had loaded it with meat, bread, potatoes, and even fresh vegetables. Good Heavens, how much had she spent on this feast? Pyotr wondered. And why?

"We're so happy to have you here with us again," she said, for perhaps the tenth time. Mikhail nodded, smiling vaguely, and then settled again into a stupor.

Pyotr raised his glass in a silent toast to both of them and then sipped from it. "You shouldn't have spent so much on this dinner," he said to Lilya. The price is too high.

"I told you before," Lilya said, "you're not just a guest, you're a family member who has returned home at last. We have a lot to celebrate."

Pyotr returned her smile and thought, Kill the fatted calf, for the prodigal son has returned. No, the sheep. Kill all the sheep.

Suddenly, Mikhail roused himself. "What time is it? Almost ten? Good Heavens, Petya, come on! I told Sergei we'd be at their apartment by now."

"Sarge," Pyotr corrected him.

Mikhail stared uncomprehendingly at him for a moment, then said, "Oh, yes. Of course. Oh, never mind that anymore. You're one of us now. You're even more than family."

Yes, I'm a fellow saboteur, Pyotr thought.

He was amazed at the change that came over Mikhail. The stupor had vanished and so had the clumsiness. Mikhail pushed his chair back and rose to his feet. He seemed filled with energy and enthusiasm. "Lilya, we have to go out now. I warned you earlier that we would be leaving for a few hours. We'll be back quite late. Please go to bed whenever you want to."

Lilya looked at the food on the table, so little of it eaten, and sighed. "But Misha, it's late already, it's dark, it's cold. It's probably raining again, maybe even snowing. Why don't you just stay home and we'll all have a pleasant evening together. I can get the couch made up so Petya can spend the night here instead of having to go home in this nasty weather."

Mikhail looked grave. "This is business, Lilya. Not pleasure. Very serious business. Petya understands. We have to do this. We have to go."

Lilya sighed again. "Yes, all right. Go ahead, then. Please don't make too much noise when you come back." She kissed her husband, hugged Petya, and turned to stare at the table as if wondering where to begin.

The two brothers put on their heavy coats and rubber overshoes and settled their thick hats on their heads and set out. Mikhail waited until they were outside the building, safe from inquisitive or dangerous ears, before speaking. "She'll stay up, no matter what she says." He grinned, turning to his brother as they passed under a streetlight. A mist was rising, and even as they walked through the pool of light, they began to vanish from each other's view, becoming shadows, ghosts, rather than men. Their voices were muffled by the mists, and Petya couldn't hear his own footsteps. "No matter when we return," Mikhail went on, "she'll be waiting for us. She'll pretend to have been asleep, to have just awakened, but I know her. By now, I ought to."

"A long wait."

"Oh, yes. The b—" He stopped talking and walking. Petya could just barely see him looking around, although it was a pointless action. A platoon of armed men could be following them only meters away, and there'd be no way of knowing it. Petya shivered.

"The event will be a couple of hours from now," Mikhail continued. "After that, you know there'll be more celebrating. More drinking," he added. "So who knows when we'll get home? Maybe not before breakfast!"

"It'll be a difficult day at work tomorrow," Pyotr said. His thoughts drifted away.

"Work! Oh, yes, all right, I suppose we should try to behave normally. Of course. But we'll be energized, won't we? Fatigue won't matter! This is the beginning of the new world, Petya." His voice had risen with excitement. Now he brought himself under control again and said, much more quietly, "Tonight is the real beginning of our revolution."

"Everything changes," Pyotr muttered. "The old ways die. What was, is no more. What is to come is all that matters. This is inevitable."

After a long silence, during which they walked some distance through the misty streets, Mikhail said, "Well, yes. That's what I was thinking, exactly. Very poetically phrased, Petya. I didn't know you had any poetry in you. Maybe you should be the one giving our speeches, eh?"

"That will never happen. You will not be spared, Misha. Do you know where you're going?"

"Of course! We're almost there. Their apartment is in the next block."

Suddenly, the sidewalk shuddered violently. A hot wind tore the wall of mist apart and knocked both men off their feet. They heard a roaring sound, as though a train were passing nearby. As they struggled to their feet, the sound died away, and they heard people screaming. Ahead of them, before the mist closed in again, they could see flames shooting from a third–floor window of an apartment block.

Then the mist swirled around them, but it was colored orange now, and it was mixed with smoke. Pyotr's eyes stung and teared. He heard sirens in the distance.

Mikhail coughed, tried to speak, choked. Finally, he managed to say, in a roughened voice, "My God, what was that?"

"A premature explosion," Pyotr told him. "The device the

traitors in the pay of a Western government had planned to use to damage the Paveletsk railroad station exploded prematurely in their apartment building, killing them and also, unfortunately, many of their innocent neighbors."

"What? Petya, what—?"

"That's what the announcement will say tomorrow. All the members of the so-called Fourth of June movement have been arrested and have received their due punishment. The motherland is safe."

"Petya, I don't understand!"

Shadowy figures appeared in the mist around them, moved closer, resolved themselves into armed soldiers. They surrounded the two brothers and aimed their rifles at them. The officer in command, a major, stepped up to Mikhail, who shrank back.

"Mikhail Andreyovich Rodzhinsky," the major said, "you are under arrest for treason. You are to be taken away and tried immediately."

"Petya!" It was the cry of a ghost, of a man who soon would be a ghost. "Lilya!"

The soldiers surrounded him and hurried him away. They disappeared quickly in the mist. The sounds were muffled and then vanished.

"She'll be all right," Pyotr called out. "You have my word. She's innocent. She's accused of nothing." He had no idea if Mikhail could hear him. He had no idea if what he was saying was the truth.

The major came up to him and said, "Congratulations, Comrade Major."

"Captain," Pyotr corrected him, his mind elsewhere.

The major smiled. "No, Major. You'll get the official

notification tomorrow, I imagine. Congratulations on breaking up this gang, too. A fine job."

"Can I ask you a favor? That man you just took away. My brother. Can you spare him pain? Make it quick?"

The major considered the request for a while. "I'll do my best," he said at last. "We have the others. Except for the two in the apartment with the bomb, of course. We can probably get all the information we need from the others. All right, Comrade Major. I can't promise you anything, but I'll try."

"And his wife?" Pyotr saw the expression on the major's face, and he sighed. "I understand. Too much risk."

The major looked around quickly and then leaned forward and spoke quietly. "A word of advice, comrade. You're young, and you're at the beginning of what can be a fine career. Don't let sentimentality get in the way. It can destroy you." He stepped away and said in a normal tone, "Good luck to you. As for me, I have a busy night ahead of me." He turned and melted into the mist.

For an hour or more, Pyotr Rodzhinsky stood there in the mist, trying desperately to feel nothing.

Fifteen

October 1991

Pyotr tried to match the speed of the other cars on the highway. His license plates said Virginia and his clothing was nondescript. If he had to speak, he could do so in the accent of the southern end of the state. He was just another local on a routine errand.

In theory, the Americans had no idea who he was. He had his doubts about that, but in case they really didn't know, he didn't want to draw attention to himself—especially not here. If he were stopped by an ordinary highway patrolman for an ordinary reason, his papers and his accent should pass muster. So he had been assured, anyway. But if the men who pulled him over weren't ordinary, that would be a different matter, a much more dangerous one.

Arkady Alenichev had argued strenuously against Pyotr doing this reconnaissance at all. "What's the point?" he had said. "Our mole has already given you all the information you could need!" Pyotr had responded that it was an emotional thing, this need of his to see the ground himself, to feel the environment. He hadn't said that he had little confidence in information supplied by the KGB's moles, that he considered that entire agency incompetent. Slonimsky had ordered the KGB and the GRU to start cooperating, coordinating, perhaps eventually (so Pyotr feared) integrating. He would follow Slonimsky's orders, of course, but what inept fools all these KGB men were!

And what awful weather this was! Afghanistan had been bad enough with its extremes of hot and cold, but at least there the air was dry.

He had started this drive with the windows rolled down in hopes of a fresh breeze. Now he used the power buttons to close them all, and then he turned on the airconditioning. Corrupt, decadent, bourgeois, all those things he remembered his father saying about Americans and their mechanical comforts—well, perhaps so, but Pyotr luxuriated in the cool, dry air blowing on his sweaty face. It was October! It should be cool already. Instead, it was hot and humid. If he had to live here, he knew he'd use this particular mechanical comfort all the time.

He bent forward and looked up at the tops of the trees. So tall, so thick! The undergrowth beside the road was dense, too. He imagined it would be hard to walk through. He would love to do so and wished he had time to stop.

So much green life. That was one advantage to a climate like this. It reminded him of a resort on the Black Sea where his father had once taken all of them. That was when Pyotr was eight, during a brief period when his father had been stable and loving, before his madness had possessed him again. Pyotr and Mikhail had played all day in the surf. Of course, he'd had to rescue Mikhail from drowning time after time. The older boy had never had any sense.

In the end, that foolishness had killed him. That was what

really killed him, Pyotr told himself.

Red lights flashed in his face as the car ahead slowed suddenly. Pyotr stepped on his brakes. He was grateful for the distraction.

He seemed to be caught in a line of traffic turning off at Maclean. Some of them were probably going to the very building that was his own true destination. Off to the right, above the trees, Pyotr could see the tops of two white buildings.

She was in the one closer to the highway. Or so the mole said.

All he had to do now was stay in this line of cars, bluff his way through the gate of one of America's most closely guarded complexes, park in front of that building, stroll inside, find the right door on the right floor, walk in, kill her, walk back out, drive away... So simple.

Pyotr glanced over his left shoulder, put on his left-turn signal, and pulled into the left lane and passed the cars waiting to turn off the highway. As he went past them, he craned his neck and glimpsed a tall chainlink fence in the distance. He didn't need to see the guard hut to know it was there. He could sense it.

They'd be alert, he knew, twenty-four hours a day. Only a fool would dismiss the Americans as fools. Pyotr never underestimated any enemy, not Americans, not Mujahedeen, none of them. His papers wouldn't let him drive through that gate with the other cars, he would have no chance of getting past the fence any other way, and if by some miracle he did manage to get inside the complex, he would be caught before he could get more than a few meters.

He sighed, stepped on the accelerator, and continued down Dolly Madison Avenue in the direction of Tysons Corner. The supposedly safe meeting place was just a few kilometers beyond that.

“Don’t you understand, Arkady? I wouldn’t even have been able to get past the gate, let alone into the complex. Trying to do it by force would be suicide. Pointless suicide.”

The young KGB man stared at him in astonishment. He was blond, blue eyed, ruddy cheeked, tall, handsome—in short, sickeningly well qualified to pose for the cover of *Soviet Life* magazine or for a poster depicting brave factory or collective farm workers. Whether he was at all qualified for espionage was a matter about which Pyotr was beginning to have doubts.

“But, Comrade,” Alenichev said, “you’re under orders to get to Maria Gorova and kill her! That’s why you were sent here! Who knows what she’s been telling the Americans?”

“Why, yes,” Pyotr said sarcastically, “some of it might even be the truth. Look, my orders are to kill her, not to sacrifice myself pointlessly. If my death would result in hers, that would be a different matter. That would be worth it.” Even as he said those words, he knew he didn’t mean them. He knew at last what this naïve young man had yet to learn: what counted most wasn’t preservation of one’s country but preservation of one’s self.

“That goes without saying,” Alenichev said. “You make whatever sacrifices you have to—yourself, even your family.” He went on, not noticing that Pyotr had winced. “I’m not saying that you should throw your life away pointlessly. I’m just saying that perhaps you should try, investigate the area, before you dismiss the idea completely. Every minute we sit here discussing this, Gorova is telling the Americans more. You have to do something to stop her.”

Pyotr sighed. He stood up and walked over to the window, leaned his forearms on the sill, looked at the dark green lawn.

A good place to live, he thought. Was this once farmland, in the old days, before the capital city and its suburbs had encroached? Back in the days when this country, too, was revolutionary, this old farmhouse had been here and the view from this window must have been of fields of crops spreading to the horizon.

Fields worked by slaves, he reminded himself. So much for their revolutionaries.

But for the masters, it must have been a good place to live. Masters always have a good life, anywhere, anytime.

These are unhealthy thoughts, he told himself. Counterrevolutionary. Revisionist. Etc., etc. These are the thoughts of a bitter, disillusioned old man, and you're too young for that. You should have no doubts, Pyotr Andreyovich Rodzhinksy. You should emulate this mindless KGB man.

If I were in charge, the KGB would be restricted to cleaning toilets.

He turned back from the window and eyed the other man. Even dressed in civilian clothes, he seemed to be in uniform. Pyotr had no doubt the Americans knew who and what Alenichev really was. Which meant that now they knew who and what he was, too. Alenichev had insisted that the ownership of this farmhouse was covered in so many layers of misdirection that the American security men had no idea it was actually being used by the KGB. Pyotr had managed not to laugh in his face. The GRU knew exactly where the supposed safe houses of the various foreign security services operating in the USSR were located, and he had no doubt the Americans had equivalent knowledge here.

But that was the GRU. The KGB probably had no idea where American spies gathered in the Soviet Union, and they probably assumed the Americans were as incompetent as they were.

Be all that as it may, Pyotr had to assume that the Americans had identified him, now that he had met with Alenichev. If that resulted in the failure of his mission, then on Slonimsky's head be it. The fool.

"All right. I'll drive by there again. Another pointless reconnaissance. In the meantime, contact your mole inside Langley again and find out where Gorova is now."

"She's in there!" Alenichev protested. "I already told you that."

This time, Pyotr didn't bother restraining himself. "Arkady, maybe under similar circumstances, the KGB would keep the subject in one place, but don't underestimate the Americans. They know I've driven past the entrance to their complex once, and by now I'm sure they know what I am. They'll certainly be watching me as I drive by the second time. Moreover, they are probably assuming you have at least one agent inside already. I can assure you that Gorova is no longer inside that place. See if you can find out where they've taken her."

He calmed himself and smiled. "Let's be entirely frank with each other, Arkady. We both want to do well with this assignment and please our superiors." Certainly you need to do that, now that you've messed everything up so badly. I can still blame my difficulties on the KGB. As long as I succeed in the end, that is. "We can do that if we work together. Your people can get the necessary information but without exposing themselves. Then I'll act upon that information. I'll willingly take the physical risks to complete our joint mission."

Arkady nodded slowly. "And in the process, we'd both be pleasing Generalissimo Slonimsky, who wants to see our agencies working together, instead of at cross–purposes, as in the past."

"Exactly! Everyone gains. Except," Pyotr added with a laugh, "Maria Gorova."

Alenichev laughed along with him. "Yes, exactly!"

"In fact, could you do me a favor? I need to reassure my superiors that I'm still on the job and everything is proceeding according to plan, but I don't want to reveal myself to the Americans by going to the Embassy. It's possible they still don't know me, after all. Could you transmit a message to Khodinka Airfield for me, using your encrypted systems?"

"Of course, Comrade! I would be delighted to do that."

"Good. Thank you. The text is simple: 'Gorova location pinpointed. Closing in.'"

"'Pinpointed'?" Alenichev grinned. "You were just telling me she probably isn't where we think she is."

Pyotr shrugged eloquently. "It's a game we all must play. I'm sure you play it with your superiors from time to time, yes?"

The KGB man laughed. "I refuse to answer that question, Comrade."

Pyotr laughed, too. They were, he reflected, filling the farmhouse with false laughter. "At the end of the message, you must append a code. That will assure Khodinka that the message comes from me. Here it is. Don't write it down. Memorize it." He recited a string of letters and numbers and made Alenichev repeat it until he was sure the younger man knew it. "Good. Off you go, now. Get that message sent right away."

Alenichev left.

Pyotr waited for half an hour and then left as well, beginning the drive back to his motel.

He took a long, roundabout, meandering route. He wasn't in any particular hurry, and he wanted a chance to see the scenery, which pleased him. He also liked the idea of annoying any American counterintelligence agents who were following him. Perhaps they liked the scenery, too! In that case, they'd feel some gratitude toward him. Not that that would help, if push came to shove, but you never knew what might give you a tiny edge. The merest, briefest hesitation on the part of your opponent could save your life.

He fiddled with the radio dial and chanced across WBMS. Bach, he thought with pleasure. Some Americans like good music. That's to their credit. He hoped the men following him were listening to the same station.

It was possible, although unlikely, that the Americans had had only one car following Alenichev. So it was possible that when Alenichev left, that car had followed him and Pyotr was now not being followed. More likely, Pyotr thought, they had called in a second team while he and Alenichev had been meeting in the farmhouse. Pyotr had arrived after Alenichev, so the watchers would have seen him drive up and would probably have called for a second car immediately.

The KGB had insisted on these face–to–face meetings. They were absolutely sure this farmhouse was unknown to the Americans as a KGB safehouse. They were equally sure that the Americans didn't know that Alenichev was anything but an ordinary civilian Soviet employee of the Embassy. Didn't they realize that the Americans would be following him around anyway, even if they did think he was just some Embassy clerk or secretary?

When had the KGB become so inept? The old rivalry between KGB and GRU didn't prevent Pyotr from acknowledging the KGB's admirable history of espionage. Was it Gorbachev's fault that all the good men had been forced out? We recruited some of them, he thought. But not that many. Perhaps Slonimsky has eliminated them, seeing them as a threat to his power, more frightened of that than of the consequences of emasculating their agency.

Thank God he hasn't done that to us! Not yet, anyway. That time may come, too. Not while he needs us so badly, not while he's afraid of what Gorova or others like her will tell the Americans and the other enemies of the state.

But he doesn't really care about the enemies of the state!

It was an overdue realization. Once it had come, it seemed obvious, and he wondered why he hadn't seen it before.

Slonimsky cares only about his own survival, Pyotr thought, his own power. All that matters is what threatens him. What threatens the country is irrelevant unless it threatens him personally as well. Nowadays they want me to say that I serve the Soviet Union and Generalissimo Slonimsky. But how can I truly serve both?

When will he turn against us, too? If I succeed in this mission, will I earn his admiration and protection, or will he see me as too competent and therefore as a future threat?

Wheels within wheels. Layer upon layer of deception. Never turn your back on anyone. Never trust anyone.

Part of the code he had given Alenichev was indeed an identifier to verify that the message had originated with Pyotr Rodzhinsky.

But only part.

Pyotr assumed that Alenichev would change the message so that the men at Khodinka would receive something damning, something that would tell them that the mission was in peril and that Pyotr was to blame for any failure. It was, he had to admit, what he would have done in Alenichev's place. But in fact, it wouldn't matter. The real message was contained in the rest of the code string. Some of that was a prearranged alert telling the GRU to examine all KGB communications having to do with any names mentioned in the apparent text of the message. The remainder of the code specified the location of one of the drop points in Washington where information could be left for Pyotr.

It was possible that Alenichev would add text containing other names, thus diverting some of the GRU's attention in unproductive directions. The real danger was that he would delete the name "Maria Gorova" entirely. Pyotr was betting that he wouldn't. Much more likely that he'd change the text to say that Pyotr was failing. Thanks to the code, Pyotr knew that would amuse the men at Khodinka.

Unless in the end Pyotr really failed. Then their amusement would turn to something else. He could end up like his brother.

He couldn't let himself dwell on that, on any of it. Determinedly, he focused his attention on the immediate problem.

He knew the GRU monitored all KGB communications. Now, because of his coded message, they would check for any mention of "Maria Gorova" and would see Alenichev's request that KGB agents try to determine her present whereabouts. Khodinka would understand that they must determine that themselves, and quickly, and transmit that information to Pyotr at the specified drop point.

How soon could he expect a response?

He had been told before he left Moscow that only the KGB knew where Gorova was, that all the information about her being in CIA headquarters came from a KGB mole, and that the GRU had been told even that much and called in to finish the job only because of Slonimsky's insistence that the two agencies cooperate. That might even be the truth, although it was also possible that Pyotr's superiors were playing a deep game of their own and were lying to him, that in fact the GRU had been watching Gorova through its own system of moles and already knew where she was. In that case, he could expect a response almost immediately.

But if they gave him the information he needed right away, that would in effect tell him that they had been lying, so they probably wouldn't do that. They would respond as if they had been telling the truth before. So he might as well assume they had been telling the truth and had been getting all their information about Gorova's whereabouts from the KGB.

He shook his head and grunted in annoyance. Why was all this subterfuge and double–dealing necessary? Surely it would be more efficient and effective if his agency told the truth within the confines of its own walls!

Lay it at Slonimsky's feet, he told himself. He's resurrected the old days, the Stalinist days, when no one knew what the truth was or who was telling it, when everyone worked against everyone else, when...

He sighed again and completed the thought: When brother betrayed brother.

He was letting his mind drift again. Stay focused! he thought.

Assume, then, that the time required for the GRU's response

will be as it would if they had no information about Maria Gorova beyond what the KGB had told them and would have to start their investigation after receiving his message. In that case, when could he expect a reply?

Would the CIA take Gorova out of D.C. entirely? That was possible, of course. If they did that, the game was up. Finding her in this large country with its many big cities before she told the CIA so much that there was no longer any point in killing her would be virtually impossible. So for the sake of his mission, and of his future, he had to assume they wouldn't do that.

If they kept her in the Washington area, the game of safehouse identification switched around. How many hiding places did the CIA have that neither the KGB nor the GRU had already identified? Not many, Pyotr was willing to bet. Probably none!

If they had her in one of their safehouses, then it would surely be one they thought was truly safe—not known to the opposition. That increased the odds that it was one the KGB knew nothing about but the GRU did.

People were being taken to and from those locations all the time—foreign agents who had turned, foreign agents who had been captured, CIA agents who had tried to turn but had been caught by their own agency, and nowadays, thanks to the new atmosphere in Washington, some American civilians who had spoken against their government too often, too insistently, too publicly, and—most dangerously—too effectively.

Pyotr chuckled. So much for America's long-proclaimed democracy and moral superiority. Now, when their country felt so threatened, the men in power in America were finding much to emulate in the Soviet model.

The GRU would have lists at Khodinka of all those comings and goings. With just a bit of luck, an analyst looking through those lists because of Pyotr's message would see something that would tell him which of those movements was Gorova's arrival.

Those lists would be long, though. And manpower at GRU headquarters was being stretched to the limit these days, thanks to the USSR's many new foreign adventures. It might be a couple of days before Pyotr got a response. Twenty-four hours at least. Yes, he'd give it that long.

He arrived back at his motel, parked the car, went inside, and locked the door behind him. A quick glance showed that nothing had been disturbed. He hoped that was the case, for that would mean he hadn't been identified by the Americans after all.

If they had in fact discovered him, they had sent top-notch experts to examine his room during his absence. Irrationally, that pleased him.

Despite the car's airconditioning, he felt sweaty and dirty. He took a quick shower and afterwards turned on the television set while toweling himself dry.

It was a nice television set, and many cable channels were available at no charge. The comfort level of even this cheap room was remarkable. It annoyed Pyotr to have to admit that a cheap motel room in America was luxurious compared to a typical Soviet home, but one of the things the GRU had trained him to do was to recognize and accept reality, no matter how distasteful. That training had merely reinforced his natural bent. Denying reality was not only foolish and futile. It was also, in his opinion, contemptible.

Nonetheless, the level of wealth and comfort in America seemed fundamentally unfair. Russians—Soviets—had worked so much harder for so much longer, had suffered so much more, for such smaller results. Americans seemed to think that this proved that God was on their side. To Pyotr, it was further proof that God did not exist.

The television seemed to be showing the middle of a national news program. Pyotr paused in his toweling and watched for a while.

The blandly pretty female news announcer was talking about yet another American military disaster in the Middle East.

Pyotr shook his head. He could almost feel sorry for these people. They had thought themselves on top of the world. Actually, everyone, even Russians, had thought Americans were on top of the world. Now a religious fanatic and his armies were steadily dismantling their allies, their armies, and their pride. Well, better them than us, he thought. As long as the Caliphate's main forces are concentrated on the Americans and their allies, it keeps the pressure off our own southern border.

The picture changed to the White House. This was a recording of a statement made earlier by the President. Pyotr looked at the man's silly face, at what some political opponent had famously called his "deer caught in the headlights" look, and thought that here was further proof that God did not exist. What kind of god would put such a fool in charge of one of the world's two great powers? A god with a very nasty sense of humor, perhaps.

"I want to tell all of you," the President said, "that the situation along the Jordan River remains stable. The line holds. The Joint Chiefs have assured me that our valiant men and women in uniform are doing the job we and God have asked them to. The land where Jesus walked remains safe. You will hear negative words spoken in the press. Pay no attention. The left–leaning liberal media have never been truly patriotic. I call on all real Americans to reject negative words, to support our brave men and women in uniform, and to believe in our eventual victory over the forces of evil. Thank you, and God bless America."

As the picture faded away, the President stared into the camera. Pyotr couldn't tell if he was trying to look earnest and reassure the citizenry, or if he was waiting for approval from off–camera.

The female announcer reappeared. "After this morning's attack on the Jordan was reported, carefully orchestrated and coordinated anti–war demonstrations were staged in a number of American cities. Police moved in immediately to enforce the Support Our Forces Act, which the President signed yesterday."

Her image slid down to the lower right–hand corner of the screen. A still picture of police attacking demonstrators filled the rest of the screen.

Pyotr could see that the police were clubbing some demonstrators to the ground, pulling others away in handcuffs, and destroying their signs. He couldn't see the signs well enough to read them, but he assumed that they called for withdrawing American forces from the dangers of the Middle East and suing for peace.

Unavoidably, he thought of his brother.

Poor Misha! He would have been at home among those hopeless fools.

He switched the television set off and continued drying himself.

By the time he had dressed again, it was six o'clock and he felt hungry. He had hoped he'd be done with the job and on his way back home by now. It was clear, however, that he'd be here at least another day. He'd have to make an effort to fit in.

His driver's license gave him an address in Portsmouth. If he were forced to explain his presence in Washington, he would claim to be a collector of antique glass ashtrays. He was here looking for more ashtrays, he would say. He had been astonished to learn that Americans really did collect such items. In preparation for the role, he had read a few reports on the subject and had found himself unexpectedly interested. If he had to, he could visit antique shops and talk about glass ashtrays quite knowledgeably. But he'd prefer it if it never came to that.

Still, his cover meant he could go to some local restaurant tonight for a quick meal, and if someone tried to start a conversation with him, he wouldn't have to avoid it. Tomorrow, he could wander around the city, working his way slowly, seemingly randomly, toward the drop point he had specified in his coded message.

In the end, the only person who tried to start a conversation with him at the fast-food restaurant he chose was a woman, obviously painfully lonely, who seemed to want more than idle chat. She aroused both his pity and his desire, but he knew better than to give in to either one. He responded to her coolly until she became discouraged, then he finished his meal quickly and went back to his motel room, alone, and to bed, also alone.

Unlike Aleksander Slonimsky, he knew where his duty lay.

The next day was seasonably dry and cool. Pyotr drove into the city slowly, moving with the morning traffic, with his windows rolled down. Despite the traffic fumes, the air seemed clear to him, a portent of a good day ahead. Even the sounds of other cars' engines idling next to him in traffic jams and the blowing of horns didn't bother him. He turned the volume up on the car radio and reveled in Tchaikovsky.

On the hour, the music was interrupted for a brief news broadcast. 10,000 Marines had landed at Haifa to reinforce positions along the Jordan. An aircraft carrier was on its way to the Mediterranean. All remaining US civilians in Israel who were not working in some capacity with the Defense Department were being evacuated. At the same time, American Jews were being encouraged to consider emigrating to Israel, which would grant them immediate citizenship and residency under the Right of Return. SOFA, the Support Our Forces Act, was mentioned again with an emphasis that Pyotr knew was meant to send a message. He was sure that everyone understood the message clearly.

Tchaikovsky resumed. This time, it was Romeo and Juliet. Suicidal young love and clan warfare in ancient Verona. Pyotr laughed. The world was returning to the violence and fragmentation of Renaissance Italy, but without the fine paintings and sculpture.

But we do have antique glass ashtrays, he thought, and he laughed again.

He stopped at a couple of antique shops in Georgetown. At the first one, his inquiry about glass ashtrays earned him a sneer. Apparently, he was the wrong kind of collector for this place. At the second, the owner turned out to be the kind of antique-glass-ashtray enthusiast Pyotr was only pretending to be. Pyotr found the conversation interesting and wouldn't have minded staying for a while, but he feared his quickly acquired and shallow knowledge of the field wouldn't be enough to fool this man for long, so he bought one of the owner's better pieces and left.

He wondered what the accountants at Khodinka would say when they saw his itemized expense list after this mission. Ah well, they were probably used to even stranger purchases than this one.

He drove south on 21st Street until he saw the park. He found a parking space on a side street, locked the car, and walked a block and then into the park.

It was clean and safe here nowadays. According to his reading, drug addicts, prostitutes, and muggers had once infested the park. The GRU had ascertained that this was no longer the case. That was all that had mattered to the briefing officers in Moscow, but Pyotr wondered when the change had come, and why, and how. And where were those drug addicts and prostitutes and muggers now? In some new American version of Siberia?

Why, I feel more at home in this country all the time! he thought.

He strolled across a wide, green lawn. Ahead, the ground dropped to form a natural depressed bowl. At the middle, at the lowest point, was a playground. There were slides and seesaws and elaborate equipment for climbing on. It was filled with noisy children, black and white, playing together. They shrieked and climbed and ran and chased each other. On benches nearby, young mothers sat and chatted while keeping an eye on their young.

Pyotr stood looking down at the scene and smiling. How charming! He hoped all of this would survive whatever was coming.

He turned and walked along the rim of the bowl, circling the happy scene and looking down at it while he walked. He could imagine himself married to one of those attractive young women, father to one or more of those happy children. It was a pleasant fantasy.

Working for the CIA, he thought. They'd be happy to have me. A curious thought—but really not all that improbable. He wished he hadn't thought it.

Further along, he turned away from the bowl. He lost sight of the playground almost immediately. He headed into a stand of trees. He slowed down even more, strolling along as though he were there simply to enjoy the shade, the trees, the delightful breeze. Delightful it all really was, and he really was enjoying it.

Within the stand of trees was an old oak. The tree must have predated the park and even the city around it, Pyotr thought. The trunk was immense, three meters in diameter at least. It forked at head height into two huge, thick branches. In the fork was a hole in the wood. It was deep. For all Pyotr knew, it went all the way into the heart of the great tree. He assumed it had been created by birds or squirrels.

He had timed his stroll so that the sun was shining through an opening in the trees and directly into the hole as he passed. Without turning his head, he looked as far to the side as he could. Into the hole in the oak tree. Where a small piece of paper lay, weighted in place by a pebble.

Highview Terrace. Hillcrest. He read the street address on the paper without slowing down.

There was a small risk that someone else would see that message, but you had to know where to look and what you were looking for, or you wouldn't even notice the piece of paper. Rain was likely within the next day or so. It would loosen the pebble, and the paper would fall down into the tree, never to be seen again by human eyes.

His heart beat faster. He knew where she was, and he was eager to go there immediately, do the job, and leave this country. But he couldn't do that. He had to wait. At the very least, he had to make it look like he'd come to this park just to relax.

He kept walking, not fast, as though he were enjoying the day, until he reached the far end of the stand of trees. He chose a tree to lean against, folded his arms over his chest, made himself comfortable, and did nothing.

Minutes passed. Fifteen. Thirty. Pyotr leaned against his tree, arms folded, eyes half closed, breathing slowly and deeply, a smile on his face.

Delightful! A light breeze touched the right side of his face. It brought with it the scent of flowers. Roses? He thought so. Now that he was relaxed, he could hear faintly the shouts and laughter of the children in the playground he had passed earlier. Insects buzzed somewhere nearby.

From the corner of his right eye, he saw a shadowy figure a few meters away. The man was trying to hide within the stand of trees Pyotr had walked through. Pyotr couldn't make the figure out, not without turning his head and looking at him directly. Which he wouldn't do, because that would let the other man know that Pyotr was aware of him.

Pyotr took a few deep breaths, stood up straight, stretched his arms over his head, sighed with pleasure.

Come along, CIA man. We have ashtrays to look at.

He spent the next four hours driving around the downtown area, on the lookout for antique and collectibles stores. He only found a few that looked at all promising, but he went into each one of them and managed to find something to buy in each.

Finally he was ready for the next stage. Surely the CIA man had given up by now! Pyotr hoped so. If the man was dogged enough to still be behind him, then Pyotr might end up having to kill him, and he didn't want to do that. He felt a sort of kinship with him. After all, some day they might be working for the same boss.

Wiser to adopt Begench's attitude: He got in the way.

He had memorized the general layout of the city. He knew where Hillcrest was. He had a detailed street map of the city open on the passenger seat next to him and had no doubts about his ability to find the specific house when he got there.

Traffic was a lot heavier now. Annoying, but he hoped it would help him blend in all the more.

The park was north of the Capitol. He took D Street west to 3rd, then 3rd south to Pennsylvania. He headed southeast on Pennsylvania Avenue. Once he'd crossed the Anacostia River, the traffic became a bit lighter. Pyotr slowed down, looking for the right place to turn off. The car behind him honked its horn. The driver came as close as he could to Pyotr's rear bumper without making contact and flashed his brights at him. Pyotr ignored him.

The highway began to climb a hill. Hence the name, Pyotr realized. He passed an old fire station. Very picturesque, he thought.

There it was: Branch Avenue.

Pyotr turned right and slowed down still more, as much to enjoy the wooded neighborhood as to look at the street names. Trees lined the street on either side, their branches almost meeting overhead. Too bad he didn't have time to get out and walk a bit.

If I do end up working for the CIA, he thought, this is where

I'd like to live.

Glancing at the map from time to time, Pyotr found Hillcrest Drive. He drove along the curving street, concentrating fully on house numbers. The scenery was forgotten. There was only one thing that mattered now. When he saw the house, he didn't slow down. Red brick colonial. Set on a slight rise, a meter or two higher than the street. Attractive and peaceful. Well manicured lawn, small trees to the side of the building. Similar houses to either side. Dark blue Ford Taurus parked at the curb in front of the house.

He continued until the curving street had taken him out of sight of the house. Then he pulled over and picked up the map and pretended to examine it.

He'd much prefer to try to enter the place after dark, when he could approach unseen from the rear. But he had had to determine its location for sure during daylight. Now he couldn't wait for dark. He couldn't take the chance. If he was still being followed, they'd know he had found the place and they'd move Gorova. They might be doing that right now.

No choice. Time to throw the dice, risk it all. If they knew who he was, he'd be dead very soon now. If they didn't know, or if they had momentarily lost track of him, he had a chance.

He made a U turn, sped back around the curve, drove past the CIA safehouse, made another U turn, and parked behind the Taurus.

He got out of the car, slammed the door loudly, and walked briskly up the sloping lawn toward the front door. He could feel the leather against his right thigh as he walked; it offered some comfort. He had removed the lining of the pocket that morning, before leaving the motel.

There was a heavy brass knocker on the door. Probably an antique, he thought. I should know that. He knocked loudly with the knocker. The sharp sounds echoed from other buildings in a ghostly repetition.

What would it be when the door opened? A puzzled, angry glare from some large CIA man, or a bullet between the eyes?

Much like home in so many ways, Pyotr thought.

He knocked again. He felt impatient. One way or the other, let's get it taken care of.

The door opened. It was the puzzled, angry glare. And the man glaring was indeed large. He was young, healthy, impatient, and the tank top and shorts he was wearing showed that he was heavily muscled. "Yeah?"

"I'm here to pick up the ashtray."

"What?"

"The ashtray. The ashtray!" Pyotr feigned impatience himself. "Antique. Glass. For sale. That ashtray."

"Wrong address, buddy. No one even smokes in this house."

He started to close the door, but Pyotr leaned against it. "I've got the right address. Look, I already mailed the check. To this address. Don't make me call the cops."

The young man chuckled suddenly at that. "Wouldn't want to do that. Look, sir. I can assure you you've got the wrong address. I told you, no one here even smokes."

"Of course not! You don't use a valuable antique ashtray to put out your cigarette butts, you moron! You've got my money, and you've got my ashtray, and I want it. Where is it?"

This was taking too long. He shoved against the door suddenly, without warning, knocking the younger man back a few steps. Pyotr stepped inside and pushed the door closed with his foot.

"Hey!" The CIA man was angry—but fortunately not alarmed. He stepped forward and grabbed Pyotr's shirt front with both hands, pulling Pyotr up onto his toes. Pyotr reached inside his right pocket. His hand went through the opening, down against his thigh, against the sheath fastened there, and came out holding a slender, razor-sharp, eight-inch blade that tapered almost to a needle point. Without pause, he drove the knife up between the CIA man's forearms and then forward at a thirty-degree angle.

The point entered under the man's lower jaw just behind the chin, slicing easily through the soft tissues and muscles, through his tongue, the back of his throat, into his brainstem.

He fell limply to the floor. As he fell away, Pyotr gripped the handle of the knife, pulling it out. The young man lay on his back, blood spewing from his wound. His eyes blinked rapidly, desperately. He could move nothing else.

A terrible thing to happen to a healthy young man, Pyotr thought. If there was time when all was finished, and if this poor fellow was still alive, he'd put him out of his misery.

Where was his partner? There must be at least one other man here to guard so valuable a prisoner. Or whatever they considered her.

No alarm so far. No sounds at all. Pyotr stood utterly still and quiet. He could hear nothing. The second man might be just around a corner in the house somewhere, standing just as still as Pyotr, waiting for Pyotr to make the first move.

Pyotr looked at the door. He hadn't pushed it far enough; it remained slightly ajar. He didn't want to push it the rest of the way: too much risk of a sound. The man on the floor wasn't in sight from outside, so leaving the door slightly open was an acceptable risk.

The man's eyes were no longer moving. He stared straight up, unblinking. His chest and the floor around him were covered in blood, but blood no longer flowed from his neck. Good, Pyotr thought. He was better off this way than he would have been if his brain had survived, trapped in a dead body.

The next encounter wouldn't be close work. Pyotr had come into the house armed only with the knife. He wiped the knife clean on the dead man's shorts and slid it back into its sheath. He put his hand under the man's hip and rolled him slightly to one side. As he had hoped, there was a small pistol strapped to the small of his back. Pyotr removed it, straightened, took a breath, and stepped carefully, slowly, silently into the house.

He was in a living room. Beige wall-to-wall carpet. To the right, against the wall, a long white leather couch. To the left, a large window, fortunately curtained against the sunlight. Generic bad landscape paintings to either side of the window and above the couch. Coffee table in front of the couch. Ahead, in the far wall, a fireplace with a clock above it.

Pyotr took another step. Another. Still nothing, and no sign of anyone.

There was, in fact, a glass ashtray on the coffee table. The dead man had lied about that. Collectible, too, Pyotr thought. If he had time afterwards, he'd like a closer look.

He heard a sound behind him.

He spun around.

Nothing.

Imagination, he told himself. Calm yourself, the way you were taught.

He relaxed, letting his heartbeat slow. Then he stepped forward again.

Now he could see, on the right, at the far end of the room, beyond the couch, an entranceway to the rest of the house. No doors or openings elsewhere. That simplified things.

The window? The second man might be waiting on the other side of that. No, for then he'd have to come through the curtain. Too hard to see what he was doing, and he'd alert Pyotr while pushing the curtain aside. If the window was closed, it would be impossible to enter that way without alerting Pyotr. The entranceway ahead was the most likely place, if he was indeed waiting for Pyotr.

Pyotr stood silently for what seemed like endless minutes, hoping the other man would move, would spring into view. Pyotr held his pistol ready aimed at the opening. With the other man in motion, Pyotr would have a momentary advantage.

Nothing happened.

Damn, Pyotr thought, he's not that stupid. Too bad. Okay, you wait there and I'll come to you.

He took another step forward.

The curtain to his left shifted.

Pyotr froze with his pistol pointed midway between the entrance ahead and the window to his left.

The curtain shifted again, more vigorously this time. Pyotr felt a breeze against his face. He heard faint, faraway sounds—a lawnmower, a car, a man's voice. Just the wind, then, not the other CIA man. But the window was indeed open, which increased the risk from that direction somewhat. If Pyotr took another few steps, the window would be behind him.

He hesitated, wondering if he should leave through the front door and go around the house, look for an unguarded rear entrance.

While he stood there weighing the options, the other CIA man jumped from the entranceway at the far end of the room and fired.

The shot missed.

Pyotr fired. Saw the man's right thigh blossom red, his knee give way. Realized it was not a man but Maria Gorova herself.

He froze in astonishment. She leaned against the wall, raised her gun and aimed very deliberately.

Pyotr seemed unable to move.

Something hit him in the right side, knocking him to the left, just as Gorova fired again. Pain erupted in his chest. He collapsed to the floor. Agony filled his chest. He couldn't breathe!

He heard shouts, shots being fired, glimpsed Gorova staggering away out of sight through the entranceway.

A weight fell heavily over his legs. Gasping for air, Pyotr managed to raise his head slightly. The weight was Arkady Alenichev, his face still recognizable but the back of his head blown away. A gun lay on the carpet near his outstretched hand.

Another man walked into view. He was also armed. He looked in the direction of the vanished Gorova then down at Pyotr and Alenichev, frowning in thought.

I've failed, Pyotr thought. And now the Americans will have my body to examine.

At least I won't have to do any explaining to General Artushev or anyone else at Khodinka.

He faded into unconsciousness with a smile on his face.

He came to again in a hospital bed beside which General Artushev sat on a wooden chair, watching him with interest.

"I'm alive!" Pyotr mumbled.

"Perhaps you're actually in Heaven and I'm one of the angels," Artushev said. "But I doubt if I can convince you of that. Yes, of course you survived. Thanks to one of your fellow GRU agents and no thanks to the KGB, damn them all to Hell." He grinned. "On the bright side, we probably won't have to worry about them anymore, after this bit of clumsiness on their part."

"I don't understand. What happened?"

"You fulfilled your mission brilliantly, that's what happened, but a fool of a KGB man—Ah, why am I saying that? They're all fools! A KGB man interfered at the end and let Gorova escape and almost got you killed to boot.

"We owned the house across the street. Perhaps I should have told you that beforehand. We had a sleeper agent there. His job was to watch the safehouse and in general to be available for future missions. That's the man who was watching that house and let us know that Gorova had been taken there.

"When he saw someone follow you into the house, he became alarmed. At first, he thought he shouldn't expose himself to the Americans. After all, what good is a sleeper agent whom the enemy has identified? But he knew how important your mission was to us, so he decided he had to act. A good thing he did! He entered the house just in time to see the KGB man trying to take over the mission.

"Of course those bastards wanted credit for it all! They're always trying to win the Generalissimo over to their side, to push us out of the way, to get him to make them the superior agency. No doubt they'd love to see us eliminated altogether. The bastards!" He sat for a while, breathing heavily.

Pyotr thought, Foolish Arkady. He saved my life. That's who was following me. It wasn't the CIA, after all. He wanted to help. Took the bullet, saved the mission, or at least my career. Poor boy!

After he had calmed down, Artushev said, "But this time, they overplayed their hand. It's clear to everyone, including the Generalissimo, that, despite being shot yourself, you were about to deliver the killing shot to Gorova when the KGB man pushed you, ruining your aim, and tried to take credit for the kill himself. Judging by the blood, you hit her anyway. Fine work, Petya! Too bad she killed that KGB bastard. I'd have loved to see him being questioned by the Generalissimo, I can tell you."

There was another pause. This time, Artushev stared off into space and smiled, perhaps imagining that questioning. He shook himself and said, "I've put you in for another promotion. I don't see how they can deny you it, after your fine work. When you recover, we can talk about your next assignment."

"Gorova?" Pyotr whispered. He couldn't raise his voice. The right side of his chest ached, burned. Later, he would ask how extensive his wound was, even try to get a look at it. For now, he didn't want to do so. "She escaped?"

"Yes, I'm afraid she escaped. Your fellow GRU agent decided it was more important to take care of a hero like you than to finish the job on her." He paused in thought. "He was probably right. Anyway, we don't know where she is. We did a quick search of the house and found the body of another CIA man. He was in the bedroom, in bed, naked, his neck broken. The back of his head had been caved in with the bedside telephone. To make sure he was really dead, I suppose. Gorova, of course. I assume she had, shall we say, disarmed him in the way she knew best. That was probably his gun she used on you. My guess is she had decided to get away from the Americans and intended to use the gun on her other guard, when she encountered you instead. By now, she could be anywhere, anywhere in the world. Who knows, maybe she's set her cap for that Caliph, eh?" He laughed, then turned serious and grim suddenly. "You'd like another chance at her, would you?"

Pyotr replayed the image of Maria Gorova at that final instant, leaning against the wall, her leg covered in blood, calmly taking aim at him, ignoring the agony she must have been feeling. Oh, yes, he would like to meet her again. Very much. "Yes," he said. "Again."

Smiling, he drifted back into unconsciousness.

It was pretty as long as you ignored the bomb craters.

When Ted Billings had been a new CIA recruit a little less than thirty years ago, Beirut was a plum assignment. The work was mildly risky but a hell of a lot safer than Vietnam, the food was wonderful, the women were beautiful and accommodating, and the location was God's second try at Eden. When the Company had pulled him out and sent him to a succession of other assignments throughout Asia, Europe, and the Middle East, he'd always sworn to himself that he would come back someday. When years of civil war and invasion turned Lebanon into smoking rubble from end to end, instead, he'd finally changed his mind.

And now, here he was.

It's getting better, he thought as he sat in the café sipping his immensely strong Arab coffee flavored with a dash of ouzo. The

Caliphate, whatever its sins, had money to spend and the willingness to use it to rebuild the shattered city. At the same time—as witnessed by the flavor of his drink—it was wise enough not to enforce strict Islamic law, nor to enact the restrictions on trade and travel which gripped the rest of its territory, from Damascus to Riyadh to Algiers.

The Caliphate *needed* Beirut, and so did its enemies; thus a treaty was imposed, though neither side would acknowledge its existence. You can't change a city's true nature, he thought, even by blowing it up. Beirut is a trading post, for goods and people and information. Always has been, always will be.

Cities like Beirut never had any shortage of men like Ted. Company, KGB, MI5, Mossad, leftovers from a hundred little Arab intelligence services which Rashid-al-Din Sinan had broken down and reassembled into something which served his purposes. No matter where their loyalties lay, they all had more in common with each other than with the other citizens of the countries they served. Ted had run into more old friends on the street here than he ever did back in D.C.

For God's sake, he was even using his own name. About half of the men and—amazingly—a quarter of the women on the street were in Western clothing, from jeans and t-shirts for the young to suits like Ted wore for the older, more prosperous ones. Of these, a third or so were distinctly not Arab: European, sub-Saharan African, Indian, Oriental. Here on "business," their visas would say, like his own. Keep the money flowing even in a state remade by blood and fire. The Caliphate would accept it, here and now, as long as they stayed within the lines.

And Ted was sure he could call one out of ten of them by name. The Caliphate must know that, what kind of business many of its visitors were on. Know it, accept it as the price for their own similar operations abroad. Arab intelligence services had not been terribly good at their job during most of Ted's career, but the Hashashim were the original master spies, and the Caliphate's agents were probably just as good at their jobs, and as numerous, as America's and Russia's and Israel's.

Undoubtedly, some of the anonymous Arabs here knew who Ted was. He wasn't sure if that mattered to him.

Goddamn, he thought, where's Elkins? The hero medic had proven to be a very good spy—maybe better than anyone in the Company had expected. Harry Elkins was American born and bred, from a family that had lived in Chicago since before that city had a name, but Haroun al Kindi was every bit as Arab as anyone here. Egyptians permeated the Caliphate, because there were so damned *many* of them; Egypt was simply the largest source of manpower in the Arab world and so its sons could go anywhere, fulfill any function, travel from the Persian Gulf to northwest Africa without ever being questioned. Haroun al Kindi had turned up in an amazing number of different places, and Washington had received Harry Elkins' reports from every one.

That sonofabitch had better be here. If he's going native I'll pull him out and send him back to Langley for debriefing tomorrow, I swear to God I will.

"Mr. Billings." Faint Arab accent, a bit of lengthening in the "i" sounds, but the voice of a fluent English speaker. Ted looked up, saw a small man silhouetted by the sun. He squinted, made out familiar features.

"Took you long enough, Elkins. Have a seat."

Elkins seated himself with a fluid grace he hadn't possessed the last time he and Ted had met, months ago. He looked thinner under the raghead garb, too. Healthily slender, not the starved look he'd had when he first stumbled out of the desert. "Sorry, but I do not know who 'Elkins' is. I am Haroun al Kindi."

Ted leaned forward. "Fuck that. Actually, fuck *you."*

Elkins smiled. "Did they make you a contact manager," voice pure Chicago for just a moment, "because they couldn't trust you to remember your lines as a field agent?"

Ted closed his eyes for a minute. You don't have to like the guy, he reminded himself, you just have to work with him. "You're looking well, Mr. al Kindi," he said. "Darker than the last time we met, I notice."

"Desert Shield, Desert Storm, desert tan." The accent was back. "My business takes me to many sunlit locations." If that was some kind of code, Ted had no idea what it meant. "I have acquired information which I am sure will be of interest to your corporation."

That was clear enough. Ted reached under the table and took the computer diskette from Elkins' hand.

"Obviously," a sip of the coffee, "we're interested in any information or contacts you may have in the business community in the Caliphate." Start giving us some idea who's feeding you, you close-mouthed bastard. "In Beirut or elsewhere." And next time you take off for deep desert in Algeria or Saudi or wherever the hell, give us some idea where you're going.

"You understand, Mr. Billings, that in my own interests, I must maintain a great deal of what I know as proprietary." Very polite, Arabs were always polite even when they were telling you to go fuck yourself, and Haroun al Kindi was no exception. "In fact, I will be doing so for some time in the future. I ask that you not attempt to contact me again."

"What the hell?" Ted jumped up, ready to lunge across the table and strangle Elkins. "You piece of—" Suddenly the café was filled with Arabs rising from their tables nearby, ready to handle this loudmouthed American. Ted looked around, smiled as apologetically as he could manage, and sat back down. "Okay, look, what exactly did you mean by..."

There was no one seated across from him. He jumped up and ran to the door of the café, then stood there looking at the endless crowd of Arabs walking by.

About the Authors

David Dvorkin was born in 1943 in Reading, England. His family moved to South Africa after World War II, and then to the United States when David was a teenager. After attending college in Indiana, he worked at NASA in Houston on the Apollo Project, then at Martin Marietta in Denver on the Viking Mars lander project. His aerospace career ended in 1974. Thereafter, until 2009, he worked as a software developer and technical writer. He and his wife, Leonore, and their son, Daniel, have lived in Denver since 1971.

In addition to non-fiction, David has published many science fiction, horror, and mystery novels. For details, as well as quite a bit of nonfiction reading material, please see David's website: http://www.dvorkin.com/

David is on Facebook at
http://www.facebook.com/DavidDvorkin
and on Twitter at http://twitter.com/David_Dvorkin
His blog is http://eyeblister.blogspot.com/

For information about the self-publishing service that David operates with his wife, please see https://www.dldbooks.com/

Daniel Dvorkin, a joint production of David and Leonore Dvorkin, has served in the Army and Air Force, and has a Ph.D. in bioinformatics, which was harder than anything the military threw at him, including Desert Storm. These days, he leads a more peaceful but only slightly less chaotic life as a consultant with The Bioinformatics CRO and a fellow at the University of Colorado Altitude Research Center. Non–academic writing includes two novels co–authored with David Dvorkin, and some short pieces in magazines which went out of business shortly after publishing his stories. He and his fiancée, Rebecca Lee, live in Denver, where they enjoy hiking, amateur paleontology, and rescuing the stray cats who keep turning up in their yard.